The Seaweed Gatherers

Jessica Blair

Piatkus
An imprint of
Little, Brown Book Group
100 Victoria Embankment
London EC4Y 0DY

piatkus

PIATKUS

First Published in Great Britain in 1998 by Judy Piatkus (Publishers) Ltd
This paperback edition published in 2010 by Piatkus

A CIP catalogue record for this book is available from the British Library.

ISBN 978-0-7515-4597-5

Typeset in Sabon by Hewer Text UK Ltd, Edinburgh
Printed and bound in Great Britain by Clays Ltd, St Ives plc

Papers used by Piatkus are natural, renewable and recyclable products
sourced from well-managed forests and certified in accordance with
the rules of the Forest Stewardship Council.

Joan
Only Forever

Chapter One

A shiver ran through Lucy, then her body tensed against the thud of the clay as it hit the rough wood of her father's coffin. At that moment, 1802 was a year she would want to forget.

At nineteen, Alice, a year older than her sister, sensed Lucy's reaction and gripped her hand not only to try to give her reassurance but in an attempt to find some comfort for herself.

Their mother's step faltered. Rebecca closed her eyes tightly as if that would shut out the unwelcome sound. She felt her son's grip on her arm strengthen to bolster her resolve not to give way in these grievous circumstances. At twenty, Robert had given unstinting support to her and to his two sisters through the gloom of the last four days.

The thuds came with regular monotony, signals of the finality of life. The gravediggers had hardly waited for the family to move from the graveside and now their efforts beat a mournful tattoo in Lucy's mind as she walked to the lychgate on the long path past unmarked graves and ornate stone carvings, grey, prominent, mocking, searing Lucy's mind with reminders of her father's inglorious end in the tiny bedroom of the terraced house in a respectable but poorer part of Newcastle-upon-Tyne.

She shivered in spite of the late afternoon warmth which encouraged the oak trees, lining the perimeters of the grave-yard, to show more of their buds and herald new life among the dead. The thump of the clay recalled the way the two gravediggers had stood leaning on their long-handled spades leering lecherously at her and Alice throughout the simple ceremony. She was not sorry when they reached the lychgate and left the churchyard, for it seemed to mark an escape from the immediate past and signify a step into the future. Life had to go on and though memories would still remain they would not contain the feelings she had experienced in the last few minutes. Those would be dismissed and she would remember the good things about her father.

She would miss his easy-going manner, his ready under-standing smile, his quiet attitude which could bring calm to troubled moments, his readiness to let his wife take the lead and make decisions, only adding a guiding word when neces-sary. She knew that beneath his serenity he reproached himself that he should have done better for his family. His meagre wage as a clerk to an attorney enabled him to rent a terraced house from his employer, in a district where respectability kept its head a shade above poverty, providing the essentials of life but no extra comforts. Those only came occasionally after the three children had all gained employ-ment; Robert as a junior clerk in the same office as his father, Alice helping in a dame school, and Lucy as governess to the attorney's three children. Thankful for their positions, the children were grateful that their parents had encouraged them to be interested in most things, had directed them advisedly in their special interests, and had realised that education could bring advantages. Now, with the main breadwinner gone, they would be thrust back on their fierce independence to counteract life's downward drag.

Lucy recalled times when her glance would catch her father daydreaming as if he was thinking of what might have been, and on those occasions glimpsing her mother's frown as if she knew what he was thinking and disapproved. Were those daydreams linked to the last words she had heard him utter? His whisper haunted her as they reached the main street where everyday life surged around them.

Vendors shouted their wares, shopkeepers encouraged people to step inside, acquaintances exchanged raucous greetings, bonnetted heads nodded in idle gossip, bare-footed urchins weaved among folk going about the business of their daily lives. Lucy was familiar with it all, but today it was different. She wanted to shout and stop it, to tell them life would never be the same, that she had just seen her father buried and that she would never again accompany him as part of this familiar scene.

Her mother, eyes fixed firmly ahead, never speaking, quickened her step. They left the main thoroughfare for a quieter side street, allowing the constant buzz of life to recede as they walked its full length of terraced houses all monotonously the same. They turned right into a repetition of the street they had just left. Door, sash window, door, sash window as far as the eye could see, and above the windows, replicas, and above the doors brickwork darkened by the grime and smoke from the forest of chimneys.

3

Houses, with doors wiped clean, knobs brightly polished, windows gleaming from their daily wash – no one was going to be outdone by their neighbours in keeping the outward signs of respectability. Number twenty, home, was no different, her mother made sure of that.

Lucy saw tiny groups of people gathered near number twenty, awkward, eyes cast tentatively at Rebecca and her family, solomn faces, nods, sympathetic glances, murmured condolences scarcely audible.

Rebecca acknowledged them with inclinations of her head, a flicker of recognition here, a wan smile offered there. She stopped at her front door, fished a key from her pocket and unlocked it. She stepped inside followed by Alice and Lucy. Robert stayed to greet the sympathisers who had hung back for a few moments to allow Rebecca and her daughters to prepare themselves.

Discarding their coats and bonnets, mother and daughters smoothed their dresses and, glancing in a mirror hanging on the wall of the passage which led to the kitchen at the back, patted their hair into place.

'Alice, the kettle, Lucy, the curtains.' Rebecca's orders came briskly. The girls noticed the tautness in her voice and knew she was fighting hard to keep her true feelings under control.

Alice bustled through to the kitchen where she hung a kettle over the fire. Lucy hurried into the front room where she drew back the curtains which had been kept closed since her father had died. The family would observe the rules of mourning for some time but convention dictated that the curtains could be opened again now the funeral was over.

4

She did not linger at the window but hastened upstairs to do the same in the bedroom overlooking the street. Reaching the door she hesitated. This was the room in which she had last seen her father alive and she had not been in since. She turned away and went to the back bedroom instead. As she returned to the small landing she drew a deep breath and, with a fierce determination, threw open the door of the front bedroom and strode unhesitatingly to the window. She flung back the curtains, flooding the room with light. In that gesture she felt she had brought normality back as near as she could. She glanced down into the street and saw people approaching the house, neighbours to offer condolences, mourners to pay their respects to the departed through the living, while drinking a cup of tea and tucking into the sandwiches and cakes she and Alice had prepared before the funeral.

She went downstairs where for the next two hours she, along with Alice and Robert, accepted sympathy, made trivial conversation, handed round refreshments, refilled teacups, while all the time keeping a concerned eye on their mother. They need not have worried, Rebecca had strength for them all. This was no time to break down; she had steeled herself not to give way, at least not here, not in front of everyone. Maybe tonight in the loneliness of her bedroom she would weep.

The final guest had left, the dirty crockery had been placed beside the sink in the kitchen and the three young people were preparing to wash up when Rebecca spoke. 'Leave it, we'll do it in a few minutes. Let's all sit quiet and enjoy a hot cup of tea, I'm sure none of you really had one when everyone was here.'

A few minutes later the tension they had all felt in the course of receiving commiserations evaporated. Lucy glanced at her mother, wondering if this was the moment when she would break down, but she saw a stoic resolve settling on the placid features.

Rebecca sipped her tea, thankful to have the love and support of her children. 'You have all behaved impeccably and I am grateful. Life will be different, it's bound to be, but if we help each other we will adjust. We'll miss your father but he would want us to look to the future. He would want you to do well. Without his wage, I think now might be the time for me to take a job.'

'Mother, there's no need,' protested Robert. 'You've plenty to do. We'll manage.'

Rebecca gave a wan smile. She nodded. 'Yes we could, but if we want to remain here, in the life we know, it would help if I was to earn something. I've given it serious thought since your father died, and I think it will be for the best.'

'But what will you do?' asked Alice with some concern.

'I think Mrs Dobson is looking for someone to help in her bakery.'

'But, Mother,' Alice's eyes widened in shocked protest, 'you can't go skivvying there.'

Rebecca laughed. 'No, I certainly can't. Mrs Dobson knows my reputation as a pie-maker. She approached me.'

Alice relaxed, relieved that her mother would have some authority.

Rebecca read approval on her daughter's face. She wanted the same from the other two, and saw agreement in Robert's serious dark brown eyes. But Lucy's thoughts were far away. Rebecca's lips tightened with exasperation.

It was at moments like this that she saw Isaac in his daughter. 'Lucy, what do you think?' she asked firmly, breaking into Lucy's reverie.

She started. 'Oh . . . er, yes, if that's what you want to do.' Lucy had only half heard her mother's proposal.

'Very well, then that's settled,' said Rebecca.

'Mother,' Lucy went on, a wistful note to her voice. 'What did father mean when he said, "The de Northbys owe you"?'

So that was it! Rebecca's mind stiffened, raising a barrier against what she knew. 'Nothing! I told you before they were only the words of a dying man confused by what was happening.'

'But, Mother, Father was so . . .'

'Stop!' Rebecca cut in sharply. 'I want to hear no more about it.' She frowned disapprovingly at Lucy as she stood up. 'Now, I'm going to see Mrs Dobson. See everything is tidy by the time I get back.' She walked briskly from the room and no one spoke until they heard the front door close.

'Really, Lucy, you shouldn't upset Mother at a time like this,' Robert remonstrated with his sister.

'But, Robert, you heard Father, just as I did,' Lucy protested.

'Yes, I know.' His words came with a slight hesitation.

'Mother said there was nothing to it,' pointed out Alice.

'Then why did Father say them?' put in Lucy sharply, irritated that her sister didn't have her capacity for curiosity.

'Robert, you don't think he meant anything by them, do you?' Alice looked questioningly at her brother for support. Her expression changed when she saw the doubt on his face. She looked intently at him. 'You know something?' she whispered with conviction.

Lucy had read his expression too. 'You do,' she pressed emphatically. 'Tell us, tell us.'

Robert hesitated, but the eagerness for information on his sisters' faces could not be denied. 'Well, it's something I overheard a couple of years ago. It may have no connection with what Father said but . . .' He paused.

'Go on,' urged Lucy, leaning forward with anticipation.

'I overheard Mother and Father. I wasn't eavesdropping,' he added quickly to vindicate himself. 'I'd come in by the back door and they were in here. The doors were open and I couldn't help hearing what they said. What they meant I don't know, but Father said, "I think the children should know the story." Mother was emphatic with her reply. "Never," she said. Father started to protest but she cut him short. "What is the point?" she went on. "It's all in the past, long ago. It's best forgotten. Nothing can be proved. You'd stir up trouble and get nowhere."'

Lucy's eyes were widening at this mysterious information. Ever the one with the alert inquisitive mind, Robert's revelations gripped her. 'Go on,' she urged.

'There's no more except that when Father said that he thought we had a right to know, Mother's reply was so shattering it made the whole thing stick in my mind: "If ever you breathe a word of this to them, or to anyone else, I will leave you."'

Both girls gasped. 'She couldn't mean it,' said Alice disbelievingly. 'They were so devoted.'

'She meant it indeed,' replied Robert. 'You know Mother, she never says what she doesn't mean.'

8

Lucy's mind was racing. 'There must be a connection. What Father said when he was dying must have been what Mother banned him from saying when he was alive. He took the opportunity knowing he was leaving her and that if he spoke then she couldn't leave him.' The words tumbled excitedly from her lips.

'But what connection can there be?' said Alice. 'We've never heard of any de Northbys. Who are they? And why should they owe us?'

'I don't know,' returned Lucy, 'but I mean to discover the truth!'

'But how can you?' asked Alice with a touch of scorn as if to cast doubt on the task.

Lucy's eyes narrowed into a faraway look. 'I will find a way,' she said slowly.

The portico and lawns of Howland Manor rang with the laughter of the youngsters of the local landed gentry gathered here at the instigation of Mark Cossart for an afternoon of croquet, tennis, archery and tea.

Mark's mother and father had driven into Whitby to visit friends, leaving the young people to enjoy themselves.

Zilpha de Northby was holding court as she always did on these occasions. The young men liked it, gathering round, hanging on to her every word, flirting, paying homage to the vivacious eighteen-year-old whose flashing blue eyes teased them and whose small sensuous mouth pouted kisses at them. The young women tolerated her, knowing she was a better friend than an enemy. Some had seen those sparkling eyes flash daggers when anyone had dared to suspect her flirtations with their beaux were anything more. This was Zilpha's way of enjoying life, of being the centre of attraction. The girls knew it and let it be so. The only thing they envied her was her monopoly of the handsome Mark Cossart, but they gained amusement to see him at times ignore her, leaving her stamping her feet in anger or pouting in a sulk.

They would all be willing to swoon at Mark's feet but Mark was always the gentleman, with eyes only for the girl of his choice at any one moment. Zilpha wanted to be that girl all the time. Mark would be a catch and she determined to catch him.

Six feet two, erect, his athletic figure emphasised by his perfectly fitting clothes, he sat on the steps of the portico surrounded by pretty young girls listening intently to his stories or imagining him dressed in his Hussar officer's uniform and they on his arm sweeping into the huge ballroom where everyone stopped to watch them waltz.

His handsome features were framed by his dark hair with a slight natural wave at his temples. But more than anything he created an aura. Any girl would say it was because of his French connections, which added a touch of mystery and romance to him.

He spoke the language fluently, something his French father had insisted he keep up and cultivate when they fled to England.

Emile Cossart had fallen in love with Elphrida Swinburn when he had visited the alum works at Ravenscar to negotiate a contract with Richard de Northby to supply alum for his textile and leather works in France. Richard had given a small party welcoming the Frenchman and there he had met Elphrida whose parents' estates bordered those of the de Northbys. Love had blossomed into marriage a year later. Elphrida settled easily into life near Paris and their happiness was complete when Mark was born in 1780. Eight years later, disturbed by troubled times and seeing revolution must come, Emile sold everything he owned and brought his wife and son to England to her parents' home. Comfortably off, Emile helped his father-in-law to run the estate until he and Elphrida had bought Howland Manor. He had renewed his friendship with Richard and Adeline de Northby and Mark and Zilpha had become firm friends.

Now, there were times when Zilpha wondered if their friendship of fourteen years was a drawback. Had they become too familiar? Did Mark look upon her as no more than a friend whereas she wanted romance to blossom? She knew that as a couple they were regarded as the pick of the district and everyone expected them to marry but she doubted if Mark regarded that as a certainty. But those thoughts were far from her mind as she delighted in being the centre of attraction on the steps of Howland Manor.

The early spring day was warm and the sun had encouraged the girls to put on their brightest dresses. Zilpha had chosen a pink gingham with thin dark red stripes cut to the slender look while maintaining some fullness at the back. The V-shaped neck fell wide off the shoulders to a point at the high waist. The short puffed sleeves came tight at the elbows. Her pale blue shawl lay on the step beside her, ready for the first hint of sharpness in the air. She wore a shallow bonnet with a wide brim tipped to the back of her head and tied by a ribbon under her chin. Not for her

11

to hide her good looks under its rim – that was angled to set them off, to focus attention where she wanted it.

Infectious laughter trilled off her lips. She was determined to outdo the merriment coming from Mark's group.

'Are you really going to sea, George Fenny?' she enquired in amusement at the prospect, for George was country born and bred, a fine horseman, who had always seemed at home on the land.

'Of course I am, Zilpha. What is there for me at Pike Cross, when there are three older brothers? I'll make a name for myself as an explorer.' He stuck his chest out at the proud thought.

Zilpha chuckled. 'So you'll be sick all over the world.'

'No I won't.'

'Yes you will.'

'Then I'll think of you every time I am.'

Zilpha pulled a face and glanced round the other four men. 'I hope you all think of me in better circumstances.'

They all roared their assurance.

'You, Charles, when do you think of me?' She stroked her finger under his chin.

'I . . . I . . .' He blushed.

'Oh, come, Charles, is it as embarrassing as all that?' She tempted him with her eyes. 'Do I come up to expectations?'

'Does she, Charles?'

'Tell us,' his companions urged.

'Leave poor Charles alone,' said Zilpha sympathetically and received an adoring look from him. She turned to a brawny, muscular young man sprawled across the step behind her. 'You, Chris Young, when do you think of me?'

'All the time, my love,' he returned.

12

'Even when you're with Eve?' she asked, knowing things were getting serious between them.

'That's something to warn Eve about,' put in the dark-haired youngster to Zilpha's right. Laughter ran through the group as they teased Chris about what they would do.

Chris looked uncomfortable and was pleased when Zilpha turned her attention to a fair-haired boy. 'What about you, Anthony?' She let her voice caress him.

He swallowed hard. He always found Zilpha irresistible and wished he had the charm of Mark Cossart. 'Me? I don't give you a thought.'

The others gave a howl of disbelief.

Zilpha cast a surreptitious glance in Mark's direction, hoping that the noise had attracted his attention, but she saw no reaction. He seemed to be concentrating on the girls around him. She glanced at Anthony coyly.

'Not even one tiny thought for an innocent girl?'

'Innocent? Upon my word!' cried George.

'For that insinuation there'll be no dance for you at my ball.' Zilpha showed mock hurt.

'Aw, Zilpha, don't punish me like that,' moaned George. 'I was only teasing. I know you're as pure as fresh snow.'

Zilpha pouted thoughtfully. 'I just might forgive you if you'll bring me a nice fresh drink.'

Eager to make amends George sprang to his feet and rushed into the house where he knew lemonade had been left out for their use.

'Save a dance for me.'

'Promise me the schottische.'

Requests came thick and fast.

Laughter quirked Zilpha's lips. 'You'll all have to wait

13

until the night of the ball.' She looked across the portico. 'Come, let me return you to your loves, they'll be getting jealous of me monopolising you.' She extended both arms in a gesture of needing help. Chris and Charles were on their feet in a flash, and each taking a hand pulled her gently to her feet.

George, holding a glass, rushed from the house. 'Your lemonade, Zilpha,' he pressed eagerly, wanting to keep her favours.

'I don't want it now, George.' She waved him away with a flutter of her hand. 'Drink it yourself.' She ignored the disappointment which clouded his face and swept past him towards Mark and his attentive listeners.

Casting a cursory eye across the group she said in a tone which would brook no challenge, 'Now, Mark and I will challenge you all to a game of croquet.'

Mark glanced up casually and at the same time gave the girl sitting next to him an unseen nudge as he said, 'Sorry, Zilpha, I've just arranged to partner Kathy.' He smiled to himself when he saw Zilpha's face cloud fleetingly with annoyance and her eyes flash daggers at him. He enjoyed irritating her with his teasing as he had done since they were children.

'Ah, well, if you want to be beaten . . .' She tried to pass off the rebuff lightly, but Mark knew that inwardly she was seething. She flounced round. 'Charles, you can be my partner.'

The rest of the day passed off pleasantly and Zilpha was delighted in her partner's play which enabled them to beat Mark and Kathy in the final match with everyone else taking sides, shouting encouragement and advice. After tea on the portico in the pleasant sunshine the party gradually broke up, excitedly anticipating Zilpha's birthday ball in two weeks' time.

She lingered until everyone had left and then sat down in a chair beside Mark. She gazed across the fields sloping gently away from the house. In one of them six sleek, well-groomed horses champed the grass or galloped in exuberant play. To the right an oak wood opened its new green to the sun. To the left a lake, bordered on its far side by massive rhododendron bushes, mirrored the blue of the sky flecked with white clouds.

Zilpha sighed contentedly. 'I've always loved it here.'

'But it's nothing compared to Northby Hall.'

'Far better. It's not so big and therefore cosier.'

'The views you have,' exclaimed Mark.

'But being on the top of a hill we catch all the winds, whereas here you are tucked in and protected from them, and there's no better view than that.' She indicated the slopes which sheltered the fields in front of them and how they framed the distant view of the sea. She glanced round. 'Your father showed his taste when he built that new wing and added this portico to the front.'

'Well, he employed the best designers.'

The house his parents had bought was well built but they had updated its solid construction to suit their tastes. The simple front of eight bays, each with its appropriate sash windows, lent itself to the erection of a portico in the classical style. The slight slope in the land allowed the construction of four steps leading on to the portico so making the entrance more impressive. The large attractive pediment at roof level remained untouched and had been matched by a smaller one over the single front door.

'It's always been a home to me,' commented Zilpha, wistfully recalling the many happy hours she had spent here with Mark. 'I don't know how you can bear to leave it.'

'I know, I sometimes wonder why I joined the army, but with the war following the upheavals in France, I felt I had to do something to show our loyalty.'

'And I admire you for your stance,' she offered quietly. 'But now the war's over . . .'

'It's an uneasy peace and will be until the situation with France is settled permanently.'

'You think Napoleon wants more?'

'Yes, he means to have all Europe.'

'Britain as well?'

'Yes.'

'But invasion's unthinkable.'

'I know.'

Zilpha waved her hands as if she could flick the possibility away. 'Oh let's not speak more about it. The peace has given you leave for a month, we must make the most of it. Ride tomorrow?'

'Yes, why not? I'll call for you at ten.'

Alice closed the door of the dame school behind her and started in the direction of home.

'Alice.'

She recognised the voice behind her and swung round, her eyes lighting up with pleasure. 'Paul! When did you arrive?'

'Docked this morning.' He gave her a light kiss on the cheek and taking her arm fell into step beside her.

16

'How long shall you be here?' she asked.

'Sail again Saturday, late afternoon.'

'So soon?' She frowned with disappointment.

He shrugged his shoulders. 'The way of a sailor.'

'I know,' she replied. 'But if I know Paul Smurthwaite it's a life he likes and because of that he'll do well. He won't always sail on a collier.'

'No indeed,' he said firmly. 'It suits me now. Shipping coal to the alum works at Ravenscar gets me home and here in Newcastle I see you. But one day I'll be master of one of those great merchantmen sailing out of Whitby.'

Alice sensed the ambition in his voice. She had heard it before and, though she dreaded the day when he would be away for longer periods, she knew his desire was to achieve a comfortable life for them.

She had met Paul in Newcastle a year ago when she was shopping. Two urchins in full flight from an irate shop-keeper had bumped into her, knocking her to the ground and sending her packages flying into the air. Paul had been the first to her, helping her to her feet with marked concern for her welfare. She had winced with the pain in her wrist so he had gathered her purchases and had escorted her home where a grateful Mrs Mitchell had insisted that he stay to tea.

The family had learned that he worked on a collier shipping coal from the Durham coalfields through Newcastle to Whitby and the alum works at Ravenscar a few miles further along the Yorkshire coast. His father was employed at the alum works and because his son was eager to go to sea had got him on to one of the colliers.

Rebecca took to the young man, who was polite and

17

considerate, so that when he called again the next time he was in port to enquire after Alice, hoping that she was none the worse for her fall, she invited him to visit whenever he was in Newcastle.

Alice discovered he had an amusing side, could make a joke and take one without being offended as well as having the ability to laugh at himself. She felt safe whenever she was with this well-built young man who always seemed alert to everything around him. His hazel eyes were ever moving, observing, learning. Alice revelled in his attention and before long she had to admit to herself that she was in love.

Now she felt pleasure in being beside him as they walked home.

'Paul, I've some sad news. Father died and was buried on Monday.' A catch came to her voice as she broke the news.

He was stopped by the shock and looked at Alice with concern. 'Oh, my God. I knew he was not well the last time I saw him but I didn't expect this.' He took her hand. 'And you, are you all right?'

She nodded as she bit her lips to hold back the tears at the recollection of the bad time she had been through.

'Your mother, and Lucy and Robert?' he asked.

'We are beginning to settle down. We have to get on with life.'

They started to walk slowly. 'I hope he didn't suffer.' Paul had got on well with her father who was always eager to hear about Paul's voyage, imagining it to be across the world's oceans whereas Paul knew it was only along the coast. Paul suspected that here was a man who, secretly, would dearly have loved to face adventure instead of the humdrum life in an office.

'No I don't think he did. He was speaking to us to the very end. Whispered words, most of them, as he weakened. His last words were strange.'

Paul glanced curiously at her, waiting for her to go on.

'He said, "The de Northbys owe you." I don't know what he meant or who the de Northbys are.' Alice shrugged her shoulders. 'A mystery we are not likely to solve. I think Mother knows, but she won't talk about it.'

Paul stopped and turned her to him. 'De Northby? You're sure?'

'Yes.' Alice was puzzled by his query. 'Why?'

'I know the name.'

'You? How could you?'

'It's the name of the owner of the alum works where we deliver coal!'

Chapter Two

Paul's information intrigued Alice but she did not have a chance to share it with Lucy and Robert until the following evening after Paul had returned to his ship and their mother had left for an evening's work at the bakery.

'Alice, what are you hiding? You've been on tenterhooks for the last hour or so,' said Robert as soon as the door had closed and Rebecca's footsteps had faded down the street.

Alice wet her lips and faced her brother and sister with excitement in her eyes. 'I know where there are some de Northbys!'

'What?' Lucy and Robert gasped.

'I was telling Paul about Father's death and happened to mention what he said, and Paul told me that de Northby is the name of the person who owns the alum works where his father is employed,' Alice explained eagerly.

'But that can't be who Father meant,' said Paul doubtfully. 'He wouldn't know about them.'

'He might, but not the present family,' put in Lucy. 'You

said that when you overheard Mother and Father they were talking about something in the past.'

'Well . . .' Robert drew the word out and pulled a face as if Lucy's theory was debatable.

'What connection can we possibly have with the owner of an alum works in Yorkshire?' said Alice. 'Our names aren't even the same, and Mother's name before she married was Wade so there's no link there.'

'We can find out,' urged Lucy.

'How?'

'I'll go to Yorkshire.'

Alice and Robert stared unbelievingly at their sister. This suggestion was preposterous but just like Lucy, plunging in without thinking the situation through.

'You can't!' said Robert.

'Mother wouldn't let you,' Alice pointed out.

'What about your job?' asked Robert, to curb Lucy's enthusiasm.

'Mrs Palmer is taking the children to her mother's for a month so I'm free,' Lucy explained.

'But Mother?' Alice raised the question again.

'You needn't say anything until after I've gone.'

'But how will you get there?'

'Walk.'

'Don't be ridiculous,' scoffed Robert.

'I will if I have to,' snapped Lucy.

'You'd be defying Mother who told you to forget what Father said.' Alice tried to support her brother.

'Don't forget, I heard her saying it would only cause trouble and was best forgotten,' Robert reminded her. 'So what's the point in going?

'And Father said the de Northbys owed us. Isn't that worth looking into?' persisted Lucy.

'But it may not be these de Northbys. You'd be going on a wild goose chase for nothing,' argued Robert.

'It's an unusual name.' Lucy fought back. The more her brother and sister argued against her the more determined she became.

'That doesn't mean a thing,' pressed Robert. 'Think of the anguish you'll cause Mother.'

'But don't we owe it to Father?' countered Lucy. 'Would he have mentioned it as he was dying if he had not wanted us to do something? I'm going for his sake.'

Alice knew her sister – there would be no stopping her. 'Well, you can't go gallivanting off on your own. I'll have to come with you.'

'Will you?' Lucy's enthusiasm was charged with hope. Though she had said nothing, the fact of going to strange parts on her own had been daunting; now it seemed less so.

'You shouldn't encourage her.' Robert frowned. He too knew that there would be no stopping Lucy once she had her head set but he had to make one last attempt to scupper what he saw as a foolish venture. 'And what about *your* job, Alice?'

'If Lucy insists on going, I'll have to give it up.'

'But that's taking one wage out of the family,' pointed out Robert.

'We'll get some work in Yorkshire while we look into the matter. And I'm sure Alice will have no difficulty getting a job when we return,' countered Lucy.

Robert shrugged his shoulders. There would no holding her now. He was not in agreement with what they were

22

proposing but he admired their spirit. 'Do you want me to come too?' he asked.

'We can't all leave Mother,' said Lucy, 'you are the main breadwinner now.' She paused then went on. 'We must start making plans.' She wasn't going to let the idea go cold. 'But first, Robert, promise you'll say nothing to Mother until after we've gone.'

'Of course I won't. You know that.' He thought too much of his sisters to give them away and from now would help in any way he could. 'I've a little money put by, it won't pay coach fares but you can have it.'

'We couldn't take your money,' protested Lucy.

'You must, you'll need something,' he insisted. 'I won't take no.'

'Thanks, you're a good man, Robert.' She kissed him on the cheek.

'Now, how are you getting there?'

'We'll have to walk,' replied Alice, though she did not relish the prospect.

'Wait, I've an idea,' put in Lucy enthusiastically.

Alice and Robert moaned in mock despair. 'Not another?'

'Listen, listen,' pressed Lucy. 'Next time Paul's in Newcastle, he could smuggle us on board ship!'

'What?' Robert and Alice stared at their sister as if she had gone out of her mind.

'You can't mean it?' said Robert.

'You're not dragging Paul into this,' returned Alice defiantly.

'If you were discovered he would be dismissed instantly,' Robert pointed out.

23

'If we were, no one need know he was implicated,' pressed Lucy. 'We could have smuggled ourselves on board.'

'It's ridiculous,' said Robert. 'Too full of danger. Besides, colliers are dirty ships.'

'We aren't going to hide among the coal.' Lucy gave a little laugh at the thought. 'That's why we need Paul's help. He'll know the best place.'

'No!' snapped Alice.

'It's a good chance. We'll get right to where we want to be. Better than walking.' Lucy pressed home her reasoning, hardly letting the others raise more objections until at last Alice agreed that they should see what Paul had to say next time he was ashore in Newcastle.

Throughout the next four days it took all of Lucy's will-power to curb her eager anticipation of what might lie ahead. She knew her mother was shrewd and if she suspected anything untoward she would not rest until she knew what it was.

Dark clouds had started to send down rain when Paul's ship docked in Newcastle in the late afternoon. As he splashed his way through the streets he anticipated the warmth and comfort he knew he would find with the Mitchells.

Rebecca had prepared for his arrival by having his favourite stew bubbling on the fire, and once Robert had arrived and had discarded his wet clothes they all sat down to enjoy the meal.

Lucy ate quickly as if that would hasten the moment when her mother had to leave for the bakery. It drew Rebecca's attention and Lucy's heart thumped when she remarked, 'What's gotten into you, rushing your food like that?'

'Hungry, Mother,' she replied and to try to calm herself added, 'Could I have a little more, please?'

Rebecca made no comment as she ladled some more stew on to Lucy's plate. Lucy was relieved that the moment had passed but she caught her brother's glance, warning her to be careful.

Once the meal was over and the washing up done Lucy was pleased to see her mother gather up the aprons she needed at the bakery.

'Draught tournament again?' she asked, seeing Alice take the board and draughtsmen from the cupboard, as she adjusted her bonnet.

'Too foul a night to go out,' replied Alice.

'I'll only be a couple of hours,' said Rebecca. 'Have the kettle boiling when I get back.'

'We will,' replied Lucy. She knew her mother would bring something mouthwatering back with her. She ushered her to the door and Robert and Alice were anxious in case she overdid her fussing.

The room door closed and Lucy turned. Her eyes held the eagerness which had been just below the surface ever since Paul had arrived. She stood with her back to the door, her head inclined, listening. The front door clicked shut.

'Go on, Alice, ask him!' The urgency in Lucy's voice surprised Paul. He looked at Alice when Lucy prompted her again. 'Go on.'

'Paul.' Alice's voice was quiet, tentative. 'Er, you know when you were here last.' She paused.

'Yes.' Paul nodded and waited for her to go on.

She hesitated. 'You remember as we walked home I was

25

telling . . . you met me coming out of school. Well, I told you Father had died.'

'Stop dithering, Alice. You're getting nowhere,' Lucy snapped irritably. She turned to Paul. 'Alice and I want you to smuggle us on board your ship when you sail.'

Paul gulped. The shock held back any words. His disbelief mingled with the expectancy of the others as they awaited his answer.

'We mean it.' Lucy pressed home her request.

'You can't.'

'We do, don't we, Alice?' Lucy looked to her sister for support.

'Yes,' she said weakly.

'But what's this all about?' Paul turned his eyes on Robert. 'Do you know?' he asked.

Robert nodded. He looked at his younger sister. 'You'd better explain.'

'You told Alice that a de Northby, the name mentioned when Father was dying, owned the alum works in Yorkshire. Well, we'd like to know if they are one and the same family, so we have decided to go to Yorkshire and find out and we thought going on your ship would be the easiest way, otherwise we'll have to walk.' Lucy poured the words out quickly.

Paul reeled under the implication. 'I can't,' he said. 'I'd lose my job if you were found out, and I'd probably be blacklisted and not find work on another ship.'

'No one need know you helped us,' said Lucy, determined to persuade him.

Paul shook his head.

'If we were discovered we'd say we sneaked on board on our own, no one helped us.'

26

'Too risky,' Paul replied. 'If you were found you'd be handed over to the authorities and probably get a prison sentence.'

'We'd chance that.' Lucy glanced at her sister, seeking her support.

'I wouldn't want Alice to run that risk. Nor you,' he added quickly and firmly.

'I told you it would be no good,' said Alice, sickened at the thought of prison. 'Besides, it's not fair to ask Paul to jeopardise his job.'

'Paul's in no danger,' insisted Lucy, annoyed that agreement had not been as straightforward as she had expected and that her sister's support seemed to be weakening. 'And we'll be all right if we are careful.'

'Do you condone this?' Paul asked, turning his gaze on Robert who so far had said nothing.

'Well, not entirely. I see no point in digging into the past, but Lucy is so determined she says she'll go on her own.'

'I can't let her do that so I agreed to go with her,' Alice explained.

'And if they walk they'll run grave risks, footpads, robbers. Maybe your ship is the lesser evil, besides getting them to Yorkshire much quicker,' pointed out Robert. 'I appreciate the risk you'll be taking but as Lucy says, no one need know that you helped them.'

Paul looked thoughtful, shaking his head slightly as if to convince himself that he shouldn't do it. He knew he should be firm and refuse, but he did not want to upset Alice and lose a relationship which he hoped was developing into more than friendship, so he considered he might kill the escapade with the question. 'What does your mother think?'

'She doesn't know,' rapped Lucy quickly. 'And she mustn't. Swear you won't tell her.'

Paul's lips tightened. It was as he thought.

'She mustn't have an inkling until after we have left. Robert will tell her then. Say you'll help us. You must,' Lucy pleaded.

'It'll be a dirty voyage, we carry coal.'

'We know that,' returned Lucy, 'but we won't be hiding in the coal, you'll know a cleaner place.'

Paul raised his eyebrows. 'Coal dust gets everywhere.'

'That won't put us off, will it, Alice?' She saw Paul's resolve weakening and once more sought support from her sister.

'No,' she replied.

'Well, now, let's see how we might do it,' said Paul, then added as Lucy's emotions burst into a flood of excitement, 'I'm not saying I'll certainly do it. Just looking into the possibilities.'

'Calm down, Lucy,' said Alice. 'Paul hasn't agreed yet.'

'He nearly has.' She turned to him. 'What do we do?'

Paul hesitated thoughtfully. 'We sail the day after tomorrow on the morning tide, so you'd have to come aboard tomorrow night.'

'Mother will miss us before we sail,' Alice pointed out.

'Not necessarily,' put in Lucy quickly to scotch any doubt. 'We can go to the ship after she is asleep. She'll only miss us when she gets up and then it will be too late.' For a fleeting moment misgiving touched her mind. 'We'll have sailed by then, won't we, Paul?'

'Seven o'clock.'

Lucy felt relief. 'There you are. Just about the time Mother would be waking us.'

28

'Then there'll be the devil to pay and I'll bear the brunt,' said Robert mournfully.

'You're strong enough, dear brother,' flattered Lucy.

'You'll be coming through the rough areas of Newcastle in the dark.' Paul glanced at Robert. 'You'll have to escort them.'

'I'll do that.'

'And watch out for yourself on the way back.'

'I'll be all right.'

'So what time will you want us to come?' pressed Lucy, calculating that Paul had given his approval.

'I'm still not sure it's a good idea,' he replied.

'Of course it is,' urged Lucy. 'We come aboard in the dark, you hide us, we sail and everything will be all right.' She made it sound so easy.

'You'll have to be extremely careful coming aboard,' he warned, 'but I might be able to make it easier. I'll try and change with whoever's on watch. He'll jump at the chance of another night ashore before we sail. The time you arrive will depend on when you can leave here, but if I'm on watch it won't matter. I'll be on the lookout for you.'

'Perfect!' cried Lucy.

'How will we know if you have been able to change duty?' asked Robert.

'You won't. That's another risk you'll have to take.' He looked thoughtful. 'Robert, I think you'd better come back with me tonight so we can make plans and you can see the best way to the dock and know exactly where the ship is.'

'Good idea,' he agreed.

* * *

29

The following night the girls had a cup of tea ready for Rebecca coming from the bakery but she did not arrive at the usual time.

'What's happened tonight of all nights?' moaned Lucy, glancing at the wall clock for the tenth time.

'Patience, Lucy,' said Robert. 'Calm yourself or Mother will suspect something when she does come.'

As much as she tried, Lucy could not stop fidgeting but when she heard the front door open half an hour later she jumped to her feet and busied herself with the kettle to hide her pent-up feelings.

'You're late. Have you had a hard day?' asked Alice, as her mother walked in, taking off her hat and coat as she did so.

'Aye,' replied Rebecca, sinking wearily into the chair in front of the fire. 'Young Potter slipped, hurt her ankle and dropped a whole tray of pies. I had to start and bake all over again.'

'You'll be ready for bed,' commented Lucy as if reminding her would quicken her departure.

'It will be nice to lie down,' Rebecca agreed.

'I'll bring your cup of tea up if you like,' Lucy suggested.

Robert shot her a sharp glance. He didn't want the situation spoiling at this stage by his sister's over-anxious attitude.

'Thank you, Lucy, but I'll just relax here for a few minutes while I have it.'

The next half hour passed slowly for the young folk. Knowing what was to happen they could not concentrate on the chit-chat and it was something of a relief when Rebecca suggested they all went to bed. Rebecca closed the door of the front bedroom, the two girls went to the larger of the back two rooms and Robert gave them a reassuring wink as he opened the door of the smaller.

'Is it going to work?' asked Lucy anxiously as she sat down on the bed.

'As long as we're careful.' Alice tried to be calm though her heart was beating fast. She did not really look forward to what she regarded as a mad escapade but she could not let Lucy venture to Yorkshire on her own.

'Mother would be late tonight. Paul will be thinking we're not coming.' Lucy's lips tightened. Nothing must go wrong. She felt sure that she was on the track of solving the meaning behind her father's last words. 'How long before she'll be asleep?'

'How should I know?' The thought of the risks they were running brought an edge to Alice's voice. 'Best thing we can do is to get ready quietly. Remember, plenty of warm clothes, Paul said.'

The two girls each had a cloth bag in which they packed a dress and extra underclothes. For the hoped-for voyage they put on an extra chemise, a plain woollen dress, and an ankle-length pelisse. They each took a pair of warm gloves and decided to have a large square scarf which would give extra warmth to the shoulders and would be useful as a head covering and enable them to dispense with bonnets.

'Am I all right?' queried Lucy.

'Yes. You'll be warm enough?'

Lucy nodded.

'Good.'

They sat on the edge of the bed, trying to calm their nervousness which increased with every passing moment.

'We should be going. Let's see what Robert says?' pressed Lucy, jumping to her feet.

Alice grabbed her arm. 'No, sit down,' she hissed. 'Robert said he'd let us know when the time was right.'

Lucy, her lips pouting, sat down on the bed. 'Suppose he's fallen asleep?' She moaned and rolled her eyes at the thought.

'He won't,' whispered Alice emphatically.

Lucy fidgeted but froze when she heard a light tap on the wall. She glanced at her sister.

Another tap.

Alice nodded. They both stood up and tiptoed to the door. Its slight squeak sounded like thunder to them. They looked anxiously at their mother's bedroom door as Robert appeared from his room, shielding the light from his lamp. Silently he moved slowly down the stairs. Lucy heard her mother snore and with relief followed her brother, Alice only a step behind.

Robert motioned to the front door and, once he was satisfied that Alice had unlocked it and had the key, he took the lamp to the kitchen and extinguished it. He moved cautiously through the darkened house, careful not to knock anything which might disturb his mother. He found his sisters outside, took the key from Alice, locked the door and pocketed the key. He started off down the street with Lucy and Alice beside him.

In spite of the thin cloud the half moon gave a silvery glow which accentuated the depth of the shadows. A nearby church clock struck eleven. Other nights if she was not asleep Lucy was hardly aware of it, but tonight it seemed to boom and reverberate off the houses. She was sure it would wake her mother and that any moment she would be running after them, driving them back home as she lashed them with her tongue. Lucy shivered and then realised that her imagination was running wild; her mother could never be the harridan she visualised at that moment, but nevertheless there would be ructions when she found out what they had done. She did not envy Robert trying to placate her.

Her brother led the way unerringly. Lights still glowed from many homes and shone through the steamed-up windows of alehouses from which came raucous shouts and ribald laughter. As they moved towards the dock area the streets seemed darker, more sinister and the alleys held an air of salacious mystery. Lucy almost fell over an inebriated figure sprawled across the cobbles. She shuddered and shuffled round him, jumped when a groan sent shivers up her spine and scuttled after Robert.

The alehouses got noisier, drunks tottered on the streets and catching sight of two females yelled lewd suggestions at them. One reached out, pawing at Alice, but Robert unhesitatingly clipped him on the chin and left him unconscious in the dirt.

They reached an uninviting alley. 'This way,' Robert instructed.

'Down here?' Alice questioned his judgement with distaste in her voice at the sound of scuttling rats.

'It's a short cut to the coal wharves,' he replied.

'Paul showed it to you?' she asked, a little doubtfully.

'Yes.' Without waiting he started off down the alley. He wanted to deliver his sisters safely and then get back in case his mother had a disturbed night.

Reaching the end of the alley, they emerged on to the

open space beside the river where three ships were tied up. Huge heaps of coal were piled to one side. Robert stopped.

'Well?' asked Alice.

'Quiet,' he whispered. He stood still for a few moments. The girls had to curb their agitation. 'Wait here,' he ordered and before either of them could say anything he moved off. Though the pale moon washed the scene with a faint glow, Robert was soon lost to sight against the dark background.

Lucy shivered. She didn't like it here and was beginning to wish she had never suggested going to Ravenscar, let alone being smuggled on board a ship. She swallowed hard and trying to draw confidence said, 'Which is Paul's ship?'

'How should I know?' asked Alice testily. The unsalubrious side of this adventure was beginning to irritate her. She wished she had protested more strongly at Lucy's mad idea. Their steady life had been turned upside down. She could have been snug and fast asleep in bed. Instead she was standing shivering on a dirty wharf, whether with cold or fear she did not know.

Lucy made no reply. She was lost in her own thoughts, wishing Robert would hurry.

Though they expected him, they both jumped when a figure appeared out of the blackness.

'This way,' he said. 'I've made contact with Paul.'

Both girls felt relief though neither said anything. They followed their brother round the first coal heap which kept them out of sight of the first ship. Reaching the second heap Paul moved carefully towards the next ship. When it was fully in sight he stopped, and surveyed the ground which lay between them and the gangway. Nothing moved. He waited a moment longer, then, seeing a figure come to the gangway, he knew the way was clear for the girls to go on board. He turned to them. 'See the gangway? Go straight to it, walk up it without a word, say nothing when you meet Paul, just follow him. No time for goodbyes.' He cast a glance towards the ship. 'Go, now.'

Alice moved forward, pressing his arm as she passed him. Lucy started, stopped. 'Thanks, Robert.' She stretched up to kiss him on the cheek.

'Go!' His word was sharp, compelling her to obey instantly. Every second was precious now. They must get on board and be out of sight as quickly as possible. He reached out to reassure her but she was gone.

He watched, silently wishing them well, until he saw their dark figures move up the gangway and disappear. Then he turned for home, not looking forward to the morning when he would have to break the news to his mother.

As the girls came up the gangway Paul cast a glance along the quay. All was still. Wordlessly he led the way towards the stern.

Halfway along the deck he stopped and listened intently. In those few moments Lucy glanced around at the fore and main masts towering above her in the pale moonlight, their sails furled awaiting the moment when the brig would come to life as dawn broke across the roofs of the city. Satisfied that the sound he had heard must have come from an animal scuttling around the coal heaps on the dockside, Paul motioned them on.

He stopped beside a boat slung ready for use in an emergency. 'The accident boat,' he whispered. 'You'll have to lie in there. Keep well down, out of sight. I've put in two blankets and some food. Stay still and quiet until you hear from me.'

'Will we be all right?' The tremor in Alice's voice betrayed her apprehension and second thoughts about the prudence of their venture.

'Of course we will,' put in Lucy sharply before Paul had time to reply. She started to climb into the boat.

Paul took her bag and helped her. 'Right, now you, Alice.' Once in, they steadied themselves and retrieved their bags from Paul.

'Down! Down!' Paul urged, having heard distant foot-steps on the quay.

He was gone before the girls had any chance to question him. They were on their own now and both felt a flutter in their hearts at the prospect of facing the unknown. They lay down quickly, using their bags as head supports. They groped for the blankets and pulled them over themselves. Alice, feeling the package of food, placed it so she could get at it without too much movement.

The footsteps grew louder and passed close by. The girls hardly dared breathe. Discovery would mean that their esca-pade would be finished before it had started. They heard a call but could not make out what was said. They recognised Paul's voice in the reply, and then the footsteps moved on. Relaxing, they tried to make themselves more comfortable. There was a long night ahead before sailing time.

'Do you want something to eat?' The query roused Lucy out of her half-sleep.

She stirred, her limbs stiff from the unaccustomed hard-ness of the boat. 'Yes please.'

Deciding to keep the pie and cake they had brought

from home in reserve, Alice fumbled in the bag which Paul had left. She was cold and pleased at the chance of movement to ease her aching body. They seemed to have been here for ages and yet she had just heard a distant clock strike midnight. Seven more hours before they sailed and then they must still remain here for the voyage. She gritted her teeth. She found bread and cheese and passed some to Lucy. Lucy munched gratefully at the food. With the gnawing feeling in her stomach alleviated Lucy felt a little better. She longed for a hot drink to drive the chill from her bones but had to make do with the apple Alice passed her.

With hunger satisfied, they drew closer together, seeking warmth. As the cold penetrated Lucy began to have regrets that she had ever started this escapade and Alice chided herself for not being firm and refusing to have anything to do with it. They dozed and woke and dozed again and their fitful sleep was disturbed by aching limbs which cried out for the comfort of a warm bed.

'All hands! All hands!'

Lucy stirred. The voice sounded so far off. Where was she? Who was calling?

As she came fully awake the hard wood reminded her where she was. She felt so stiff. Her neck hurt and her side felt as if it had been kicked by a mule. She started to ease her aching body. A voice close to her ear hissed, 'Keep still.'

Feet pounded past the boat.

'Are you all right?' Lucy whispered.

'Barely,' replied Alice sarcastically. 'Fools, we are.'

In silence the girls searched in the food bag for some more bread and cheese.

'Let go fore and aft!'

'Get aloft!

The orders came firm and clear.

Timber creaked. The ship eased away from the dock side.

'Unfurl top gallant!'

Lucy peeped from below her blanket and saw sails curl and catch the breeze. She eased herself and peered over the side. The gap between them and the quay was widening. Excitement drove some of her doubts from her mind. Alice tugged her back down. 'Stay out of sight!' she ordered.

The ship groaned, moving to the centre of the river and heading for the sea.

'This is smooth,' commented Lucy after a few minutes.

Alice gave a little snort of disgust at the naivety of her sister. 'We're still in the river.'

The ship met the sea, dug its bow into the waves and rolled with the movement of the water. Lucy gulped. She felt an unusual twinge in her stomach. More sail billowed overhead, caught the wind and took the ship further and further from the protection of the land.

The motion increased. Lucy felt squeamish. 'Alice, are you all right?' she asked, her tone apprehensive.

'Yes,' hissed Alice. 'Be quiet.'

'I feel funny,' moaned Lucy.

'You're all right,' Alice replied firmly.

'I'm not. I feel sick.'

The ship heaved and rolled, the motion becoming more noticeable.

Lucy moaned. 'Wish it would stop.'

'Don't be stupid,' snapped Alice. 'Settle down, we've a long way to go yet.'

'Oh, no.'

'You shouldn't have had this mad idea,' Alice admonished impatiently.

Lucy bit her lip, fighting the nausea rising in her stomach. She clenched her fists tight. She gulped and put them hard against her mouth. She felt hot. She needed air and started to throw the blankets off. Alice grabbed them and jerked them back.

'Stupid,' she hissed. 'We don't want to be seen.'

'I don't care,' cried Lucy. 'I'm going to be sick.' Alice could do no more than throw back the blankets and shout, 'Over the side.'

Lucy leaned over the side of the boat and retched and retched until she thought her stomach would be torn out. Her head felt awful, light and swimmy yet pressed down by the sickness which overwhelmed her. 'I wish I were dead,' she moaned.

Alice, who had knelt helplessly by, put a comforting arm round her sister. 'There, you've got rid of it. Everything will be all right.'

Lucy thought she would never be right again. She groaned and sank back, only dimly aware of voices crowding in on her.

'Come on, Lucy, we've been discovered.' Alice was trying to help her sister to her feet. Then someone was beside her, taking over. Strong arms lifted Lucy and passed her over the side to another sailor waiting to take her. He stood her on her feet. She staggered and would have fallen if he hadn't steadied her. Hands helped Alice to the deck. She saw Paul was among the group of sailors who had come to the boat. She caught his eye but he feigned lack of recognition.

Some ribald remarks were cast in their direction once the sailors had got over their initial surprise at finding two female stowaways.

'Belay there!' A voice boomed across the deck. 'Bring the stowaways here.'

Alice saw a broad-shouldered man, feet astride, braced against the roll of the ship, standing beside the helmsman. There was an air of authority about him and she guessed they were being taken before the captain. He was dressed in light blue, wide-bottomed trousers with a matching shirt tight at the throat, over which he wore a thick jersey. His mark of authority, apart from his aura, was his peaked pork-pie hat. His black beard ran to thick sidewinders which merged with the flow of hair along his temples. He looked down at the two intruders with dark eyes but as Alice met his glance she reckoned there was understanding, fairness and compassion just below the surface. She determined to try to use them.

As the two girls walked towards him, he was surprised to see that his first expectations were incorrect. These were not a couple of sluts who had hoped for illicit liaisons with the crew only to find they had not banked on seasickness. He had never had them attempt to sell their wares on board his ships before. No, there was something different about these two. The cut of their clothes was not disguised by the crumpled appearance after a night spent in the accident boat. They held themselves in a way which spoke of respectability, even the one who showed signs of having been sick. In spite of her discomfort she tried to appear normal.

'Well, who are you?' he boomed, showing some annoyance at having his ship invaded.

Alice tilted her head proudly. 'I'm Alice Mitchell and this is my sister, Lucy.' Having decided that it would be better to stand up to this man, she met his gaze without flinching.

'And what are you doing on my ship?'

'Sir, we want to get to Ravenscar.'

'How did you know that's where I was bound?'

'We made enquiries.'

'From whom?'

'That I will not say.'

His lips tightened but secretly he admired this young woman who would not disclose the source of her information.

'How did you get on board?' he demanded.

'We sneaked on when it was dark and the watch's back was turned.'

The captain cast his eye around those of the crew who were standing by. 'Any of you on watch last night?'

'Aye, sir.' Paul stepped forward without hesitation.

'See anything?'

'No, sir.'

'Asleep were you?' he asked gruffly.

'No, sir.'

'Well you weren't wide awake letting a couple of females outwit you. Such carelessness demands dismissal.'

'Aye, sir,' replied Paul glumly.

The captain noted Alice shoot Paul a glance of alarm. It was only momentary but it was sufficient to make him suspect that these two were in league. He had heard that Paul was seeing a girl in Newcastle. Could this be her? Most likely. She had said they wanted to get to Ravenscar and that was where Paul's family lived. If she was the girl then he had chosen one with some spunk in a crisis.

'But you're a good crew member and I need good men,' the captain went on, 'so for this once I'll overlook your neglect.' He knew Paul's ambitions. The young man's father had told him when he had asked him for a place in his crew for his son.

'Aye, aye, sir.'

The captain had been aware of the relief in both the girls' eyes. 'Now what do I do about you two? Why do you want to get to Ravenscar, godforsaken place?'

'Trying to trace some relatives,' Lucy put in, the first words she had spoken since their discovery. The fresh air was clearing her head. Though her stomach still felt queasy the nausea was passing. 'If we hadn't stowed away we'd have had to walk and that would have been more dangerous.'

The captain turned his gaze on her. She was the prettier of the two and he could detect fire in her eyes. He guessed maybe she would have done the talking if she had not been seasick. 'Do you think so?' An amused smile twitched the corner of his lips. They must have been helped by one of his crew, who would have known they would be safe on his ship. It could have been different on some others. 'Suppose I was to hand you over to my crew?'

'Don't! It could have . . .' started Alice.

'You wouldn't dare!' Lucy's voice was sharp and challenging as she cut in.

'Wouldn't I? I could let them do what they want and then throw you overboard. Only the crew would know and they wouldn't look for trouble by reporting what happened.' He let out a boom of laughter when he saw alarm and fear mask the faces of the two girls. 'But I won't. You're safe enough on my ship. I should take you back and put you ashore but that would upset my schedule.'

'You'll not keep them on board, cap'n?' The mate, standing at his shoulder, voiced his misgivings.

'We want no bad luck.'

'Doomed if we take 'em.'

'Turn back, I says, or the sea'll have us.'

Murmurings came from those members of the crew who supported the mate.

The captain gave them a withering glare. 'Superstitious nonsense!' he snarled. 'You ought to know better, Mr Mate. I'll not turn back, but I'll not take them to Ravenscar.'

'Then what . . .' asked Alice, bewildered and puzzled.

'I want no one in the way of unloading there. All our attention must be on that. I have to unload some coal in Whitby so I'll hand you over to the authorities there.'

'No, sir, don't do that,' cried Lucy. 'Put us ashore there but don't hand us over or we'll never get to Ravenscar.'

The captain hesitated. It would be going against rules and regulations.

'The authorities would send us back to Newcastle and we need to get to Ravenscar,' pressed Alice to add weight to her sister's suggestion. 'Please put us ashore in Whitby and say nothing.'

The captain eyed them both. Their pleading looks could not be denied. 'Very well, I'll do that. You'll have to walk from Whitby to Ravenscar.'

Chapter Three

'Robert!'

He started, for a moment wondering where the noise was, and then he came wide awake.

'Robert!' There was panic, annoyance and disbelief in his mother's voice.

He groaned. He knew what was coming.

The door of his bedroom burst open.

'The girls aren't in their room. Their bed hasn't been slept in.'

'What?' He pretended surprise as he sat up in bed and ran his hand through his hair.

'Alice and Lucy have gone!'

'Gone? What do you mean?' He tried to make his questions ones of genuine dismay but when he saw distress being replaced by suspicion on his mother's face he knew he was not making a good job of it.

'Robert Mitchell, I think you know something about this. Where are they?' She brought her hands to her hips and set her face with a warning that he should not try to deceive her.

'At this moment they should be at sea,' he muttered.

'At sea! Don't you play tricks with me!'

'I'm not,' he protested, wanting to avoid the lash of his mother's tongue. 'They should be on Paul's ship bound for Ravenscar.'

Rebecca looked stunned. That name said it all. There was no need for Robert to tell her why they had gone but nevertheless she demanded a full explanation of what had happened. She listened intently without interrupting.

'So they dragged Paul into it. Didn't they realise the risk he would be running? He might lose his job. Stowing away on board ship is a serious offence. Those girls could be handed over to the authorities if they are discovered.' There was a cry of distress at the thought of what might happen to her daughters. Her lips set in a grim line. 'I might have known our Lucy wouldn't let it rest even though I told her to forget the whole thing.'

'What thing, Mother? What's it all about?' pressed Robert.

Rebecca hesitated, wondering if she should tell him, but then she shook her head slowly. 'There's nothing to be gained from knowing. It's best forgotten, but now it could all be dragged up again and it could cause trouble. It's never worth it, nothing can be proved.'

'About what?'

Rebecca stiffened. 'Nothing. Forget it, Robert, forget it.' The steel which had returned to her voice and now appeared in her eye told Robert he should question no further. 'You get yourself to Ravenscar and if they haven't been arrested bring them home immediately.'

'But, Mother, I can't just go like that. The office . . .'

'You must arrange to have some time off for important

45

personal business. I'm sure Mr Palmer will understand. I have a little money put aside so you can book a passage.'

When Robert returned later that day he was able to tell his mother that the first ship he could get did not leave until Tuesday.

'Five days.' There was a touch of despair in Rebecca's voice. 'Let's hope you are not too late.'

The two girls turned up the collars of their coats, removed the shawls from their heads and enjoyed the freshening wind blowing through their hair which they allowed to fall free. Lucy's upset passed and with Alice she enjoyed the sharp tang bringing colour to their cheeks.

Lucy laughed with the exhilaration and admired the sight of the billowing sails taut with the wind. The ship rolled and pitched gently, sending water hissing along the sides.

Alice was drawn by the magic of the motion of the ship and the ever-moving sea and she began to understand why Paul was drawn to the life though she guessed there could be danger with the sea in its more tempestuous and frightening moods.

Some sailors going about their work still muttered their superstitious misgivings, others paused and had a brief word with them. Paul took advantage of this and on the pretence of pointing out something on the coast, which was rarely out of sight, told them to take the Scarborough road out of Whitby and when they got to Ravenscar to go to the alum works and ask for Mrs Smurthwaite's cottage. He hoped to be there before them.

The ship altered course and the two girls sat enthralled

by the sight of the ruined abbey and the red-roofed town clinging precariously to the cliffs on each side of the river.

'Whitby,' Paul informed them as he went by to the bow to get ready for docking.

The ship became a hive of activity and Lucy was amazed at the agility of the sailors who swarmed aloft to furl the sails. Orders were shouted and instantly obeyed. There was no mistaking that the captain was in charge and his crew knew it. He guided, with eyes alert to every situation. His judgement was perfect as the ship passed between the piers to find the calm of the river. Taken in hand the ship was manoeuvred through the bridge which had been opened to allow passage upstream to the quay where the coal would be unloaded. Ropes curled out, thrown with accuracy to the waiting men who gathered them and wound them round capstans to bring the vessel gently to the quay. The gangway was run out. The crew unbattened the hatches and prepared to cooperate with men ashore to unload the coal, knowing their captain wanted it done quickly so he could be on his way to Ravenscar.

When everything was to his satisfaction he came to Alice and Lucy. 'This is where you leave. Take the Scarborough road, that's it yonder.' He pointed to a trackway climbing from the riverside. 'About seven miles and you'll find a track to Ravenscar. Best of luck. I hope you find your relatives.'

'Thank you, sir,' said Lucy with a touch of perkiness.

A flicker of amusement touched the captain's lips as he recalled how green she had looked when she was discovered but he banished it quickly and adopted a stern note. 'Don't ever try stowing away again. You might not find such an understanding captain.'

47

'Yes, sir. And thank you again.' Alice added her gratitude.

'Now, off my ship and on your way.'

The two girls scuttled to the gangway and as they started along the quay there were shouts of good wishes from some of the crew, among them Paul who knew his call carried more significance than the others.

They shuffled more comfortably into their clothes, eased the bags in their hands and fell into stride. They were soon climbing out of Whitby, only pausing to gaze back with admiration across the red roofs to the gaunt outline of the ruined abbey.

The breeze was more noticeable on the higher ground and they tightened the shawls around their heads.

'Will we get there before dark?' asked Lucy, noting the lowering sun.

'If we find the right track,' replied Alice. 'And I expect it will be worse than this,' she added, casting her eye along deep ruts and hoof marks hardened by the sun. 'Careful you don't twist your ankle.'

They had been walking about twenty minutes when they heard the sound of squeaking leather, rumbling wheels and the snort of a horse straining against the weight of a vehicle. They stopped and looked back to see a two-wheeled chaise, its hood drawn up to shield its passenger from the breeze.

As it neared them they saw that the sole occupant was a young woman about their own age. Envious that she should have money enough to afford such a vehicle to get her across this rough terrain they waited for her to pass. Instead she pulled the horse to a halt beside them.

'Are you two going far?' Her enquiry was pleasant, friendly.

Alice decided this person had summed them up before stopping and had concluded that they were respectable. 'Ravenscar,' she answered.

'I'm going near there. Would you like to ride?'

'Yes please.'

'Climb on.'

Lucy smiled her thanks as she shuffled along the seat so that Alice could sit beside her.

'Bit crushed, but we'll manage,' said the driver, holding the horse steady as it champed impatiently. 'I'm Zilpha de Northby. I live at Northby Hall near where you are going.'

Alice, sensing Lucy was about to burst with questions, gripped her arm tightly in warning to say nothing.

'We are pleased to know you and are very grateful for the ride,' put in Alice quickly.

Zilpha set the horse in motion and the chaise swayed and squeaked as the wheels negotiated the ruts.

'Sorry the track isn't smoother,' apologised Zilpha. 'It'll be a bit better when we turn off, not used so much. This one goes to Scarborough. Have you come far?'

'Newcastle,' said Lucy brightly.

'By ship into Whitby?'

'Yes. First time we've been to sea. We enjoyed it.'

'First time to Ravenscar?'

'Yes,' said Alice, wanting to make the explanation in case Lucy gave away the reason for their visit. 'I'm friendly with a sailor and I've come to see his family.'

'Who? Maybe I know them.'

'Smurthwaite.'

'Oh, yes I do,' cried Zilpha. 'A nice family. Mr Smurthwaite works at the alum works which are owned by my father.

Mrs Smurthwaite puts some time in at the Hall. She's a motherly woman, you'll like her.'

Alice was glad to hear such a glowing report for she had some misgivings about meeting Paul's family for the first time, especially as she and Lucy would be throwing themselves on their good nature. Paul had told her everything would be all right, and now she felt a little more reassured.

'She'll be helping next Wednesday evening at my birthday party. That's why I've been in Whitby today, collecting a dress and a few other things.'

'Then a happy birthday if it's not too soon,' said Lucy brightly.

'Thank you,' replied Zilpha with a gracious inclination of her head.

The three of them chatted pleasantly and all the while Lucy was wondering what her father's last words could mean. How did he know about a family living in a remote part of Yorkshire who were so well off, and who, judging by the girl beside them, must be pleasant? What could such a family owe the Mitchells?

Questions she was dying to ask Zilpha were spinning in her mind but Alice's grip had warned her and she respected her judgement.

Zilpha pulled the horse to a halt at a fork in the track. 'This is where I turn off. You carry straight on about a mile and you'll see the alum works. Mr and Mrs Smurthwaite live in one of the cottages.'

'Thank you very much for the ride,' said Alice. 'We'd have been a bit weary by the time we had walked here.' She dropped to the ground and turned to take their two bags from Lucy.

'Thank you,' smiled Lucy and jumped from the chaise. 'Goodbye.' The two girls set off in the direction indicated by Zilpha.

She watched them for a few moments. Pleasant girls, she thought. Lucy the prettiest, in fact she could turn men's heads. She gave the reins a flick and the chaise rumbled forward.

Alice and Lucy looked back and waved.

'A nice person,' observed Lucy.

'I feared you were going to reveal why we are here.'

'It was a good opportunity to ask if there was any connection between our families.'

'I think we make some outside enquiries first.'

'Ever the cautious one,' commented Lucy lightly. 'But maybe you're right this time. They're certainly well off. Did you see the quality of her coat?'

'I certainly did,' replied Alice in a tone which revealed she appreciated the cost of the garment. 'And no doubt she has collected a dress for her party just as expensive.'

'But she was agreeable, and not proud of her standing.'

'No,' agreed Alice. 'I liked her.'

They topped a rise and stopped. Their attention was drawn to the bay which lay before them. Away to their left grey towering cliffs lowered as they swept round a bay to rise again even higher and more precipitous. The starkness of the landscape was only relieved by the red roofs of a tiny village which clung precariously to the cliff to their left. It seemed as if the houses, with smoke curling from their chimneys, must fall into the sea at any time.

The ground fell away gently in front of them towards a complex of red-roofed buildings with a tall chimney

51

belching smoke in their midst. In the evening light they could make out men moving about, pushing wheelbarrows to and from a coal heap, or rolling barrels from one of the sheds to waiting horses and carts. Steam rose from some of the buildings and from open pits, adding a macabre atmosphere to the scene.

'It's strange,' muttered Alice half to herself.

'And smelly,' added Lucy as she caught the whiff of a sharp pungent smell wafted on the breeze.

The smell grew stronger as they drew nearer the buildings but if they wanted to find the Smurthwaites they would have to ignore its unpleasantness.

'I don't know how they work among it,' commented Lucy, wrinkling her nose.

'They must be used to it,' said Alice. 'Maybe it's not so bad when you're nearby.' She stopped.

'What's wrong?' asked Lucy.

'We'd better go to the left, there's a quarry just ahead.'

Lucy followed her sister's gaze and saw that indeed they were heading for the edge of a quarry. She cast her eyes quickly across the immediate landscape.

'Yes, to the left, and further over. Those must be the cottages.' She indicated some rows of buildings from one of which she had just seen two women emerge.

'I wonder if that's Paul's ship?' Alice pondered, pointing towards a two-masted vessel which, far out on a tranquil sea, was altering course towards the cliffs.

'I believe it is,' said Lucy. 'We'll be at his home before him.'

'And that means an explanation to his mother,' said Alice, a little apprehensive at this prospect. She drew a little comfort remembering Zilpha's assessment of Mrs Smurthwaite.

Having been directed to the Smurthwaite cottage by one of the workers, the girls found Zilpha's opinion to be correct for the woman who opened the door held a motherly aura in spite of her look of puzzled enquiry at finding two young women standing on her doorstep.

'Mrs Smurthwaite?' Alice asked tentatively.

'Aye.' She glanced from one to the other. 'What can I do for you?' It was unusual to find two girls, strangers, here, and from their dress, plain but well cut, she judged that they came from a respectable family.

'I'm Alice Mitchell and this is my sister, Lucy.' Her timbre was nervous. 'I'm . . . er . . . a friend of Paul.'

For a moment Mrs Smurthwaite was taken aback by this unexpected announcement. Her mind raced. Surely Paul hadn't got this girl into trouble! Alice caught her automatic glance downwards.

'Oh, no, Mrs Smurthwaite, it's nothing like that,' she added quickly. She saw relief in her eyes and went on, 'I'd hoped Paul would be here before us so that you would have had an explanation. I think that will be his ship coming in now.'

'I'm sorry, lass, but when strangers like you turn up saying they know my son, well, a mother . . .' Her voice trailed away. 'I think you'd better come in and tell me what this is about, where you are from and how you got here.' These girls looked respectable and it was good to know that her son had found such a person and not got entangled with a girl like some who haunted the ports.

The two girls found themselves in a large square room

with a sink under one of the two windows which faced the sea. A fire burned brightly, casting a cosy warmth into the room. The black oven, which it also heated, shone with regular care. Two Windsor chairs were positioned near the fire and a sofa stood along one wall. The centre of the room was occupied by a scrubbed white-wood table with a wooden chair placed on each side.

'Put your bags down, lasses, take off your coats and sit down. You'd like a cup of tea?'

'Yes please, Mrs Smurthwaite,' said Alice.

As she poured water from the kettle she asked, 'Have you come far?'

'From Newcastle.'

Mrs Smurthwaite, teapot in hand, straightened with surprise. Her eyes widened, their whites emphasising the deep blue which now sparkled with curiosity. 'Newcastle? How did you get here?'

'Paul's ship.'

Mrs Smurthwaite flopped down on one of the chairs beside the table as if dealt a blow by the information. 'What?'

Alice went on quickly to tell her how Paul had smuggled them on board and that the captain had insisted that he put them ashore at Whitby.

Mrs Smurthwaite listened without speaking, merely shaking or nodding her head in surprise and incredulity.

'You walked from Whitby?' she asked when Alice paused.

'We started to,' put in Lucy, 'but we were given a lift by Zilpha de Northby.'

Mrs Smurthwaite raised her eyebrows. 'Aye, that's

54

Zilpha, grand lass, always willing to give a helping hand. Mind you she can be headstrong and being an only child is spoilt, especially by her father.' Her gaze passed between the two girls. 'That tells me how you got here but not why, nor how you know Paul.'

'Paul helped me home after I had been knocked down in Newcastle. Because he was so kind Mother invited him to visit us whenever he was in port,' explained Alice.

'If your mother knows then that's all right,' approved Mrs Smurthwaite. She frowned as a diquieting thought struck her. 'If she approves why did Paul have to smuggle you on board his ship?'

'Oh, she doesn't know we're here.' Lucy's words brought alarm to Mrs Smurthwaite's face. 'Well, she will now. Robert, our brother, will have told her after we had sailed.' She saw a mystified look come to this kind lady's eyes and decided she deserved a full explanation. She glanced at her sister and saw that Alice had thought this too. 'It's really all my fault,' went on Lucy. 'After a fashion.' She went on to explain how her father's dying words had raised her curiosity and determination to find out what he meant even against her mother's wishes. 'We had no idea who the de Northbys were but, when Alice told Paul what Father had said, he told her that a de Northby owned these alum works.'

'So you decided to come here without your mother's approval.' There was a slight admonishment in Mrs Smurthwaite's voice as one parent upholding the decision of another. Lucy nodded. 'And I suppose Paul said you could stay here?'

'Yes,' replied Alice quietly. 'I hope that's all right?'

Mrs Smurthwaite looked sternly thoughtful.

'Oh, please say yes, Mrs Smurthwaite,' pleaded Lucy. 'We've nowhere else to go.'

She had been carefully studying the girls throughout their explanations and she had been taken by their forthright attitude. They appeared to have hidden nothing. She liked their open countenances, their simple dress. The look she had put on to show the girls that she didn't fully approve of their escapade vanished and she smiled, relaxing the atmosphere to one of friendliness. 'I wouldn't be Sarah Smurthwaite if I turned anyone away.'

'Oh, thank you, thank you.'

She laughed at their relief. 'Right, let's have another cup of tea.' She brewed some fresh tea and as she was filling their cups she said, 'I suppose you want me to tell you what I know about the de Northbys.'

'Yes, please,' urged Lucy, hoping she was on the verge of finding out what her father had meant, but her hopes were spoilt when Sarah said, 'It's very little, I'm afraid.'

'Anything might help.' Lucy was not to be put off. 'Have you heard our name, Mitchell, connected with them?'

Sarah looked thoughtful for a moment but then shook her head slowly. 'Can't say I have. Did your folk come from these parts?'

Lucy shook her head. 'Grandfather and Grandmother were natives of Newcastle, before that I don't know.' She glanced at Alice.

'I never heard Mother nor Father mention any links with Yorkshire.'

'There are no Mitchells hereabouts so I can't see any connection with the family at the Hall. I work there from time to time and I haven't known anyone speak of Mitchells.'

'How long have the de Northbys owned these alum works?' Alice asked.

'I don't know how long, since far back in the past. Richard, Zilpha's father, is the present owner; he inherited it from his father and I suppose he did from his and so on and so on. His father built the Hall out of profits, bought a lot of land and built cottages for farm workers and brought a lot of waste land into cultivation. Though they have never been known to pay their workers well, and I should know with my husband, Tom, employed here, they have done a lot of good in the countryside. Folk would be worse off without them. The present owner is a bit of a tyrant, expects his workers to know what they owe him, touch a forelock and all that. His wife, Adeline, is kind and Zilpha takes after her. Only child, I suppose she'll inherit Hall, land, alum works, the lot. She'll be a right catch so I hope she gets the right man. Everyone expects him to be Mark Cossart from Howland Manor.'

'And will he do?' asked Alice, absorbed by Sarah's information.

'Aye, he'll do. Fine young man.'

Lucy had only been half listening, for her thoughts were glumly taken up with trying to see some connection between the Mitchells and de Northbys. It seemed as if Robert would be right, they were here on a wild goose chase.

Suddenly she sat upright, hopeful excitement on her face. The movement drew the attention of Alice and Sarah.

'What is it?' asked Alice.

'Suppose it isn't Mitchell.'

'What do you mean?' Alice was puzzled.

Lucy's words came slowly at first. 'Father did not

mention Mitchell, he merely said "the de Northbys owe you". Suppose he didn't mean the Mitchells?'

'Then who?'

'Mother's family.'

'Wades?' Lucy's implication was beginning to dawn on Alice.

'Yes, he could have meant Mother's family.' Lucy's words came faster with excitement at what could be a different interpretation of his meaning. She looked expectantly at Mrs Smurthwaite and saw from her expression that the name did mean something.

'Wade, now I have heard that name mentioned. Some trouble in the past, a long time ago I believe.'

'Trouble?' pressed Lucy.

'I don't know. Never bothered my head with it.'

'Can't you remember anything?' cried Lucy.

'Sorry, love. I only heard a rumour that there had been some trouble, but what it was about I do not know. I can only tell you the name Wade was mentioned.'

'There, we have discovered something.' Lucy's voice filled with joy.

'We don't know yet. We may not have,' put in Alice trying to calm her sister's over-exuberance.

'We'll soon find out. We'll go up to the Hall now and demand to see Mr de Northby and ask him to his face.' Lucy jumped to her feet.

'You can't do that,' Sarah protested with alarm. 'It's more than Tom's job's worth. We'd be turned out and have nowhere to go.'

'He wouldn't know we'd been here.'

'He'd soon find out.'

'We told Zilpha where we were coming,' pointed out Alice.

'But . . .'

'No buts,' interrupted Alice. 'We have got to think of other people and proceed calmly. There may be nothing in it. So sit down.'

Lucy stared hard at her sister for a moment then, as the wisdom of her words dawned on her, obeyed.

Before any more plans could be made the door burst open and Paul rushed in. 'Ma! Ma!' He pulled up short and the words died when he saw the two girls. 'Oh, you've got here.' He turned to his mother, his face reddening. 'Ma, you've met . . . er . . . is it all right?'

Sarah laughed at her son's embarrassment. 'Of course it is, lad. Alice and Lucy have explained everything.' She became serious. 'You took a risk smuggling them on board ship.'

'I knew they wouldn't give me away if they were discovered.' He smiled his thanks at Alice.

'We've found a link between us and the de Northbys,' cried Lucy, her eyes brightening with the good news she had to tell him.

'Then it was worth coming,' said Paul, eager to hear what she had to say.

Lucy explained. 'I wanted to go up to the Hall and confront Mr de Northby but your mother cautioned against that.'

'We'll do some investigating quietly. Maybe we could go and thank Zilpha for giving us a ride and maybe contrive to talk of the past.'

'She'll be too involved with her birthday party to bother about thanks,' warned Sarah.

'Ma, you'll be working at the Hall that night?' said Paul.

'Aye.'

'And Mrs de Northby generally engages a few local lasses to help at the party?'

'Aye.'

'Well, you could get Alice and Lucy a job and they could see the place and maybe get an opportunity to thank Zilpha.'

Sarah nodded. 'A good idea.' She turned to the two girls. 'But on one condition: you don't bring up any of this that evening. I don't want involving in any trouble. As I said it's more than Tom's job and this roof over our heads is worth. You'll see the de Northbys and can make up your own minds about them.'

'Very good, Mrs Smurthwaite,' Alice agreed. She looked at Lucy. 'And you keep your impetuosity under control. We'll work things out gradually.' She looked back at Sarah. 'How long can we stay?'

'As long as you like, lass, provided you let your mother know you're safe.'

'We will. Thank you.'

Sarah looked at her son. 'Are you staying the night?'

'No,' he replied. 'I'll be sleeping on board. We sail early tomorrow morning.'

'Back to Newcastle?'

'Aye.'

'Then you can make sure that Mrs Mitchell knows her daughters are safe and sound here with me.'

'I will,' he promised.

'But don't tell her that we might have found a connection,' Alice requested. 'If you get an opportunity you can tell Robert.'

'Very good. Now I must be off. I only slipped away to warn Ma that you would be coming.'

When he had gone Alice made one more observation to Mrs Smurthwaite. 'We don't know how long we'll be here if anything comes of our enquiries or how long they will take, but we should be back in Newcastle within the month, Lucy's due back in her employment then.'

'And what might that be?'

'Governess.'

'What about you?'

'I gave up my job as a teacher in a dame school. I couldn't let Lucy come alone. So if there is any work around here we could take it would help us and we must contribute something to our keep.'

'That's thoughtful of you.' She pondered for a moment. 'Probably the easiest way would be to gather seaweed for the alum works. It's burnt to produce ash which is used in processing the alum. Folk are paid for what they gather.' She looked a little doubtful. 'Maybe that isn't the kind of work . . .'

'We'll do anything,' cried Lucy.

'Well, you'd earn some money and at the same time have freedom to take time to follow up your enquiries. All I ask is that when you are making them you are careful.'

'We will be,' promised Lucy, grateful for the opportunity Mrs Smurthwaite was giving them.

When she closed the door after showing them the bedroom they could share, the two girls smiled broadly and flung their arms round each other, joyful in their good fortune.

'Hope Mother hasn't been too upset,' commented Alice as she sat down on the bed.

'She'll have given Robert her tongue.' Lucy grinned ruefully at the thought.

'It will help when Paul gets there and reassures her that we are staying with his mother.'

'We've got to find out what lies behind the trouble in the past which Mrs Smurthwaite mentioned, and the sooner the better,' said Lucy, focusing their minds on why they had come. 'Maybe there's an old retainer at the Hall who might know something. We might find out something when we are at the Hall for the party.'

'Oh, do be careful, Lucy,' Alice cautioned.

When Tom came home he was surprised to see the two girls but a brief explanation was sufficient for him to make them as welcome as his wife had done. He agreed to their plan to gather seaweed and to see that they were provided with baskets and to show them the easiest way to the shore.

The following day he showed them the huge quarries in which pickmen hacked shale from the rock face. A line of barrowmen carted the shale to clamps, smouldering fires, situated in the lower flat parts of the quarries.

'Those fires are kept burning with brushwood for about a year,' he explained. 'You see those pits.' He pointed them out near the clamps. 'The burnt shale is steeped with water from reservoirs above the quarry. Those men you see working there are the liquormen and then when the alum liquor is removed the wet shale is taken away by pitmen and dumped in heaps further down the slope.'

'Where is the seaweed used?' Alice asked.

'I'll tell you in a minute,' replied Tom. 'Let's go further.' They moved towards the main complex of buildings. He indicated some storage units sunk in the ground and covered by a wooden roof supported by stout timbers. 'The alum liquor from the steeping pits is stored in there before going to the clearing house, that building with the tall chimney at the end. There it is boiled to get rid of any impurities before passing to the evaporating pans where it is boiled again, maybe for a couple of days to get rid of a lot of the water and leave a concentrated fluid.'

He led the way through some of the buildings, nodding to some of the workers as he went. Alice and Lucy realised that Tom must have a position of authority, probably a foreman or overseer under the manager whose house, with an office next to it, he had pointed out to them in a position overlooking the main buildings.

He stopped in front of some open pits of liquid. 'The concentrated liquor is left in these settling tanks so that any impurities which are left can settle to the bottom before the liquid is run off into these cooling tanks.' He had led the way into a building alongside the settlers. The girls screwed up their noses at the smell, which had become stronger when they had moved inside. 'Now comes the process where we use the seaweed. The liquid which is obtained from burning seaweed and that from . . .' He paused and looked a little embarrassed as he eyed the girls, who were finding his explanation fascinating. 'Er . . . well, let's say the liquid which is shipped in barrels from London and once occupied . . . the city's chamber pots . . .'

Both Alice and Lucy stared wide-eyed at him.

'Really?' said Alice in disbelief.

'You're teasing us,' exclaimed Lucy, the corners of her

lips twitching in amusement at the picture she had conjured up.

'No,' replied Tom in all seriousness.

'Then that is what's making the unpleasant smell?' said Alice.

'Mostly,' he agreed.

'I shouldn't like to work here too long.' Lucy wrinkled her nose.

'You get used to it after a while.'

'And what happens when those liquids are added?' asked Alice.

'Alum crystals are formed. They are taken to the alum bing where they are stored prior to boiling in the roaching pans. That removes the rest of the impurities. While the liquid is still hot it is poured into casks in the tun house. Then, in just over a week, the barrels are split open and there are huge blocks of crystal. They are left for about another week during which time any remaining liquid drains off. That is taken away for reboiling and the blocks of crystal are taken to the warehouse where they are broken up and ground and stored ready to be taken down to the harbour for shipment.'

'Harbour?' Lucy looked a little puzzled. 'Aren't we on the edge of a steep cliff?'

Tom smiled. 'Yes we are. I said harbour, but really it's a dock, a jetty. We have to get coal in some way – you know that through Paul. So there is a track up the cliff used by packhorses and there is also an inclined track of rails. Trucks are loaded below and hauled up by means of a winding engine, the rails taking them into the coal yard which you saw near the boilers. So we use the same means to ship the alum out.'

'Where does it go, Mr Smurthwaite?' asked Lucy.

'Chiefly to the textile industry to fix dye in the cloth and to the leather industry because it helps to make leather more supple. Some goes to harden candles and it also helps to make things waterproof.' As he took them into the open again he said, 'We're a bit isolated here; that's why cottages were built for the workers.'

'Yours is a bit bigger than some of them,' Alice observed.

'The bigger ones are occupied by the housemen, they are the supervisors and it will be one of them who will check your loads of the seaweed. Now, to get to the beach – the safest way is via Stoupe Beck, yonder cutting that runs down to the shore between here and Robin Hood's Bay. That's the village you can see over there.' He indicated the houses clinging to the cliff across the bay. 'Dangerous to try to get round the cliffs and come up the packhorse path or the incline, easy to get cut off by the sea, and the tides can be dangerous.'

The girls nodded their understanding. 'When do we start?' asked Lucy.

'Mrs Smurthwaite tells me she's going to try to get you some work at the Hall on the night of the party, so I'd say wait until after then, no good tiring yourselves out before. It's only four days away and I have no doubt Mrs de Northby will want to see you the day before so she can tell you what to do.'

Later that day Mrs Smurthwaite arrived home from the Hall, where she had been working in the kitchen, with the news that Alice and Lucy could help at the party. 'Mrs de Northby will want to see you on Monday and again on

Tuesday – she wants everything to be perfect for the party on Wednesday.'

'Remember not a word to anyone about our interest in the de Northbys,' Alice warned Lucy as they got ready to accompany Mrs Smurthwaite to the Hall on Monday. 'We don't want trouble for Mr and Mrs Smurthwaite.'

'My tongue is tied,' said Lucy lightly.

'And see the knot doesn't slip,' returned Alice, knowing Lucy's impetuosity.

The day was fine, the air crisp, making everything stand out sharply. Alice and Lucy enjoyed the walk, revelling in the open air and panoramic views after being used to the enclosed atmosphere of Newcastle. It opened a whole new world to them, which widened even further as they walked up the long drive towards Northby Hall.

'I'll take you up the main drive so that you can see the front of the house, before we go to the back entrance,' said Sarah.

The gravelled driveway twisted between rhododendron bushes which Mrs Smurthwaite told them would be a blaze of colour later in the year. These gave way to shrubs on the right and a small wood on the left. The drive curved round the end of the wood to reveal a large house standing imposingly at the top of gently sloping grassland which gave way to immaculate lawns in front of the house.

The girls stopped in their tracks and gaped. They had never seen anything like this. They had read about and been told of such places but had never dreamed they would ever see one, let alone go inside one.

'This for one family?' gasped Lucy, her eyes wide.

'Aye, lass,' smiled Sarah. 'See nothing like it in Newcastle?'

'Nothing,' agreed Lucy. 'And Zilpha lives here?' She could not get over the size of the building.

She could see the drive sweeping round and widening in front of the stone-built house. The single door with small but enhancing pediment was centrally placed, complementing the symmetrical aspect. Two large sash windows were placed on each side of the doorway and exactly above them, with a fifth over the doorway, were identical windows. Above them, set into the roof, were five more windows of the same pattern but slightly smaller in height. The pantile roofs over these windows were miniatures of the two roofs which covered the two wings protruding beyond the main frontage.

'Mr Leo de Northby built the present Hall about forty-two years ago,' Sarah informed them. 'He knocked down a house built by his grandfather.'

'Why did he do that?' asked Lucy

'I suppose he wanted a bigger place but to still use the site his grandfather had chosen because of the beautiful views in every direction. You'll see better when we get to the house. I don't like the change he made to the gardens.'

'How did he do that?' queried Lucy, ever inquisitive.

'You see that area of shrubs we passed? Well, that was all laid out in nice formal gardens. I can remember them because I used to run around them as a little girl when my mother came to work at the Hall. But Mr Leo had them all changed. "Back to nature," I heard him telling the gardener one day. "It's the new way, created wilderness, but under control." He talked of a lake at the bottom of yon field but it was never done. We'd best be on.'

She kept to a brisk pace up the slope but paused before

heading for the back of the house to allow the girls to take in the view. They saw exactly what she meant by the magnificent position. Set as it was at the top of the rise it enjoyed panoramic views on all sides. Fields lay before it where cattle grazed and to the left there was an unrestricted view to the sea which today lay tranquil under a blue sky. To the right lay more fields and beyond them were glimpses of moorland.

Lucy sighed when she thought of her mother and Robert hemmed in by houses and looking out on to grimy streets and not far away the noisy thoroughfares crowded with folk.

Sarah escorted them to the back of the house, which though more practical with its service yard and nearby stables and coach house was just as symmetrical as the front.

When she opened the back door they were into a small vestibule. 'Hang your coats up here, lasses.' She indicated the row of pegs, several of which already held coats, scarves and bonnets. She opened another door and they found themselves in a huge kitchen. Two large wooden tables with a space between occupied the centre of the room. A wide roasting range was let into an outside wall. Three spits situated in front of the fire rested on hinged arms and were turned by chains passing round pulley wheels. Close to it, utilising the same flue, was a large iron range with an oven and its own fire. Lucy gaped at it in amazement as she thought of their own small range at home and that, thanks to a sympathetic landlord, was better than most people had. Other tables were dotted around the room against the walls and here kitchen maids were busy preparing fruit and vegetables and at one bigger than the others two young women were making pastry.

'Good morning, Mrs Kemp.'

The stout woman, in white mob cap and white apron over a blue dress, who was busy at the centre tables supervising the making of fruit fillings, looked up. 'Good day to you, Mrs Smurthwaite.' She eyed Alice and Lucy. 'These are the lasses you were telling me about?'

'Yes.' Sarah introduced them and added, 'Mrs Kemp runs the kitchen, her word is law. What she tells you, you do instantly.'

Mrs Kemp gave the two girls a friendly smile and said, 'Remember that and we'll get along very well.'

'Yes, ma'am,' said both girls, a little overawed.

'Don't ma'am me. I'm Mrs Kemp to you. Ma'am is for Mrs de Northby.'

'Yes, Mrs Kemp.'

'Good.' She glanced at Sarah. 'The other temporary staff for Wednesday are with Mrs de Northby in the ballroom now, so you'd better get along there.'

'Very good,' said Sarah. 'This way, girls.'

They followed her out of the kitchen along a wide stone-flagged corridor past three doors on each side. 'Storerooms,' she informed them. They passed from the corridor through a doorway into a room which she told them was used to assemble food prior to taking it into the dining room.

'That's it.' She indicated a door opposite them when they came into a corridor running at right angles across the house. They entered an immense room which ran to the front of the main building and beyond to the full extent of one of the wings the girls had seen when they approached the house. 'The ballroom,' she whispered.

Both Alice and Lucy stopped in their tracks and gazed in

amazement. They had never imagined a room so big. It was flooded with light from the large sash windows, showing the ivy-patterned wallpaper to advantage. The white plasterwork of the ceiling was ornate with hanging pendants shaped as bunches of grapes. The shining floor was being given a further polish in readiness for Wednesday.

'Ah, Mrs Smurthwaite, and the two girls you said you could bring.' A lady dressed in a high-waisted, rose-patterned, ankle-length frock detached herself from a group of twelve girls and moved gracefully to greet them.

'Yes, ma'am.' Sarah bobbed a curtsey. 'This is Alice and Lucy Mitchell.'

The girls imitated Sarah's curtsey though not as smoothly.

'This is Mrs de Northby,' Sarah informed them, though they had guessed that.

'Ma'am,' they said together.

Her long face seemed to carry a touch of severity but that was immediately demolished by a smile which revealed an attractive brand of beauty. Her blue eyes, attentive, observing, carried a brilliance which held the attention of whoever she was with. Her dark hair was simply dressed, piled high on her head and held in place by four jet combs.

'I'm so glad you could come. Mrs Smurthwaite tells me you are from Newcastle. This will be quite a change for you.' Her voice was soft with a pleasant lilt.

'Yes, ma'am.' Both girls were charmed by her and that impression deepened as, along with the others, she directed them in what she expected of them on Wednesday. Her instructions were precise and clear. Ambiguity was not part of her make-up.

'Food will be set in the dining room for guests to help themselves as and when they desire. You will be in attendance to help them and also to see that there is always plenty of food available. Wine will be at a separate table in the dining room but I want two of you,' she paused and looked round the girls, 'you, Alice and Lucy, to go among the guests at various intervals throughout the party, with glasses of wine and also filling up glasses if guests require it.'

When her instructions were finished and she had requested that all the temporary staff report again tomorrow to rehearse she took them into the assembly room where, as she had instructed, cocoa was available for the girls before they left for their homes.

As they walked away from the Hall Alice and Lucy expressed their awe at its size and at the opulence they had seen.

Sarah laughed. 'You'll see even more on the night of the party. Nothing will be spared. The food will be exquisite, the wine will flow, and you'll be envious of the dresses and the attention the smart young men will lavish on the girls. There'll be music and dancing and gaiety everywhere.'

'My goodness,' said Lucy, 'will we be able to cope? We've never done anything like this before – and serving wine!' She raised her eyes heavenwards as if that was the end of the world.

Alice agreed glumly. 'I hope we don't make fools of ourselves.'

Sarah laughed at their self-doubt. 'You won't. Harold, he's the head butler, Mrs Kemp's husband, he'll keep you right. You'll meet him tomorrow.'

The two girls felt some measure of relief that they would not be entirely on their own to see to the wine.

In the afternoon they decided to go for a walk along the cliffs and discover Stoupe Beck so they would not have to spend time finding the way on their first day of gathering seaweed.

They enjoyed the walk with views across the bay and out to sea. They found the beck and followed it to the shore. The tide was out exposing long scaurs, flat lines of rock, covered with seaweed. That, together with seaweed washed up on the beach, was being gathered by several young women. As they strolled towards the water's edge Alice and Lucy saw that the seaweed gatherers were putting the harvest into large baskets. Two of the women had filled theirs and they helped each other fasten them on their backs by shoulder straps before setting off for the climb to the alum works via Stoupe Beck.

'We'll probably manage that better than the wine on Wednesday,' observed Alice.

'Oh, I don't know,' said Lucy. 'I've got used to the idea, especially after Mrs Smurthwaite told us about Harold. In fact I'm rather looking forward to it and seeing how other people live.' She frowned. 'After that visit it makes you wonder just what Father could mean by, "the de Northbys owe you".'

'I know,' agreed Alice. 'How could he know of such a family living in a place like that? They must be rich beyond imagination. I don't see what connection we can have with the family. Maybe we should give up and go home.'

Lucy stopped and, grabbing her sister's arm, turned her

72

to face her. 'We won't and don't you start thinking like that. There was something behind Father's words. Don't forget it seems more likely that the connection is through Mother's family. Mrs Smurthwaite thought she had heard something about Wades.'

'But what?' said Alice.

'That's what I am determined to find out.'

Chapter Four

The following day as they were making their way to the back of Northby Hall they saw Zilpha coming from the stable yard.

'Doesn't she look lovely?' whispered Lucy, admiring Zilpha's riding habit. The dark blue cloth almost straight from the tight waist was worn under a long-sleeved waistcoat of light blue. A neck-fitting white cravat was frilled at the front emphasising her delicate features, pink from the morning ride. Her hair was held at the nape of her neck by a blue bow and was enhanced by a small red tricorne hat perched at a jaunty angle. Black riding boots peeped below her dress which she held so that it did not drag across the cobbles.

She stopped when she saw Mrs Smurthwaite and the two girls.

'The Mitchell girls,' she exclaimed with a friendly smile. 'You found Mrs Smurthwaite without any trouble?'

'We did, and thanks to you sooner than we expected,' replied Lucy brightly.

'Will you bring them to help at my party, Mrs Smurthwaite?'

'Yes, Miss Zilpha.'

'Good. Is Mother rehearsing you?'

'She is that, Miss Zilpha, and if we don't hurry we'll be late.' She bustled away with Lucy and Alice in her wake.

The rehearsals went smoothly. They found Harold, whom they judged to be in his fifties, likeable and helpful. He told them he had been in the employment of the de Northbys ever since he was twelve. His deep sonorous voice instructed precisely and he got through as much work as anyone in an easy, efficient fashion. The girls felt confident about what they had to do and how to do it after they had spent a couple of hours with him. He enjoyed teaching them and found in Lucy someone who could have rivalled Zilpha in attracting the young men if she had been one of the guests.

They learned which glasses should be for which wine, which to use for spirits, which wine should be kept at room temperature and which should be kept cool when the ice was brought from the icehouse. He showed them the best way to carry a tray of glasses and after several practices under his critical eye they were looking forward to the following day.

'Now, don't worry, Mother. Everything will be all right. If it wasn't I'm sure we should have heard by now.' Robert's voice was strong as he picked up his bag.

Rebecca raised her eyes heavenwards. 'I hope you're right. My poor bairns could be in some gaol now.'

'I'm sure they are not. Now I must be off. I'll do my best to have them with you very soon.' He kissed his mother.

She watched him to the end of the street where he turned and waved.

In one way he was looking forward to the voyage. It was a new experience for him and took him out of the office routine which at times bored him. He had never said anything to his parents for he knew how much they wanted him in a steady job; a regular wage was essential to them, more so now his father was dead, leaving him the principal breadwinner. But he yearned to do more with his life. Now an opportunity to see something of the world outside of Newcastle had been thrust upon him and he was determined to make the most of it even if it was short-lived.

When he stepped on board the *Elizabeth* bound for London with a stop at Whitby, where he had been told he would have to disembark, he felt exhilarated, and a sense of freedom enveloped him. He watched with interest the activity on the quay with people bustling to come on board, sailors loading merchandise, small groups making their goodbyes and old men, past their sailing days, come to revive memories of going aloft to unfurl the sails.

Sailing time came, ropes were cast off, the top sails caught the breeze and, under thinning grey clouds, the *Elizabeth* moved gracefully down the Tyne.

Robert's full attention was on the sights along the river. Ships at quays loading and unloading, small craft toing and froing, the raucous shouts of sailors wishing them a good voyage, the noise of hammers from the shipyards, warehouses, cranes, the whole life of the river pulsated before him. He was fascinated, just as he was by the collier beating its way to the mouth of the river as the *Elizabeth* met the first waves.

* * *

Once the collier had docked and he had finished his work, Paul lost no time in making his way to the Mitchells'. His knock on the door was answered by Rebecca.

'Paul!' she gasped. 'Come in. You've a lot to tell me.' He could not mistake the admonishment in her tone.

'I'm sorry for my part in what happened, Mrs Mitchell,' he apologised sheepishly as they entered the kitchen.

She ignored his apology. 'My girls? Are they all right?'

'Yes, Mrs Mitchell.' His eyes widened brightly with his reassuring smile. 'They are well and with my mother.'

Rebecca, her anxiety banished, sank on to a chair. 'Thank God for that. They weren't discovered?'

'Yes, they were,' he replied and then, seeing alarm cross her face, went on quickly. 'But the captain was understanding, said he would take no action against them and put them ashore in Whitby where they made their way to Ravenscar and contacted my mother as I told them to.'

'Thank goodness. So Robert will have no difficulty finding them.'

'Robert?'

'I've sent him to bring them back. He sailed today.'

Paul said nothing but he wondered if Robert would have any success with the headstrong Lucy.

Alice and Lucy fussed with each other preparing to help at the party – ironing the creases out of their dresses, Alice's a pink striped poplin flaring slightly from waist to ankle, Lucy's a green striped and even tighter at the waist. Mrs Smurthwaite loaned them each a fichu of white cotton which they draped around their throats and shoulders and tied in a bunch above their breasts. They drew their hair to the nape of their necks and fastened it with a pink ribbon.

'You look right smart,' said Mrs Smurthwaite standing back to admire them.

'What about aprons and caps?' asked Alice.

'Mrs de Northby will provide them. Now, we'd best be off.'

When they reached the Hall it was four o'clock and the kitchen was buzzing with activity. Kitchen maids were busy at all the tables, preparing salads, filling glass dishes with pickles and boat-shaped jugs with sauces. Others were checking the silver condiment sets, filling them where necessary. Huge glass bowls were being set with fresh fruit, jellies turned from their moulds and decorated in their dishes, individual glasses held fruit compote or fruit-flavoured creams. Biscuits, tarts and cakes of every description were already being carried through to the dining room. Beef, chickens, pork and lamb were now being carved cold and laid out on silver salvers. Over all this activity Mrs Kemp kept a watchful eye, ordering here, complimenting there, cajoling, scolding, advising and ready to deal with any emergency.

'You know your job, Mrs Smurthwaite,' she called as soon as they entered. 'You girls report to Mr Kemp right away.'

'Yes, Mrs Kemp,' they chorused and having quickly dispensed with their coats and shawls went to find Harold in the dining room.

He welcomed them with a warm smile. 'My, you both look pictures,' he praised. 'Could be the belles of the ball. You'd turn all the young men's heads if you were in ballgowns.' He chuckled at the thought but added, 'Sorry, girls, all I can provide you with are these aprons and caps.' He picked them up from a table and handed them over.

The girls tied the white lace-edged thigh-length aprons around their waists and fiddled with the mob caps until they had them to their liking, using a long wall-mirror to see how they looked.

'Now, can you remember all I told you yesterday?' Harold asked as he indicated the tables of glassware which had been set out at one end of the dining room. Behind the three large tables were several small ones with bottles of red wine already in place. Others held jugs of fresh lemonade and the juice of squeezed oranges.

'What about the white wine, Mr Kemp?' asked Alice.

'That will be brought in shortly and placed in those containers.' He indicated square lead-lined receptacles on the floor between the tables and packed with ice from the icehouse.

'Mr Kemp, will all those candles be lit?' asked Lucy staring up at the chandeliers, her mind far from the work they would have to do.

'Oh, yes, every one. All the glass has been specially polished for this evening. They'll sparkle like diamonds. And all those in the sconces.' He nodded at the brass fittings on the walls. 'The mirrors behind them reflect the light from the three candles in each sconce. But this is nothing to what the ballroom will look like. There are fifteen chandeliers there, as well as the sconces. They look magical, and when the light is reflected in the ladies' jewellery there's a real colourful beauty in that room.' Harold suddenly pulled himself up. He liked talking about the Hall, especially when it was to girls as pleasant as these two. 'I'd go on forever,' he smiled, 'but we'd better get back to what we are here for.' He turned to the tables. 'Now, do you remember which glass is for what?' He questioned them, holding up various glasses in no particular order, and was pleased that the girls had good memories. 'Now we must practise with trays.' He set some glasses on two trays, watched them pick them up and walk around the room with them. He nodded his satisfaction. 'Good,' he praised. When they had set the glasses down he said, 'Now, you can spend your time giving the glasses an extra polish. I'm off to see about the white wine and the supply of ice.'

The girls set about their task. When Harold was out of earshot Lucy said, 'Maybe Harold can tell us if there's any connection between the de Northbys and us. He must have worked here for forty years so . . .'

'Not tonight,' Alice cut in. 'No searching questions until we know a little more.'

'But how are we going to find out if we don't ask?' Lucy demanded.

'Discreet enquiries,' returned Alice. 'You be careful or we'll be packed off out of here. And I don't want Paul's family jeopardised.' She looked at her sister with a warning eye. 'Do you promise to be cautious?'

'All right,' said Lucy. 'But even if nothing comes of it I'm glad we came to see all this. I never imagined anyone living in such splendour. The furniture is beautiful.' Though she could not recognise the individual Chippendales, Hepplewhites and Sheratons she knew perfection in the making when she saw it.

'Just look at that sideboard.' Alice indicated the long, bow-fronted mahogany piece across the room.

'I know. And the food. Did you ever see anything like it?' said Lucy, glancing at the the trays and dishes arranged with succulent fare.

'How on earth will they get through it all?' wondered Alice.

'Let's go and take a peep in the ballroom,' suggested Lucy daringly.

'Do you think we should?' asked Alice doubtfully.

'Why not? There's no harm in looking,' Lucy reassured her. She put her cloth on the table.

The double doors were open and they stopped in their tracks at the sight of the room. They had been in it when Mrs de Northby was rehearsing them but now it looked even more imposing. The candles had been lit, shimmering magically. Footmen were closing the wooden shutters on the windows and drawing the heavy crimson velvet curtains, imparting a warm feeling even to a room of this size.

'It's magnificent,' whispered Alice.

Lucy stood in awe, her thoughts running. What possible connection with such opulence could her father have known? This was a different world. Surely her family could never have been close to this life. There could be no link. Her mother must be right, her father's words had been the garbled delirium of a dying man. And yet Mrs Smurthwaite had heard something about Wades. Maybe Harold would know.

'Hello, you two.' A voice stopped her speculations.

'Miss Zilpha,' they both gasped guiltily.

She laughed at their discomfort. 'Not supposed to be

here? I'll not tell.' She smiled at their obvious relief. 'I suspect you have not seen anything like this before?'

They shook their heads.

'It is rather beautiful on occasions like this. A bit cold and severe at other times.'

Lucy had been eyeing Zilpha's dress. 'It's gorgeous,' she whispered as if she could not believe what she was seeing. The cut was simple but it had elegance, revealing the hand of an expert dressmaker. The bodice and skirt were one, the skirt falling straight at the front from a slightly high waist but at the back the train gave it its flowing line. The white India muslin was striped in a gauze weave and embroidered in strips of a pale blue leaf motif. The neckline was a simple curve slightly lower in the front than the back and the long sleeves were frilled at the wrist.

'I'm pleased you like it,' replied Zilpha, 'after all, you escorted it part of the way back from Whitby. I gave Mother a surprise when I got it home. She had wanted me to have short, puff sleeves, and wear elbow-length gloves but I persuaded the dressmaker to make it a long-sleeved dress.' She wrinkled her nose. 'I don't like those sort of gloves. I declare, they make me feel old.'

'It fits you beautifully,' said Alice. She glanced anxiously towards the dining room. 'We'd better get back, Mr Kemp might have returned.'

'Wait till you see it when the dances are in progress.' Zilpha glanced across at the other door into the ballroom. 'Ah, the musicians have arrived. I must speak to them.' Moving away, she gave them a warm smile.

Lucy stared after her, admiring the way she seemed to

glide across the floor. 'She's beautiful, whether in riding habit or evening gown.'

'And you'd be just as beautiful in those clothes.' Harold's voice in her ear startled them both. He laughed at the shock on their faces. 'Come, back to work.' He put a bark in his voice but from the light of gaiety in his eyes they knew there was nothing behind it.

After speaking to the musicians and choosing the music which would open the dancing, Zilpha hurried up the stairs to her bedroom. She checked the fall of her dress in the long mirror and gave a final preen to her hair before going to her parents' room. She knocked and at her father's call went in.

Her father, his hands clasped behind his back, was looking out of the window. Her mother was standing in front of a mirror adjusting the silk fichu at her neck. She stopped when she saw her daughter and her eyes sparkled with admiration and love. She nodded. 'You were right, my dear, long sleeves suit you. You look beautiful.'

Zilpha smiled. 'I can't match you.' She kissed her mother on her cheek. 'You still like the older style,' she added, moving back to look more critically at the dress her mother had kept a secret until now.

'It suits me,' she replied glancing over her shoulder at herself in the mirror. The light from the lowering sun filled the room with a gold sheen which made the yellow silk frock shimmer. It was a little fuller in the front than Zilpha's but most of its fullness was in the back though it had no train. The sleeves, trimmed with white lace at the cuffs, were wrist-length. The vandyked collar in a deeper yellow was complemented by the fichu which Mrs de Northby continued to tuck in and allow to overflow the neckline.

'Don't you think Mother looks lovely, Father?'

Richard de Northby turned from the window. He smiled. 'You are both as pretty as pictures. I'll be a proud man tonight for there'll be no one to match you.' He gave a little bow to add respect to his words.

He was a tall man, holding himself to his full height of just over six feet. His slim figure was the result of daily exercise; he often walked along the cliffs. He did not worry that his dark hair was greying at the temples for he knew it gave him a distinguished look. Anyone in conversation with him, especially if it was connected with his alum business or the working of his estate, often had difficulty in holding his penetrating gaze, which gave the feeling that he already knew the attitude and reasoning being presented. On occasions like tonight's his dark eyes would mellow a little though his guard would never be down. He prided himself on the way he had built on the already flourishing family business and had successfully expanded the development of the estates.

'You look smart, Father,' said Zilpha, admiring the perfect fit of his red tailed jacket cut to waist length at the front and held snug by five buttons running to the long drop collar which was trimmed with dark red velvet. At his neck he wore a grey cravat, neatly tied and pinned, matching the colour of his admirably tailored trousers which touched the top of his highly polished black shoes.

'Thank you, my dear.' Hearing the sound of wheels and the scuff of hooves on the gravelled drive, he turned back to the window. In the dying light he saw two carriages approaching the house. 'The first guests. We'd better go down.'

When they came on to the corridor from which they could look down into the hall they paused. He cast a quick glance to confirm that the servants on duty to receive the guests were in position. He held his arms out, so that his wife and daughter might each take one. Side by side they walked steadily down the wide staircase with its elaborately carved bannister and exquisite creations of birds at each corner.

Their movement caught the eyes of the servants, who watched in admiration as they came down the stairs. It pleased him that they made such an impression for it emphasised his authority.

From the moment the first guests arrived the Hall buzzed with activity and conversation. Maids took their outdoor clothes and bustled to a room set aside as a cloakroom where they were tagged so that they would be returned to the rightful owners without any confusion. A butler announced the guests who were received first by Zilpha, hostess for the night of her birthday, then by her mother and father.

Alice and Lucy stood by with trays of wine, offering them to the guests as they passed further into the house.

Gentle music drifted from the ballroom where the chairs around the perimeter were gradually occupied by the older ladies who would not partake of the dancing but would enjoy watching the younger guests display their talents while sharing opinions about them and approving or disapproving associations which seemed to be forming.

'Mr and Mrs Emile Cossart and Mr Mark Cossart!' The butler's voice rang around the entrance hall.

Even in the middle of greeting a guest, Zilpha's heart gave a flutter at hearing Mark's name.

'Mr Cossart,' she said politely, accepting his compliments with a gracious smile. But conscious of Mark's presence she hardly heard them.

'Mrs Cossart.' She liked Mark's mother especially. She was a gentle lady, with an aura of unflustered serenity. Yet below that surface was a quiet steeliness; there had to be for her to uproot herself to go and live in a foreign country of which she knew nothing. Everything about her was ruled by the deep love she shared with her husband. Zilpha hoped that same love would grow for her and Mark.

'Mark.' His hand was in hers and she squeezed it with affection.

He bowed. 'Zilpha, a happy birthday.' His voice was soft, caressing.

'I'm so pleased to have you here,' she returned.

'It is my pleasure. I look forward to dancing with you.'

'Every one,' she replied, a catch in her voice.

'There is nothing I should like better,' he smiled, 'but you have other guests and I should not be greedy.' He let his hand slip from hers and moved on to allow Zilpha to welcome George Fenny.

Lucy returned to Alice's side after replenishing her tray and saw Mark talking to Zilpha.

'Who's that?' she whispered, her voice betraying the impression he had made.

'Mark Cossart, the butler said,' replied Alice in an undertone.

86

Lucy's eyes were fixed firmly on him as he passed from Zilpha to Mrs de Northby and then to Mr de Northby. She was not aware of guests taking drinks from her tray. Then Mark was coming towards her. Her heart started to race. He was truly handsome, a fine figure in exquisitely cut clothes. The deep purple tailed coat, the yellow trousers, the matching cravat flouncing at the throat and filling the low neck of the brilliant white shirt had obviously all been chosen to create an eye-catching display. But it was his eyes which held Lucy's attention as he drew near, for they were dark, like brilliant pools of water which wanted to draw her to their depths. Yet she felt that she had not come under his gaze.

She was wrong.

He knew the effect he could have on the opposite sex and he liked it when it happened. He sensed it now on this pretty girl with the tray of drinks. His eyes twinkled with amusement. He pretended not to have noticed and then flicked his eyes straight on hers. The fleeting moment that they met was gone as she diverted her gaze, but he kept his eyes firmly on her for he knew her look would be back almost instantly. He was right. Then he was close, taking a glass from her tray without taking his eyes off her. Suddenly he felt he should not be teasing her.

She was different to the usual girls who helped at these events. There was something about her which set her, and the girl beside her, aside from the maids and serving girls. They expected the sons of the landed gentry to flirt with them. He sensed she was not expecting him to do so for she was showing more than a passing interest in him. Though there was a serious expression in her attractive brown eyes, there was also sympathy and understanding. But he noted too that they could sparkle with interest and enjoyment, that life was an adventure to her. Beyond her eyes he was aware of a distinctive beauty. He found himself wanting to know more about her.

He made his thanks and moved away to the ballroom.

Lucy's mind was a whirl. She had been conscious of the teasing light in his eyes and had immediately rebelled against it but when she saw it suddenly vanish she knew this man had considered her above a mere dalliance. Then she pulled herself up sharply. What had got into her? How could he be interested? She was not of his class. If only she was Zilpha, with all her fine clothes, these surroundings, things might be different.

When she saw Zilpha hurrying to the ballroom she chided herself. 'Well, that's that, foolish Lucy Mitchell.'

'Wake up, dreamy head.' Alice cut into her thoughts. 'We're to go to the dining room, now all the guests have arrived.'

Lucy started. 'Oh, yes.'

Zilpha, a radiant figure, swept into the ballroom. Her smile embraced everyone. She returned their nods, acknowledged their compliments as she hurried past, and failed to hear the comments.

'Isn't that dress gorgeous.'

'It suits her and fits so well.'

'She's always full of life.'

'Such a lovely girl.'

She paused and glanced quickly round the room. Many seats were already taken by the older people, heads together in gossip or admiring dresses across the room. Men in little groups passed judgement on the political situation, the likelihood of the resumption of war, or commented on the latest trading prospects in Whitby. The younger set were engrossed in stories and laughter while awaiting the commencement of the dancing.

Zilpha spotted Mark. She had promised him the first dance after offering it to her father, but he, knowing where her heart lay, had suggested that it would be better if she and Mark opened the dancing. And that was exactly what she wanted and then to go on dancing, dancing and dancing. She glided across the room.

'Mrs Stevens, Mrs Barnes.' She acknowledged the two middle-aged ladies sitting sipping their wine while talking to Mark who was standing in front of them. He smiled admiringly at her as she slid her arm through his. 'Am I permitted to steal him away from you?'

'Of course, my dear.'

Mark bowed. 'It has been a pleasure talking to you.'

The ladies watched the young couple cross the floor towards the musicians.

'Such a handsome pair.' Mrs Stevens inclined her head towards her companion.

'It will be a fine wedding.' Mrs Barnes leaned close to Mrs Stevens's ear.

'You know something?' Eager to learn more she raised her eyebrows questioningly.

'No, no.' Not wanting her friend to jump to conclusions, Mrs Barnes hastened her denial. 'Nothing definite but the whole countryside expects it.'

Zilpha and Mark had reached the musicians. A brief

word to the leader, a nod of understanding and the musicians stopped playing. A hush descended on the room. At an announcement, gentlemen escorted their partners on to the floor where they took up their positions for the quadrille, the dance which usually started a ball.

The dancers moved in time, elegantly, sedately, smiling at their partners, hands lightly touching. The elaborate patterns performed so expertly by the group led by Zilpha and Mark brought murmurings of delight from the older watchers. The dance finished and was immediately followed by the minuet and then the gavotte. The tempo rose with some country dances, the general, Tringhams fancy, and the spaw stage chase. Dresses swirled in bright colourful rotation, jewels caught the light from the candles casting shimmering fires of red and blue as necks turned and hands gesticulated. Many a gold necklace encrusted with diamonds had been brought out of safekeeping to lend enchantment to the evening.

The ländler was followed by the lavolta, which Emile and Elphrida Cossart had brought with them from France. After demonstrating it at the ball given by Richard de Northby to introduce them to the local gentry, they had been pressed for lessons. It had captured the attention of the younger set and had to be danced time and time again at any local ball.

Hearing the music for the lavolta start, Harold Kemp, who had noticed Lucy's and Alice's feet tapping to the music earlier in the evening, and realising this was a slack moment in the dining room, said to them, 'Go and take a peep.'

'Can we?' Lucy queried excitedly. The music had set her

pulses racing and she had been longing to see the splendid display she had imagined in the ballroom.

He nodded. 'Off with you, don't be long. You know the stairs next to the kitchen. Up those, take the passage to the right. Go to the end. Start up another flight of stairs. Halfway up you come to a small landing with a window on the right. It looks into the ballroom.'

The girls nodded and tripped away quickly in the direction Harold had indicated. They were soon looking down on a gyration of colour as the dancers whirled to the beat of the music.

The girls were struck silent for a few moments, drinking in the excitement of the scene.

'Isn't it gorgeous,' breathed Alice in awe. 'Look at those dresses, and that jewellery!'

Lucy did not answer. Her eyes had fixed on Mark. He swung Zilpha with graceful ease as she followed his steps in perfect time.

'Look,' whispered Alice, 'couples are leaving the floor.'

One by one the dancers moved to the sides of the room. They knew this was Zilpha's favourite tune for the lavolta. She and Mark should have the floor to themselves.

'Don't they look fine together,' murmured Alice.

'Yes,' Lucy whispered automatically, for in her mind she was there on the floor with Mark's arms around her, his eyes fixed intently on hers as if the world was only made for them.

The music stopped. Mark bowed to Zilpha as she curtseyed to him and spontaneous clapping broke out around the room.

A sharp dig in the ribs brought Lucy back to reality. 'Come on, we must go.'

Lucy followed her sister back into the mundane world.

'What do you think to that lot?' Harold asked, beaming enquiringly when they returned to the wine table in the dining room.

'Wonderful,' replied Lucy, ecstatic at what she had seen. 'Such dresses, such colour!'

'And the jewels!' added Alice. 'I never thought there were so many.'

'Nobody leaves their best at home when there's a party here. Now get ready with that wine.' The music had paused for a moment at the end of a dance and Harold knew it would be the start of an influx into the dining room.

Eventually when things did subside a little Harold went to the entrance to the ballroom. Dancers were creating a kaleidoscope of colour as they swirled around the floor like vivid spinning tops, but his experienced eyes were only casually aware of them as he surveyed the room. After a moment he was back with Alice and Lucy.

'There are a few people in there without a drink. Take a tray each,' he ordered.

Lucy picked up a tray of glasses filled with white wine and Alice took the red.

'Careful of the dancers. Keep to the outside,' he warned. 'I want no accidents.'

The two girls started round to the right offering glasses to the guests as they went. Lucy, entranced by the lively music, kept stealing a glance at the dancers. Zilpha was there with Mark. Lucy's mind drifted from her job. Oh, how handsome he looked and how elegantly he led Zilpha through the intricate steps. He smiled with enjoyment as he swept Zilpha round and round, faster and faster, and she threw her head back with laughter, delight on her lips. Lucy tried to imagine how she must feel in the arms of the handsomest man in the room.

'Watch where you're going,' Alice whispered sharply in her ear.

Lucy started. She had been holding the tray out automatically, hardly knowing what she was doing. Now it was half empty. She hadn't realised so many glasses had been taken.

They were approaching the second corner of the room where a group of younger people, among them Chris Young and George Fenny, having decided to forgo this dance, were sharing comment, gossip and jokes. As the two girls approached them, Chris reached the climax of his story. He flung his arms wide and swung round delighted at the reception his tale had received from his companions. He did not see Lucy behind him. His arm caught the tray, sending the glasses crashing to the floor, and, hitting Lucy on her side, sent her tumbling among the broken glass.

The resounding noise caused cries and gasps of dismay. Curious glances shot across the room as people tried to see what had happened. The music ceased. The dancers lost their steps and stopped. Everyone stared in the direction of the upheaval.

Lucy, the breath driven from her, lay stunned, for a moment unaware of what had happened.

Chris froze in horror at what he had done.

Mark and Zilpha were near when it happened and, without hesitating, he went to kneel beside Lucy.

His hands were on her shoulders, helping her to her

feet. 'Are you hurt?' he asked, his voice gentle as people gathered round.

'No, no, I'm all right,' Lucy was bewildered by the attention she was getting. Her hands hurt. Bemused, she stared at them. Blood trickled from her fingers and across her right palm.

Zilpha was beside her. 'It's the glass. We'll get you to the kitchen, Mrs Kemp will see to those cuts.'

Lucy gaped at the floor. 'Oh, what a mess,' she cried, a catch in her voice.

'Good God, girl, what were you doing?' The words snapped from Richard de Northby.

Lucy, jolted by the accusation, stared at him, to be met by anger smouldering in his dark piercing eyes.

'I'm sorry, sir,' she mumbled.

'Sorry! Sorry! Damned careless,' he stormed.

Tears came to Lucy's eyes.

'Sir, it was my fault.' Chris hastened his apologies. 'I didn't see . . .'

'She should have been alert for anything,' cut in de Northby, irritated that one of his guests should want to take the blame from a girl who was a mere servant.

'Richard, quieten down, it's not a tragedy.' His wife spoke softly and laid a calming hand on his arm. Without giving him time to say more, she took charge. She glanced at Alice. 'Tell Mrs Kemp to send someone to clear this mess.'

'Yes, ma'am.' Alice hurried away.

Lucy felt easier in spite of de Northby's lashing tongue. His eyes were still ferocious but Mrs de Northby was sympathetic.

'Zilpha, see that she gets these hands attended to. Mark, go with her.'

They started to lead Lucy away but Chris stopped them. 'I'm terribly sorry, miss,' he apologised with embarrassed concern.

'No, no, it was my fault, sir. I should have had my mind on my job instead of on the dancing,' replied Lucy, anxiously biting her lip.

'It was a pure accident and there's no harm done,' said Mrs de Northby. She cast her husband a warning glance to say no more. 'Richard, get the dancing started again.'

The music was soon flowing as if it had never stopped and the dancers picked up their steps again. Two maids dealt with the shards of glass and spilt wine and the party continued as if there had been no disturbance.

Once they had seen Lucy to the kitchen and Mrs Kemp had reassured them that she could soon take care of the cuts, Zilpha and Mark returned to the ballroom.

'Who is she?' asked Mark. 'I've never seen her here before.'

'No, you will not have done,' replied Zilpha. 'It's the first time. Mrs Smurthwaite brought her and her sister.'

'Relations?'

'No. The older girl, Alice, is Paul Smurthwaite's young woman. They came visiting.'

'And this one?'

'Lucy. She simply accompanied her sister as far as I know. I picked them up the other day on my way back from Whitby.'

'They aren't from around here?'

'No. Newcastle.'

'And what do they do there?'

'I don't know. Why?'

'They just seem different. There's something about them that . . .'

'Sets them aside from serving girls.' Zilpha finished for him when he hesitated.

'Exactly.'

Zilpha, recalling her opinion of Lucy when she watched them from her carriage, eyed him suspiciously. 'You seem more than interested?'

Mark shrugged his shoulders. 'Strangers, one always wonders about them,' he said casually.

Would you if she wasn't pretty? she queried without voicing her thought, determined that his interest would develop no further.

Chapter Five

Robert thanked the carrier and bade him a cheerful good-bye. He hitched the small bag more firmly on his shoulder and strode out towards Ravenscar.

He was thankful that he had met a carrier bound for Scarborough as he climbed the track out of Whitby. The voyage from Newcastle had been uneventful except, like his sisters, he was plunged into a new world and his horizons expanded beyond the confines of Newcastle and the mundane life of an attorney's office. Even in this short time away the new experiences were having their effect. The ship, the sea, contact with strangers, the buzz of life around Whitby's harbour, and the cheerfulness of the carrier, pleased at company to whom he could regale his tales of the Yorkshire coast, all fascinated his sharp mind.

He wondered if his sisters had felt the same. He had a week's leave from the office. Maybe he wouldn't be in a rush to whisk them back to Newcastle.

The wind sharpened. Robert was thankful that it kept the grey clouds moving, lessening the threat of rain. The track was hard and rough but it would have been much more unpleasant if it had been turned into squelching mud. He lengthened his stride, breathing deeply on the salt tang of the air.

It did not seem long before a dip in the landscape revealed the distant alum works. When he saw the cottages he swung to his left and as he approached them he saw a man emerge and pause to light his pipe.

'Hello, there,' Robert called, wanting to make contact before the man went on his way. He started to trot as the man looked up. 'Sorry to delay you,' he panted, 'but I wonder if you can help me? I'm looking for my two sisters. I think they should be staying with the Smurthwaites.'

'Aye, I can, lad. I'm Tom Smurthwaite. If you're Alice's brother you'll know our Paul. I'm his father.' He held out his hand and smiled at the relief on Robert's face.

'I'm pleased to see you, Mr Smurthwaite. I'm Robert. My sisters?'

'They're all right. Nice lasses. They're up at the Hall with Mrs Smurthwaite.'

'The Hall?'

'Aye. The de Northbys had a party last night for their daughter's nineteenth birthday. Mrs Smurthwaite and your sisters were up there helping and today they're giving a hand with the clearing up.'

Robert's mind grasped at the name. So his sisters already had some contact with the de Northbys, albeit in servants' duties. What else might they have learned?

'Should I go to the Hall?' he queried.

'Might not be a bad idea, lad. I don't know what time

they'll be back and I'm just off to work so I'd have to leave you on your own. You can wait here if you like.'

'No, I'll take a walk up to the Hall.'

'Right, put your bag inside.' After Robert had deposited his bag, he told him how to get to the Hall. 'Go round to the back, you'll find the kitchen, ask for Mrs Kemp, she'll get the lasses for you.'

Once he had climbed away from the houses and reached more level ground, Robert quickened his pace. He was anxious to see Northby Hall, the home of the people his father had mentioned. If they owned the alum works and vast tracts of land, as Mr Smurthwaite had indicated, they must be wealthy. What on earth could the connection be with his humble family?

So engrossed was he in his thoughts that he had not been paying enough attention to the direction he was taking and, instead of the long carriageway mentioned by Mr Smurthwaite, he found himself striding across fields with the house set a long way ahead at the top of a steady rise. He stopped, looked back, and realised what a magnificent view there must be from the front of the house. In the fields to his left cattle grazed contentedly. To his right a wood hid the carriageway which he should have taken. He could see it emerge beyond the wood some distance ahead and climb towards the Hall. He weighed up his options. There was no point in going to the drive; with the Hall in sight he would be all right across the fields.

He started off again. Five minutes later he pulled up sharp on hearing a crashing in the wood's undergrowth as if something or somebody was rushing to get out. He froze. His eyes widened with shock as two huge mastiffs burst

99

into the open and dashed towards him. Robert sensed they could easily knock him down. His instinct was to turn and run but he took a grip on himself. He couldn't outrun them. To try would be fatal. He must stand and show no fear. His heart was beating fast but outwardly he presented a relaxed calm, hoping these two magnificent creatures sensed it. Their loud barks were deep and hostile but he determined to take no notice. He called out, keeping his voice soft and friendly and focused his eyes on theirs. The dogs slowed. He detected the hostility replaced by a momentary puzzlement. He spoke a little quicker but still keeping a warm, friendly tone. They were near. Would they leap? If they did he knew he had no chance against their powerful impact. Their strides became shorter. Their barking subsided to a low, unsure growl.

Then they were close, sniffing, circling him. He kept up his soothing chatter. When he felt the hostility had gone he dropped to one knee to put himself on the same level.

'You're a couple of fine fellows, aren't you? Where are you from? Should you be out here on your own?'

The dogs hesitated, their dark hazel-brown eyes watching him.

'Come here. I'm a friendly lad.' He reached out tentatively but with a gesture that encouraged closeness.

The mastiffs shuffled the last few inches towards him. They made no resistance to his gentle touch on their flat coats. They nuzzled him with their short black muzzles and Robert laughed soothingly as he hugged them round their necks.

At this point he was aware of someone hurrying towards them from the direction of the wood. He looked up and was struck immediately by the delicate features of the girl whose face expressed surprise and wonder. Even though she was breathing hard, she retained a serene composure.

'I've never seen that happen before. Usually I have to call them off. They'd dashed out of the wood before I knew why. It's amazing.'

'They're a fine pair, miss.'

'Rupert and Bracken.'

He hugged them again and then rose slowly to his feet. 'You must be used to dogs?'

'No.'

She raised her arched eyebrows in surprise. 'You must,' she repeated disbelievingly.

'No, miss. Really. I've never had a dog, nor even been associated with one.'

'Well, that makes it even more surprising. It's a wonder these two didn't sense that, but from what I saw you showed no fear and that would help.'

Robert gave a little chuckle. 'When I first saw them I must admit I was tempted to run.'

'A good job you didn't,' replied Zilpha. 'You aren't from these parts but you must be from the country and have an affiliation with animals.'

Robert's smile broadened. 'I'm sorry to contradict you again. I have no connections with the countryside. I'm from Newcastle and this is my first time out of the town.'

'Then it's in your make-up. If you can get on with these two then you'll get on with any animal.' She looked at him curiously. 'From Newcastle?'

'Yes, miss. I've come for my two sisters. They're staying

with the Smurthwaites near the alum works. I was told they were at the Hall.'

'Yes they are,' she replied. Noticing the surprised look on his face, she added, 'I'm Zilpha de Northby and they are there with Mrs Smurthwaite helping to straighten up after my birthday party last night.'

Robert stifled his gasp. He had not expected to meet a de Northby let alone one who had set his heart racing with her bewitching beauty. Her sensuous mouth with bowed lips was perfectly balanced by a small nose and curving nostrils as if some great sculptor had been concentrating on the perfect work of art. Her blue eyes sparkled with vitality and a desire to enjoy life even in a wild and venturesome way. Her dark hair hung loose to the nape of her neck, having been released from the scarf which she now held between her long fingers.

'I'm on my way home. I'll show you the way, though with the Hall in sight you'd hardly get lost,' she offered.

'Thank you, miss,' he replied. 'I had strayed from the path somewhere and I hoped I wasn't trespassing.'

'Nobody would have bothered unless you were up to no good. The danger would have been from these two, but you certainly had no trouble with them.' She gave a slight shake of her head. 'I'm still amazed.' She started to walk. 'Come, you two, off you go.'

Robert fell into step. Rupert and Bracken made no attempt to run but ambled along beside him. Zilpha halted, her hands on her hips. Robert stopped and looked questioningly at her.

'Look at those two.' She indicated the dogs who nuzzled his hands. 'You've certainly made a conquest there. No one will believe this.'

As she was speaking she was aware of his eyes on her. She met them and was flattered when she saw a look of awareness of her as a woman. There was nothing salacious about it, but there was a genuine pleasure in being in her company even after this brief meeting. It aroused a deeper interest in him. From his square chin she deduced that he was a determined character but from the softness in his brown eyes he would not ride roughshod to get his way. She felt sure he would be considerate and after his empathy with the dogs she knew he would be gentle.

By the time they reached the Hall, Robert had been captivated by her beguiling charm and she revelled in the spell she knew she had cast.

She led the way to the back of the Hall where a dog handler met them, surprised that Rupert and Bracken had not come dashing into the yard but instead were walking calmly beside a stranger.

Zilpha laughed. 'What do you think of that, Leo?'

'Astounded, miss. Come on, you two.'

They took no notice of the familiar voice but nuzzled at Robert's hands.

Zilpha and Leo showed even more surprise.

Robert rubbed Rupert's and Bracken's necks with a farewell touch. 'Off you go,' he said gently but firmly.

The two dogs loped to Leo and followed him to their caged run.

'Well, you'll find no opposition from them if ever you come to the Hall again,' commented Zilpha as she turned for the back door.

'And I hope from no one else,' said Robert.

'No reason why you should,' replied Zilpha coyly. They

entered at the back door and walked down a passage to a door on the right.

'Mrs Kemp,' she said pleasantly as she entered the kitchen. 'Where are Alice and Lucy?'

'In the ballroom with Mrs Smurthwaite, miss,' she replied, then eyed Robert questioningly.

'Robert Mitchell,' said Zilpha to allay her curiosity. 'He's come to take his sisters home.'

Robert was already overawed by the size of the building and the extent of the kitchen overwhelmed him but when he entered the ballroom he stopped in astonishment. Never in his life had he imagined a room like this. His eyes widened with disbelief, the shock making him miss Zilpha's words. She touched him on the arm and repeated them, 'There they are.'

He became aware of his sisters, at the far end of the room, staring at him in amazement. He glanced at Zilpha. 'Thank you.'

She smiled and left the ballroom.

'What are you doing here?' asked Lucy when she reached her brother.

'Is Mother all right?' queried Alice with concern.

'Yes, she's well, and has sent me to take you home.' He lowered his voice. 'She said you are to forget the whole thing.'

'We can't, not now,' hissed Lucy. Hearing footsteps she turned. 'This is Mrs Smurthwaite.' She glanced at her and added, 'Our brother, Robert.'

'I'm pleased to know you, lad. You've two fine lasses for sisters.'

'Thank you,' he smiled. 'And I'm pleased to know you. Thank you for looking after them.'

'It's been a pleasure. You are here . . .?' She looked enquiringly at him.

'Mother sent me to escort them home. She was concerned about them, not knowing whether they had arrived here safely.'

'You've not heard from Paul?' asked Alice.

'Not before I left.'

'I told him to contact your mother as soon as he reached Newcastle in order to reassure her,' explained Mrs Smurthwaite.

'I must have sailed before he reached port.'

'Well, she'll know by now so there's no hurry to leave,' said Lucy. 'When are you due back at work?'

'I have a week off,' replied Robert.

Lucy turned to Mrs Smurthwaite. 'May we stay a little longer, please?'

'As far as I'm concerned you can stay as long as you like but you must think of your mother.'

Lucy brightened. 'Oh, thank you, Mrs Smurthwaite. There you are Robert, it's settled.'

'But where will I stay?'

'We'll manage,' put in Mrs Smurthwaite. 'Mind you, you may have to sleep on the settle.'

'That will suit me,' he replied.

'Very well. Now you'll have a lot to talk about so I'll finish off here. Tell Mrs Kemp on the way out. Take your brother home. Here's a key. I'll be along later.'

They took their leave of Mrs Kemp and Robert was soon telling them of their mother's reaction to their leaving. 'I think you'd better forget the whole thing.'

'I can't,' said Lucy vehemently. She stopped and turned

round. 'Look at that,' she added, looking back at the Hall. 'Think of all the land attached to it, remember the alum works, and then recall Father's words. There must be something behind them.'

'Have you found a link with the Mitchells?' asked Robert.

'No. But there may be one with Mother's family, the Wades.'

Robert raised his eyebrows. That was something he hadn't thought of, having automatically assumed it would be his father's side.

'Mrs Smurthwaite remembers hearing something about de Northbys and Wades from back in the past, before her time, but she can't remember what,' put in Alice.

'So you think there might be something?' Robert's interest was beginning to be aroused, though he added a caution. 'It may not be Mother's family, it could be some other Wades.'

Lucy smacked her lips with exasperation. 'Rubbish. Father wouldn't have said what he did if it hadn't been Mother's family. I mean to find out what happened and why Father said the de Northbys owed us. If neither of you are interested then go home to Mother, but I intend to stay.'

Alice and Robert glanced at each other. They knew their sister and that it was no good arguing with her when she was in this mood.

'Very well,' said Robert. 'I can stay four days. If nothing develops and you don't come back with me I'll have to make some excuse to Mother.'

'No need for excuses,' put in Alice. 'Tell her the truth, maybe then she'll tell you what she knows. I'm beginning to think she knows more than she's said and didn't really regard Father's words as those of a confused dying man.'

'Where have you thought of enquiring?' Robert asked Lucy.

'She was all for marching right up to Mr de Northby and asking him outright,' explained Alice, 'but Mrs Smurthwaite pointed out that to antagonise him would rebound on them. So we have to be discreet.'

'Robert, you came in with Zilpha. How did you meet her?' The excitement which had come into Lucy's voice made him beware.

He explained what had happened. In his telling, the tone which came into his voice revealed that he had been attracted.

'I didn't know you had a way with dogs,' laughed Alice.

'Nor did I until a short time ago.'

'Well, you must have impressed Zilpha,' commented Lucy. 'Maybe you could find out something about the de Northbys and the Wades from her. Go to the Hall on the excuse of wanting to see the dogs again.'

'I can't do that,' protested Robert.

'Of course you can,' pressed Lucy.

He grasped her arm and stopped her. 'No! I'll not do it and risk offence from her.'

'Ah, so that's it!'

Robert's face reddened but there was no slackening of his determination not to be persuaded by his younger sister. 'Forget this, Lucy.'

'You won't help?'

'Not in that way.'

'I think we'll need to ask someone older,' put in Alice to support her brother.

'All right,' conceded Lucy. 'But who?'

'What about Harold?' she suggested.

Lucy brightened. 'That's a good idea.' She added by way of explanation to her brother, 'He's the head butler and has served all his life at the Hall. He may have heard something of the past.'

'And he seemed to take to us,' Alice pointed out.

'But will you be at the Hall again?' asked Robert.

'Mrs Kemp was satisfied with us and said we could help whenever Mrs Smurthwaite is at the Hall. We can combine that with the seaweed gathering.' Alice went on to explain that in fairness to Mrs Smurthwaite they had decided to do some work so that they could pay her for their keep and bed.

Robert approved his sisters' thoughtfulness. He offered to make his own contribution but Mr and Mrs Smurthwaite would not hear of it as his stay was going to be short. They liked the three of them and were pleased that their son had met such a pleasant family in Newcastle.

The following morning, when his sisters had gone to the shore, Robert took a walk along the cliffs. It was a pleasant warm day. The gentle breeze carried a salt tang and a freshness which he had never experienced in the smoke of Newcastle. The wide open spaces seemed to have an exhilarating effect, beckoning him to throw off the confines of town life. He had to pull himself up sharply for he found himself beginning to regret that he had to return north.

He stopped and gazed out to sea, wondering what lay beyond the far horizon. His eyes drifted down to the shore where he saw two figures gathering seaweed. Would they be dissatisfied with life at home when they returned?

His thoughts were interrupted by distant barking. He turned and saw Rupert and Bracken bounding towards him and in the far distance two riders.

'Hello, you two.' He greeted the mastiffs with a broad smile as he dropped to one knee. The dogs were upon him, yapping with pleasure as they pushed against him, almost tumbling him to the ground. He laughed loudly at their antics as each tried to curry more of his favour than the other. As he hugged them his eyes fixed on the riders again. He could guess the identity of the rider who rode sidesaddle. But the other? That rider was astride the horse.

Robert was startled by the feeling of jealousy. His muscles tensed as if he was facing opposition, as if he had to combat a rival's affections for a woman he had only met once. Such feelings were foolish. Zilpha de Northby, with her station in life, would not think twice about him. Yet she had shown a friendship yesterday, been pleasantly companionable, and he could have sworn that he had seen a certain regard in her eyes. Rubbish! He was just being fanciful, seeing what he wanted to see. But his chiding was weak and he found his attention fixed on Zilpha.

How elegantly she sat her horse. Poised with an expert grace, she looked attractive in her riding habit, her features rosy with the exhilaration of the ride.

They pulled their mounts to a halt in front of him and he straightened, allowing the dogs to nuzzle his hands hanging limply at his side.

'Good day, Robert Mitchell,' called Zilpha. She steadied her horse as it champed at the ground, annoyed that its run had been stopped. 'Are you as good with horses as you are with dogs?' There was a hint of challenge in her voice.

'No, miss.'

'No?' She raised her eyebrows in mock surprise.

'Never been around them.'

'I suppose not in Newcastle.' She glanced across at her companion. 'Mark, this is the person I told you about. Don't you think there is something he's not telling us, judging from the way Rupert and Bracken reacted?'

'Most surely,' replied Mark readily. The imperious look he gave Robert from the height of his horse annoyed him.

'I've never had anything to do with dogs,' repeated Robert firmly.

'Come now.' Mark gave a little mocking laugh of disbelief. 'Rupert and Bracken don't take to strangers the way they took to you.'

'If they like me it must be a natural affinity that I didn't know I had,' replied Robert tightly. The glance of disbelief which passed between the two riders annoyed him. He was honest. Why should anyone doubt his word?

Zilpha saw anger flare in his eyes and, not wanting her teasing to provoke an argument, quickly intervened. 'And when you return home will you remember them?' The lilt in her voice and the smouldering look in her eyes implied that he might remember their owner as well.

'Maybe I will,' he replied.

'Come, Mark, we must continue our ride and leave our friend to his musings.' She turned her horse and tapped it into a trot.

Mark wheeled his mount after her without a glance or

a gesture to Robert. The dogs paused a moment, then raced after the horses.

Robert watched them, his mind confused. 'Beautiful, attractive, teasing? Aye, you are, but you're a damned flirt and if it came to it you'd have nowt to do with the likes of me. All you want is men at your feet and that fine fellow who rides beside you.' Mark steadied his horse to match Zilpha's pace which she changed to a walk when he reached her.

'Zilpha, you're a flirt,' he called, amusement in his eyes.

'Would you have me any other way?' she asked with a coy inclination of her head.

'I would not. But you left that young man bewitched and beguiled.'

'He liked it.'

'And that pleases you?'

'Just as your flirting pleases you.'

'I don't flirt.'

'Yes you do.'

Mark shook his head. 'No. Having admiring young ladies around me doesn't mean I flirt. They have the choice, I don't encourage them. If they are interested in being in my company who am I to deny them that pleasure? You encourage, you let them think there's a chance, even though they know that that is remote, just as that fellow will be thinking now. By the way, you addressed him as Robert Mitchell. Is he related to the girl who cut her hand?'

'Brother. He's come to take his sisters home.'

'So soon? They've only just got here from what you told me.'

'A short visit, probably.'

'Then why would they be gathering seaweed?' he asked, nodding in the direction of Stoupe Beck a short distance away.

Startled by his question, Zilpha saw Lucy and Alice, with baskets fastened to their backs, emerging from the cutting which carried the beck to the sea.

Lucy's pulse raced at the sight of Mark, a lithe, powerful figure in command of his horse. But she also felt a stiffening of jealousy: the rider beside him was Zilpha.

'Good day, young ladies.' Mark doffed his hat as he pulled his horse to a halt.

Zilpha nodded to them and would have ridden on but when Mark stopped she was obliged to do so.

'How is that hand?' asked Mark, his eyes directly on Lucy.

'It will be all right, sir,' replied Lucy, feeling her face reddening under his gaze.

'Gathering seaweed, now. It doesn't seem to be the right employment for visitors. You must be staying some time?'

'We must earn something to pay for our keep with Mrs Smurthwaite,' explained Alice, trying to divert Mark's attention from Lucy. She had sensed her sister's reaction on seeing him and it had alarmed her.

'Then you must be staying a while, but Miss Zilpha told me your brother had arrived to take you home.'

'We may not go with him,' replied Lucy. Aware of his interest in her she felt she must let him know. Alice's lips tightened with exasperation. The fewer people who knew what they were doing, the better.

'Then I hope your stay will be enjoyable.' Mark replaced his hat and tapped his horse. As it moved past Lucy his eyes carried a message only to her that he hoped he would see her again.

With a smile which held no warmth Zilpha followed him. Annoyance was beginning to boil towards anger. Mark had not flirted but he had been interested in Lucy and that was more dangerous. She was about to challenge him but he spoke first.

'I wonder why they aren't returning home with their brother? What is keeping them here?'

Chapter Six

'Ah, my two bonny helpers.' Harold Kemp gave Lucy and Alice a beaming smile when they followed Mrs Smurthwaite into the kitchen of Northby Hall the following afternoon.

They had needed little persuasion to accompany her when she informed them that their help would be appreciated in preparation for a small dinner party Mr de Northby was giving that evening. Unused to so much bending they had found seaweed gathering hard on muscles they never knew they had, and their arms and legs ached with the effort. They had slept the sleep of the exhausted which, followed by the walk to the Hall in the bracing air, had revived them. They had agreed that they would seize any opportunity to discreetly elicit information from Harold.

'Good day, everyone,' they called cheerily above the clatter of preparation which filled the room.

'You did so well polishing glasses for the party that you can help me set the table and decant the wine.' Harold pushed himself from his chair at the end of the table where he had been enjoying a cup of tea.

114

'Not so fast, Harold,' his wife chided. 'Give the lasses time to get their coats off. And maybe you could find a cup for them out of that pot.'

'Reckon I could,' he agreed and chatted idly to them while they drank the tea and ate a slice of Mrs Kemp's sponge cake. When he saw their cups were empty he stood up. 'We'll make a start.'

He took them to the dining room where a long table occupying the centre of the room had been covered with a white damask tablecloth trimmed with a broad band of lace. In the centre of the table a silver fruit dish rested on a pedestal supported by four silver dolphins. Twelve places had been set for a seven-course meal, the tableware patterned with a deep crimson lattice work enhanced by a gold rim.

Alice's and Lucy's eyes widened at the sight. They had seen elegance and fine presentation at the buffet served for Zilpha's birthday party, but this meal was obviously for something special.

'We must polish all the glassware,' Harold indicated the array awaiting attention on the long oak sideboard, 'and place them precisely at each setting.' He handed both girls polishing cloths.

They worked vigorously but with extreme care. Lucy, recalling the accident, showed signs of nervousness but Harold's chatter reassured her.

They followed his example of holding each glass to the light to make sure no mark remained and then placed each one on the table as he directed.

'This must be a special occasion?' Lucy queried casually.

'It is indeed.' There was a touch of pride in Harold's

115

voice as if he deemed it a privilege to be setting the table for this particular meal.

'Is the family still celebrating Miss Zilpha's birthday?' asked Alice, following Lucy's lead.

'Oh no. She won't be here. She's dining with Mr Mark and his parents.' Lucy tensed at this information but banished it from her mind as Harold went on. 'You could call this a business dinner. Mr de Northby will be entertaining five friends and their wives. Merchants, shipowners, bankers and the like from Whitby. There could be some deals struck tonight after the ladies have retired to the parlour.'

'Mr de Northby has interests other than the alum works?' prompted Lucy.

'My goodness, yes. He has shares in merchant ships, a partnership as a ship's chandler and . . .'

'Ship's chandler?' Alice looked puzzled.

'Yes. Supplying goods to ships for their voyages, particularly cordage, canvas and so on.'

'And other businesses?' Lucy wanted to know more.

'Yes. He has interests in shipbuilding, and has just gone into the jet trade. He's inherited a business sense from his father and grandfather.'

'But they made their money from alum in the first place?' suggested Alice.

'Oh, yes. They invested in other enterprises, bought land and let it out to tenant farmers.'

The table was beginning to sparkle as more and more glassware was put into place. Harold moved to the table and made a slight adjustment here and there.

'How did they come to have the alum works?' asked

Lucy, having sensed that Harold liked to air his knowledge about his employer.

'That's a long and interesting story,' he replied. He glanced at the clock on the wall. 'You carry on with the glassware, I'll see that the red wines are brought in so that they'll get settled to room temperature and then I'll tell you about it.'

When he had left the dining room the two girls looked at other with glee.

'We've got him talking,' said Lucy, her eyes gleaming. 'We might discover something!'

'We did that very well,' agreed Alice. Her voice took on a serious tone. 'But we must be careful not to let him suspect anything.'

They went on with their task and only casually observed Harold supervising the arrival of the wine.

Once they were alone with Harold again he directed them to polish the decanters ready for the wine. Lucy, receiving a nod of approval from her sister, took an opportunity to bring Harold back to his story.

'In the sixteenth century Sir Thomas Chaloner of Guisborough, about twelve miles northwest of here, was travelling in Italy and saw the alum works on the Pope's estates. On his return he noted that there was shale on his land which might be turned into alum and make a nice profit for him but he didn't know all the necessary processes to turn the shale into alum. The story goes that he returned to Italy and persuaded some of the Pope's workers to come and work for him, bringing their knowledge of the process. This contact was made secretly and Sir Thomas devised a scheme whereby the workers were

117

smuggled out of Italy in barrels. It is said that the Pope was furious when he learned what had happened because it undermined his monopoly of the alum trade.'

The two girls were agog with interest, hoping Harold would go on. 'And did Sir Thomas prosper?' prompted Lucy.

'He did that.'

'If his alum works were on his estates, how did this one develop and how did the de Northbys come to be involved?' Alice asked.

'The de Northbys are said to be descended from one of those Italian workers.'

'But that name isn't Italian,' protested Lucy.

'No. What their name was I've never heard but it is supposed that at some time one of them changed it and because he was living in the north took that as part of his surname. I suppose, he added the "de" to remind his descendants that they were of foreign extraction.'

'Sounds rather romantic,' commented Alice.

'And one of them found the right shale here?' asked Lucy. Then, a little puzzled, added, 'But they wouldn't own the land?'

'True. I think it was Miss Zilpha's great-great grandfather, who was visiting this part of the coast and saw what he believed was good shale for alum.' He paused, rubbing his chin thoughtfully. 'He must have been a thrifty man for he approached the owner, whose name escapes me, and proposed that they go into partnership to produce alum.' He snapped his fingers. 'Now I recall, the owner was named Wade.'

The name sent waves of emotion coursing through the girls. Had they a lead at last?

118

'But there is no Wade now?' asked Alice, hiding the tremor in her voice.

'No. There is a story that some time later, the next generation I think, there was a dispute. The Wade of that time left and de Northby became the sole owner.'

Dispute! The word pounded in Lucy's mind. Was this behind her father's last words? Had he known something or was it just a tale which had grown up over the years? If he had had definite facts then her mother must be aware of them. But she had discredited his implication. She had to find out what it was, but where to start? Question Harold further and he might become curious about them, and that could be risky as he was devoted to his employer. She had seen a warning look in her sister's eyes.

'An interesting story,' remarked Alice, cutting out any comment from Lucy, who with her imagination stimulated by Harold's information, polished the last decanter vigorously.

'Here, lass, don't rub it away.' Harold's chuckle broke into her thoughts. He took the decanter from her. 'You've both done well,' he praised as he surveyed the table with a critical but satisfied eye.

'I tell you, Robert, I believe there's some truth behind Father's words,' enthused Lucy. 'You must question Mother when you get back home. When she knows what we have learned she might be more forthcoming.'

After the evening meal the two girls had taken the opportunity of a stroll along the cliffs to acquaint their brother with Harold's story.

As it unfolded he had become swept up in their

119

enthusiasm to know more. 'What do you propose to do now?' he asked.

'We don't know,' said Alice. 'Have you any suggestions?'

Robert looked thoughtful. 'I don't think you should press Harold further. It seems he knew nothing about the dispute itself, if indeed there was one.'

'I'm sure there was and that the Wades came out of it badly,' said Lucy with an edge to her tongue as if she could see no reason for her brother to think otherwise.

'You may be right but don't let your enthusiasm ruin things. We may be seeking something which is to our advantage but it might be difficult to prove, as it happened so long ago.'

'Not so long,' insisted Lucy. 'Remember Harold said he thought it had occurred in the generation following the start of the partnership so that would make it our great-grandfather, Mother's grandfather. It's just possible that she may know all about it.'

Robert nodded thoughtfully. 'Possibly,' he murmured half to himself. Then with a firmer tone he said, 'I wonder if I might learn anything over there.'

'Where?' asked Alice.

He stopped. 'Yonder.' He nodded in the direction of Robin Hood's Bay. 'They're close enough to de Northby land to pick up stories. I might glean some information from the older generation.'

Robert strode along the cliff. The morning sun had dispersed the curls of mist which had tumbled towards the shore and now the gullies and the tops were bathed in warmth. He felt contented, filled with a determination to

120

glean some information from the people who lived in the village which clung to the cliff as if its very life depended on its tenacious foothold.

Straggled across the beach below were small groups of girls gathering seaweed and Robert stopped to locate his sisters. He recognised the hard work of bending, loosening the seaweed from the scaurs, loading the baskets and trudging up to the alum works. He grieved that his sisters should have to do it but he admired their courage so that they could contribute to Mrs Smurthwaite's housekeeping. The sooner they had some answer to their father's belief the better, then they could all get back to living their normal lives.

He scrambled down into Stoupe Beck and up the other side, having decided to take the next gully to the beach and approach the village from the shore. The tide was well in and he relished walking close to the water, avoiding the running waves as they swept up the sand and then retreated.

Gulls sighed on the gentle breeze making for the cobles, the boats skilfully used by the fishermen of the village, which were drawn up on the beach where the birds screeched, dived, and fought over tasty morsels of fish and bait left behind after the morning's fishing. At some of the cobles men still sorted the marketable fish into baskets. They cast Robert what appeared to him only casual glances but he sensed that he was being watched with curiosity and suspicion reserved for strangers. He was tempted to stop and pass the time of day but he felt that an interruption of their work by an unknown would not be welcome. Instead he turned towards the sharp slope which led up from the beach to the village.

As he did so an almost overbearing atmosphere seemed to press down on him from the buildings which climbed high on the cliff and huddled together as if in massed protection against intruders. Did they harbour secrets which precluded them from welcoming strangers? Was one of those secrets related to his ancestors on his mother's side? Should he heed his mother's warning that probing could bring trouble and unsavoury information? Should he retreat from the unknown?

Robert stiffened his shoulders and his resolve. He strode purposefully up the incline scarred by the marks of boats where they had been dragged to a safe haven away from the sea. Again he resisted the temptation to get into conversation with the men tending their boats, their voices lowered, their eyes suspicious. He wondered if he was wasting his time. Would he be able to break down the barrier of reticence in this close-knit community? Maybe the inn he had noted on his right as he climbed from the shore would provide the means.

He slipped his way past the cobles on the landing with hardly a glance at the fishermen. The Fisherman's Arms stood tall and gaunt, with few windows, its stonework salted by the sea spray when tides and winds were running high. He pushed open the door to find himself in a long, gloomy passage only dimly lit by one oil lamp. A faint murmur came from behind a door on his right. He pushed it open and tentatively stepped into the room. Four men sat round one upturned barrel which acted as a table. At another were seated two fishermen in deep conversation. A fire burned brightly in the grate, which, apart from warming the room, added a little light to that coming from three lamps hanging from the dark oak beams. It was altogether a dour atmosphere. The bar was little more than a table with a solid front extending across one wall in which there was a door.

A broad-shouldered man leaned with his forearms on the wooden top. His hair was close-cropped, emphasising the massivness of his heavy jowled head. He straightened when he saw a stranger hesitating in the doorway. Robert almost recoiled, for the man seemed to fill the space behind the bar and his tight shirt revealed muscular strength in his arms and chest.

As Robert crossed the room he knew he was being closely scrutinised by the man whose eyes were small for the size of his head and whose nostrils flared as if he was sniffing the newcomer out.

Robert was also aware that conversation in the rest of the room had flagged and that he had become the centre of attention.

'Good day.' He steadied his nerves. 'A tankard of ale if you please.'

The man behind the bar, his heavy lips drooping at the corners, stared at him for a moment, then grunted and left the bar. A suspicious tension had filled the room but it gradually lessened with each passing moment. Robert knew it could be back in an instant and his welfare be in jeopardy if he was not careful.

The man returned with a foaming tankard and placed it before Robert, slopping a little ale as he did so. Robert passed over a coin which the man looked at before dropping it in a bowl on a shelf behind the bar.

'Stranger hereabouts?' he growled, his head thrust forward.

'Yes, first time in Robin Hood's Bay,' replied Robert brightly, trying to lighten the atmosphere.

The man straightened to his full height, chuckling as he did so, amusement relieving the dour look. 'Hear that lads?' he called across the room.

'Aye, he's a stranger all right,' called a small stocky man, a broad grin on his face which was matched by those on the faces of his companions. 'Thee tell him, Luke.'

'Robin Hood's Bay?' Luke chuckled again. 'That gives thee away. Thee ain't even from as near as Whitby. If thee were thee'd be calling it Baytown.'

'You're right,' returned Robert amiably. 'I'm from Newcastle.'

'Thee's a long way from home. What's thee doing in these parts?' Suspicion had crept in again.

'I'm visiting my sisters.'

The man cocked his head on one side. 'They live around here?'

'No. They're staying with Mr and Mrs Smurthwaite up at the alum works.'

'With Tom?'

'You know him?'

'Aye.'

Though Luke did not put another question, Robert offered an explanation. 'One of my sisters met Paul Smurthwaite when he was in Newcastle. He sails on a collier, you know.'

Luke nodded. He knew.

'My sister wanted to meet his parents, so here we are.' Robert felt his explanation had been satisfactorily accepted by everyone. Suspicion had gone and the room had returned to normal.

Outward hostility had vanished from Luke, though, ever cautious about strangers in Baytown, he remained alert for the merest hint that Robert was not telling the truth. No one in Baytown wanted their lucrative, illegal trade of smuggling upset and every stranger was regarded as a government man until proved otherwise.

Robert, aware that he had taken a step towards acceptance, knew he must still be careful in what he had to say. He took a drink of his ale and smacked his lips as he swallowed. 'That's a drop of good.'

'Aye, we keep a strong brew. Our fishermen like it that way.'

'Dare say they have some tales to tell.'

Luke gave a little laugh. 'Aye, they have that. Thee interested?' Was this young man being nosy?

'Yes. Stories always interest me. I write for a journal.'

Luke nodded, weighing up quickly whether he should let this line of conversation run on. If he did he could learn more about the stranger. 'He's the one to talk to.' He inclined his head towards the bearded man at the corner of the bar. 'We'll have a word.' He moved towards the old man and Robert picked up his tankard and followed. 'Amos, this young fellow,' he glanced at Robert, 'Didn't get your name.'

'Robert Mitchell.'

Luke nodded. 'Right.' He turned back to Amos. 'Robert here writes for a journal. He'd like some tales of the sea. I told him thee's the man.'

Amos puffed at his pipe, his eyes intent on Robert. 'Aye,

I am that. Fifty years at sea, man and boy. I can tell thee tales to make thy hair curl.' His eyes narrowed as if searching the distant horizon, remembering when he stood on the deck of a rolling ship or was on the yard furling sails before the storm hit. 'I've sailed far and wide but allus came back to fishing from Baytown.'

'Stories of fishing from here are the ones I'm most interested in.'

'Right, young fella.' His beard quivered as he dampened his lips.

Robert indicated to Luke to fill up Amos's empty tankard. 'And one for yourself.' He turned his attention back to the old man. 'You were born here?'

'Aye. Eighty years ago. Was brought up on fishing but got restless when my pal got married. I've sailed the oceans of the world.'

'And never regretted returning here?'

'Nay. Had a good life.'

'Never married?'

'Oh, aye.' His blue eyes shimmered wistfully. 'Bonniest lass in whole village.'

'No family?'

'Two sons, both lost at sea. Our coble was hit by a freak wave. Turned turtle. I was lucky.' A catch came into his voice at the recollection.

Luke slid Amos's tankard to him. He took a sip, recomposed himself and started to regale Robert with his stories.

Robert let him tell five before he felt he had won Amos's trust and changed tack. 'Most interesting, Amos. Maybe you can tell me something about the people who owned the land where the alum works are now?'

Amos hesitated. 'The de Northbys?'

'I heard tell that they bought the land from,' Robert paused thoughtfully, rubbing his chin, 'ah, someone called Wade.'

He had been so intent on watching Amos for any reaction that he did not notice Luke stiffen at the mention of the name.

The old man took a drink of his ale. He wiped his mouth with the back of his hand and nodded. 'Aye, thee's right. Jacob Wade was the pal I mentioned. He used to come fishing with me. It was his father, Alex, who went into partnership with the de Northbys to produce alum on Wade land. Jacob was dragged into the business by his father.'

'Dragged?'

'Aye. Jacob's heart was never in it. He wanted to go to sea with me but his father wouldn't let him.' Amos's voice had hardened. 'Twister.'

'Twister?'

'Aye. There was a dispute and Jacob was accused of swindling his partner Peter de Northby, Alex's son. Wish I'd been here. I might have been able to help him.'

'You weren't here?'

'No. It was when I was sailing out of Whitby. Came back from one of the voyages and Jacob and his family had gone. No one knew where.'

'A mystery?'

'Aye. Then I was away to sea again. The years went by and I never did trace them. So I never heard Jacob's side of the story.'

'And the de Northbys were biased?'

127

Amos shrugged his shoulders. 'Who knows? I only heard that side. Seems de Northby out of deference to his father and grandfather, who'd had a good understanding with the Wades, did not press the charges as he might have done – it could have meant deportation for Jacob. There were stories and stories. I could never really find the truth without hearing Jacob's side as well.'

'Was he the type of person who would do anything like that?'

Amos gave a wry smile and a slight shake of his head. 'Not the Jacob I knew, but who knows how circumstances can change a man? And I had been away for some time. As I said, his heart wasn't in the business and he was a person who could easily be taken in.'

Luke frowned. This young man was asking too many questions. Was he really after stories for a journal? Or was there something else behind his probing?

Robert's attention was riveted on the old man. His mind was racing with facts and possibilities. He was tempted to press Amos but caution began to exert itself. He had been lucky so far and he did not want anyone to become suspicious of his motives. He had learned something, though not as much as he would have liked. The dispute and accusations must have been serious for Jacob Wade and his family to make sure they left no trace of their whereabouts.

Robert was tempted to reveal his identity to the old man and let him know what had happened to his friend, but he held back, remembering his mother's warning that enquiries could lead to trouble and heartache. This was the time when a still tongue made a wise head.

He bought Amos another tankard of ale and had another

himself, and allowed the conversation to drift away to generalities without questions.

Twenty minutes later it was a very thoughtful Luke who watched Robert leave the Fisherman's Arms. He even went to the door to see if the young man got into conversation with anyone outside.

When Robert reached the beach and set off towards Ravenscar without stopping, Luke returned inside still bothered by the course of the exchange between Robert and Amos. He went to the kitchen, ordered his wife to look after the customers, took a jacket and cap and left without so much as telling her where he was going. She, knowing his moods, judged it best not to ask.

He turned away from the beach up the rutted ground which was the main street to the cliff top. Houses crowded in on either side as if they were attempting to shut out the sun. In the maze of narrow streets houses seemed to sit one on top of another. Some were cared for, some were shabby, the ground was clear and neat or littered with rubbish. But Luke had no eye for either. His mind was set on one purpose and the sooner he got it over the better, whether there was anything in his suspicions or not. Let Mr de Northby be a judge of that.

He was breathing heavily by the time he reached the cliff top but, on flatter land, immediately fell into a steady stride.

Reaching Northby Hall he was thankful to see Richard de Northby sitting alone on the portico, smoking a cigar.

The sound of footsteps drew de Northby's attention. He raised his eyebrows in surprise when he saw the huge bulk of the landlord of the Fisherman's Arms. His curiosity sparked, for, though he had a certain hold over Luke, it was unlike him to come to the Hall.

'Good day, Luke, what brings you here?' he asked.

Luke snatched his cap from his head and held it with both hands in front of him. 'Well, sir, I . . . er.' His voice was hesitant and quiet.

Richard smiled to himself. It always gave him pleasure to see men behaving like this in his presence. Bulk strength, such as Luke's, meant nothing when dominated by an opposing personality of such magnetism as his.

'Get on with it, man.' Richard took a pull at his cigar and blew a smoke ring into the air.

'Well, sir, knowing how you turn a blind eye to certain activities which are conducted through the Fisherman's Arms . . .'

Richard chuckled to himself when he thought of the brandy, lace and tobacco, even the cigar he was smoking, which had found its way to Northby Hall via the cellars of the Fisherman's Arms.

'And I want to show you how grateful I am for the last time you prevented the law . . .'

'Yes, yes, man,' Richard waved a hand. 'Get on with it. What is it you want to tell me?'

'A young fella's just been in the Fisherman's Arms and seemed to be interested in the Wades.'

'What?' De Northby sat up, his penetrating gaze searching Luke's face.

'I thought you ought to know.'

'Why?'

'Well, sir, occasionally stories still go around about how

130

Jacob Wade tried to swindle your grandfather, and I thought you wouldn't want it dragging up again.'

'Quite right, Luke. It would do no good, only cause my family pain. A sorry business it was. Who was this fellow?'

'Young man by the name of Robert Mitchell, said he was gathering stories for a journal, sea stories from old Amos, but I got a bit curious when he asked about the alum works and the partnership.'

'Mitchell? From Newcastle?' Richard shook his head. 'Where is he staying? Might be advisable to have a word with him, see he sticks to his sea stories.'

'He's with the Smurthwaites at the alum works. He came visiting his sisters. It seems one of them knows Paul Smurthwaite.'

Richard nodded thoughtfully. He had made the connection. The two girls who had helped at Zilpha's birthday party. His lips tightened. And one had broken those wine glasses. If this Robert was looking for stories for a journal and was interested in the Wades, might his sisters be helping him? Prying strangers needed to be watched lest they uncover the truth.

As he walked back along the beach, Robert examined what he had learned. He felt sure that whatever Jacob Wade had been accused of, Amos had thought him innocent. Was that out of loyalty to an old friend? And why had Amos never been able to learn more? Maybe that was because he was away so much and the lapse of time had blurred the happenings. But the more Robert thought about it the more he felt sure that there was a story which needed uncovering.

Where to start? He had only a stronger confirmation that there had been a scandal of some sort involving the de Northbys and the Wades. He wished he could remain longer but he must return to Newcastle. He could not jeopardise his job. With luck his sisters would be able to learn more.

He saw them gathering another load of seaweed and as he helped them with their baskets he acquainted them with what he had learned.

'But couldn't you have got more from Amos?' pressed Lucy.

He shook his head. 'I thought I had gone far enough. After all there were other men there and Amos was not trying to hide what he was saying.'

Lucy's lips tightened but she nodded her understanding. 'You'll have to see him again.'

'That would make folk curious,' he pointed out, 'besides, I've got to go home.'

'Maybe you and I could see him?' She put the question to Alice.

'That's not a good idea. You can't go to the inn. And for someone else to be making enquiries along the same lines would certainly raise suspicions,' Robert pointed out.

'Who will be bothered?'

'If there's something to hide who knows who might be? Remember Mother's warning. You must be careful. Promise me that.'

Robert turned up the collar of his topcoat against the morning fog which clung to the River Tyne. The voyage had been uneventful and the fog had only been encountered as they approached the river. He hoped the gloom was not a foreboding of his encounter with his mother.

She frowned and looked askance at him when she saw that he was not accompanied by his sisters. 'Well, where are they?' she demanded after he had kissed her.

'They are well, Mother,' he hastened to reassure her.

'I told you to bring them home.'

'I couldn't. I tried but they refused.'

'You didn't try hard enough.' She turned away in disgust and sat down on a chair beside the table.

He sat beside her and took her hand. 'I did at first.'

Rebecca sent a piercing look at her son. 'At first?'

'Yes, but they resisted.'

'And you weakened.'

'Not exactly. We learned things which makes us believe that there was something behind Father's words.' He looked intently at his mother. 'What is it?' he pressed. 'There's something you haven't told us.'

She looked grave and yet Robert detected a little sadness in her eyes. Was she regretting that her husband wasn't here to speak for her? She hesitated, pondering whether it was wise to say more. She was frightened of what it might stir up and the trouble it might lead to, but did she owe it to them as Isaac had said?

She took a deep breath, gave a shiver and realised her son's hand was cold. 'What's a mother thinking about? Her son arrives home after a cold voyage and she hasn't even offered him a cup of tea.'

'It's better that we talk.' Robert tried to detain her but she slid her hand from his, stood up quickly and turned to the fire where a kettle hung on the reckon. She welcomed the activity of tea-making to give her time to make up her mind about what she should do.

Robert wisely did not interrupt her thoughts. He sensed he might learn more by not pressing her too much.

When she had poured the tea she sat down again. She met his enquiring gaze and gave a small thoughtful nod. 'I suppose with the way things have developed I should tell you what I know, though I'm afraid it's scant. It happened when my father was only ten so he was not of an age to be told anything. So what I tell you has only come down as a story and stories have a habit of growing out of all proportion. What I heard I took with a grain of salt but your father, although he was not a Wade, believed them, maybe because of his anxiety to always be able to provide for his family. Every so often he would bring these stories up and want to try to pursue them but I always held him back. I was content with our life. We had security, we loved each other and we loved you three and when you were able to earn, things were a little easier.'

She paused and took a sip of her tea. Robert waited for her to go on. She picked up a spoon and stirred her tea which gave her something to do while she chose the point at which she should begin.

'It was said, and I believe it is true, that the Wades were part-owners of an alum mine in Yorkshire. Where? I had never bothered my head about it and was unaware of its location until Paul linked the de Northbys to Ravenscar.'

'That's right, Mother. I saw an old man, Amos, who was friendly with a Jacob Wade.'

Rebecca looked up sharply. 'My grandfather! You saw someone who knew my grandfather?' Her voice became charged with emotion and excitement. 'I really never knew him. All I have is a hazy recollection of a tall man who used to lift me high above his head, tickle me and make me laugh.'

'He sounds a jovial sort.'

'What did this Amos say about him?' pressed Rebecca, eager for information.

'Amos was friendly with him when they were boys. Amos went off to sea. Jacob wanted to go with him but his father wouldn't let him. Amos said Jacob was not keen on the business but did become a partner with Peter de Northby when their fathers died. One day when Amos visited home, Jacob and his family had gone, nobody knew where, and the de Northbys had the alum mine. He said there had been some scandal but being at sea he had never bothered to look into the matter. I got the impression that he believed Jacob wouldn't do anything underhand.'

Rebecca nodded. 'I can tell you no more except the scandal, a dispute over something, could easily have led to Grandfather Jacob being transported. Things were hushed up, and Grandfather brought his family to Newcastle. I think my father knew a bit more but he wouldn't talk about it, saying that he respected his father's wish that the matter be forgotten.' She shrugged her shoulders. 'And maybe that's why I feel Grandfather Jacob's wish should be respected.' She gave a slight, regretful shake of her head, 'I wish those girls had come back with you.'

Chapter Seven

Mark reined his horse to a halt close to the edge of the low cliff. He had seen several girls with baskets on their backs making their way up Stoupe Beck from the beach. They were obviously aware of the deteriorating weather sweeping in from the sea. It would not be long before the rain hit the bay and they wanted to deposit their loads and find shelter before it did.

But one remained, intent on filling her basket to achieve the maximum pay. She worked quickly, pulling seaweed from the scaur on which he saw she was not too sure of her foothold. He focused his attention on her for he had recognised the girl whose looks and personality had attracted him the night of Zilpha's party.

He sat, holding his horse steady, watching her and though she was some distance away in his mind's eye he could see her face clearly. He surprised even himself that he could remember so vividly the mass of natural curls framing a bonny face made more attractive by the slight up-turn of her petite nose. He recalled the sparkle in her brown eyes which was doused for only a few moments in the embarrassment of dropping the glasses, to be replaced by anguish when de Northby had scolded her.

He saw her straighten and glance seawards at the darkening clouds and then turn quickly back to her basket. In her rush she slipped on the wet rock, lost her footing and fell heavily. She lay still for a moment then tried to struggle to her feet only to fall again. He saw her sit up and grasp her right ankle.

Perturbed, Mark turned his horse and sent it quickly along the cliff edge until he found a negotiable way to the shore. Reaching the beach he put the horse into a gallop towards Lucy. Another attempt to get to her feet had failed.

She looked up at the sound of hooves thrumming on the hard sand and, in spite of the pain, she felt a surge of elation when she recognised the rider.

He pulled the horse to a sliding halt and was out of the saddle almost before it had stopped. He dropped to his knees beside her, his handsome features clouded with genuine concern. 'Let me look.'

She made no protest but submitted willingly to his ministration. She leaned back on her elbows and watched him as he raised the hem of her dress above her ankle. She winced when he touched her foot even though she knew his fingers were as gentle as they could be. She had envied Zilpha de Northby having Mark beside her but now here he was, so close to her.

He looked up and met a vibrant and enticing brightness in her gaze, and she saw in his eyes the same feeling she was experiencing. Words were not needed. It was as if the world was theirs and theirs alone.

'You've sprained your ankle.' His voice quietly interrupted the intimacy of the moment.

She scowled at this information. This was most annoying, but she drew some consolation even amidst her despondency. If it hadn't happened she wouldn't have had Mark looking after her.

Thunder rumbled out to sea, warning of the storm to come. Mark glanced anxiously across the water. The wind had strengthened and was beginning to pile the waves on one another as they ran for shore.

'Can you manage with my help?' he asked.

Lucy nodded. She pulled her shawl from her shoulders where it had slipped when she fell and draped it around her head. She drew confidence from his strong hands as they helped her to stand. She gave a little gasp of pain as her right foot touched the ground. Then, almost before she knew it, he had picked her up in his arms. Automatically her left arm came round his back for extra support.

'You can't carry me all the way.' She made a tentative protest, hoping that was exactly what he would do.

Merriment danced in his eyes. 'I'm not going to. My horse will do that.'

He eased her on to the animal's back and then, taking the reins, started out for the nearest gully leading up the cliff.

He quickened his pace as the thunder rolled nearer and nearer and lightning forked from the darkening clouds.

They were just leaving the sand when the first big drops hit them. He glanced back. The veil of rain, blotting out the sea, swept towards them.

'I'll ride with you!' he shouted above the screech of the

wind. He swung up behind her and she sank back against him as his arms came round her to control the reins.

They moved into the gully unaware of the figure on horseback some distance along the cliffs who had witnessed the scene. Zilpha admired Mark's gallantry, and she would have ridden to help but at that moment the rain swept up the cliff and she knew the wisest thing was to ride for home as quickly as possible. Jealousy swamped her as she visualised Lucy nestling in Mark's arms.

The rain closed on the land, covering everything in a cloak of concealment.

When they reached the top of the cliff Mark settled his horse into a gallop towards the alum works. In spite of the fast pace Lucy felt confidence in his handling of the horse. Though her ankle hurt and the rain drenched her she ignored them in the pleasure of being so close to Mark.

The path forked and he took the right-hand track, the shortest way to the workers' cottages.

The sound of thrumming hooves brought Mrs Smurthwaite hurrying to the door wondering who rode with great urgency in such dreadful weather. She gasped when she saw Lucy and Mark hunched against the driving rain. Water streamed from them.

Mark slid to the ground. 'There's been an accident!' he yelled by way of an explanation as he reached up to take Lucy into his strong arms.

'Inside, quick,' cried Mrs Smurthwaite.

He carried her quickly to the cottage and lowered her gently on to the sofa which faced the fire glowing in the blackened grate.

Mrs Smurthwaite closed the door and, startled by the

sight of Lucy's pale and drawn face, asked with grave concern as she came to her side, 'What happened?'

'Miss Mitchell fell and sprained her ankle on the beach,' explained Mark. 'I happened to see her when I was riding on the cliffs.'

'Wasn't her sister with her?'

'She'd filled her basket before me and had left,' explained Lucy.

Sarah nodded and knelt down beside the sofa. 'Now let me have a look at that ankle.' She smiled reassuringly at Lucy, who was beginning to shiver. 'Does that hurt?' she asked as she carefully handled Lucy's foot.

Lucy winced. 'Just there.' The pain which darted through her almost brought tears to her eyes.

Sarah grunted knowingly and looked up at her. 'A bad sprain. It's bed for you, my girl, but first we must get you out of those wet things.' She straightened and looked at Mark who had anxiously awaited her assessment of the injury. 'I thank you, sir, for bringing Lucy. A good job you saw her, she could have been lying there yet in this storm.'

'She's in good hands now.' He smiled as he wiped some water from his face. 'I'd best be going and getting out of these wet clothes.' He looked at Lucy. 'I trust you will rest now, young lady.'

'I will. And thank you for what you did.'

As he started for the door, he stopped and turned round. 'Mrs Smurthwaite, will you mind if I call to see how the invalid is?'

'Not at all, sir. I'll be here all day tomorrow and no doubt Alice will too, if she isn't gathering seaweed.'

'Thank you, Mrs Smurthwaite.' He glanced at Lucy and

saw that his suggestion had brought her pleasure, then left the cottage and rode quickly to Howland Manor.

'Now, Lucy, we must get you upstairs,' said Sarah as soon as Mark had gone. 'Can you manage?'

'I'll try. But where's Alice?'

'She must be sheltering at the works. Now, swing yourself round and let me take your weight as you stand up.'

Lucy winced as she struggled upright and put her foot to the floor.

'Hold on to me,' said Sarah as she put her arm round Lucy's waist. 'All right?'

Lucy nodded but bit her lip. They started forward slowly towards the stairs.

It was a struggle and Lucy cried out with pain on two occasions when her injured foot touched the steps. She was sweating with the exertion by the time she was sitting on a chair in the bedroom but her teeth were beginning to chatter with the cold creeping from her soaked clothes.

'Start taking your things off,' ordered Sarah and hurried from the room. She returned a few moments later with two towels, and helped Lucy to remove the rest of her garments, being especially gentle as she eased her stockings off. She took no notice of Lucy's embarrassment at being naked. 'A good dry down,' she said, starting to rub vigorously, 'will get the circulation going and warm you up.' After a few minutes she handed the towels to Lucy. 'Keep doing it. I'll be back in a moment.'

When she returned she was carrying a small bucket of cold water and some bandages. Satisfied that Lucy was looking a little better, she handed her her nightgown. 'Put that on and this shawl, then I'll see to your ankle.'

For the next ten minutes Sarah gently applied a cold water compress to the sprain and then carefully bandaged the ankle.

'Now, into bed,' she instructed.

They completed the task without causing Lucy too much pain. She experienced relief from the softness of the feather bed and pillows. It was good to be comfortable and to feel warm again.

As she tucked the bedclothes round her Lucy looked at her with appreciation. 'Thank you, Mrs Smurthwaite. I'm most grateful to you.'

'Not at all. It's a good job Mr Cossart saw you. He's a nice young man.' She smiled to herself when she saw Lucy's eyes light up at the mention of his name, but then Mark Cossart would turn any girl's head.

Mrs Cossart was crossing the hall when Mark hurried in from the stables. She stopped and stared at him with horror.

'Where on earth have you been to get so wet? Why didn't you shelter?' she cried.

'I will explain when I come down,' he said without stopping and then took the stairs two at a time.

She shook her head thoughtfully and smiled at the exuberance of the young before continuing to the drawing room.

She settled herself in a high-backed chair to one side of the fire. It was a room she liked, large but cosy. Straight-backed chairs and small tables were set at intervals around the walls which were covered with a lightly patterned paper. There was a large landscape painting on each wall, and one between two long windows which gave a view of a walled garden. She adjusted a small table so that she could read Thomas Bewick's *A History of British Birds*, a recent present from her husband.

She became so absorbed that only when her husband came in ten minutes later did she realise the rain no longer beat at the windows and the storm had passed.

'Hello, Emile,' she greeted him pleasantly.

She never ceased to bless the day when he had come into her life. A tall, thin man, he held himself with a degree of pride and dignity, qualities with which he had contested the blows life had dealt him, forcing him to escape the onslaught of revolution, impoverished, and seek refuge and the goodness of his in-laws in a strange environment. His thin, angular face bore a warm smile. His brown eyes, though appearing lazy, were alert to everything around him, something which he had cultivated when running his textile and leather works in France, and which had been strengthened in outwitting the revolutionaries who would have had his head. His greying hair was always neat. His thin moustache gave him a debonair look which was added to by his well-cut clothes.

He crossed the room and gave her an affectionate kiss.

'You completed your business in Whitby?' she asked.

'Yes. Very satisfactory.'

'The storm?'

'On my way back. I had to stop until the worst had passed. I was all right under cover in the carriage but the horse nearly bolted with fright. I just managed to calm her.'

'Mark got soaked. He's changing now.'

143

'Where was he?'

'I don't know. He should be down in a few minutes.'

When Mark arrived his father had a glass of Madeira waiting for him.

'I hear you got caught in the storm,' he said, handing him the drink.

Mark nodded and, after his father had sat down opposite Elphrida, he took a chair beside his mother.

He told them what had happened.

'Was she badly hurt?' asked his mother.

'She has sprained her ankle. The injury is not too grave. I'll find out tomorrow. Mrs Smurthwaite said I could visit.' Mark noticed the sharp glance which passed between his parents. He smiled. 'It's all right, Mrs Smurthwaite will be there as well.'

'Maybe I'll accompany you.' Elphrida's words were half query and half statement – an answer to her own supposed question.

'A good idea, my dear,' put in Emile. 'You could take her some sweetmeats and maybe some fruit.'

The following morning was sunny with the air fresh after the storm when Mark drove his mother to the Smurthwaite cottage.

Sarah, on hearing the creak of an approaching carriage, pushed the edge of the lace curtain aside so that she got a better view from the window. She started when she saw Mrs Cossart. Oh, if only she had known, she would have had things much tidier, though, house-proud as she was, there was little out of place. She quickly took off her coarse apron and stuffed it behind a cushion, straightened her dress, and glanced in a mirror to make sure her hair was tidy, her collar flat and the jet brooch at her throat straight.

She opened the door just as Mark was helping his mother to the ground.

'Good day, Mrs Smurthwaite,' Elphrida smiled pleasantly.

'Good day, ma'am.' Sarah bobbed a little curtsey.

'I thought I'd come with my son to see how Miss Mitchell is today. I hope none too worse for her ordeal.'

'Her sister told me Miss Lucy has not had a bad night, restless at times, but on the whole she slept well. But come in, ma'am, and see for yourself. She wanted to come down. It was a struggle but she's a determined young miss.'

Sarah fussed her way back into the cottage, and Mark closed the door.

'Two visitors for you,' she announced.

Both Lucy and Alice were surprised to see a lady accompanying Mark but when he introduced her as his mother they recalled having seen her at Zilpha's party.

'Now, young lady, how are you feeling after your unfortunate accident?' Elphrida's voice was gentle, her eyes showing genuine concern. She acknowledged Alice offering her a chair.

'Nicely thank you, ma'am.'

'Does your ankle hurt?'

Lucy screwed her face. 'Sometimes.'

'Those scaurs can be treacherous,' Elphrida commented. 'I've brought you a little present.' She passed the small basket to Lucy, who inched back the white cloth to discover the sweetmeats and fruit.

Elphrida had caught the smile exchanged between her son and Lucy and sensed that he had been attracted to this girl. She could see why. She was pretty with striking features framed by a mass of brown curls.

'You aren't from these parts. Are you relations of Mrs Smurthwaite?'

'No, ma'am,' said Alice. 'I'm friendly with her son Paul. We came on a visit. We're from Newcastle.'

'So you had no experience of those slippery scaurs?'

'No, ma'am. We only decided to gather seaweed to earn a little money to pay Mrs Smurthwaite for our keep. It was the handiest thing to do.'

Elphrida nodded her understanding.

'So what do you do in Newcastle?' She was curious. Their confident manner made her feel that there was something different about these girls.

'I'm a governess to an attorney's children, my sister's a teacher at a dame school,' Lucy explained.

'Capable sisters,' commented Elphrida, inwardly pleased that her judgement had been right.

'Our parents encouraged learning.'

'And rightly too,' approved Elphrida, recalling how her parents had done the same. 'Your father?

'He died a few weeks ago.' A catch came to Lucy's voice.

'I'm so sorry.' Elphrida made her commiserations and then added, 'Are there any more in the family?'

'A brother. He is a clerk to the attorney I work for.' Recalling Robert's explanation to the villagers in the inn at Robin Hood's Bay, she added quickly, 'He also writes for a journal.'

'What sort of things?' Elphrida's interest had been aroused.

Lucy's mind was sent racing by this unexpected enquiry

and was already wondering if it might be turned to advantage. 'Stories about people, about their work, particularly if it's something unusual.'

'He should be able to get plenty around here,' Elphrida smiled.

Lucy wondered if she should follow up this lead with a query about the Wades but before she had made a decision Mark spoke. 'You should talk to my great-grandmother. She'd tell them some stories, wouldn't she, Mother?'

'She certainly could,' smiled Elphrida. 'Her memory's a trifle vague at times, but when she's feeling refreshed she's truly a mine of information.'

'You'll like her,' put in Mark with obvious affection.

'She used to be a governess just like you, Lucy. She married her employer's younger brother. His family were against it but she won them over and they were thankful that she did. She had a shrewd brain and when their merchant business was heading for disaster she persuaded her husband to let her help. She saw what was going wrong and what it needed to rescue the business. They survived and went on to better things. She's been a great influence on the family, even my husband who is French. He came from a well-to-do family, and French people of that standing would have looked down on one of them marrying below their status. But my grandmother made him change his outlook and he's a much more tolerant man because of it.'

'She sounds a remarkable person,' said Lucy. 'I would love to meet her.'

'I'll take you to meet her one day,' said Mark.

Lucy smiled her acceptance but her look contained a

measure of admiration for the man who made the offer. It was not lost on Elphrida.

'I think we have been here long enough, Mark. We must not tire Miss Mitchell.' She rose from her chair. She looked at Lucy. 'I am pleased that your injury, though bad enough, was no worse. I hope you make a speedy recovery.'

Alice and Lucy did not speak until they heard the carriage start to move.

'Isn't he handsome?' sighed Lucy.

'You be careful, don't go getting ideas about him. Don't forget what we are really here for.'

'Yes, and he might be able to help. He said he'd take us to see his great-grandmother. She might remember the Wades.'

'He's probably forgotten that already.' Alice tried to dampen her sister's enthusiasm, for she knew how badly disappointment could hurt Lucy.

'I'll make sure he remembers.'

'You may never see him again.'

'I will. I know I will.'

She sighed and settled into the feather bed. She dozed with thoughts of Mark and the pursuit of the truth.

'A pretty little thing,' observed Elphrida as Mark drove to Howland Manor. 'She'll turn a few heads.'

Mark made no comment, but agreed silently. Yes, she was pretty. There was laughter in her eyes, though he did not doubt they could be serious even if she was making light of a situation. She was pretty in a way which could make men's heads turn again once they had noticed her, even though she might hold a shield which would only be removed for a man she truly loved. But there was something more which attracted him. He had not only felt the urge to sweep her into his arms but he had sensed there was some hidden and enticing quality which carried an air of mystery about it, and he would not rest until he had uncovered it.

He started. He shouldn't be thinking this way. It was Zilpha he was expected to marry. Everyone presumed it. He and Zilpha had spent almost all their lives together. But now this slip of a girl had entered his life and something he had never felt before had stirred in him.

Zilpha yawned and stretched beneath the covers. The sun had driven the night away from her bedroom. Before retiring she always drew back the heavy curtains and opened a window so that she could feel the cool night air as she lay snug in her feather bed, blankets tight around her, and was ready for the early morning light to wake her.

She glanced across at the sky beyond. It held no clouds, the day promised well. The storm had long since gone but the air was still fresh from its passing.

Thought of the storm recalled seeing Mark helping Lucy Mitchell. They must have been soaked before he got her home. She had been caught and had had to change all her clothes, and they had the longer ride to the Smurthwaites. Then Mark had to return to Howland Manor. She really must go and see how he had fared.

Following her usual habit, she got up and crossed to the window. She loved the view and never ceased to enjoy it no matter what the mood of the weather, for the constant change of light was forever altering the picture. Today the early rays of the sun were beginning to bathe the garden in a soft light and shadow the woods with mystery. Beyond the fields she glimpsed the tranquil sea.

She inhaled the tangy air deeply then dressed quickly, choosing to go down to breakfast in her dark green riding habit, which she knew Mark particularly admired.

As she headed for the stables Rupert and Bracken saw her and, with tails wagging, raced to the fence of their large compound. Their friendly barks came in joyous anticipation of a long run with their mistress.

'Hello, you two.' She stopped and stooped to their level. 'Sorry, you can't come with me this morning. Leo will take you for a run.' She pushed her hand through the fence and rubbed them under their chins. 'And don't expect to meet Robert Mitchell. He'll have gone home.'

Even as she spoke she wondered why he had come into her mind. As she walked to the stables she found herself recalling the look in his dark brown eyes which had caught her attention; she had responded in the way she enjoyed, teasingly flirtatious. She knew she had struck a chord in him and she wondered how he would respond the next time they met, if ever they met again.

She reached the stables and found the groom had followed the instructions she had sent to him earlier.

Her favourite horse was ready. She stroked its muzzle and spoke softly to it. Its response was to rub endearingly against her shoulder. Then she climbed into the saddle and took the horse at a walking pace out of the stable yard, watched enviously by four other horses from their stalls.

She kept to a leisurely pace, taking the path towards the

cliffs along which she would ride before turning across country towards Howland Manor.

As she rode along the cliff top she noticed six girls were already gathering seaweed but she did not recognise any of them as the two girls from Newcastle, one of whom she had last seen on Mark's horse with his arms around her. What had happened after the rain had obscured her view? Maybe she had been too shaken by her fall to be on the beach today.

A groom came briskly from the stables on hearing the clop of hooves coming into the yard. Seeing Zilpha he hurried to steady the horse while she dismounted.

'Good morning, miss. Nice day for a ride.'

'It is, Jack,' Zilpha agreed. 'Keep her saddled. No doubt Mr Mark will join me.'

' 'Fraid not, miss.'

'No?' She stared at him. She and Mark always rode together.

'He's driven his mother to the Smurthwaites' cottage.'

Zilpha tensed. 'Smurthwaites'?' She could guess the reason for the visit.

'That's what Mrs Cossart said and also that they wouldn't be long.'

'In that case I'll wait. Is Mr Cossart at home?'

'No. He's gone to Whitby.'

'Look after her, Jack.' She patted the animal affectionately on the neck and left the stable yard.

She went into the house through a side door used by the family, knowing she was welcome any time. It had been that way ever since the families became friendly after the Cossarts fled from France.

As she crossed the hall towards the parlour a maid was coming down the stairs.

'Good morning, miss. I'm afraid no one is at home.'

'I know, Lena. I'll wait.'

'Very good, miss. Would you like some hot chocolate?'

'That would be nice, thank you.'

Zilpha settled herself in a chair from which she could see the garden.

Twenty minutes later she was drinking her second cup of chocolate when Elphrida and Mark walked in.

'Jack told me you were here,' said Mark. 'I'm sorry I was out. Mother and I went to see how Miss Lucy Mitchell was. She fell on the scaurs yesterday. I happened to see her and went to help. The storm had drenched us by the time I got her to Mrs Smurthwaite.'

'How is she?'

Elphrida noted that Zilpha's voice held little concern.

'She's quite well. Sprained ankle. None the worse for the soaking.'

Zilpha made no comment, but said, 'I came expecting to go for our usual ride.'

'And we shall,' replied Mark. 'When Jack said you were here I told him to saddle Freya.'

Zilpha wondered if a special meaning for her lay behind his choice. She recalled the time when she was with him when the horse was born. He had asked her to name the new foal and she had whispered, 'Freya.'

He had sought an explanation.

'The Norse goddess of love,' she had replied.

As she watched him now, she wondered if he had ever really read the meaning she had implied in her youthful

152

suggestion five years ago. If he had was it being eroded by the presence of the girl from Newcastle?

She had to know and brought up the subject as she and Mark were riding out of the stable yard.

'Did you have to go and see that girl?'

Mark was taken aback at her sharp tone. 'I thought it only polite to do so. After all I helped her.'

'And no doubt she revelled in riding with you.' Zilpha's eyes flared.

'You saw us?'

'Yes! And the sooner she goes back to Newcastle the better.'

'You're jealous!' He gave a mocking laugh.

'Jealous? Don't be ridiculous! Me, jealous of a seaweed gatherer?'

'She's not a seaweed gatherer.'

'That's what she was doing when you saw her fall.'

'She's only doing it as a convenient way of getting some money to pay Mrs Smurthwaite for her keep.'

Zilpha gave a snort of derision.

'She is,' protested Mark. 'She's a governess really.'

'Well then, at the best she's only a governess, the type of person once employed by your mother.'

'The type of person my great-grandmother was and don't you disparage her, not even by implication,' snapped Mark.

Zilpha drew back. She had nearly gone too far. 'I meant nothing against your great-grandmother, but she was exceptional.'

'Yes, and there's more to Lucy Mitchell than there appears.'

'You'll see only what you want to see. There's none so blind . . . Are you intending to see her again?'

'I might.' Wanting to calm the situation he added, 'It would only be polite to make enquiries about her recovery.'

Zilpha knew that to argue further would only heighten Mark's defiance of her wishes. Instead she would use her charm to outplay Lucy Mitchell.

Their exchanges slid into familiar idle chatter. They enjoyed the ride, marvelled at the views and drifted into the pleasures of each other's company, forgetting the differences they had aired.

They turned inland, keeping to the ground above Robin Hood's Bay, pausing to gaze across the red roofs of the tiny village to the sea and the enormous headland at Ravenscar across the bay. They rode up to Ness Point and after a pause gave the horses their head. The vigour and power of the animals beneath them as they galloped along the cliff top exhilarated the riders.

With the ruined abbey at Whitby distantly in sight, they pulled their horses to a halt. Mark slipped from the saddle and as he walked to her side Zilpha watched him carefully. Would he react as he always did in these circumstances? She waited. He reached up towards her waist and lowered her to the ground.

He held her, looking down at her with soft eyes, holding this moment for them alone. He saw her jealousy had gone, a transient thing which had flared in a moment of pique. For her, this special place was where they had shared love.

She had purposely ridden this way because of that, hoping it would drive all thoughts of Lucy from his mind, reminding him that there were things they shared that she could not reach. She was determined to wipe Lucy from his mind. Her eyes mesmerised his. The brush of her lips tantalised and, as her kiss became stronger, he was unable to resist the whirlpool of desire she created. Her arms came round his neck, gripping him tight, clinging as if breaking the hold would lose him.

'Mark! Mark!' she whispered passionately as their lips parted but for a moment. His arms tightened around her and in the tautness of his body she felt victory.

Chapter Eight

Two days later Mark rode to the Smurthwaites' cottage. Sarah heard the sound of hooves and came to the door.

'Good day, Mrs Smurthwaite. How is the invalid?'

'She does nicely, thank you, sir. The sprain wasn't as bad as I first thought.'

'May I see her?'

'Certainly, sir. Miss Alice is with her.'

He followed Sarah into the house.

'Good day, both the Misses Mitchell,' said Mark breezily. 'I'm pleased to see you looking so well, Miss Lucy.'

'Thank you, kind sir,' she replied. Her heart was racing. The hoped-for visit had materialised. 'But, please, it's Lucy and Alice.'

He inclined his head in acknowledgement. 'Then I should be Mark. Now, that ankle?' He indicated the foot which Lucy was resting as she reclined on a horsehair sofa.

'Improving,' she said with a smile. 'Soon I shall be able to take a few steps outside.'

'Good.'

'We really must thank you again for helping Lucy,' said Alice. 'I really shouldn't have left her on the beach.'

'There's no blame on you. Your basket was full,' said Lucy. 'I dawdled. But thank goodness Mark saw me.'

'How fortunate I was on the cliff,' he replied with a smile. Lucy's heart missed a beat. How handsome he was.

He stayed a quarter of an hour, all three enjoying their conversation, but the glances exchanged between Lucy and Mark told of their wish that they were alone.

After Mark had left and Mrs Smurthwaite was busy in the scullery Alice looked warningly at her sister. 'Be careful, sister.'

'What do you mean?' queried Lucy innocently.

'Don't get your fingers burnt playing with Mark's affections.'

'He feels as I do.'

'Don't talk ridiculous,' snapped Alice. 'This is typical of you, acting impulsively. Jumping in without thinking. You don't know him.'

'Do you need to, to fall in love?'

'It helps to avoid a mistake.'

'Don't you believe in love at first sight?'

'Of course, but . . .'

'Then, no buts.'

'You can't possibly know he feels the same.'

'I just sense it here.' She pressed her hand to her heart.

'You could be mistaken.'

'No.'

'You could be dazzled by his kind of life. And that's something we're not used to.'

'Not now. Don't forget his great-grandmother was a

governess just like me and she must have coped with a new life. Besides, deep down I know that our family was once one of means and looked up to around here. Mark's, Zilpha's sort of life should be ours.'

Alice raised her eyebrows. 'Don't get carried away by impossible dreams.'

'They aren't impossible. You shouldn't think like that.'

Alice shrugged her shoulders. 'Well, be careful of Zilpha. She has her eyes set on Mark and jealousy can be a formidable enemy.'

'There's nothing to stop us being friendly rivals.'

'Friendly? Could you be friends with her if he chose her, and what do you think Zilpa would do if she thought you were trying to take Mark away from her?'

'If it comes to it it will be up to him to choose.'

'Don't get your heart broken.'

'I won't.'

Alice's warning was far from Lucy's thoughts when two days later, with the aid of a stick, she ventured from the cottage. Buoyed by the fine weather, she walked further than she had intended. Feeling weary with the exertion she sank to the ground. A few minutes' quiet and she would be all right. On the distant scaurs and sand she could see the seaweed gatherers and wished she was there helping Alice.

The sound of a horse swishing through the grass broke into her thoughts.

Mark!

She thrilled at the sight of his lithe body swinging from the saddle. His smile enveloped and caressed her. 'How nice to see you out,' he said with genuine pleasure in his voice. He dropped to the grass beside her so he could look into her eyes.

He saw they were filled with delight but he also realised that there was something more, a feeling towards him which set his mind racing.

'And I'm pleased to see you.'

'Tired?'

'A little. I did not realise how weak I would feel.' She paused then added, 'It was nice to meet your mother the other day.'

'She's wonderful, in fact both my parents are. I'm very fortunate.' He told her a little of their history.

Lucy decided to take the plunge. 'Would they know anything about the partnership between the de Northbys and the Wades? Robert would be interested for his journal.'

'No more than is generally known. Three generations back the partnership existed, then the Wades disappeared from these parts without trace. My great-grandmother might remember something.'

'You said you would take me to meet her. Will you?'

'Of course. When you are better. She's eighty-two. Mother and Father have wanted her to move in with us but she won't. She has a cottage on the estate and she has a companion housekeeper and a maid to look after her.'

'She sounds intriguing. I'd love to meet her.'

'Then you shall.'

Lucy shivered.

'I think you should return,' said Mark.

Lucy took the concern in his eyes to heart. 'I don't want to but I suppose I should.'

Mark stood up and then held out his hands to her. She

took hold, thrilled by his touch, feeling support in the strong confident hands. He helped her carefully to her feet, wary of causing her pain.

Their eyes locked on each other, speaking volumes. Slowly he bent forward. His lips brushed hers. She shivered, untwined her hands from his and slid them slowly round his neck. When his lips met hers again she held him tight as if she would never let him go. His arms came round her slim waist, drawing her close. Passionate feelings swamped them. Time stood still. The world was theirs and theirs alone.

'I think we'd better get you back,' gasped Mark as their lips parted.

Lucy wanted never to let him go but he had already slipped from her grasp. He picked up her stick and the reins of his horse. They said little as they walked back to the cottage. There was no need for words. Each was lost in their own thoughts.

As Mark rode home he dwelt on his moments with Lucy. She had bewitched him. Then his thoughts descended into upheaval, sometimes drifting with a nervous uncertainty through a fog from which a face, expressing love, needed to be plucked. At other times his thoughts pounded his mind like some roiling sea pushing hard for the cliffs. In that maelstrom a face of tempting beauty cried out for help.

Reaching home he went straight to his bedroom, his mind in confusion.

His gaze moved around the room taking in all that was familiar, his large bed covered by a colourful quilt made by his mother, his desk, a present from his grandparents, an armchair facing the large window offering panoramic views to the west from which he loved to watch the setting sun paint the sky with slowly changing colours. This was home, here were his father and mother, loving, tolerant and understanding, here their love for each other created a womb of stability, memories of which had kept him sane when the upheavals of army life threatened to swamp him. Could all this be destroyed by a stranger, a wisp of a girl to whom this station of life could mean nothing?

He walked across the room deep in thought and started to change out of his riding clothes.

His mind drifted to the girl he had just kissed. There was something different about her but he just could not focus on what it was. He tried to recall their conversation. It had been straightforward. Nothing unusual in it. She had been keen to meet his great-grandmother. She had asked if his parents knew of a partnership between the de Northbys and the Wades. Why? She was a Mitchell. Was there more behind her interest than a story for her brother?

His lips suddenly set in a tight line. He chided himself. Why was he so interested in this stranger? Why had she come into his life complicating the situation by charming his feelings? There had been Zilpha and only Zilpha. Hadn't they a future set for them? Now that future had been shaken to its foundations and a new aspect of life presented itself to him. He was being questioned where his love lay.

He could ignore Lucy. He had just met her. He could forget her and pretend she never existed, but deep down he did not want to.

The following morning with Zilpha not expected he rode to the place where he had seen Lucy, hoping she might be there, to assuage his desire to see her again. He slowed his horse to a walking pace, his eyes scanning the distances. Then he saw her. The tension vanished and in its place came the pleasure of anticipation of being with her again.

'I hoped you'd be here,' he said as he sat down beside her.

'And I hoped you'd think I would be,' she whispered.

He leaned towards her and kissed her. Their lips held each other, hers sending confusion into his mind – Lucy, Zilpha, which one really held his heart? Zilpha, so much a part of his life, or this girl from Newcastle who might soon be gone?

'Once you are well, will you be going home?'

'Don't let's think of that, Mark.'

'It must be faced. Your world is in Newcastle and mine is here. They are far apart.'

'Maybe things will change.'

'How? What do you mean?'

Lucy hesitated for a moment, wondering if she should tell him why she had come to Yorkshire, but then said quietly, 'I cannot say.' She diverted her gaze, looking down at her hands, ashamed that she gave the impression that she could not trust him.

He shrugged his shoulders at this unexpected affront. Was this to do with the Wades? Should he ask her? But if she would not tell him, if she had something to hide, was it a sign that she did not trust him? He stood up. 'Very well,' he said coolly.

She raised her eyes quickly. 'Please, Mark, sit down. Don't go like this. Please try to understand. I would tell you if I could but there are more people involved than I. I will tell you as soon as I can. Please trust me.'

He stared at her for a moment and then his heart melted. He could not ignore the pleading look with which she had transfixed him.

He sat down slowly. 'Very well.'

'Friends?'

He nodded.

She held out her hand and when he took it in his he felt a shiver of relief in her touch.

But he did not feel at ease for he felt a barrier had been raised when she would not confide in him.

By the time he reached home he had resolved to go away for a few days to try to sort out his feelings. He'd visit his army friend, David Hughes, who lived in York. He left the next day after a morning ride with Zilpha, telling her he would probably be back in a week.

For four days Lucy faced disappointment. Though she had gone to the same meeting place every day at the same time Mark had not appeared. She began to fret that she had offended him by not trusting him with the real reason for her presence at Ravenscar. And she feared that she might have lost the chance of contacting his great-grandmother and learning something about the Wades.

Alice recognised the symptoms but refrained from saying, 'I warned you.' Instead she concentrated on helping her sister to get over her sprained ankle. It eased quickly as she walked a little further each day until finally she reached the beach and decided that she would start gathering seaweed again.

Ten days later amidst the chatter and jovial banter of the other seaweed gatherers, local females who had come to accept the girls from Newcastle, Lucy's mind turned once again to Mark. It had been painful at first to think of him but as the days passed she began to believe that Alice had been right and that now she really should be forgetting him. He had not tried to see her. It hurt to think he had played with her affections, used her, without any consideration for her feelings. It seemed out of character with the man she knew. But that thought reminded her of Alice's warning: Do you really know him?

She straightened and eased her back. As she did so she became aware of movement on the cliff top. Riders. Two. Mark and Zilpha. The seaweed gatherers, the scaurs, the sea, the distant cottages of Robin Hood's Bay clinging to the cliff face, all faded into limbo and she was only aware of the shock which gripped her body.

Mark was there and he rode with Zilpha. So that was why he had not come to her. Zilpha had occupied his full attention.

She bit her lip, trying to hold back the dampness in her eyes and prevent tears from flowing. She must not let anyone see that happen. She saw the two figures turn away from the cliff edge to disappear from sight.

Lucy said little as she filled her basket and even less as she and Alice walked back to the cottage. Alice knew what was the matter for she too had seen the riders on the cliff and had noted her sister's reaction but she said nothing. No words would help Lucy get over what she was feeling at seeing the man she said she loved with the girl the whole countryside expected him to marry – Zilpha.

The following day Lucy could not help herself from constantly glancing at the cliffs as she gathered seaweed. She did not want anyone to notice her doing so and drifted away from the other girls. Many of them, their baskets full, had left when she saw the horseman. She held her breath, half expecting to see a second rider, but Mark was on his own! She pulled her racing thoughts up short. What difference did that make? If he had wanted to see her he would have made contact before this. She went on with her seaweed gathering but she could not stop the pounding in her heart.

When she looked up again he was not there. Then a movement caught her eye. A horse negotiating a cleft towards the sands.

He reached the beach and turned the animal in her direction but kept it to a casual pace. She went on gathering seaweed, pretending not to have noticed. Only when she was aware of the horse stopping close by did she look up. Her eyes met his, searching for some expression of what he was thinking.

He doffed his hat. 'Good day, Miss Mitchell, I am pleased to see you well again.'

Her mind was cool. Formal. Did this indicate that a relationship was over? Or was it for the benefit of anyone who might be left in earshot?

'Thank you, sir. It is pleasant to be able to walk comfortably again.' She kept all feeling out of her voice.

'Be careful you don't fall again.'

'I will.'

He glanced round and then leaned from the saddle. 'I must see you, Lucy,' he whispered. 'Tomorrow, where we last met, when the tide is in and there'll be no seaweed to gather.' He straightened and said more loudly, 'Good day, Miss Mitchell, take care.'

As she watched him ride away her mind and heart were racing. Had she misjudged him? Had there been some reason for his absence?

Alice sensed her sister's more buoyant mood as they climbed the cliff with their baskets. She had observed the meeting from a distance.

'Well?' she prompted.

'He wants to see me tomorrow.'

'Why not before now?'

'He didn't say.'

'Then be careful, sis. Remember he was with Zilpha yesterday.'

'You saw them?'

'Yes. Remember what I told you. Don't get carried away.'

Lucy did not want to pursue the matter of her feelings now that Mark had made contact again so said merely, 'Now we might get that chance to see his great-grandmother and learn something about the Wades.'

The following day Lucy was at the appointed place. She sat patiently gazing over the sea, watching the white-caps raised by the freshening wind. She tried to examine her feelings for Mark. It hurt that he had not contacted her for so long.

But that was driven away when she heard the approaching horse and a few moments later Mark was making an apology.

'I've been away, Lucy. I'm sorry I couldn't let you know.'

Lucy felt relief at this news, but he made no move to sit down beside her.

'And I can't stop now. I've to take my mother into Whitby.' He saw doubt mask her face. 'It's true,' he added quickly. 'She asked me just before I came out. I'll have to get back. Will you meet me this time tomorrow?'

'Here?'

'No. You know the cleft where I rode down to the beach yesterday. Meet me at the top.'

'Very well.'

He was already swinging into the saddle. 'Until tomorrow.' He turned the horse and was gone, leaving a dazed and disappointed Lucy behind.

If she had any doubts about Mark's intention it was dispelled when she saw him waiting at the appointed place. He had tethered his horse and was sitting gazing out to sea.

She paused and studied the handsome profile which sent a longing surging through her.

He felt her presence and scrambled to his feet and as she came forward he held out his hands to her. She felt them strong, confident, reassuring yet gentle in their touch. Their eyes locked in mutual admiration and desire, in a way that dispensed with words. He kissed her gently, a kiss which she returned.

'Let's go down on to the beach,' he said. 'The tide's in but there's a narrow strip of sand.'

They started down the gully slipping and sliding, laughter on their lips as Lucy tumbled, righted herself and grabbed his arm.

Mark was caught up in her enjoyment. Was she really the girl for him? Indecision was still there. His stay with David had done nothing to help and he left York when he

167

realised he was only delaying the moment of finding where his love truly lay. Whoever he was with took precedence over the other. Two days ago Zilpha had meant everything to him. Now it was Lucy.

They walked close to the water's edge enjoying each other's company, holding hands and chatting idly as only lovers can.

Mark stopped and turned her towards him. He saw an invitation she was not bothering to hide. He drew her closer. His lips came to hers and she arched her back against his arms as they came round her in a hold which said he never wanted to let her go. Lost in their world they failed to notice the figure who turned slowly away from the cliff top.

Chapter Nine

Zilpha stepped back from the cliff edge, numbed by what she had just seen. She was frozen in shocked disbelief and yet the scene was so vivid it confirmed the truth.

Her steps were leaden as she walked in a daze towards her horse. The pleasant ride she had anticipated had turned sour. She had seen Mark's horse, Freya, and thought to give him a surprise but now the turmoil of her emotions ranged through nausea and anger. Had her naming of that horse meant so little to him? She wanted to plead, to cry, to fight.

She rode away at a walking pace. The reality of what she had witnessed overwhelmed her and tears flowed down her cheeks.

The horse seemed to sense her misery and twitched nervously. She leaned forward and patted it comfortingly on the neck. She anticipated its desire to run. 'Come on, let's go home.'

The need for consolation overpowered her. She would find it with her mother and father in the security of her own surroundings. Anger began to dominate. She tapped the animal into a quicker pace. The hooves thrummed on the soft ground, sending clods of earth flying. She rode hard and fast. The rush of air and the vigour of the animal beneath her brought exhilaration to combat the anger. Her mind began to clear, as if the the flaying hooves and powerful energy of her mount had driven out the demons which had clouded her judgement.

As she hauled on the reins and brought the horse to a halt, she recalled that her father had gone to a meeting in Whitby and her mother had taken the opportunity to go with him and visit friends. Despondent that there was no one to turn to she sat in the saddle staring out to sea. It misted through the tears which flowed silently.

How many minutes passed she never knew but she became aware that the tears had stopped. She bit her lip, forcing herself to feel again and to think. She drew a handkerchief from her sleeve and wiped her eyes. Life began to come into focus again. The undulating sea stretched endlessly as if indicating that there was a future and it was up to her to take it under her control.

Her eyes narrowed. Anger at Mark rose again. Hadn't he held her in his arms in their favourite place along the cliffs? Now . . . Her fists tightened. She subdued the anger and brought into its place a determination to fight. Why should she give up easily? The shock had blurred her thinking. Had the kiss she had witnessed been just of that moment? A result of flirtation? But Mark wasn't a flirt.

She would face him. Test his feelings and do all in her power to make him see that it was she to whom he should be giving all his attention. She knew he loved her and . . .

That thought brought her up with a jolt. Did he? Or had they slipped into a relationship which had developed from a childhood companionship and had she assumed therefore that he loved her? She must do something about it. She turned her horse back.

She was still some distance away when she saw Mark riding towards Howland Manor. Her instinct was to gallop after him but she checked herself. In her present state she might say things to him which she would regret. Lucy must be walking back along the cliff edge. She turned in that direction. This could be the opportunity to strike, warn her off. She had no right to Mark. He was hers.

She waited until Mark was out of sight, then rode slowly until she saw Lucy emerge from a dip in the path whereupon she put her horse into a gallop.

Lucy was startled by the pounding thrum of the hooves. She looked up in alarm and froze when she saw who galloped towards her.

Zilpha pulled her mount up in an earth-tearing halt. She let the animal swing around for a few moments, causing Lucy to flinch every time it came near her. Zilpha laughed at the uneasy fear in her eyes, then she calmed the horse and slid from the saddle.

'You've no right to him! You don't belong here!' Zilpha drove her words home with an intensity which made sure that Lucy was in no doubt about what she meant.

Lucy stared at her for one moment in the realisation of what must have happened. 'You saw us?'

'Yes. I saw you!' she hissed. 'And don't tell me it was just an innocent kiss.'

Lucy gathered herself from the shock of discovery. 'It

wasn't.' There was a touch of triumph in her voice. 'He loves me and I love him.'

Zilpha's lips tightened. She gave a slight shake of her head. 'Oh no. It's me he loves.'

'He didn't tell me that.'

'Did he tell you he loved you?'

'Yes.'

'Liar.' The word spat from Zilpha. She glared at Lucy with mounting hatred.

Lucy's eyes flared with anger at this accusation. 'I'm never that,' she protested.

Zilpha ignored the rebuff. 'And what happens when you go home? Do you think he'll come chasing you to Newcastle? His home's here. He'll stay. His family mean more than you'll ever do. Gone, you'll be forgotten.' She saw some doubt creep into Lucy's eyes and she pressed on. She guessed exaggeration might be the arrow which would hit gold. 'He's like this with all the girls. Leads them on and then lets go. But I'm always here. I belong to him and he belongs to me.'

'Stop! Stop!' Lucy's voice rose. Her eyes widened with disbelief.

Zilpha laughed scornfully. 'You don't want to hear any more, do you? You're frightened by what you might learn.'

Lucy stiffened, getting a grip on herself. She must not give way. She must not let Zilpha dominate her.

'I don't believe you. Not after what Mark just told me.' She saw a flicker of wary curiosity combat the scorn. 'Now who's frightened of what she might hear?'

Zilpha sharpened her mind. The feelings she had let slip for one moment were under control again. Her thoughts were ice-cool. She must maintain the upper hand but had she been using the wrong tactic in exaggerating Mark's outlook? Maybe she should play on Lucy's love for him, for she had no doubt that the girl was deeply smitten.

'If you love him, as you say you do, consider his feelings, consider his future. What would it be? Would he want to give up everything he has here?'

'He wouldn't have to. As his wife I'd come here.'

'Could you cope with it? Wouldn't you be an embarrassment to him? Just think, most of his friends have seen you as a serving maid at my party . . .'

'I'm not that! I'm as good as you!' cried Lucy.

Zilpha's head went back with a laugh filled with scorn. 'What? You? Never!'

'I am,' snapped Lucy, riled by Zilpha's mockery. 'The Wades were as good as the de Northbys.' The words were out before Lucy realised she had let the name slip.

Zilpha's laughter grew. 'I've never heard of the Wades. You're making it all up. If you thought anything about him you'd not indulge in these lies. You'd leave and not ruin his life. Don't delude yourself. It's me he loves! It's me he'll marry!' She sensed she had sown doubt in Lucy's mind. Her voice lowered into a mesmerising monotone. 'Think carefully about it, Lucy, you'd never fit in here. Leave Mark to the life he knows.'

Lucy stared at her, not knowing what to say. If only Mark was here.

Zilpha smiled a smile of triumph, of right which would withstand all challenges. Lucy felt a chill grip at her heart. Zilpha climbed on to her horse, looked disdainfully down at Lucy and left her deep in disturbing contemplation.

Had Mark been using her? Tears dimmed her eyes as her troubled thoughts almost overwhelmed her.

What would he have said if he had been here to face Zilpha? There was only one way to find out, confront him. But how would she know he was telling the truth? How could she really know that the words he had uttered but a short while ago were genuine, that he really did love her? Or was he just leading her on for his own gratification? That thought brought more tears. How long she stood there racked by sobs she did not know but by the time the ache had left her she had begun to analyse and think more rationally. She concluded that challenging Mark might not lead to an answer which would convince her. She chided herself for her mistrust but she could not escape the fact that it was there. Maybe the best way would be by testing him without him knowing.

'Maybe we should think about going home?' said Lucy when she and Alice were alone.

'Is something wrong?' Alice asked, having sensed an uneasiness in her sister.

Lucy went on to tell Alice about her meeting with Mark and confrontation with Zilpha.

'I warned you,' said Alice.

'I know,' Lucy lamented.

'Oh, why did you let yourself get into this situation? Do you really love him?'

'Yes,' she cried but then drew back. 'I thought I did but after what Zilpha said I don't know.' She looked at her sister as if appealing for help.

'Don't look at me for help. I can't tell you if you're in love. Only you can judge that. But I do think that you are

174

right not to confront him and I can see why you want to be away from here. Separation is probably the best thing now. It will give you both time to really know how you feel.'

Lucy drew a little comfort from her sister's agreement that they should leave, but she still looked downcast.

'There's something else you're not telling me,' said Alice, seeing her sister's discomfort.

'Oh, Alice, I mentioned the Wades. She got me so riled I blurted out that they were as good as the de Northbys.'

Alice drew a deep breath. 'Well, what's done can't be undone. Did you say they were family?'

'No.'

'What was Zilpha's reaction?'

'She laughed. I believe she thought I was making it up.'

'So she may think no more of it.'

Emile Cossart climbed the stairs to the offices of the Whitby Shipping Company overlooking the harbour.

'Good day, Mr Cossart.' A clerk in his mid-thirties jumped from the tall stool from which he had been working on a large sloping desk arranged along one wall of the outer office.

'Pleasant day, Roger,' commented Emile with a smile.

'It is that, sir.'

'Too nice to be working inside.' Emile gave a little secretive grin as if to say, no one will know if you slip out.

Roger smiled as he took Mr Cossart's cane and hat. He liked the Frenchman who had made himself so much at home in Yorkshire, adopting Yorkshire ways without trying to impose any of his French outlook. He was much pleasanter than that often sour-faced, stern looking Mr de

Northby whom he had just shown into the other office. He liked to keep you in your place. Never a smile or even a 'Good day' came for anyone like a clerk. But he'd put on a different face for his partners. Roger had heard him, though even in that office his voice would sometimes rise in intolerant argument.

Emile opened the door and stepped into a large room with an oak desk across one corner. A similar one occupied another corner with a fireplace in between. Today four chairs were drawn up in front of one of the desks with two more behind it.

De Northby and the two men with whom he was in conversation turned on hearing the door open.

'Ah, Emile, a pleasure to see you.' The tall thin man stepped forward and extended his hand. As the senior partner Joss Storm always greeted new arrivals. 'We have an hour in hand, gives us time to agree the course of action we should take.'

'Emile.' The stout, jovial, red-faced man smiled and shook Emile's hand vigorously. William Hirst was always enthusiastic in all he did whether it was in greeting people or going about his business in running the practical side of the shipping business these four men had founded.

Richard and Emile, who saw more of each other than the other two, exchanged nods as William fussed with a glass of wine for Emile so that he could join the others who were already on their second.

'Let's be seated,' suggested Joss. 'As arranged, the attorney for Mr Alan Dewey arrived in Whitby yesterday. He called here, made himself known and we arranged a meeting for this morning. Mr Dewey sends his apologies for having to put the matter of negotiating into the hands of his attorney but he has every confidence in him. The attorney, a Mr Palmer by the way, is familar with Mr Dewey's full wishes.'

'Why is Mr Dewey unable to attend?' asked de Northby huffily as if he thought they should not be dealing with anyone whom he regarded as an underling.

'Ill-health,' replied Joss. 'He is anxious to complete this deal if we are in agreement. If we had waited for him it might have taken some time.'

'Poor man,' said William. 'I hope it's nothing too serious.'

'Palmer assures me it is not, but I believe Mr Dewey has taken precautions in case anything untoward happens to him.'

'Sensible man,' commented Emile. 'And with negotiations having gone so far already it is as well to have them completed. Mr Dewey's future and his stake in this company, should we agree to it, is his own private affair.' He glanced at de Northby. 'You're frowning, Richard, is something troubling you?'

'I think we ought to know who will inherit Dewey's partnership should he . . . well, die,' he stated firmly. 'After all, we don't want to be in partnership with someone who is undesirable.'

'Quite so,' said Joss. 'I think in all probability Palmer will be able to reassure us.' He steepled his fingers in front of his chin and glanced round his partners. 'Are we all happy about the fact that he is bringing four ships to our three?'

'I don't think it's a question of numbers but one of soundness of ship, and tonnage,' said Emile. 'I'm satisfied with the reports we have received about them.'

William nodded his agreement.

'But three of his are only colliers,' pointed out Richard. 'He brings one merchantman to our three. A little one-sided, don't you think?'

'Ah, but the colliers bring a good income, shipping coal from Newcastle to London and places in between,' Joss pointed out. 'You should know that, Richard. They're bringing coal vital for your alum works.'

Richard grunted morosely, having been caught out.

'I think the deal is fair enough,' said William. 'It does take us readily into the coal trade and that extra merchantman will soon be adding to our profits. There are two points we should insist on.'

His fellow investors were all attention. William might appear easy-going but they knew there was a nimble brain behind the façade. He could often see advantages and disadvantages beyond the immediate future. 'One, we should insist that all repairs and alterations to the ships are carried out in Whitby. Our shipbuilders and repairers are second to none and I'm all for keeping as much trade as possible here, it's good for the local economy. That should please you, Richard, with your investments in those trades.' Though he was pleased, de Northby remained impassive. He didn't want anyone to think they were doing him any favours. 'Secondly,' William went on, 'I would like to see an agreement on fitting out and insist that that be shared equally between Whitby and Newcastle or as convenient when the ship docks.'

There was a murmur of agreement and when Joss looked directly at Richard and Emile they both nodded approval. 'Very well, gentlemen. Are we agreed in principle that we accept the idea of a partnership with Mr Dewey's company, subject to a consideration of his proposals in detail?'

His three partners gave their assent. In the interval of waiting for Mr Palmer's arrival they discussed the possibilities of the fragile peace with France breaking out into hostilities again and the course of action they would take to continue trading.

At precisely the minute they expected Mr Palmer Roger announced his arrival.

Joss came from behind his desk to greet him warmly. 'You're a man of impeccable timing.'

The small man, neatly dressed in a charcoal-grey suit, shook hands firmly. 'I believe in punctuality, that way no one wastes time.' His dark blue eyes indicated a man whose expression, in negotiations, would give nothing away until a point had been won or lost.

Joss introduced him to his partners who expressed their pleasure at meeting him. Only de Northby's lacked the warmth of the other two and Seth Palmer was immediately on his guard against him. If there were going to be any difficulties this might be the man who would cause them. Seth always prided himself on being able to judge a character at first meeting. This man would be one who would look after his own interests even at the expense of friends. But he had no doubt that he could handle any problems de Northby might raise.

Introductions over, Seth turned to a young man who had followed him into the room and who was standing beside the door which Roger had closed. 'Gentlemen, I have brought my clerk with me. I would like him to make notes of this meeting so that, provided we come to a satisfactory conclusion, we can draw up the necessary documents before we return to Newcastle. I am proposing to take a little time off, and have booked our return passage to Newcastle for a week yesterday. That should give us ample time to sort details out and finalise the documents for signing. I hope this meets with your approval.'

Joss received nods from his partners and he voiced their agreement.

'Good,' said Seth with a feeling of satisfaction, 'then I'll introduce Robert Mitchell.'

Robert, who had been startled when he heard Mr Palmer introduced to Richard de Northby, had kept his attention on the man whose ancestors had once been in partnership with the Wades, the man who was Zilpha's father. He was an impressive figure, holding himself to his full height, which Robert judged to be over six feet, something he cultivated to give the impression of domination. Robert guessed that he would be loyal to his family and that he would dote on his daughter for whom nothing or no one would be good enough, unless it be that fellow, Mark, whom he had seen on the cliffs. Robert met a penetrating gaze from him and he was forced to look away. He felt he had come under close scrutiny and thought it might be because de Northby disapproved of a mere clerk sitting in on this meeting. He would have been alarmed if he had known the real reason for the interest.

Richard watched Robert cross the room to the un-occupied desk, which Joss had indicated he could use, and meticulously set out his three quill pens, ink and paper. So this was the person whom Luke had told him had shown interest in the story of the Wades. This must be the brother of those two girls who had caused havoc at Zilpha's party and who were staying at the Smurthwaites'. Were they also interested in the Wades? If so why? Was this young man really seeking stories for a Newcastle journal?

He received another jolt when Emile spoke up. 'Robert Mitchell? Surely this can't be a coincidence? Do you have two sisters, Alice and Lucy?'

Robert was taken by surprise. How did this man who spoke with a slight foreign accent know them? He had been introduced to Mr Palmer as Emile Cossart and Robert decided that he must be Mark's father. 'Yes, sir, I have.'

'They came to visit Mrs Smurthwaite?'

'Yes, sir. I hope to see them.'

'You know your sister, Lucy, had an accident?'

'No, sir.' Worried concern tensed Robert.

'She fell on the scaurs and sprained her ankle when she was alone. Fortunately my son saw her and took her to the Smurthwaites'. I believe she's up and about again. No doubt she'll be delighted to see you.'

The meeting went well and when the final details were sorted out all participants were satisfied.

'Mr Dewey will be pleased with the progress we have made,' Seth Palmer assured them. 'I'll have all the necessary documents drawn up for signature the day before we sail. Shall we meet at three in the afternoon?'

The four partners agreed.

Robert had started to gather up his papers when Seth spoke. 'You have all you need, Robert?'

'Yes, Mr Palmer.'

'Good, then I suggest you return to your room, work

on them now, so that you can contact your sisters tomorrow as you requested.'

'Very good, Mr Palmer, and thank you.'

As he politely took his leave of the four men he felt himself come under the critical gaze of de Northby and he found it something of a relief to escape from it.

'Capable young man,' commented Joss.

'Excellent.' Business over, Seth Palmer allowed his reserve to fall. There was approval of Joss's comment in his eyes.

As conversations developed de Northby sought to speak privately with Palmer.

'You do find Mitchell reliable and trustworthy?' he asked guardedly.

Seth spread his hands. 'Would I have brought him here, would I have him draw up such important documents if I did not?' He gave a little shake of his head. 'He is highly efficient and steady. He gets that from his late father who worked for my father and for me. Robert came into the office under him. He was a quick learner and showed a nimble brain. He has it in him to become a fully fledged attorney one day. That sharpness comes from his mother's family.'

'Interesting,' said Richard, then asked cautiously, 'Has he any other interests that would get in the way of that ambition?'

Seth gave a little laugh. 'Oh, no,' he said emphatically. 'None outside his work, except a devotion to his family, his mother and two sisters.' He pursed his lips thoughtfully. 'I've always found them interesting. Father and mother encouraged learning with the result that one of his sisters is a governess to my children and the other is a school teacher.

182

I've always felt there's more behind that family than appears on the surface. There's been breeding somewhere.'

'I heard you mention that Mitchell's sisters were with the Smurthwaites,' commented Richard casually as he and Emile left the office. 'Do you know what connection they have with one of my employees?'

'The elder girl, Alice, is friendly with Smurthwaite's son, Mark tells me.'

Richard nodded.

'They seem to be interested in your alum works. Looking for stories for their brother for a journal he writes for in his spare time.'

'That can't be the real reason,' mused Richard to himself.

He said goodbye to his friend and, as he headed for Bagdale where his wife was visiting friends, he had much to think about. The story that Robert Mitchell wanted items for a journal was false according to his employer. So why was he interested in the Wades? After what Palmer had said about breeding could that lead the Mitchells back to the Wades? After all, Jacob Wade and his family had disappeared. Could they have gone to Newcastle? Could Robert Mitchell be a descendant? It would have to be on his mother's side, and Palmer had indicated that he thought that his clerk's astuteness had come from there.

Robert Mitchell and his sisters must be watched.

Chapter Ten

Zilpha felt much more at ease with herself as she rode home. She had put that damned shrew in her place. Fancy her thinking herself as good as the de Northbys. The cheek of it. Her just a governess, and that position couldn't be up to much if she was prepared to work as a serving maid and a seaweed gatherer. Well, now she knew where she stood and the sooner she left the better.

Zilpha smiled to herself when she remembered the startled expression on Lucy's face, but she became more serious when she recalled the name Lucy had mentioned. Wade. From where had she dreamed up that name? Probably something that had just leaped into her mind. But there had been a serious note in her voice. And why link it with the de Northbys? Just a means of fighting back? The name kept imposing itself on her mind. She knew no one called Wade, hadn't even heard the name in this district. Though she tried to put it from her mind it kept recurring until she decided she would have to ask her mother and father if they knew any Wades.

The opportunity did not arise until their evening meal. Mr and Mrs de Northby had arrived home from Whitby later than they had intended and had immediately gone to their room to change.

Though pleasantries were exchanged during their first course, Zilpha's mind was elsewhere until she decided to come straight to the point.

'Does the name Wade mean anything to you?' she asked.

Taken aback by the unexpected question, her father paused in cutting up his meat. As he looked up he saw anxiety cross his wife's face before his gaze swept on to his daughter.

'Where have you heard that name?' he asked.

The nature of his question answered hers. 'You do know it.' A tremor of excitement touched her voice. Her eyes, now intent on her father, awaited his reaction.

'Where did you hear it?' he repeated his question so firmly that Zilpha knew she would not get to know any more until she had told him.

'You remember the two girls who came with Mrs Smurthwaite to help at my party?' Her father nodded. 'Well, the younger one sprained her ankle on the beach, Mark saw her and took her to the Smurthwaites'. It's given her ideas about him. I saw them together today and I don't think it's the first time they've met. I had an argument with her after Mark had left.' Zilpha's eyes narrowed when she recalled the confrontation and there was malice in her voice as she went on. 'She thought too much of herself. I had to bring her down to earth.'

'What's this got to do with the name Wade?' cut in Richard with a snap in his voice.

'When I told her she was no better than a serving girl, or a governess at best, she remarked that the Wades were as good as the de Northbys. I told her that I'd never heard of them.'

'Did she say any more about them?'

'No, but I had a feeling that there was something she wasn't telling me. From the way she said it I got the impression that she believed the two families knew one another at some time.' A puzzled frown creased her forehead. 'But that would have meant that the Wades had lived around here. I've never heard of them. I thought you might.'

Her father did not reply immediately and she knew better than to speak when he was in this thoughtful mood. When he glanced at her mother she saw that he received an almost imperceptible nod from her.

From his grave expression Zilpha knew that he expected her to listen carefully and digest what he was about to say.

'Yes, we know of the Wades. They lived around here, but not in my time. Your great-great-grandfather recognised the potential of the land here for making alum. That land belonged to Wades. They established a partnership and the business boomed. Their sons, your great-grandfather, Peter, and a Jacob Wade carried on the partnership until Jacob tried to take more money out of the business than he was entitled to. There was a scandal but your great-grandfather was generous towards the family and did not press charges. I don't know what happened but apparently the Wades disappeared overnight and were never heard of again. I have never heard the name for a long time until now.'

'So, if Lucy Mitchell mentioned the Wades she must believe she's descended from them,' said Zilpha thoughtfully.

'If that's the case does she know she comes from a cheat and a rogue?' mused Adeline. 'I think it's as well you know the story. You can warn Mark against her.'

Zilpha had already recognised this possibility.

'I wonder what the three of them are really doing here?' mused Richard.

'Three?' Adeline looked surprised.

'Yes, Mother. There's a brother, Robert. I met him the day after the party. He came to the Hall to see his sisters who were helping with the cleaning up. He had come to take his sisters home but I believe he had to return without them.'

'Ah, but he's here again now,' revealed Richard, and went on to tell them how he had met Robert. 'To all outward appearances a personable young man but I wonder if his presence in these parts has a more sinister purpose, especially as he has two sisters here as well.'

'But if they are connected with the Wades would they want to rake up the past and the scandal? Surely that would sully their name whereas at the moment they are protected by the anonymity of Mitchell?'

Richard shrugged his shoulders. 'Who knows? But if you hear any more or have any suspicions let me know.'

Zilpha smiled to herself. She'd do just that. It would be better for Lucy Mitchell if she went home.

The next day Mark was waiting along the cliffs at the appointed time. The weather was fine, with the sun shimmering on a gentle sea. He felt eager to take Lucy in his arms again. He kept looking in the direction from which she would come and as soon as he saw her he was on his feet and hurrying to meet her. He was still some distance away when he sensed something was wrong. Her step was not brisk. It carried no sign of an eagerness to reach him.

Nearer, he felt her mood was subdued with regret, and her face reflected disappointment and sorrow.

'Is something wrong?' he asked, a worried frown creasing his brow. He took her hand and felt little response from her. 'Lucy, what is it?'

'We've decided we should go home.' Her voice was weak.

'No! You can't!' he cried as if the words would prevent her.

'I think it's best.'

'Not after what has grown between us,' he protested. 'Something has happened. What is it?'

'No, Mark. Only that I've had time to think.'

'About what? You do love me?'

Lucy's heart was wrenched in two. She wanted to express how much she cared for him, but hadn't Zilpha pointed out that that might be the wrong thing for Mark, that a love for him could change his life, take him out of the environment he knew so well, in which he fitted so admirably, and even if that life went on she could be an unwelcome intruder?

'I don't know,' she said with an anguished shake of her head.

'But yesterday . . .'

'Heady moments,' she cut in.

'Not for me.'

'But we've only known each other such a short time.'

'Long enough.'

'We can't be sure. Our lives are so different. You couldn't give up the life you are used to.'

'You would share it.'

'But I don't know this sort of life. No, Mark, we must not commit ourselves now and find ourselves in a situation that we might regret.'

'But I love you, I know what I want – you.'

She touched his lips. 'Don't say such things until you are certain.'

'I am.'

She shook her head. 'I mean with absolute certainty which can only come with time when every aspect has been considered. I need that time if you don't, but I believe it would be better for both of us.'

He looked into the sadness in her eyes. 'If that's the way you want it. But I'll not give up the attempt to make you love me.'

She wanted to cry out, 'I do,' but she bit the words back. Mark must be given the chance to see if parting brought a change of heart.

'When will you go?'

'Nothing has been arranged yet, but it will be soon.'

'Then I will see you again?' Eagerness was back in his voice.

'I don't know,' she said quietly, while her heart longed to say yes.

'Oh, yes you will. There is one thing I must do before you leave.'

Lucy stiffened. She feared he was going to make public his love for her and she would be placed in a compromising situation. But her fear vanished and she knew he respected her wishes when he continued.

'You mentioned you would like to talk to my great-grandmother. I'll drive you to her cottage in the morning.'

Lucy thought that they might have an opportunity to find out more about the Wades.

'Alice must come too,' she said.

Although he had hoped to have Lucy to himself he complied with her wishes.

'Thee looks two fine young ladies,' commented Mrs Smurthwaite the following morning, her eyes casting an approving look over the colourful flowered dresses Alice and Lucy were wearing for their visit to Mrs Swinburn. 'You shouldn't be seaweed gathering because of me.'

Mark was pleased to see that Lucy had thrown off some of her despondent mood of yesterday, and it raised his hopes that she had had second thoughts about her decision. For the moment he must accept her as she was. He helped them up into the carriage and once they were settled he picked up the reins.

When they had discussed the situation in their room the previous evening Lucy and Alice had come to the conclusion that, with Mark present, they would have to be guarded in their questions and would have to assess the situation as it developed.

They said goodbye to Mrs Smurthwaite, who after being told who would be calling for them wondered if Lucy was getting out of her depth for she had detected that the girl had special feelings for the man regarded as Zilpha's. She shook her head, hoping no one would get hurt, as she watched them drive away.

'I've news for you two,' Mark informed them. 'Your brother's in Whitby.'

'Robert?' They were both taken aback.

'Yes. Father mentioned it. There's an amalgamation going on with a firm in Newcastle. The attorney Robert works for is acting for the Newcastle party. Robert is with him.'

'I wonder if we'll see him,' said Alice excitedly.

'Oh, we must,' cried Lucy. 'I wonder how long he will be in Whitby.'

'When we've seen my great-grandmother, I'll drive you to Whitby to see him.'

'Oh, Mark, would you?' Lucy looked at him hopefully.

'Of course,' he laughed and flicked the horse into a trot.

After a pleasant drive along a winding path across the estate, Mark reined the horse to a halt when the building tucked in a sheltered hollow came in sight. 'Charming, isn't it?'

'Beautiful,' said Lucy.

'Bigger than I expected,' commented Alice.

Mark raised an eyebrow. 'What did you expect?'

'A small cottage.'

'Not for Great-grandmother. She had been used to something similar to Howland Manor but when Great-grandfather died she eventually decided to move. We wanted her to come and live with us but she wouldn't hear of it so mother suggested this cottage which was empty. Great-grandmother thought it was a good idea but it wasn't big enough in her view so she had it enlarged at the same time as the renovation.' He let the horse walk slowly down the slope.

The pathway ran parallel to a stream and over a hump-backed bridge to turn along the front of the house, which was raised two steps above it on a paved area which ran the full length of the house. Its two storeys held twelve large sash windows giving a lightness to the stone façade.

191

Mark helped the girls from the carriage. Once inside they gazed round the hall in admiration. Light shafted from a window on the landing halfway up the oak staircase. The carpet, patterned in light colours, calmed the heaviness of the two oak armchairs and chest which occupied one wall.

'Great-grandmother is sure to be in here,' he said, starting towards a dark oak door. 'Hello, Grandma,' he called lightly as he stepped into the room. 'I've brought two visitors to meet you.' He stood to one side while Alice and Lucy tentatively entered the room.

An armchair was placed so that the light from the window fell across the book an elderly lady was reading.

'Mark! And visitors. Splendid. I like visitors. Come, come, introduce me.'

Mark laughed at his great-grandmother's impatience and raised an eyebrow at the two girls as he went to greet her. 'This is Alice and Lucy Mitchell from Newcastle.'

Both girls took her proffered hand in turn, expressing their pleasure at meeting her. As Mrs Swinburn smiled her welcome her eyes narrowed a little as if she was trying to bring them into focus but they knew they had come under close scrutiny. Her great-grandson had arrived with two young women and she had to give her approval if only to satisfy herself.

'Sit down, sit down.' She gave little waves of her right hand in the direction of the chairs opposite her. 'Newcastle, you say. What brings you down here?' Mark knew that question also hid one for him, 'How did you meet them?'

'We came to visit Mrs Smurthwaite at . . .'

'Smurthwaite? Smurthwaite?' Mrs Swinburn interrupted as if trying to recall if she knew such a person.

'Mr Smurthwaite is a foreman at the alum works.

192

I know his son,' Alice explained. 'He came to my aid when he was in Newcastle. I'd fallen and he helped me home.'

'Just so,' grunted Mrs Swinburn.

'And that's how I met them. It seems the Mitchell sisters are always falling,' said Mark with a teasing laugh. 'Miss Lucy fell on the scaurs and hurt her ankle. I saw it happen and took her to the Smurthwaites'.'

During his telling his great-grandmother kept giving little grunts of commiseration and approval.

'You're quite well again, my dear?' she asked.

'Yes, thank you, ma'am.'

Mark was pleased at his great-grandmother's term of endearment. It meant that so far she had approved of her visitors. Now might be the moment to move on to the real purpose of their visit. 'Grandma,' he paused to see if he had her full attention.

There was no doubt about it when she said, 'Oh, my, when you use such a serious tone you're going to make a request.'

Mark smiled, glanced at the girls, and looked back at his great-grandmother. 'You're very shrewd.'

'I know you, Mark Cossart.' She gave a little laugh, pleased that she had read him right. 'What is it?'

'Well, it isn't so much for me as for Alice and Lucy, or rather not for them but for their brother.'

Mrs Swinburn shook her head with irritation. 'Now you are talking in riddles. It's not for you, it's for them, but not for them but someone else.'

'That's right, Grandma. They have a brother, Robert.'

'Is he as agreeable as them?'

'I've only met him briefly.'

'All right, all right. Get on with your asking.'

193

'I'll let one of them do that.'

Mrs Swinburn looked at the girls.

Lucy began. 'My brother is a clerk in an attorney's office but he also writes for a journal. He heard there once was a partnership in the alum works at Ravenscar. He thought he might write about it.'

'Partnership?' Mrs Swinburn looked thoughtful.

'Wasn't the original owner of the land called Wade?' put in Mark. 'I've heard so.'

'Wade?' She said the name half to herself.

Lucy and Alice were on tenterhooks as they waited for her answer.

Lucy was about to say something but she caught Mark's eye. He gave a slight shake of his head, warning her to say nothing. She assumed he knew his great-grandmother not to interrupt her thoughts.

Mrs Swinburn's lips moved silently, her forefinger moving up and down as if she might be trying to work out the generations. Suddenly she looked up, her eyes wide with delight. 'I have it. Peter de Northby, Zilpha's great-grandfather.'

Lucy and Alice felt relief. Maybe there was more to come.

'A sneaky man,' she was going on. 'I never did like him. Richard takes after him.' She raised her hand to her mouth as if she had said something she shouldn't have. She looked guiltily at Mark. 'Sorry. I know he's Zilpha's father and one day will be your father-in-law, but I can't help my feelings.'

Mark felt embarrassed as he glanced at Lucy and saw her eyes go cold.

'Now don't anticipate events, Grandma,' said Mark, hoping that would convey something of his feelings to Lucy.

194

'Can you tell us any more about Mr Peter de Northby?' put in Lucy quickly, not wanting the old lady's train of thought to be diverted. 'Or about the people he was in partnership with, the Wades?'

'Ah, now it's all coming back. Jacob Wade. A fine man, a man I was drawn to, but his love was elsewhere.'

'What happened to him?' Lucy pressed eagerly.

'I don't know. He and his family just left. Gone one night. Nobody heard of them again.'

'Something bad must have happened,' Lucy urged, trying to keep Mrs Swinburn's recollections coming.

She did not answer. The faraway look came to her eyes again but then she spoke quickly. 'Some scandal. Fraud. Yes. There were rumours of fraud. Things seemed to get hushed up. Everything happened so fast. Accusations. Denials. Evidence. Then everything went quiet. The Wades had gone.'

'It looks as though the Wades were to blame,' said Mark.

'You don't know that!' Lucy's eyes flared with anger at Mark.

He was taken aback by her sharp reaction. 'But, if there was fraud and the Wades left . . .'

'That's no proof,' snapped Lucy. She ignored the warning glance cast at her by her sister. 'They could have left for any number of reasons.'

'It appears no one knew they were leaving and it seems to me that they didn't want anyone to know where they went. That looks suspicious to me.'

'It would, you being so close to the de Northbys!'

The barb hurt but Mark did not respond to Lucy's taunt.

He did not want an upset in front of his great-grandmother who, deep in thought, showed no reaction to the exchange. Instead he turned to her. 'Grandma, can you recall any more about what happened?'

She shook her head and grimaced with sadness. 'Oh, dear, that's all I can recall.'

'Never mind,' Alice reached forward and patted her hand sympathetically. 'You've been a great help.'

But Lucy was not going to let the matter rest. 'Mrs Swinburn, can you remember any more about Jacob Wade?'

A little smile crossed her lips. 'He was a handsome man, who broke a few hearts when he married Eliza Fenton, a rich farmer's daughter from over the hill. Mind you he had an eye for beauty, had Jacob, and he picked a bonny lass in Eliza.'

'I hear he had a love of the sea?' said Lucy, hoping to gain confirmation of the story Robert had heard from Amos.

She did not miss the look of surprise which crossed Mark's face and she knew he was wondering where she had obtained this information.

'Aye, he had but his father insisted he kept up the family association with the alum works. Jacob didn't like it.'

'Could that be the reason he left?' interjected Mark.

His great-grandmother shook her head. 'No. There was more to it than that. If that had been the reason they could have gone to Eliza's family but they didn't.'

'Could any of her family know where they went or what happened?'

'They were as mystified as anybody. They wouldn't talk about it but I did hear tell they regretted their name being tarnished by what happened.'

'But you don't know what that was?'

'No.' Again she shook her head regretfully. 'No.' As she drew the word out a light appeared in her eyes. 'That's it. I knew there was something else.' She had everyone's attention back, expecting a momentous revelation. She looked thoughtful for a moment longer then said slowly, 'Frederick Wilkins. Manager of the alum works. He had something to do with it.'

'What?' pressed Lucy eagerly when Mrs Swinburn paused.

'His name was mentioned at the time but nobody knew what his connections were. There were those who said he had discovered discrepancies in the accounts.'

'He might be able to help us. Where can we find him?' Excitement sharpened Lucy's question.

'I don't know. Shortly afterwards he left and I heard tell he'd gone to France.'

'Oh, no!' Lucy's dismay was shared by her sister. The chance, suddenly there, had been snatched from them.

'And he might be dead,' pointed out Mark.

'How old was he at the time?' asked Alice.

'He'd be about my age, maybe a year or two younger,' replied Mrs Swinburn.

'So he could still be alive.'

'I suppose so.'

'But we have no chance of contacting him,' moaned Lucy. 'Just think,' she added in exasperation, 'he might have been able to tell us what happened.'

Alice and Lucy were despondent when they said goodbye to Mrs Swinburn and left the house.

Mark was curious. They seemed more down than they

should have been. He was beginning to suspect that there was more to their enquiry than a story for Robert.

Trying to brighten them, he said, 'Now for Whitby and your brother.'

After they had travelled a short distance he voiced his suspicions. 'I think there's more behind this than you are telling me.'

The girls exchanged a quick glance but neither spoke.

'Your hesitation tells me I'm right,' he insisted. He pulled the horse to a halt and turned to face them. 'Why are you so interested in the Wades?' His expression held a determination to know.

Lucy watched him closely as she said, 'If we tell you, you must swear to tell no one else.'

'Whatever you say is safe with me,' he said quietly, his eyes never leaving hers.

Lucy told him the story of their father's dying words and their determination to find out if anything lay behind them.

'And what have you learned so far?' he asked, wanting to link any information with what they had heard from his great-grandmother.

They told him about Robert's visit to Robin Hood's Bay. 'Amos's opinion of Jacob Wade coincides with your great-grandmother's. He couldn't be bad,' concluded Lucy.

'But he and his family disappeared without trace and that looks suspicious. People are not always what they seem,' he replied.

Alice saw Lucy's temper rising at this insinuation and intervened quickly. 'True,' she agreed, 'but I think there's more behind this than there appears. After all, the de

Northbys were left with everything, a successful business and land.'

'But no one knows what the Wades got.'

'Precious little, I imagine. We have never been well off,' replied Alice.

'Your ancestors could have wasted it.'

'You seem determined to paint the Wades black,' put in Lucy.

Mark shook his head. 'No. But if you are still going to pursue this matter . . .'

'Of course we are,' interrupted Lucy vehemently. 'Just because our best contact may be in France, if he is still alive, and we can't contact him doesn't mean we have to give up.'

'All right,' Mark agreed, 'but I think you've got to be prepared for the worst. You might uncover something unsavoury.'

Lucy hesitated then said defiantly, 'I don't think it will be.'

'My great-grandmother and Amos have mentioned scandal,' warned Mark.

'And that may not be what it seems. I'm prepared to take the chance,' declared Lucy. She glanced at her sister for her reaction.

'So am I.' Alice was firm in her backing.

'Very well. We'll see what Robert has to say.' Mark headed for Whitby.

Zilpha stretched in her bed. This would be a good day. Mark would know the truth about that brat from Newcastle, and she had no doubt about what the outcome would be. The sooner he knew the story of the Wades the better.

She was dressing when she remembered. 'Drat, my music lesson.' In her eagerness to confront Mark she had almost forgotten it. Mrs Jefferson, a genteel lady whose husband had drunk and gambled away a fortune leaving her penniless, would be here at ten o'clock. Zilpha's mother had heard of her talents as a musician and embroiderer and had engaged her to expand Zilpha's accomplishments. Zilpha liked her, so it had become routine to have a cup of chocolate on her arrival, following it with a music lesson and after a short break embroidery before lunch after which Mrs Jefferson would depart.

Zilpha knew she would have to disguise her impatience throughout the morning and hope that Mark would be at home when she arrived in the afternoon.

Immediately she had said goodbye to Mrs Jefferson she rushed back into the house, calling to a maid to inform a groom to have a horse ready for her in a few minutes.

She was grappling with hooks and buttons almost before the door of her bedroom had shut behind her. She flung her dress across the bed and grabbed a riding habit from the wardrobe.

When she reached the stable the horse was saddled and Zilpha was soon urging it into a gallop along the shortest route to Howland Manor.

'Are we going to contact Robert first?' asked Alice as they neared Whitby.

'But we don't know where he is staying,' Lucy pointed out.

'We could enquire at the offices of the Whitby Shipping Company,' said Mark. 'Father's partners should know.

Most probably he'll be at the Angel. We'll go there for our meal and make enquiries.'

He guided the horse to a stable, and then escorted Lucy and Alice to the Angel.

'Good day, Mr Cossart.' The landlord greeted him with a broad smile. 'Good day, ladies.'

'Can you find us a table, Sam?'

'I can that, sir.'

Sam led the way into the dining room and signalled to a serving man.

'Sam, before you go, have you a Robert Mitchell staying here, he's with . . .'

'Aye, we have, sir. Nice young fellow.'

'Can you tell him we're here? We are his sisters,' exclaimed Alice.

Sam raised his arms in a gesture of regret. 'Alas, I cannot. He has just gone out.' He saw disappointment cross their faces. 'I can tell you where. He left a message for his employer, Mr Palmer, to say he was going,' he glanced at Mark, 'to see his sisters.'

'Then we must return at once,' said Alice.

'And we might miss him again,' pointed out Mark.

'But we might not see Robert at all and I would like to know how Mother is,' countered Alice.

'Oh, you'll have other opportunities to see him,' Sam put in. 'Mr Palmer has rooms booked for another four days.'

'Well then, we may as well eat a leisurely lunch, take a stroll and come back here. If Robert has not returned we'll leave a message that you'll call tomorrow afternoon to see him. I'll bring you.'

As that seemed the sensible course to pursue the girls agreed.

Lucy and Alice, enjoying dining in such surroundings, were flattered by the glances which were cast in their direction and recognised the inquisitiveness of people who wondered at the identity of the two presentable young ladies escorted by the eligible Mark Cossart.

Lucy smiled to herself. What would Zilpha think if she could see her now? But even with this amusement came a niggling reminder of Zilpha's words about her place in Mark's world.

When Zilpha learned that Mark had taken Lucy and Alice to meet his great-grandmother she refused the invitation to wait at Howland Manor until his return. She was in no mood for small talk and gossip, saying she would take her ride now and return later.

And when she did he'd get a few home truths about that deceiving little minx, Lucy. Coming here pretending to be what she wasn't, trying to worm her way into his affections for her own ends – she'd find she'd met her match in Zilpha de Northby.

Topping a slight rise in the land she saw a figure striding briskly along the track from Whitby.

'Robert Mitchell,' she whispered. She halted her horse and watched him. She recalled their first meeting, his friendliness with Rupert and Bracken, and then her father's words thundered into her mind. Had his coming to these parts 'a more sinister purpose?' Her thoughts were in confusion. Was he a threat? Had his visits and that of his sisters something to do with the past? Were they here to rake up the scandal all over again? Surely not. When she had first met them she had been taken by their friendly dispositions. It was only Lucy she had come to regard with hostility and that was because of Mark. But after her slip in mentioning the Wades what else was behind their presence? Her father had expressed a desire to know. Maybe she could help. Maybe the young man striding across the landscape could unlock the mystery.

She had liked him when they first met and she had detected in him an interest in her. She could not deny that he had an appealing aura about him and he was good-looking. There had been an immediate rapport between them. Maybe she could turn that to advantage.

She tapped her horse forward towards the track from Whitby.

Robert's stride faltered. The rider had caught his eye. He stopped. 'Zilpha!' Her name came slowly, savoured for the excitement it gave him. Then momentarily he was astonished at the way the sight of her had affected him. After all they had met only twice and on the second of those occasions she had been in the company of Mark Cossart. Yet even then some sort of bond had sparked between them. Then he recalled his thought that she liked flirting and would toss him aside for the likes of Mark Cossart. And yet, hadn't their first meeting been more indicative of a relationship which might develop if handled correctly? But she was a de Northby and he had Wade blood in him. Could whatever there had been in the past destroy a future?

Robert, the breeze playing with his hair as he removed his hat, watched her approach.

'Good day, Miss de Northby,' he called amiably as she pulled her horse to a halt.

'And good day to you,' she called with an inclination of her head. 'You must like these parts to be here again so soon.'

'Business. Did your father not tell you?'

'Yes, he did. But you've escaped.'

'Only temporarily. My employer decided to take a few days away from Newcastle, and, while I still have work to do, I'm taking the opportunity of contacting my sisters. I'm on my way to see them now.'

'I have just come from Howland Manor. Mrs Cossart told me her son has taken them to see his great-grandmother.'

Disappointment and annoyance fleetingly touched Robert's face. 'Then I've wasted my time.'

'Isn't meeting me some compensation?' A teasing smile twitched her lips while her gaze fixed intently on him to catch his reaction.

For a moment Robert was caught off guard. His face reddened. 'Well, I . . .' He paused, but then just as quickly regained control. He could play her game. 'If I had known I would meet you I would have been here all the sooner.'

'And if you had you'd have missed me for I've only just come this way.'

'It must be fate that has brought us together.'

'For what purpose?'

'Who can tell?'

'Then help me down. I'll walk with you and maybe we'll find out.'

Chapter Eleven

'How are Rupert and Bracken?' asked Robert to break the silence which had settled uneasily on them.

'Full of life.'

'But not with you today.'

'No. I had a special purpose in visiting Howland Manor. They would have been in the way.' She paused then, deciding the situation provided an opportunity to strike, went on. 'It concerned your sister, Lucy.'

'Lucy?'

'Yes. I think you ought to know that she is making a fool of herself.'

'How?' Robert frowned.

'She's playing with Mark's affections.'

Robert stopped and stared at her in disbelief. Surely Lucy wouldn't jeopardise the real reason for coming to Ravenscar.

Zilpha was amused by his expression. 'It's true. She's throwing herself at him.'

'I don't believe you.'

'You ought to,' she advised forcefully. 'And you'd better take her home with you.'

'You're jealous!' Robert's loud laugh was derisory. 'And you can't stand a rival.'

'Oh, I can do that but I don't like her making a fool of Mark.'

'My sister wouldn't do that.'

'Maybe you don't truly know her. She's a schemer when there's something or someone she wants. It would be a disaster for Mark to get involved with someone below his station.'

Robert glared. 'Don't you get on your high horse. We Mitchells are as good as you de Northbys. You wouldn't be where you are if it wasn't for my family.' The words were out before he realised it.

'Your family?' Zilpha pretended surprise.

'Aye. The Wades.'

'Wades?'

Robert gave a contemptuous grunt. 'Don't pretend you've never heard of them.'

'I hadn't until Lucy mentioned them yesterday. Attempting to put herself on a level with us, all to try and get Mark. But it won't work. I came to Howland Manor to see him and tell him what my father told me, that the Wades were fraudsters and cheats. Jacob Wade took more money out of the business than he was entitled to. He . . .'

'Was a good man,' Robert interrupted sharply. 'According to Amos it was your great-grandfather, Peter, who was the rogue.'

'Nonsense!' snapped Zilpha. 'He was generous; hushed the matter up so that there would be no public scandal.'

She looked at him with contempt. 'You're no better than your ancestors, supposedly here to take your sisters home, and to collect stories for a journal. I see it now. Those were excuses to cover the real reason – to try to extract money from my father. Well, you won't succeed.'

Robert's voice was icy quiet. 'All I want is the truth.'

'Even if it shocks you?'

'I'll take that risk.'

'Even if it shatters your world?'

'Yes.'

Zilpha could not but admire his determination, his willingness to accept whatever the outcome, and his strong belief that he would be right.

'Will you be able to do the same?' he added, his eyes searching for the true character behind the unsavoury attitude she was wearing now. In that he could see much of her father. But he believed the real Zilpha was the friendly person he had met that first day as he walked to Northby Hall.

She met his gaze without flinching. 'I will. But how do we prove who is right? What is your family's story about what happened?'

Robert gave a regretful shake of his head. 'We don't have one.'

'What?' She stared at him in astonishment. 'Yet you come here making accusations for which you have no foundation. Creating trouble for nothing. Is that why your sisters came in the first place? Was the story of Alice wanting to visit Paul Smurthwaite's family all a lie?'

'No, no,' Robert hastened to deny her assumption. He went on to explain how it was that they came to visit Ravenscar.

She listened intently, taking in every word. Maybe she would learn some of the answers her father wanted.

'So you only have the word of an old man in Robin Hood's Bay to go on.' She gave a short laugh of disbelief.

'That's all I have, but my sisters may have learned more since I last saw them.'

'That's unlikely, seeing as how Lucy's been more concerned about Mark.'

'We shall see.'

'When?'

'Well, you say they've gone to see Mrs Cossart's grand-mother so I may as well return to Whitby. I'll try to see them tomorrow.'

'No doubt our paths will cross again for one reason or another.' The haughtiness in her voice had softened.

'No doubt.' Robert's tone still carried an edge.

As he neared Whitby Robert was aware of a carriage coming towards him. Lost in his thoughts of the confrontation with Zilpha, he took little notice of it until he heard a shout which drew his attention. His sisters! His serious expression vanished. He waved back. Then his pleasure was momentarily marred by a frown. Mark Cossart was driving the carriage. Could there be something in Zilpha's assertions about Lucy?

With greetings exchanged Robert added, 'I thought you had gone to see Mr Cossart's great-grandmother?'

'We did,' explained Lucy. 'When we left, Mark drove us to Whitby to see you.'

'That was good of you,' Robert acknowledged Mark's thoughtfulness. 'Sorry I wasn't there, but I had learned Lucy had hurt her ankle and I was concerned.'

'How did you know we'd gone to see Mark's great-grandmother?' asked Alice.

'I met Miss de Northby. She had been to see Mr Cossart.' He was aware that Lucy scowled at this information.

Mark made no comment but said amiably. 'We'll take you back to Whitby.'

'I can't put you to that trouble, Mr Cossart.'

'Nonsense. Your sisters have something to tell you and I'm sure they'll want news of home. And it's Mark. No more formality please.'

He climbed up beside Mark who turned the carriage back on the track to Whitby.

Once he had reassured his sisters that their mother was well, Lucy, bursting to tell him what they had learned, started on her story when she caught a warning look from him and then a glance in Mark's direction.

'It's all right,' Lucy reassured him, 'Mark knows everything. We told him after he had heard what his great-grandmother had to say.' She went on to disclose what that was.

Robert listened eagerly, wanting something definite to uphold the views he had expressed to Zilpha, but when Lucy had finished he looked despondent. 'Even though Mrs Swinburn confirms Amos's opinion we are no nearer getting any solid proof. What a pity Mr Wilkins went to France. He probably could have contradicted Mr de Northby's condemnation of the Wades.'

'How do you know about his attitude?' asked Alice.

'Miss de Northby told me.'

'And that's because I let the name of Wade slip to her,' said Lucy.

Mark frowned. 'To Zilpha? When did that happen?'

'Two days ago. I met her on the cliff on my way to the Smurthwaites. She had seen us together,' Lucy explained.

Robert was a little taken aback by her revelation. Was there truth in what Zilpha had told him?

'And,' prompted Mark when she stopped.

'There was a scene and I let the name slip. She must have gone home and asked her father about it.'

'And naturally believes him,' said Robert. 'And unless we can prove otherwise she will go on believing it.'

When they left Robert he told them that he would be too busy to see them the next day, so Mark arranged to bring them to Whitby in two days' time.

After taking Alice and Lucy to the Smurthwaite cottage he drove straight to Northby Hall. As he approached the house he saw Zilpha walking the dogs. He pulled the horse to a halt knowing that she had seen him, for she turned in his direction. He jumped down from the carriage and strode towards her.

As his eyes fixed on her he felt a confusion of emotions. The anger he had felt towards her when Lucy had revealed Zilpha's verbal attack had been tempered by the subsequent drive and now evaporated. After all this was the person he had grown up with, with whom he had shared so much, whom he liked, whom he admired. He found he was doing just that, taking in her slim figure, enhanced by the close-fitting dress in the colour which suited her best, blue. The gentle breeze flicked her hair into movements like enticing ripples on a dark mysterious pool. Her eyes shimmered with pleasure at seeing him. How could he have thought of anyone else? But immediately that disturbing thought had entered his head he dismissed it, for he knew he would have to decide where his love really lay.

'I believe you were looking for me.'

'Yes, Mark, I was, and it's good of you to come.' She watched him as he patted the dogs. 'I needed to warn you about the Mitchells.'

'Warn me?' Mark feigned puzzlement.

'Yes. I know Lucy's set out to charm you.' She raised her hand to stop the protestation she saw coming. 'Don't deny it and don't deny that you like her attention. I saw her kissing you. But be careful, Mark. They are not what they seem.'

'What do you mean?'

'They are troublemakers.'

'Troublemakers?'

'Yes. They maintain they are descendants of the Wades who were once partners with my family in the alum works.'

'How do you know this?'

'Lucy let the name slip.'

'When?'

'I was hurt, Mark, deeply hurt when I saw you two kissing. I came back to confront you both but I saw you riding away.'

'So you decided to tackle Lucy on her own.'

'Yes. And it's fortunate I did. After hearing the name Wade I asked my father if he knew of them and he told me the sordid story of how the Wades tried to cheat his grandfather.'

'And how do you know that was the truth?' asked Mark coolly.

211

'Mark!' cried Zilpha with indignation. 'My father isn't a liar.'

'I didn't say he was,' he responded. 'But is what he says happened really what did happen?'

'What do you mean?'

'The truth can get twisted and distorted depending how you look at it. Couldn't there be another side to the story, which might be the truth?'

'You're doubting me?'

'No. Just wondering what is the truth. You see my great-grandmother gives a different impression.'

Zilpha's eyes narrowed. 'So that's why you went to see her. I see it all now. Lucy twisted you round her little finger and got you to take her to see the old lady.' She gave a little snort of contempt. 'She's duped you, Mark. She's a conniving hussy out for her own ends. She'll ruin your life. Can't you see that? Or are you so besotted you don't want to?'

'She's not like that,' he protested. 'She wouldn't mean me any harm.'

'She's using you to get at the de Northbys for something she thinks happened in the past. She sees parting us as a means to that end.' Her voice rose, desperate in its pleading. 'Mark, don't let it happen. Don't let her ruin our love, our future together.'

Zilpha knew she had struck doubt into his mind. The resoluteness which had been there on his approach had been weakened.

'Can we really know people on such short acquaintance?' Her voice was low but incisive. 'A girl from nowhere? Think carefully, Mark. Don't ruin your future and all it can hold for one brief obsession.'

She turned away and started towards the Hall, bringing the dogs to heel with a snap of her fingers.

Mark stood watching her, recalling their times together, knowing the expectations of their families. She swirled, vivacious and teasing, elegant and adventurous, to be lost in the mist of confusion as another emerged, pretty and enticing, perplexed and in need of his help.

He had to find the truth.

On reaching Northby Hall Zilpha sought out her father, knowing he would be interested in what she had learned and hoping it would help him discredit the Mitchells.

'Father, I've seen both Robert Mitchell and Mark,' she announced as she crossed his study. He was sitting behind a large oak desk on which maps of the coast and its immediate hinterland were spread out.

He sat back in his chair, nodded and waited for her to continue.

She sat down opposite him. 'I met Robert Mitchell first. He was on his way to see his sisters. There is no need for me to go into the details of our conversation but it emerged that the Mitchells are descended from these Wades.'

'So that must be on their mother's side,' he mused.

'They have no definite story about what happened in the past and have only come here on the word of their father who, when he was dying, told them that the de Northbys owed them. They didn't even know who the de Northbys were but by chance Alice Mitchell had met Paul Smurthwaite, a sailor on a collier bringing coal to your alum works, who of course knew the name.'

'So that's how they come to be here.' He gave a little

incredulous shake of his head. 'And Mitchell knew no more?'

'Not when I spoke with him, but he may now.'

'How?'

'Well, I told you I met Mark later. He had taken the Mitchell girls to meet his great-grandmother and she had told them what she knew.'

De Northby's eyes narrowed. 'And she was alive when the scandal took place. I wonder how much she remembers?'

'Mark said very little about that.'

'Could be that she doesn't remember much. It's a considerable time since I've seen her. You'll have visited her with Mark. It might be an idea to do so again and find out how much she recalls.'

'Her memory is failing, though it is sharper about the past. If she had said anything of significance I think Mark would have said.'

'Did you learn anything else?'

'No.'

'Well, if you do, don't forget to let me know. It might be as well if you saw young Mitchell again. His story about wanting information for a journal is only a cover. His employer told me he has no interests in that direction.'

Robert's concentration on the accuracy of the document he was drawing up was so intense that he was startled by the knock on the door of his room. For a moment he thought he was mistaken but the knock was repeated.

'Sir, there's a young lady to see you,' one of the servants informed him.

'I'll come down.'

He shrugged himself into his tailed coat and hurried from the room, a little annoyed that his sister had ignored the fact that he would be busy today.

He ran quickly down the stairs and pulled up sharply at the bottom when he saw Zilpha.

'Good day, Mr Mitchell,' she said with a smile and a slight inclination of her head.

'Good day, Miss de Northby. When I was told that a young lady wished to see me I expected to see one of my sisters.'

'And that would have displeased you?' She feigned astonishment.

'Well, no, but I am busy today.'

'Oh, dear. I shouldn't have called. I've interrupted something important. I'll go.' She started to turn towards the door.

'No, please don't.' He reached out as if he would stop her.

She paused. 'But I don't want to be in the way.'

'You won't be. It is a pleasure to see you. I'm flattered that you called. Was there anything special?'

'Oh, no, Mr Mitchell,' she replied, though she hoped she would gain more information for her father. 'I was in Whitby and I thought that as we had not parted on the best of terms yesterday I should call and apologise.'

'My dear Miss de Northby, there was nothing to apologise for. It is I who should be doing that.' He glanced around. 'Oh dear, I'm forgetting my manners. Will you take a cup of chocolate with me?'

'It is such a lovely morning I would rather take a walk. But maybe you are too busy?'

'Not at all,' replied Robert. His enthusiasm at the prospect of walking with her was evident and it pleased Zilpha to know that she could charm him. 'I'm sure our walk will sharpen our appetites, the Whitby air does that to me, so will you do me the honour of taking a meal with me on our return?'

She inclined her head in acknowledgement of his gesture. 'It will be a pleasure.'

Robert called the landlord and asked him to make a setting for the young lady at his table. He excused himself to Zilpha in order to collect his hat.

He bounded up the stairs delighted that she had deigned to call on him and the thought that dining with her . . . but was there some ulterior motive behind her visit? De Northbys? Wades? What did it matter? His chance of proving anything was so remote that maybe it was best forgotten. Why ruin a possible friendship with a beautiful young woman?

The day was mild, with little breeze. Thin high cloud hazed the sun. Life surged around them as they made their way past the bridge spanning the river and turned into Haggersgate before continuing along the west bank of the river. Housewives about their shopping paused to exchange news and gossip with each other, artisans hurried about their business, clerks hastened to shipping offices, and vendors shouted raucously. The port bustled with activity. Across the river ships from the Baltic unloaded timber, sailors prepared the vessels for the next voyage taking on board food to sustain them in their absence as they delivered alum to the Continent, local produce to Newcastle or passengers to London.

They paused to watch weatherbeaten fishermen unloading their catch. Seagulls screeched in protest when they were beaten to a tasty morsel which had fallen on the quayside. Zilpha and Robert shared every moment in undisguised enjoyment at the life going on around them.

'There's talk of us getting a lifeboat later this year,' Zilpha informed him when she pointed out the area opposite Scotch Head pier which had been designated as the site for the building to house the boat.

'An important asset,' he agreed. They moved on to the pier beyond the protection of the cliff and felt the fresher breeze. 'Do you want to turn back?'

'No,' she shook her head. 'Remember, we're working up an appetite.' She glanced at him thoughtfully. Could she elicit any more information for her father? She did not want to spoil the empathy she was experiencing. He was a likeable person and had about him an air of confidence to a degree she would not have expected in an attorney's clerk. It was as if it had been bred in him. 'I hope this is not interrupting your work too much?'

'No,' he replied. 'I'll complete it before we are due to leave, but it takes time making sure everything is worded correctly. After all it is an important document for your father's firm and Mr Palmer's client.'

'Then I shouldn't be taking up so much of your time.' Zilpha pretended penitence. 'Maybe I should go home.'

'I can't let you do that. I ordered a meal.' His tone was forceful, daring her to refuse.

They continued their leisurely stroll, paused to watch the ships sail with the tide and, when it neared time for their meal, made their way back to the Angel.

They had passed the offices of Chapman and Fishlock, ship's chandlers, and therefore failed to see Mark leave the building.

As he stepped on to the street, he pulled up sharp. He stared disbelievingly at the two people who strolled arm in arm a few yards away. Zilpha and Robert Mitchell! What were they doing together?

He felt a pang of jealousy as memories of Zilpha came flooding back – her laughter torn away by the wind as they raced their horses, her face aglow with the pleasure of their walk beside the sea, the feel of her close to him as they swirled around the ballroom, and most of all the sheer pleasure of being with her. But Lucy had stepped into his life, pretty, enchanting, a magical bewitching presence that captivated him. Whom did he really love?

Automatically, he followed them and received a further surprise when he saw them enter the Angel together.

Should he tell Lucy or keep this his secret?

He had not decided by the time he reached home but there his dilemma was driven from his mind.

'Thank you for this,' said Zilpha when they were seated for their meal. They had ordered soup and freshly caught fish. 'When will you be seeing your sisters?' she asked casually as she dipped her spoon into the soup.

'Oh, I've already done so. I met them on the way back to Whitby after I left you yesterday.'

'I didn't know they'd been to Whitby. I thought they'd been to see Mrs Swinburn, Mark's great-grandmother.'

'Oh they had and then decided to drive into Whitby to see me.'

218

Zilpha's annoyance smouldered. Mark must have fallen for Lucy's wheedling ways again. She curbed her feelings to make her enquiry sound casual. 'They had news for you?'

'About the Wades? Yes. Mrs Swinburn's story differs with yours.'

His remark only exacerbated the annoyance she was feeling. 'You'd believe a forgetful old woman before me?' she said, her words sharp.

'She's not so forgetful, and I think what she says is nearer the truth.'

'You call me a liar?' Zilpha snapped with indignation.

'No. Mistaken, believing what your father told you,' replied Robert.

'Do you now call my father a liar?' Zilpha glared.

'Maybe he has twisted the truth.'

'Why should he?'

'To save the family name, because he's ashamed of what his grandfather did. Because he has something which is rightfully ours, something your family cheated mine out of.'

'Cheated?' Her voice rose with indignation. She put down her spoon with a clatter. 'I'm not staying here to listen to slurs on my family.' She started to rise from her chair.

Robert reached out quickly, grasping her wrist and forcing it hard against the table. 'Sit down!' His voice was low but it demanded obedience.

'Let go!' she hissed, trying to force herself free, but his powerful fingers were like a vice. She could do nothing but sink back on her chair, inwardly fuming at his audacity.

'You're my guest, you must stay!'

She stiffened, astounded by his effrontery. She tried to stare him down, but he met her gaze until she was forced to look away.

He felt a little of the tension go from her. 'That's better. Don't try it again or there'll be an unholy scene.'

She was under no illusion that he meant it. Their actions had already attracted one or two curious looks from nearby diners. She did not want her name bandied around Whitby. She pouted and picked up her spoon.

He leaned forward and whispered, 'And don't behave like a spoilt brat with me!'

Zilpha felt exasperation. Her thoughts were awhirl. Her heart was racing with a mixture of annoyance and pleasure. For once she had not had her way, had not influenced the man she was with and it hurt, but she had been thrilled by his dominating attitude. This was another side to Robert and she found she admired it, even liked it, though she would not admit that to him now.

'Now, let us eat our meal,' he said gently, offering an olive branch.

'How can I,' she snapped, 'when you adopt this attitude?'

'I don't think you mind.'

Zilpha cursed to herself. Could he see through her too? She shrugged her shoulders and tasted the soup.

'Good,' he approved. 'Now, to return to the topic of our conversation. I may believe the de Northbys cheated the Wades but I'll admit I can't prove it. It appears that the person who might shed light on it, a Mr Wilkins who was manager of the alum works, went to live in France. There's little chance of us contacting him, he may even be dead, and if he's not he'd be an old man whose memory may well be vague.'

'So is that the end of the matter?' asked Zilpha.

'It would seem so. Is it worth trying to follow up when there's little hope of discovering anything?'

'I suppose not.' Her father would be pleased with the information she had gleaned. 'So your sisters will accompany you home?'

'Possibly, though they have minds of their own. I cannot vouch for their actions.'

Maybe, thought Zilpha, but with a little persuasion . . .

Mark was crossing the hall to the stairs when his father came hurrying from his study.

'Mark, Lieutenant Hughes is in my study waiting to see you. He's been here over an hour and is becoming anxious.'

Mark's face became serious. His friend must be here on urgent army business. Without a word he hurried past his father into the room.

'David!' Mark held out his hand.

A tall young man jumped nimbly from his chair. He smiled as he took Mark's hand in a firm grip but there was no smile in his eyes, only deadly seriousness. 'You've to return to our unit immediately.'

'What's this all about?' asked Mark, concerned at the pressing note in his friend's voice.

David pulled a face. 'I don't know but I was despatched with the utmost urgency to fetch you.'

Mark nodded grimly. It was no good speculating. He would find out soon enough. Outside, he found his father waiting in the hall. 'Father, I've to report back to headquarters immediately. Come.' He stepped aside for his father to enter the study. 'David Hughes is a good friend of mine.'

'You'll have a meal before you go?' suggested Emile. He was already pulling the bellsash to summon the maid.

'A quick one. I'll go and get ready. Look after David, please.'

The maid arrived. 'Agnes, tell cook a quick meal for two,' Emile ordered amiably. 'Mr Mark and his friend have to leave as soon as possible.'

'Yes, sir.'

'And then find Mrs Cossart and tell her I would like to see her immediately.'

The maid nodded and hurried from the room.

As he changed into his uniform Mark remembered that tomorrow he had promised to take Lucy and Alice into Whitby to meet Robert. There was no time to see them now to explain, so, as soon as he was dressed and had packed the few belongings he wanted with him, he left the house for the stables. He instructed one of the grooms to collect the Mitchell sisters at Mrs Smurthwaite's at ten o'clock the next morning, apologise for his absence and take them to Whitby and be at their disposal for the rest of the day.

When he returned to the house he found his mother and father and Lieutenant Hughes waiting for him in the dining room.

Mrs Cossart could not hide her worry at this sudden recall and speculated that the government must think war was likely to break out again.

'It's time this upstart Bonaparte was put in his place,' commented Emile.

The statement coming from a Frenchman in undisguised outrage did not even raise a querying eyebrow from David. He knew only too well from Mark that Mr Cossart was truly loyal to Britain and the country's opposition to the upheavals and personalities emerging from the confusion of the French Revolution.

'He will be, Father, if David and I have anything to do with it.' He winked at his friend. 'Seems we're wanted to settle the matter.'

'Then see you do,' replied Emile, undrawn by the light-hearted acceptance of their recall by the younger men.

After an emotional goodbye Elphrida found a comforting arm around her shoulders as she and her husband watched their son and his friend be driven away from Howland Manor by their coachman. In Whitby they would catch a coach for York where they would take another to London.

When Zilpha returned to Northby Hall she was in good spirits. She had enjoyed her day in spite of the altercation, maybe because of it. It pleased her to toy with Robert's feelings and tease him with her attention. He had been different to other men with whom she had flirted. Only Mark had a special place in her affections, but he had never been assertive in the way Robert had.

She threw off the confusion. The Mitchells would soon be gone, Mark would be hers, Robert forgotten, and life would return to normal.

She sought out her father, finding him sitting alone on the terrace perusing some documents.

When he heard footsteps he looked up and smiled when he saw his daughter.

223

'Hello, Father,' she said brightly.

'You seem quite pleased with yourself,' he remarked.

'I've had a pleasant day in Whitby and I think I have good news for you.'

He looked at her curiously. 'News for me?'

'Yes, I saw Robert Mitchell and . . .'

'Mitchell?'

'You said if I learned any more about the Mitchells you wanted to know, so I went to see him, used my charm.'

'And?' he prompted.

'Well, Mark took Robert's sisters to see his great-grandmother.'

'Why?'

'I don't know, it may have been a social visit or it may have had other motives, but whatever the reason, the question of the Wades came up. Mrs Swinburn mentioned that the person they wanted to see was a Mr Wilkins who had gone to live in France. Do you know of him?'

'He used to be manager at the alum works but I know little more.' Richard did not want to reveal Wilkins's part in the scandal.

'Well, Robert accepts that they won't be able to contact him even if he is still alive and said there seems little point in pursuing the matter. So there it is.'

'How interesting,' said Richard. 'Thank you for the information.'

'It was my pleasure,' said Zilpha as she rose from her chair. 'I'll go and change.'

Richard watched his daughter as she walked away. This was valuable news but could he really believe that the Mitchells would not try to investigate further? If the girls went back to Newcastle with their brother then maybe their interest had waned, but in the meantime he would not let his guard drop.

Hearing the approach of a carriage Lucy hurried outside the Smurthwaites' house in anticipation of seeing Mark.

Mrs Smurthwaite and Alice gave each other a knowing look having recognised in Lucy's impatient fidgetings, while awaiting Mark's arrival, the reactions of a lovelorn girl.

Lucy pulled up sharply on seeing the carriage driven by Cossart's coachman. Disappointment drained her face. She looked appealingly to her sister even though she knew Alice had no answer.

The carriage came to a halt and the coachman jumped down.

'Good morning, miss.' He glanced at Lucy and Alice in turn and then at Mrs Smurthwaite. 'Good morning, ma'am. Mr Mark Cossart instructed me to drive the two young ladies into Whitby to see their brother at the Angel Hotel.'

'But, Mr Mark? Is he ill?' A concerned tremor filled Lucy's questions.

'No, miss. Mr Mark is well, but he was called away urgently yesterday. Army matters I presume for he left in uniform. He told me to apologise and say that he would return as soon as possible.'

Lucy nodded, trying to suppress tears.

'Come, let's go and see Robert,' put in Alice quickly to try to ease Lucy's disillusionment.

It was a quiet ride to Whitby and Alice's attempts to brighten it were met with monosyllabic replies. The coachman took them straight to the Angel where Robert had ordered hot chocolate to be served on their arrival.

Once they were settled, Robert asked, 'Are you coming home with me?'

'No,' was Lucy's sharp refusal.

'But what's the point in staying?' he asked. 'There's no sense in pursuing the matter if our only chance of solving the mystery is in France, if alive.'

'You're giving up?' demanded Lucy. 'Well, I'm not. There may be something we've overlooked.'

'But, Lucy . . .'

'No buts.' She turned to Alice. 'Are you also giving up?'

'Well, Robert has a point.'

Lucy tightened her lips. 'Do you think Father would want us to?'

'Are you sure you're not using this as an excuse to be here when Mark returns?' Alice asked. She saw her brother raise a querying eyebrow. 'He's been called away to his regiment, and she's in love.'

'And what if I am?' retorted Lucy.

'Aye, maybe you are,' said Robert. 'He's a likeable fellow, but what about him? Is he in love with you?'

'I know he is,' replied Lucy emphatically.

'Are you sure? He and Miss de Northby . . .'

'That proud creature!' Lucy spat the words viciously.

Robert received a warning glance from Alice. They both knew what Lucy could be like in this mood.

'So you're going to stay?' he said.

'Yes.'

'What about you, Alice?' he queried.

'If Lucy stays then I'll have to.'

Robert nodded. 'Do I tell Mother why?'

'No,' put in Alice quickly. 'Tell her something has developed which needs our attention.'

Lucy made no objection to this proposal. Better to make sure that Mark still felt the same about her when he returned before saying anything to Mother.

'Very well,' agreed Robert. He paused thoughtfully then added, 'You know, Lucy might be right, there might be something we've overlooked. If there was a partnership and it was broken there could be some documents which would verify the arrangements and throw light on what happened.'

Lucy's eyes brightened at this new possible line of enquiry. 'Where do we start?' she asked.

Robert gave a wry smile. 'Steady on, Lucy, it isn't as easy as that.'

'You work for an attorney, you should know,' she pressed. If there was an opportunity she wasn't going to let it slip away.

'That document could be anywhere. De Northby's copy will be under lock and key. In his own home? More likely with an attorney in Whitby, or even Scarborough. Or it could be with documents relating to the alum works wherever they may be.'

'Would the Wades have one?' asked Alice.

'We don't know what broke up the partnership. If it was done legally then Jacob Wade, I think, would have been given a copy.'

'Where could that be?' asked Lucy.

Robert shrugged his shoulders. 'Who knows? Whitby? Newcastle? Or anywhere else the Wades went.'

'Mother! She might know.'

'She'd have said.'

'I'm not so sure,' said Alice. 'She didn't want us to come here. She wanted the whole thing forgotten. Maybe she never mentioned it on purpose.'

'I think she'd have said something when I went home last time and told her you were determined to find out more. She did tell me more of the story, but she never talked about a document. I'll try again when I go home tomorrow.'

Zilpha wondered if she was just giving way to habit as she rode to Howland Manor. When Mark was at home it had become the normal practice to ride together. Her mind would always be on the pleasant company she would share but today was different. Another young man kept drifting in and out of her thoughts. He began to occupy them more than Mark did until she reminded herself that Robert really had no part in her life. Mark was hers and that schemer Lucy should not have him. A ride with Mark this morning would make sure of that.

In the stable yard a groom touched his forehead as he said, 'Good morning, miss.'

Zilpha returned the greeting brightly and added, 'Is Mr Mark's horse ready?'

'No, miss. He's not at home, miss.' The groom went on before she could query Mark's absence. 'He was called away urgently yesterday afternoon. Army matters I think. He left in uniform. Samuel drove him and another officer into Whitby to catch the coach.'

'He left no messages?'

'I wouldn't know, miss. Maybe with his father or mother, miss.'

She nodded and slid from the saddle. 'Is Samuel around?'

'No, miss. Mr Mark left instructions for him to take the two Miss Mitchells into Whitby to see their brother, something he was going to do himself.'

She felt a tightening in her chest. Mark had thought of Lucy before leaving but not of her, unless there was a message awaiting her with his parents.

But her disappointment intensified when she learned that he had left no word.

'Didn't Mark let you know that he'd been called away?' Mrs Cossart asked with surprise.

Zilpha shook her head. 'No. I came expecting our usual morning ride.'

'How remiss of him. Didn't he even inform you that he had promised to take the Misses Mitchell to see their brother and wouldn't be taking his usual ride this morning?'

'No.' Zilpha held back her rising anger. He'd thought more of Lucy than of her! She hardly heard Mrs Cossart scolding her absent son, but, with a shrug of her shoulders, said. 'Well, I'll leave and have my ride.'

'I'm sorry, my dear. I'll let you know whenever we hear anything from him.'

As she rode away she cursed Mark for his omission. He'd hear about it when he got back.

Richard de Northby pondered the situation carefully. Was he reading too much into the Mitchells' presence and enquiries? Was he becoming obsessed that the past should remain undiscovered? He could lose so much if the truth should ever be revealed. Zilpha thought that Robert Mitchell had given up, but an inbred caution still told him to be wary until he knew for certain that all the Mitchells had returned home. Would they all be sailing tomorrow? Maybe he could find out today when Palmer presented the final agreements for signature.

Joss Storm and William already had the Madeira and glasses ready in anticipation of a successful conclusion to the new agreement between the Whitby Shipping Company and Dewey's Mercantile when Richard arrived at the office a few minutes after Emile. They had barely had time to exchange greetings when Seth Palmer and Robert arrived.

While the men passed the time of day, Robert spread out two identical sets of documents on the desk he had used during their earlier visit.

'Well, gentlemen, I would like you each in turn to peruse the wording,' Palmer suggested.

Richard and Emile were the first to do so and replaced the documents on the desk without comment so as not to influence their partners' judgement.

While Joss and William studied the papers, Richard took the opportunity to engage Robert in conversation. 'You have a fine and presentable hand, young man. Those documents are beautifully written.'

'Thank you, sir,' said Robert.

'Have you enjoyed your few days in Whitby in spite of the work?'

'Yes, sir. So different to Newcastle.'

'But you'll be pleased to get home?'

'To see my mother, yes, but the town is so crowded and smoky. Here you can soon be free of that.'

'You're not happy in your job?'

'Oh, yes, sir.' Robert put enthusiasm into his voice. 'Don't misunderstand me. Mr Palmer is a kind and understanding employer.'

'Good, I'm pleased to hear it. No doubt you'll settle with him and find Newcastle not such a bad place. You've been able to see your sisters while you've been here?

'Yes. I was glad to find them well in spite of Lucy's mishap.'

'Are they returning with you tomorrow?'

'No. They want to stay a little longer. I know Mother will be disappointed.'

As Joss and William finished reading the documents with a nod of approval and a satisfied mutter, their conversation ceased but Richard was satisfied. He had found out what he wanted to know.

'Well, gentlemen,' Joss glanced round his partners. 'I think the agreement is satisfactory.'

'Capital, capital,' agreed a beaming William.

Emile and Richard added their endorsement.

'Now for the signing,' said Joss. He moved to the desk where Robert had quills and ink ready.

The four partners and Mr Palmer signed the two documents, one of which was taken by Joss and the other by the attorney from Newcastle.

'Well, gentlemen, let us drink to a successful conclusion to the agreement and to a happy and profitable partnership,' Joss suggested and turned to the table where William was already pouring the wine.

* * *

231

As he returned home Richard considered the decision of the Mitchell girls to stay behind. Had they an ulterior motive? Were they still determined to pursue the subject of the Wades in spite of what Zilpha had told him? Why else should they want to stay when they had a chance of returning home with their brother?

He took pleasure in the drive when the house came in view. It always gave him great satisfaction that this imposing building and the land as far as he could see were his. As he watched the Hall come nearer he steeled his determination not to let anyone deprive him of even one small item of his possessions.

When he reached home he went to the estate office and called three of his most loyal estate workers, Albert Johnson, Edward Norton and Jarvis White, to see him.

'I've a special job for you three,' he told them. 'But it must be kept a secret. Not a word of what I want you to do must go beyond these four walls.' He glanced from one to the other, looking for their understanding and agreement.

'Yes, sir, you can trust us,' said Albert in an assured voice.

'Aye, you can that,' confirmed Edward.

'No word will pass our lips, sir,' added Jarvis.

'Good. There are two young women staying with the Smurthwaites. I want them watched at all times, and their movements reported to me. Two of you must always be on watch together so that one of you can get a message to me, if necessary, without the surveillance being broken. You can arrange working times between you.'

'Night and day?' queried Albert.

'Yes.'

'Are they likely to move around at night?' queried Jarvis.

'I don't know.' A snap had come to de Northby's voice. 'But I want to know if they do.' He saw the men were puzzled.

'Do what I tell you and there'll be extra money for you.' That promise he knew would hold their tongues even though their curiosity had been aroused by his strange orders.

Chapter Twelve

Robert had much to ponder as he walked home after the ship had docked in Newcastle.

The narrow streets, the row upon row of houses, the grime from the chimneys, the smoke which disguised the blue of the sky, all were so far removed from the openness and wide vistas but a short stroll from Whitby. There he had experienced a sense of freedom far different from the oppressive pulsations of the city. Somehow he had felt at home in that new environment. But now he recalled Mr Palmer's encouraging words about his prospects. He could go far if he set his mind to it.

He should have persuaded his sisters to return home with him, but headstrong Lucy had deemed otherwise and now he was committed to enquiring about the possibilities of a document which would probably only prove that there had been an agreement between the de Northbys and the Wades.

'Robert!' His mother greeted him with delight when she opened the door. Then she looked past him. Her face clouded. 'No girls?'

Robert grimaced. 'Sorry, Mother. Lucy insisted on staying,' he said as he stepped past her into the house.

She shut the door and followed him along the passage to the kitchen where he put down his cloth bag and removed his coat.

'What's got into that girl? You should have made her come home,' snapped Rebecca.

'Mother.' Robert spread his hands in a pleading gesture. 'I could only advise. I couldn't make her. Lucy's a young woman with a mind of her own.'

Rebecca stared at him for a moment. She felt rebuked. 'I suppose so,' she muttered reluctantly. 'And Alice stayed with her?'

'She couldn't leave Lucy on her own.'

'There's been no trouble?' A mother's natural alarm tinged her question.

'No.'

For one moment she looked at him with doubt then asked, 'You'd tell me if there was?'

'Of course I would.'

'Then did she and Alice learn any more about the Wades?'

Robert detected a genuine interest even though his mother tried to disguise it. 'Yes, they did. I'll tell you about it while I have something to eat.'

'Forgive me, I'm forgetting you'll be hungry after all that sea air. You go and wash and change if you want to while I get you something to eat.'

'Thanks.' He gave his mother a kiss. 'It's good to be home.' He picked up his bag and left the kitchen wondering if he really meant it.

Soon the appetising smell of frying bacon wafted up the stairs. He decided he was indeed pleased to be home. His roots were here. He had known no other place until these two visits to Whitby and they had served merely to unsettle him.

The tempting aroma drew him back to the kitchen.

The whitewood table was set and a board held a white loaf. A sharp knife lay beside it. His mother turned from the fire with the frying pan in one hand and served out sizzling slices of bacon on to two plates, then took an egg each from the pan.

'This is a homely smell,' said Robert, pulling a chair from under the table.

Rebecca smiled at his comment and sat down. 'Now, tell me what happened in Whitby.'

As he ate his bacon and egg, dipping fresh white bread into the fat, he related his story, emphasising what Lucy and Alice had learned from Mark's great-grandmother.

'She knew Jacob?' Rebecca displayed a keenness to know more about her relative.

Mark nodded. 'Aye, and thought highly of him.'

'I can only just remember him, but I've always carried an impression of a smiling man with strong hands when he lifted me on to his knee.' She looked wistful. 'I'm glad she liked him.'

'He sounds a man who would not be wilfully involved in scandal or fraud,' commented Robert.

'I know nothing about what happened, no more than what I've told you.'

'But wouldn't you like to know the truth?' he pressed.

'Not if it's going to hurt us. And will we ever, when the

man who might be able to help went to France and more than likely is now dead?'

'But, as I said to Alice and Lucy, there might be something we have overlooked. Could there be a document dissolving the partnership which might throw some light on what happened? Did you ever hear one mentioned?'

Rebecca looked thoughtful. 'No.' She shook her head slowly as if still considering the question. Then she looked her son straight in the eye. 'No,' she said firmly. 'I was too young to bother about what was going on.'

'And you've never heard one talked about?'

'No. I suppose you could be right. If a partnership was dissolved there must have been some agreement drawn up and signed. After all Mr de Northby has everything now, so he must have proof that it is all his. But where could that document be?'

Robert smiled to himself. His mother was taking an interest. 'Well, more than likely there would be two, one for de Northby and the other for Jacob Wade. His could be with an attorney in Newcastle or placed with one in Whitby before he left. De Northby's could have been lodged anywhere, Whitby, Scarborough, or even London if he was in the habit of going there. Or they both might have been kept in their private possession. There were never any papers handed down?'

'No. Who knows what Jacob would do with it if he had one? Maybe he wanted to forget the whole affair and destroyed it.'

Robert agreed. 'Or it may be among masses of papers in some attorney's office, here or in Whitby.'

'And impossible to trace.'

237

'Not necessarily. Maybe I'll ask Mr Palmer's advice.'

Rebecca's eyes widened with alarm. 'Robert, be careful. I know he thinks highly of you. He told your father that he saw you as a partner in his firm if you continued to work as diligently as you do. Don't ruin that by disclosing anything unsavoury in the family's past.'

'If I decide to seek his help, I'll be discreet.'

Two days later Robert started to put a hypothetical case to his employer but before he had got very far Mr Palmer raised a hand to stop him. Robert's words trailed away. He knew he had been caught out and was embarrassed by the admonishment in the look Mr Palmer gave him.

'Robert,' he said firmly. 'Can't you be completely open with me? You're talking about your own family, aren't you?'

'Yes, sir.' Robert looked downcast.

'Well, then, let's begin all over again,' he said gently.

Robert told him the whole story. He listened without interruption, making the occasional note. When Robert had finished Mr Palmer spent a few minutes in thoughtful consideration.

'You are quite right. Such documents as might have been drawn up could be anywhere. However we must start somewhere. I cannot make enquiries about Mr de Northby's but I can about your great-grandfather's, if indeed he had a copy. I would think that if your great-grandfather had a document and did not keep it in his own possession, he would most likely put it in the hands of a Whitby attorney for safe keeping.' He paused a moment and then continued. 'You say that your great-grandfather just disappeared? No one knew where he went?'

'That's right. It appears that he and his family just left without telling anyone, even his wife's family, where they were going.'

'In that case the document could lie forgotten, for unless your great-grandfather got in touch with him the attorney would not know where to find him and there would be little he could do.'

'So where can I start, sir?' asked Robert, a little despondent.

'Don't look so glum.' Mr Palmer gave a little smile. 'All is not lost. I'll write letters to various attorneys in Whitby asking if they hold any documents in the name of Jacob Wade probably dated about . . .?' He looked enquiringly at Robert.

'I would think about seventeen fifty.'

'I'll dictate a letter and you can pen them to the attorneys concerned. We'll get them away by the coach the day after tomorrow.'

'I think I can get them into Whitby before that,' said Robert. 'Paul Smurthwaite, Alice's friend, arrived this morning and sails early tomorrow. I'm sure he would deliver them if you are agreeable.'

'Admirable. The sooner they are in Whitby the better.'

When Robert returned home he was full of hope that something would result from Mr Palmer's letters. His enthusiasm spilled over to Paul when he told him of the situation. Paul said he would be able to get permission to go ashore at Whitby and rejoin his ship at Ravenscar where it would unload the rest of its cargo.

'Then you can tell Alice and Lucy that something is

being done and they should return home,' put in Rebecca, hoping that this positive move would put a stop to Lucy's madcap ideas.

At that moment those ideas had taken a new turn.

Earlier in the day when the sisters were carrying seaweed from the beach Lucy made a remark which sent misgivings shuddering through Alice.

'I think we should look here for the document Robert mentioned.'

Alice tensed. She knew Lucy's impetuosity but surely this couldn't be a serious suggestion? She saw Lucy surveying the alum works as if searching for a likely place.

'You must not do such a thing,' she said firmly.

'But Robert suggested that de Northby's copy might be here. Isn't it likely that he would keep all documents relating to these works in the office which Mr Smurthwaite pointed out to us?'

'It might also be with an attorney in Whitby or even in safe keeping at Northby Hall.'

'It's worth looking,' insisted Lucy.

'Robert is asking Mother so we . . .'

'Waste time,' Lucy put in. 'I'll look even if you don't.'

This was a ploy always used by Lucy. Alice knew she was cornered. She could not let her sister go into this madness alone.

'Even if you're right, the office will be locked. We can't go breaking in,' Alice protested.

'We may as well have a look. We've got to start somewhere.'

'And when is that to be?' asked Alice, exasperated by her sister's persistence.

'Well, we won't be able to use a lantern. The moon is almost full, it should give us plenty of light, so the first time there are few clouds.'

Alice kept her counsel. She knew it would be useless to try to talk Lucy out of this escapade. She walked on quietly under her load. She startled herself when she realised that she had been unconsciously studying the position of the windows and the approaches to the rectangular building close to the manager's house. She reckoned that they had every chance of reaching it without being seen from the house.

Two nights later when they went to bed Lucy, looking out of the window, announced, 'It'll be tonight.'

She came and stood beside her sister. The land was bathed in a white light, the sky was crystal clear, the moon's brilliance outshone the stars.

'We shouldn't do it, Lucy.' She had to make one last protest though she sensed that the charged excitement in her sister would not be denied.

'Don't be silly.' Lucy rounded on her with a snap. 'This is just the night and I have a feeling we are going to find something of importance.'

'And what if we're caught?'

'We shan't be caught. We wait here until Mr and Mrs Smurthwaite are sound asleep then we leave and, if necessary, we wait until the lamps go out in the manager's house. If there is a disturbance we'll have time to get away and even if we are caught, which is extremely unlikely, we'll think of some excuse. The thing is not to get caught in the building.'

241

'If we can get in.'

'Exactly. If we can, I'll go in and you can keep watch outside. If you hear or see anyone give me the warning and we'll be away.'

'It sounds easy but I don't like it.'

'Now hush and listen for Mr and Mrs Smurthwaite coming to bed. And put something warm on, the night air will be a bit sharp.'

They were in the middle of getting ready when they heard footsteps start to mount the stairs. Lucy held up her hand and they both froze. They listened intently. Lucy mouthed the words 'Mrs Smurthwaite'. They heard the bedroom sneck and a faint squeak as the door was opened. They waited. The sound of bolts being pushed home came from below. Then there were footfalls on the stairs heavier than the first. They heard the bedroom door close and the sneck fall into place. They relaxed and continued their preparations. Ready, they sat on the edge of the bed and waited, Alice content to follow Lucy's actions.

Fifteen minutes later the sound of snoring drifted across the landing. Alice glanced at her sister. Lucy held up a cautionary hand. Time moved on. Alice wondered why they were waiting. Ten minutes passed. She was getting anxious. Then Lucy inclined her head, listening. Alice caught the sound of a second snoring. It grew louder and was out of rhythm with the first. Lucy smiled and nodded. 'Both asleep,' she whispered and stood up. Alice realised that her sister had been planning for such a possibility as tonight by studying the Smurthwaites' sleeping habits.

Lucy moved quietly to the door. Carefully she lifted the sneck and stepped out on to the small landing. Alice, close behind her, quietly closed the door. They started down the stairs hoping that the odd creak would not disturb the sleepers.

They breathed a little easier when they reached the outside door. Lucy eased the top bolt back. She stooped to the bottom one. It was unyielding. She pulled a little harder. It gave suddenly and shot back with a noise which to them sounded like a clap of thunder. They stiffened, listening for any sound of movement, but the snoring went on undisturbed. Some of the tension slipped away. Lucy drew the door open, thankful that Mr Smurthwaite was a meticulous man who liked to keep the hinges well oiled. Outside they paused to get their bearings, unaware that their presence had awakened the attention of two watchers.

The movement startled Albert Johnson, driving away the drowsiness which had threatened to addle his mind. Keeping watch was monotonous especially through the long hours of the night when he knew the two girls were probably sleeping the sleep of the innocent. Neither he nor his companions had seen any reason for de Northby's order but order them he had and if they valued their jobs they had better obey and make no slip.

Two figures moved from the shadows into the moonlight.

He dug Edward Norton twice in the ribs to awaken him.

'What is it?' he whispered, not too pleased to be dragged from the warmth of his dream.

Albert pointed in the direction of the two figures.

'The lasses?' asked Edward, now wide awake, realising that their mission was still very much part of their lives.

'Aye.'

They remained still. They had made themselves as comfortable as possible in a hollow on the slope which gave them a good view across the cottages and the alum works. Now they watched Alice and Lucy walking quickly in the direction of the path which led between the works and the manager's house.

'Where the hell are they going at this time of night?' asked Edward.

'We'll soon see,' replied Albert. The older man calmed his companion's irritation. He could understand it for he too would rather have been snuggling up to his wife in a warm bed.

The girls reached the path and turned up the slope towards the manager's house.

'Now what are they up to?' muttered Albert half to himself. 'Come on. Be careful, we don't want to be seen.'

They kept to a slight hollow which ran across the slope and gave them a certain amount of cover. They crouched low, pausing every now and then to check the situation.

The girls continued the climb and were so intent on their objective that they did not consider the possibility of being followed.

'They're going to call on the manager.' Edward sounded puzzled.

'Can't be. The house is in darkness. Mick will be in bed,' Albert pointed out. 'Let's get to that wall.' With that he started at a crouching run.

Edward waited a second and then followed. They reached the wall without mishap, and, after pausing a moment to regain their breath, raised themselves so that they could peer over the stonework.

'The office,' whispered Albert on seeing their quarry making for the building a few yards from the manager's house.

'What on earth do they want there?' muttered Edward.

From their hiding place the two men had a good view of the building. They saw the girls pause close to one corner, look around and then study the house for a few moments.

Satisfied that the household appeared to be in bed, Lucy whispered, 'Let's see if we can find a way in.'

As expected, they found the front door of the office locked.

'Windows,' said Lucy.

The sneck on the first sash window was firmly in place. They moved to examine one on either side of the door.

'This one!' Alice's whisper carried to her sister who was quickly at her side. Alice raised the window, thankful that it moved easily and with the minimum of noise.

'You keep watch. I'll go in.' Lucy was firm, but she need not have worried, for Alice would have chosen the task Lucy had allocated for her.

With her sister's help Lucy scrambled through the window.

It was this moment, when their full attention was on breaking into the office, that Albert seized the opportunity to make a move.

'Up there and round the back,' he whispered.

The two men walked quickly round the corner of the wall and then to a gate. Seeing that it was hidden from the girls' view by the side of the building, he slipped quietly through to the back of the office. The men paused a moment. Albert signalled to Edward to remain where he was while he stepped to a side window which gave him a view into the room.

He was thankful for the moonlight for it afforded him a sight of Lucy. It was obvious that she was searching among papers. He was puzzled. What was she looking for? Did it matter to him? Was this the time to move on them, catch them? Was this what de Northby would expect him to do? Caught on the spot with Edward as witness they could not deny that they had broken into the office. Challenge them afterwards and they would deny everything.

He moved silently back to Edward. 'One's inside. The other must be keeping watch.'

'What are they after?' asked Edward, keeping his tone low.

Albert shrugged his shoulders. 'You go round the back to the other side. When I challenge them you cut off any escape.'

Edward nodded and slid silently away. Albert returned to the window and watched until he felt certain that Edward was in position. The girl was still searching, opening drawers, examining papers. He moved to the corner of the building and peered round. He could almost feel the agitation and anxiety of the girl keeping watch. He half smiled to himself anticipating the shock he was going to give her. Albert stepped round the corner.

'What are you two up to?' His voice shattered the silence which until then had only been marred by the gentle swish of the distant sea at the foot of the cliffs.

Alice started, frightened out of her wits. Her mouth opened to shout but it seemed an eternity before the word came out in a piercing scream. 'Lucy!' She turned and ran but she seemed to hit a brick wall. Then she felt arms close tightly around her and a voice close to her ear. 'Gottcha, lassie.'

'Good work, Edward.' Albert turned back to the open window. 'Come out of there. You're caught.'

Lucy had frozen with shock when Alice's scream shattered the night. Then she came alive, knowing she must do something. She looked round in desperation for a means of escape. The hopelessness of the situation bore down on her like a heavy cloak. She was trapped. There was no way out. Despair engulfed her as she came to the window, hoping that Alice had made her escape.

'Now, miss, what are you doing in there?' Albert demanded. 'Out with you.'

Lucy scrambled out of the window and felt broad hands grip her. She saw Alice held by another man. They were in deep trouble and she was to blame. She looked at her sister. 'Alice, I'm sorry.'

'We are together, Lucy,' answered Alice.

A flare of light in an upstairs window of the manager's house turned to a steady glow. A window opened noisily and a man looked out.

'What's going on down there? Who's there?' The voice was gruff with annoyance at being disturbed.

'Mick, it's Albert Johnson and Edward Norton from the estate. We've caught two lasses breaking into the office.'

'What? Bring 'em over here. I'll be right down.' The head disappeared and the window rattled down.

Each with an arm held in a vice-like grip, Alice and Lucy were marched to the manager's house. After a few minutes a broad-shouldered man, still in his nightshirt, held an oil lamp high to view the folk who stood at his door.

'Come in,' he snapped and stood to one side.

The two men pushed the girls inside where they saw a short dumpy woman, with a coat over her nightdress, still wearing her frilled lace nightcap. She too held a lamp. Her severe look took in the group.

'Sorry about this, Mrs Weatherall,' Albert apologised.

'Nowt to do wi' me.' Her words came sharp as if each was bitten off. 'But with lasses concerned I thought it best if I was here.'

'Quite right, ma'am.'

Mick had closed the door and scrutinised the girls. 'I've seen you two around. Staying with the Smurthwaites, aren't you?'

'Yes,' replied Alice meekly.

Mick frowned. 'Do they know you are out?'

'No, sir,' Lucy put in quickly, not wanting any blame to be put on the people who had been so kind to them.

'So, what are you up to breaking into the office?' The manager looked severely at them.

When they did not answer Albert put in a word of explanation. 'I don't know what they were after, but Mr de Northby must have suspected them of something. He's had us watching them for a few days.'

Mick raised his eyebrows. 'I was wondering how you two came to catch them.'

This news of de Northby hit the sisters hard. What had made him suspicious? If he had wanted their every move watched, breaking into the office might bring dire consequences. Tears of fear began to dampen Lucy's eyes.

'Please don't report us. We meant no harm.' She felt she had to make the plea though she suspected that there was little chance of it being heard.

Albert gave a shake of his head. 'It's our duty.'

'Are you taking them to Mr de Northby now?' asked Mrs Weatherall.

'Yes, ma'am.'

'Will he want disturbing at this hour?' queried her husband.

'From his attitude I reckon he wants to know immediately anything untoward happens,' replied Albert.

Mrs Weatherall nodded. 'Mick, you get dressed and let Mr and Mrs Smurthwaite know what has happened.'

Alice was startled by the sudden realisation that they might bring trouble on Paul's mother and father. She turned to the manager. 'Please reassure them we meant them no harm. We'll make sure that Mr de Northby knows they had nothing to do with this.'

'Very well.' He turned to Albert. 'Anything else?'

Albert shook his head. 'We'll get on our way. Sorry you were disturbed but thankfully we have your evidence of what happened.'

It was a tiring walk to Northby Hall for the two girls and for the most part they were silent, lost in their thoughts.

Lucy now regretted that she had insisted on the search and chided herself for her foolishness in thinking that they would find anything incriminating. She had got her sister into a hazardous situation which could jeopardise her relationship with Paul. What must he think of a girl as an accomplice to a break-in? But what was done was done and there was no going back.

Her thoughts turned to de Northby and the fact that he had hired these two men to watch them. What had led him to be suspicious? Zilpha? Robert's actions? Had Mark said anything after their visit to his great-grandmother? Oh, if only he were here now she felt sure he would help.

Alice was numb with the thought of what was happening to them. Branded as thieves even though they had not taken anything; the fact that they had broken into the office would be taken as an intention to steal. What consequences would that bring? She shuddered at the possibilities but consoled herself that Mr de Northby might not go to extremes. Then she was shattered by the thought that this would be the end of her relationship with Paul.

Albert gave the bell-pull at the back door of Northby Hall a vicious tug. After several attempts to rouse someone he heard footsteps and a disgruntled voice muttering as the bolts were pulled back. A dark scowling butler held a lantern high and peered at the faces it revealed.

'What does thee want at this time o'night?' he growled. Then, recognising the two estate workers, he said, 'Oh, it's you.' He recognised the girls who had helped at Miss Zilpha's birthday party. 'What's going on?'

'We must see Mr de Northby,' replied Albert.

The butler gave a little grunt of derision. 'At this time of night?'

'It's important,' snapped Albert.

'Aye, important,' agreed Edward.

'What is it, Ralph?' The voice was accompanied by footsteps in the corridor.

Ralph stepped to one side. 'Albert Johnson and Edward Norton, Mr Kemp.'

When he reached the doorway his eyes widened in surprise when he saw the two girls. 'Miss Alice? Miss Lucy?' He shot questioning looks at the estate workers.

'We must see Mr de Northby,' said Albert.

'Now? At this time of night? He won't take kindly to being woken,' warned Mr Kemp. He appeared to be wanting some explanation but Albert was not offering it.

Instead he said, 'Harold, I'll take the responsibility, just tell him we are here.'

Still Harold hesitated. He sensed trouble and that it concerned the two girls he had taken a liking to when they had helped at the party. He wanted to save them any more distress if he could. 'Can I deal with it?' he asked.

'No you can't,' rapped Albert firmly.

Harold looked at the two girls but there was no explanation coming from them. 'Close the door and take them into the kitchen,' he told Ralph. His footsteps echoed in the corridor as he hurried away.

When Ralph had shown them into the kitchen there was an uneasy wait until they heard someone approaching.

The door opened and Richard de Northby strode into the room in a red dressing gown over his nightshirt. He wore matching red slippers. The powerful colour gave him an authority which filled the room and made Alice and Lucy wish they didn't have to face his wrath.

He nodded at Albert and Edward, then turned on Harold and Ralph. 'I shan't need you two, go back to bed. Light me one of those lamps before you go.' His voice was brusque.

Ralph's hand shook as he lit the lamp. He had seen his master in this mood before and he did not relish seeing it again. He was thankful when he closed the door after Mr Kemp had left the kitchen.

De Northby eyed the two girls fiercely while the footsteps faded then he turned to Albert. 'Well, what happened?'

'They broke into the office at the alum works, sir.'

'Did they indeed? Did you see what they were doing?'

Albert explained what he had seen.

'And what were you looking for?' He glowered at the girls, daring them to lie. Before either of them could speak he held up his hand. He looked at Albert and Edward. 'You two can wait outside. I'll call you when I want you.' De Northby waited until the heavy door closed. 'Now, an explanation?'

His penetrating gaze carried a threat. Lucy met that piercing look. She had had time to think and she was determined not to be cowed by this man's demeanour. Attack him with what they knew and maybe he would reveal the truth.

'I think you know what we were looking for,' she replied, defiance in her voice. She sensed Alice's shock at her attitude and had even surprised herself at her temerity.

'Do I?' De Northby gave a small smile.

'Yes. A certain document.'

'Document?' He frowned as if puzzled.

'Yes, one drawn up by your grandfather.'

'If there was one, of what interest is it to you?' His voice was smooth, icy, challenging.

'Lucy.' Alice spoke as a warning to say no more but Lucy ignored her.

'Jacob Wade was our great-grandfather and we believe he was cheated by your ancestor.' Her words came full of accusation.

'Prove it.' He gave a supercilious laugh. 'You can't.'

The door opened with a clatter. Annoyed by the interruption, Richard swung round, chastisement quivering on his lips, but he calmed quickly on seeing his daughter.

'I heard a noise. What's going on?'

'Nothing for you to bother about,' her father said.

'But Albert Johnson and Edward Norton are outside.' She was puzzled. Was there a connection between the estate workers and the two girls?

'Yes,' Richard replied, realising he could not fob his daughter off. 'These two were caught breaking into the office at the works.'

'What?' She looked from one to the other.

'They were looking for a document, prepared to steal it.' He saw protestations rising to Alice's lips. 'Don't deny it. That's exactly what you would have done if you had found it, supposing one does exist.' He turned to his daughter. 'Zilpha, there is nothing to concern you now. I have these two thieves to deal with. I suggest you return to bed. On the way look in on your mother. Just reassure her that all is well.'

As she made her way through the house, Zilpha's thoughts dwelt on the incident. Lucy and Alice would be branded as thieves. What would her father do? Though they had taken nothing, they had broken into the office with intent to steal. He could really put them in terrible trouble.

After she had acquainted her mother with what had happened she returned to her own bed. As she snuggled down, drawing the eiderdown over her shoulders, she smiled to herself. Now Mark would see Lucy in her true light and realise how he had been duped. One way or another, the Mitchell girls would soon be out of their lives for ever, and no doubt Robert too. Was he branded by his sisters' action? Had he suggested that they make a search? If so he was as guilty as they were. He had indicated that the matter would be dropped. She had believed him and had passed on the information to her father. Had that been Robert's intention, hoping to make it easier for his sisters to investigate further? Her father had been too clever for that.

As the kitchen door shut behind Zilpha, her father turned a look of triumph on Alice and Lucy. They read no mercy in it. He was going to exact full justice for he had seen a means of getting rid of them and their troublesome investigation once and for all.

'You have committed a serious offence and I cannot let it go unpunished. You will be taken tomorrow to Whitby to appear before a magistrate.'

Both girls were shocked. They knew they faced dire punishment unless de Northby lessened his charge, and they feared he would not do that.

'But, sir, we took nothing,' protested Alice.

'You intended to; besides, you broke in, damaging property, and you were trespassing.'

Lucy's eyes flashed. 'No doubt you'll think up more with which to accuse us. And you'll influence the man who'll judge us. It seems you de Northbys are all alike! But our brother won't stand for it.'

'Lucy!' Alice was shocked by her sister's outburst. Better at this stage not to antagonise de Northby any more.

'Your brother?' He laughed contemptuously. 'No doubt he put you up to it. He's as guilty as you. Let him return to

Whitby and see what awaits him.' He chuckled as he went to the door. He opened it and looked into the corridor.

'Johnson, Norton.' The two men followed him into the kitchen. 'You did well. Now, I want you to lock these two in one of the storerooms. Then get some sleep. Tomorrow I will want you to accompany me when I take them into Whitby where they'll be brought before the magistrate. You will be called as witnesses.'

'And no doubt he'll pay you well to embellish what happened,' cried Lucy.

'Get them out of here!'

De Northby watched with satisfaction as the two men bustled the girls out.

Chapter Thirteen

The *Aquarius* lay on a tranquil sea, darkness cloaking her in anonymity. She drifted slowly down the Channel with the breeze and the tide. The French coast which had been a mere smudge on the horizon had disappeared with the dusk.

The captain was satisfied. He would be in the right place at the right time. After leaving Dover he had held close to the English coast, only leaving it when he judged that he would not attract the attention of watchers across the Channel. In these uneasy times he had no doubt that English shipping movements were noted by the French and this was one activity he did not want them to record.

The sailing had been made when clouds hid the moon so that their presence in French coastal waters in the Baie de la Seine close to a lonely, low-lying stretch of land would not be seen.

Even so he exercised the utmost caution and, as he had briefed his crew before sailing, orders were now passed on in whispers.

One such came a few minutes later from the captain.

'Lower boat.' He watched as the boat slid towards the sea, pleased that the sheaves in the blocks had been well greased to eliminate any sound.

Almost before the boat touched the water two sailors swarmed down the rope ladder to steady the boat and to be ready to cast off as soon as their two passengers joined them.

When he was satisfied they were ready the captain turned to the two men standing beside him. He held out his hand. 'Good luck.'

'Thanks. A week this time,' Mark said as he took the firm reassuring grip.

'We'll be here.'

Mark turned and slapped his companion on the shoulder. 'Over you go, David.'

David said nothing, shook the captain's hand, and went over the side. Mark followed. As soon as they were seated in the boat the sailors cast off, slipped their muffled oars into the water and headed for the beach.

Not a word was spoken. The boat was beached. Mark and David jumped out. The sailors quickly got the boat waterborne again and rowed away into the darkness.

The two men hurried across the sand to the dunes where in a hollow they regained their breath and settled into their new roles.

They were dressed plainly. Mark's calf-length coat was dark green and David's dark blue. They wore matching breeches, waistcoats, and stockings of fine grey wool. Each had a black felt hat with forward peak but turned up at the back. They had chosen stout but comfortable black leather shoes, and both carried a walking stick.

They slapped the sand from their clothes for they wanted no trace that they had come ashore.

'French from now on,' whispered Mark.

David nodded. Although he could speak French fluently and had never attracted any suspicion on two previous spying missions he wished he was as skilled as Mark.

Their brief now was to gather information as to the likelihood of the British being able to use any anti-Napoleon groups should the uneasy peace be shattered by war. Concern that this could happen soon had resulted in the urgent recall of the two men.

'Marcel Davout's house,' said Mark. 'Rest, and the coach to Paris.'

The two men started off at a steady pace away from the coast and found the road running inland. Six miles would bring them to the rendezvous with the man whose sympathies had been turned to Britain when revolutionaries had confiscated his land.

They reached the house without mishap, approaching it cautiously even though they had watched it for ten minutes before making their final move. Mark rapped the door with a signal Marcel would recognise for he knew that the agent sent in to make the arrangements for their arrival had returned to England and had reported that they would be expected.

'Ah, my friends, it is good to see you.' The man who greeted them was in his early fifties, thin, his face lined by the worries which had assailed him since the Revolution. There was genuine warmth in his smile and his pale blue eyes shone with pleasure. He embraced both men and then stood back to survey them. He nodded his approval of their disguise. 'What this time, gentlemen?'

'We thought, minor government officials who had been in Normandy assessing land which might be taken over by the government.'

'Ah, something I know about, but, how you say? From the wrong side of the fence.' He smiled wryly. 'That is good. I can brief you on what happened when such men visited me. Now, come this way, gentlemen. While you eat I'll put the finishing touches to the papers you will require, now that I know what your proposed profession is.'

He led them into a large kitchen where a white scrubbed table in the centre of the room was set for two. A portly lady was standing by a big black range stirring the contents of a large pan from which there arose a most appetising smell. She glanced over her shoulder when they entered.

'Madame Davout.' Both Mark and David made the greeting with a small bow. She acknowledged it with a smile but said nothing. Though she did not relish the risks her husband was taking she understood his attitude after the humiliations he had suffered because he had disapproved of many of the revolutionaries' methods. He had been lucky to escape with his life but they knew the local community held him in high esteem for his benevolence, apart from which his knowledge of local farming was useful to them. This had not stopped them from taking most of his land, of which they said it was not right for one man to own so much. Had he been of aristocratic descent he could well have lost his head by now.

'Sit down.' He indicated the chairs at the table. 'We eat in here, my friends, because there is not enough fuel to heat other rooms.'

Madame Davout ladled mutton stew into plates. A stone jug and a bottle stood close to two glasses.

'Cider,' Madame Davout indicated the jug. 'And local red wine.'

'Thank you.' Mark reached for the bottle.

Madame nodded with approval and returned to the range where she proceeded to prepare the next course.

When Marcel returned he handed them two small pieces of paper each. They were worn as if they had seen much use. 'One is your identification, stating you are a government official from Paris. The other is a travel permit which should give you unquestioned passage.'

Mark expressed his thanks. 'The coach for Paris?'

Marcel looked a little perturbed. 'You go to Paris, monsieur? You must be careful. There is still a current of unease as some see war coming. Napoleon has done much for France and is looked on as a saviour by many Frenchmen through his annexations to bolster the French economy. They see French dominance as magnificent but,' he shook his head sadly, 'it can only lead to war. No nation is going to bow completely to French subjugation.' He threw up his hands. 'Oh, messieurs, forgive me, I go on so.'

Mark smiled his understanding and sympathy for a man who saw trouble for his beloved France. 'The coach for Paris?' he prompted again.

'You'll catch it in Caen. I'll drive you there early tomorrow morning.'

The morning mists cleared early, leaving the countryside of orchards and meadows bathed in a warm sun. Cows grazed quietly. Peasants tilled the land. War seemed a million miles away. Marcel's carriage carried them through tiny villages, past half-timbered houses and on to Caen.

He indicated the coach for Paris and was gone before too many people noticed them.

Mark and David had little trouble obtaining seats on the coach, for government officials, though regarded with some suspicion and apprehension, were offered deference for fear of offending which could bring reprisal, an attitude which allowed them the best beds at their overnight stop.

Word that they were government officials having filtered through to the other passengers there was little conversation, for no one wanted to say anything which might be noted and passed on to the authorities. This suited Mark and David: the less they spoke the better.

Once their destination was reached, close to the centre of the city, the passengers quickly dispersed, thankful that the journey had been uneventful.

The two Englishmen were soon among a maze of streets on the left bank of the Seine. Their knock on the door of a house, with no features to distinguish it from the rest of the row, was quickly answered. No words were exchanged for the woman in her early thirties recognised Mark from a previous visit. She led the way to a room at the back. It was square, compact, with a cooking range on one wall, a table beside the one opposite and a dresser with crockery against another. A door, open, in the fourth wall, revealed a room with sink.

A man in his sixties rose to greet them. He was short and stocky, almost rough in his appearance for he was not one who carried his clothes well, but Mark knew that behind that façade was a gentle man, a man of high intelligence, who had once held high office until the Revolution.

He had escaped the drastic attentions of the revolutionaries to settle quietly with his daughter Madeleine.

'André.' Mark felt the firm handshake of a man genuinely pleased to see them.

'You arrived unnoticed?' Though he knew Mark would have taken every precaution he put the question not so much out of concern for himself but for his daughter.

'Yes.' Mark nodded.

André turned to David and shook hands. 'It is good to see you again too. Come, gentlemen, let us go into the other room. Madeleine will prepare some food.'

'Have you any news for us?' Mark asked anxiously, as they sat down.

André shook his head. 'Sorry, Mark. I did take tentative soundings of men who I thought might be sympathetic to England and her allies should war break out but they are either too wary of the authorities, too frightened for their families, or too satisfied with the new life under Napoleon. They see him as the saviour of France, as someone who will make their country great again, with all Europe subjected to France. I tell you, there can be little chance of insurrection within the country if it comes to war.'

'Is it so hopeless that David and I could be wasting our time?'

André shrugged his shoulders. 'Who can tell? Maybe there are a few who could rally others if ever an invasion took place.'

Mark glanced at David questioningly.

'If André can give us the names of the most likely ones, we can make contact and reassure them about English

262

intentions should war become inevitable. At least we will know the genuine opponents of the present regime.'

Mark turned to André. 'Will you supply us with the names and addresses of those most likely to help us and brief us about them?'

'Certainly.' André wrote quickly.

Mark looked at the list. Ten names. Not as many as he would have wished but at least it was something.

'It is a pity Monsieur Wilkins is not still alive, he would have rallied more in spite of his age.'

The words hardly registered with Mark, so intent was he on the list but they had struck a subconscious chord. He looked up suddenly. 'Wilkins?'

'Yes. He was an Englishman who came to France many years ago. You would have had his support after what the revolutionaries did in consficating his property and trying his two sons for treason, proving them traitors on false evidence, merely because their father was English. They finished on the guillotine.'

'What happened to him?'

'Their fate only made him more anti-government and his subversions eventually also led him to the guillotine.'

Could this be the Frederick Wilkins to whom his great-grandmother had referred? Surely it was too much of a coincidence for two Englishmen of the same surname to be in France?'

'What was his first name?' asked Mark. It seemed an eternity before André replied but it was only a couple of seconds.

'Frederick.'

Mark's heart raced. 'Tell me about him.'

'He was about thirty when he came to France. I got to know him in seventeen sixty when he married the daughter of a friend of mine, Claudette Coutard. She was twenty years younger but they were deeply in love. He apparently had money when he came to France and set up in the clothing business. He became very much a Frenchman except that he would never give up his English citizenship. It was this which led to his downfall, for he became regarded as an English spy. Nonsense, of course. The revolutionaries tried to break him by taking his sons away but it only made him all the more determined to oppose the regime.'

'What about his wife?'

'She is still alive, living here in Paris with her daughter, Louise. She was safe, she was French and knew certain people in high places, not sufficiently well-placed to save her husband, nor her sons. Even people with some authority in those turbulent days dared not be seen to sympathise with the condemned. They were able to save her, but because of her marriage to an Englishman she was watched closely. She still is, though not as strictly.'

Even as he was absorbing these facts he was wondering if this woman would know anything of her husband's past. He would dearly love to talk to her but would he have time, dare he risk his mission for the sake of a private matter?

'André, can you give me her address?' There would be no harm in being prepared for the opportunity should it arise. He imagined Lucy's surprise if he returned with information.

'What is there to be gained? She knows nothing. You could jeopardise her liberty.'

'Her husband might have left names that you don't

know of. We've got to explore every possibility. We will take every precaution so that she is not compromised.'

Still André hesitated. Claudette had suffered so much and he did not want to be the cause of more trouble for her. 'It is nearly nine months since I even heard of her, let alone saw her, she might . . .'

'The address, André, please,' Mark pleaded. 'You have cast doubts about the help we might get if war breaks out. Contact with Madame Wilkins could make this mission worthwhile. I assure you we will exercise the utmost care.'

'On one condition, monsieur. You do not contact Claudette until the rest of your mission is over.'

'So that if we do not have time there will be nothing to associate us with her,' added David.

André nodded. 'Exactly.'

When they left André's the following morning Mark and David mingled with the crowds converging on Notre-Dame Cathedral for morning Mass. Without appearing to, they eavesdropped on conversations, gathering the mood of the people. When they met again at the west door their information was not promising. Apart from everyday exchanges the talk had been of the anticipated glories of France under Napoleon, the power of France as the greatest nation in Europe, and the stability within the borders of France itself.

There seemed little chance of subversive action even by those still looking back to the old life before the Revolution with regret at its passing. The changes in France had been momentous, but people were settling down to them and though the authorities still ruled with suspicion and an iron fist most people wanted no upheaval.

265

'Abandon the mission?' queried David as they strolled casually beside the Seine.

'We can't do that,' replied Mark. 'We need verification of our feelings and this can only be gained by making contact with the names André gave us. There still might be a glimmer of hope of some help from within if war comes.'

'Are we splitting up?'

'You take five and I'll take the others. We'll meet in three days outside the main door of Notre-Dame, midday.'

'And if delayed?'

'Wait half an hour. We don't want to be conspicuous. After that the rendezvous will be André's.'

Thick grey clouds drifted over Paris carrying with them the threat of rain. The weather was in marked contrast to the day they had parted on their separate missions three days before. Then Mark had been full of hope but that had been dashed.

He had met with little success and he saw that any hope of help within France, if war broke out, would first have to come from outside, from the Royalist exiles in England. People who might have given support feared betrayal for even neighbours could not be trusted. To show any sympathy could bring reprisals, arrest, prison or even the guillotine. He doubted if David would have met with any better support.

He turned the collar of his coat up as he sauntered past the west front of Notre-Dame. Pretending to admire the architecture, his eyes sought David among the people passing the church in the course of their business.

He was not there.

Time passed, and Mark became anxious.

When the half hour was up, Mark wondered if he should

266

wait longer. He shouldn't break his own rules. Besides, this was the afternoon he had assigned to contact Claudette Wilkins. He wanted David with him as a witness in case she had anything of importance to tell him. He looked round once more but still there was no sign of his friend. He would have to see Mrs Wilkins alone. He started to walk away, unaware that his action was observed by two men in the employment of the secret police, who had kept him under surveillance since his last contact.

He quickened his pace. Had he paused and turned to look back he would have seen his friend rounding the corner of the cathedral.

David was breathing heavily when he paused to let his eyes sweep across the flow of people. He was annoyed that he was late but it could not be helped. His last contact, whom he had hoped to see early that morning, was not to be found at the address he had been given. Tracking him down had taken time. He wouldn't have minded if something worthwhile had come from it but as in his previous meetings he detected wariness and fear.

He could not see Mark. Maybe he had slipped into the cathedral. His eyes moved to the doorway. Two men stood there, deep in conversation, their gaze intent in one direction.

Automatically he followed it. Mark! Some distance away but he could catch him up. He made one step then stopped, looking back at the two men. They had started to move. Were they following Mark? He waited and watched and after a few minutes he was certain they were. Well, he too could play cat and mouse. He judged his distance carefully so that he would not be conspicuous to the men he was following.

He pondered the chances of out-walking the two men and warning Mark but, observing the way they stalked him, he realised that would be impossible.

But he had to do something otherwise André would be in danger as well. Should he hurry by another route and warn André? He was growing anxious, thwarted by his inability to find a way out of their dilemma, when he realised that Mark was going in the opposite direction to André's. Was he aware that he was being trailed? But he showed no sign of trying to shake off his followers. What was Mark up to? Suddenly David realised. Madame Wilkins! David's anxiety deepened but there was nothing he could do. They were too near her home for him to outwit the two men and warn Mark.

He saw Mark stop and knock at a door. The two men also stopped and appeared to be having a casual conversation. He slipped quickly into an alley on his right from where he could keep all three under observation without being seen.

The door opened and he saw Mark speak to a young woman who glanced along the street, pointed and waved her hands as if giving directions at the same time as she was speaking. Mark touched his hat and turned back along the way he had come. David's heart raced. What had happened? Mark would have to pass the two men. Would they stop and question him?

His friend walked briskly nearer and nearer his followers who were still talking, appearing to take no notice of him. They did not even look at him. He was past. They waited, looked after him for a moment and then walked quickly in the opposite direction.

David realised they must be going to call at the house

Mark had visited, no doubt to enquire what Mark had wanted. He weighed up the various distances. If only Mark would quicken his pace and reach him before the two men arrived at the house. Dare he step out of the alley and risk one of the men turning round? He must chance it.

Mark was startled to see David appear. His friend's gesticulations brought instant reaction from him. He tumbled into the alley, his mind awhirl with questions. He did not have a chance to put them, for David was whispering close to his ear.

'You were followed. Two men are at the house now.'

Although startled Mark reacted quickly. 'They'll come back. You grab one. I'll take the other.'

They heard feet hurrying in their direction.

The two men hardly knew what was happening. Hands grabbed them, dragged them into the alley and despatched them into unconsciousness.

'They'll be out for quite a while. Come on.' There was urgency in Mark's voice.

'Where now?' asked David.

'Madame Wilkins. She'd moved just a couple of weeks ago. That young woman gave me her address.'

'You'll be putting her in danger,' David protested. 'Those two will have got the address. They've been following you since Notre-Dame. I spotted them when I arrived.'

'A good job you were late,' said Mark.

'What about Madame Wilkins? If you don't call she can deny all knowledge of you and will no doubt have witnesses to say that she has had no visitors. André asked you not to jeopardise her freedom. Judging from the reaction I got from our contacts, if this Frederick Wilkins has a list of sympathisers, it will be useless. Lots of attitudes have changed since his death.'

'I agree,' replied Mark. 'I shan't ask her about any list. It's a private matter. She may have information which will help a friend of mine back home.'

'You shouldn't mix private and military affairs.' There was teasing in David's admonishment.

'Not even for a beautiful girl?'

'Ah!' David raised his eyebrows. 'Matters of the heart overrule everything.'

Mark hurried on, hoping he was on the verge of discovering information which would help Lucy.

With the letters safely delivered to the attorneys in Whitby, Paul Smurthwaite strode home filled with the expectancy of seeing his beloved Alice again. It was a shock when he was confronted by serious-faced parents and his mother burst into tears when she saw him.

'What's wrong?' he asked in mystified alarm.

'Alice and Lucy have been arrested,' replied his father.

'What?' He stared disbelievingly at his parents.

His father explained how they had been woken by the manager who broke the news of what had happened.

'Where are they now?' asked Paul.

'We don't know.'

'You haven't seen them?'

'No. They sent a message with Mr Weatherall that they would make sure we were not implicated. He told us that they were being taken to Mr de Northby.'

'But . . .'

'I don't dare interfere,' explained Mr Smurthwaite, hoping his son would understand.

'But I've got to find out what's happened to them. I'm going up to the Hall.' Paul started for the door.

'Paul!' Alarm rang in his father's voice but he was gone.

The walk to the Hall calmed Paul somewhat. He began to think logically. He could not demand to see Mr de Northby but someone at the Hall might be able to tell him what had happened to Alice. He recalled her telling him that Mr Kemp had been kind to them. He might know something.

His knock on the kitchen door was answered by one of the kitchen maids.

'Could I see Mr Kemp please?' he asked. 'It is important.'

Before the maid could react, a voice called from the kitchen. 'Who is it, Rosie?'

'Someone asking for Mr Kemp,' she called over her shoulder.

There was no answer but someone approached the door. Rosie opened it wider and Paul saw Mrs Kemp.

'Oh, it's you.' Mrs Kemp's greeting held sympathy and understanding. She turned to Rosie. 'Find Mr Kemp quickly and tell him Paul Smurthwaite wants to see him.' She turned back to Paul. 'Come inside. This is a bad business. I'm sorry it happened. They're such nice lasses. I can't understand why they did it.'

'I want to know where they are. I thought as Mr Kemp had been kind to them at Miss Zilpha's party he might be able to tell me.'

Before Mrs Kemp could say any more Mr Kemp hurried in. 'You're here about Alice and her sister?' Knowing the

271

answer he did not wait for one. 'I'm afraid things look bleak for them. They were caught in the office where they had no right to be and I believe Mr de Northby will press charges to the full.'

'Where are they now? I must see Alice. Let her know I'll do all I can to get her freedom.'

'Mr de Northby took them to Whitby to the gaol where they will await trial at the Quarter Sessions in four days' time.'

'But surely he can't leave them in that terrible place,' cried Paul. 'The conditions are appalling and they'll be among common criminals, and they aren't that. I know they aren't.'

'So do I,' replied Harold sympathetically. 'They shouldn't be there but there's nothing anyone can do. Mr de Northby is determined they shall be treated as criminals.'

'Take me to him.'

'Sorry, it's impossible.'

'You mean you won't,' cried Paul with disgust.

'No,' replied Harold gently. 'It would do no good and might only antagonise Mr de Northby further. I'm hoping his determination to charge them might mellow.' He put his arm round Paul's shoulder and turned him towards the door. 'Are you due to sail to Newcastle?'

'Tomorrow. But I'm not going. I must see Alice.' The determination in his voice almost convinced Harold that he should say no more but he steeled himself to continue with an opinion.

'I think you should sail.'

'How can you say that?'

'Listen.' Harold fixed him with a firm gaze. 'I think you would serve her better if you contacted her brother and told him of the situation. I believe he works for an attorney.

Maybe he could get the girls some help which it is unlikely they'll get here.'

'But . . .' Paul looked perplexed, his mind torn between wanting to stay and wanting to go.

'Believe me it will be for the best if you go to Newcastle.'

Reluctantly Paul agreed and left. His heart felt so heavy that he almost succumbed to the idea of returning to Whitby here and now in order to try to contact Alice. But better judgement prevailed and he journeyed homeward.

Realising he was already late in reporting back to ship he quickened his pace. Given permission to deliver the letters in Whitby on condition that he went on board immediately he arrived at Ravenscar, he knew he should not have gone to the Hall but the circumstances were exceptional. He hoped his captain would understand.

He acquainted his mother and father with what he had learned and of Mr Kemp's advice. They were relieved for they feared that he might do something foolhardy if he stayed. He bade them goodbye and hurried to his vessel lying below the cliffs. Immediately he went on board he set-to, helping with the preparations to sail in the early morning for Newcastle.

The voyage was no longer than usual but to Paul, impatient to see Robert, it seemed interminable.

Once the ship had docked and he had completed his duties Paul lost no time in going ashore. Knowing Robert would still be at work he went straight to the attorney's premises.

'Paul! What is it?' Robert read trouble in the serious expression which clouded his friend's face.

'I must speak to you. I think we should go outside.'

'Very well.' Robert frowned as he followed him into the street.

'Your sisters are in trouble.'

'What? How?'

Paul went on to explain what he knew.

'Oh, what idiots,' cried Robert in exasperation. 'I suppose it was Lucy. Why didn't she wait, leave it to me? She knew I'd be making enquiries.'

'What can we do?' asked Paul, almost beside himself with worry.

'It's not going to be easy. I reckon de Northby has something to hide so will throw all the charges he can at them and that could mean transportation to Australia.'

'No!' Paul's cry filled with anguish.

'Paul, come inside while I acquaint Mr Palmer of the facts and see what he suggests we do.'

He ushered Paul back inside the building and then hurried to see Mr Palmer.

'I am sorry to bother you, sir, but I need some advice.' Robert's face was grave.

Mr Palmer leaned back in his chair. 'Sit down, my boy, you look as if you've had something of a shock.'

'I have, sir.' He went on to tell his employer what had happened to his sisters.

Mr Palmer listened carefully. He frowned when Robert had finished. 'It is a serious offence to break into premises with the intention to steal.'

'But we don't know if that was what they were intending to do. They may have only wanted a sight of the document if there was one.'

Mr Palmer gave a small smile. 'Come now, Robert, you

274

don't think for one minute that any magistrate or jury would believe that they did not intend to steal. Besides, if I know de Northby, he'll want to build up the worst possible charges. This makes me think all the more that documents do exist and he doesn't want it known.'

'What can I do, sir?'

'We must get to Whitby as soon as possible.'

'But, sir, I can't expect you . . .'

Mr Palmer held up his hand to silence him. 'Nonsense. It will give me great pleasure to spike de Northby's guns but it might prove a hard job. He has influence in Whitby and district and he'll use it to get what he wants. First, we need to know when the next sailing is to Whitby.'

'I can tell you that, sir,' replied Robert. 'I have a note of the sailings here. I hoped I might get to Whitby again before long.'

'To see the young lady who laid her charm on you?' Mr Palmer suggested.

Robert ignored the question, but it did make him wonder if the information gleaned from him by Zilpha had been passed on to her father who as a result had put the two men on to watch his sisters. Had she duped him?

'There's a ship sailing tomorrow.'

'Then we'll be on it. What about Alice's friend, when does he return?'

Robert left to confer with Paul and returned a few minutes later to inform Mr Palmer that Paul would leave his ship and sail with them.

'Admirable. We'll enlist his help to see if any of those attorneys in Whitby have found the document we are looking for. While it would not exonerate your sisters completely it could mitigate their circumstances especially if it showed some flaw in the original transaction.' He eyed Robert seriously. 'What about your mother? Are you going to tell her?'

'I think I shall have to. It will be a shock to her but it would be a greater one if at some time we had to break even worse news. I believe she would want to know now.'

Mr Palmer nodded. 'I think you are right. Now off you go and get ready for tomorrow. I'll see you on board ship.'

'You're home early, is something the matter?' Rebecca asked when her son walked in accompanied by Paul. It struck her as strange that they should arrive together. 'The girls? What's happened?' She looked wildly from one to the other.

'I think you had better sit down,' said Robert gently. 'They are all right,' he added quickly, realising she was thinking the worst. 'But they are in serious trouble.'

'I knew it. I knew it. This stupid obession with what your father said. I knew it would lead to trouble.'

Robert explained the situation to her as mildly as possible without hiding anything from her for he knew she would want the whole truth.

'Oh, Robert, Paul, what are we to do?' There were tears in her eyes.

'It is already being done, Mother. I explained the situation to Mr Palmer and he will help. He and I sail for Whitby tomorrow.'

'And I'm coming too!' Rebecca had felt immense relief at the thought of Mr Palmer's assistance. 'Don't try to persuade me not to. My daughters are in trouble and my place is with them.'

276

Chapter Fourteen

Alice and Lucy were bewildered by the swiftness of de Northby's action to be rid of them. He had them woken early and bundled aboard his coach before the majority of the household was astir. He said nothing as the coach tossed them around on their seat, but he played on his commanding and intimidating presence.

Drawing up at the gaol he called for the door to be opened and once it gave them admission he had the girls bustled inside. There he called on the chief gaoler to lock them up pending their appearance before the magistrate.

The gaoler knew de Northby had influential friends in Whitby and any questioning of his right to bring these two respectable-looking girls here could bring undesired repercussions for him. He noted their names and the charge against them.

Once that was done de Northby hurried away without a word to them. Outside the gate he felt an immense satisfaction. Prying busybodies were out of the way and would be for good after the trial which he anticipated would be brief. To make sure of that and that the verdict he wanted was enforced, he made his way to the house of the man whom he knew would be conducting the trial. He left there knowing the man, who owed him a favour, would repay it in the way he wanted.

Alice and Lucy hoped that at any minute they would wake up from a nightmare from which there was no escape. The room they were in seemed to close in on them, its bare stone walls and flagged floor cold and uncompromising. The gaoler in his grey, dirty trousers held up by a thick leather belt below a stomach which showed a liking for ale, was as unyielding as the surroundings. He was a short, broad man with powerful arms which threatened to burst the sleeves of his tight shirt, open at the front to reveal a dark mat of hair. He wore a small woollen cap which only made a half-hearted attempt to keep his unruly hair under control. His ears were large, his lips were thick and when parted revealed broken yellowing teeth. His piercing eyes were given a look of terror by the unusal caste in them.

As the door shut behind de Northby the gaoler straightened from his writing and looked leeringly at the two girls who shrank before him. 'Now, my pretties, life in here can be hard or easy, depends what thee has to offer.' He chuckled meaningfully but the next word he spoke was put as a question. 'Money?'

'We have none,' said Alice weakly.

'Your folk.' The way he looked at their apparel left no doubt in his mind that their nearest kin would be able to line his pocket for a few favours for the prisoners.

Alice shook her head. 'We aren't from these parts.'

'Ah.' The gaoler's disappointment was obvious. He ran his tongue round his thick lips. 'Well then, maybe there's something else thee'd like to give me.'

'We have nothing,' said Lucy tentatively.

The gaoler laughed raucously. 'Ah, now that's where thee's wrong. There's always summat that thee has which will be very acceptable. And if thee's not sure then maybe thee'd like to come into my room,' he nodded at a door, 'and I'll explain. Thee first?' he asked Lucy.

Lucy's eyes widened in horror. This nightmare was getting worse and it was all her fault. She looked at her sister, pleading for help. Tears started to well in her eyes.

Appalled by the implication behind the gaoler's words Alice stiffened her determination not to be overwhelmed by their situation. Everything that was happening to them was foreign to their life but overcome it they must or they would sink into the abyss of despair. She drew herself up and stared defiantly at him with a look which had barbs of steel in it. 'Don't you dare touch us,' she hissed with venom. 'My brother, who is an attorney in Newcastle, will hear of it and he'll wreak a revenge on you which will have you hanging from a scaffold.'

For one moment the gaoler stared at her then he gave a derisive laugh. 'Rot. Thee's lying, trying to scare me.'

Alice detected an element of doubt in his tone. She seized on it. 'It's no lie.' She held his gaze, casting further doubt in his mind.

He hesitated, then wilted. He dared not risk the repercussions if what she said was true. 'This way!' he grunted in a mixture of frustration and bad temper. His big bunch of keys hanging from his belt clanged against his thigh as he stepped towards a heavy wooden door.

Lucy, trembling with fear, tried to draw confidence from Alice who, knowing she had to be strong for her sister, hid her own inner quakings. The door crashed loudly against the stone wall.

'Temper, temper, Lugs.' The female voice, filled with mockery, was accompanied by shouts of derision at the gaoler.

'Couldn't thee get 'em to play?'

Raucous laughter burst from the cells on either side of the stone-flagged corridor.

'Failed again, Lugs?'

'Lost y' charm?'

'Kept it hidden again.'

'Quiet! Shut up!' Lugs yelled.

Lucy moved a little nearer Alice. They were both shocked by the sight of the unkempt females crowded in the cells. They pushed at each other to get a place at the open bars to see the newcomers, those behind straining to see over the heads of their cellmates.

The stench of sweating bodies, of unclean cells was almost too much for Alice. She gagged and had to force the nausea down.

'Pretty pair, these.' There was a touch of mockery in the voice. It was taken up by others.

'Gaol's getting classy.'

'We'll need soap and water now, Lugs!'

'I say, isn't this a frightfully nice place?' The mimicked accent brought shrieks of laughter and coarse expletives resounding off the walls.

The gaoler stopped at a cell containing ten females. 'Get back, get back,' he yelled at them, rapping the hands which held on to the bars of the door with a heavy blackjack he had drawn from a pocket. He unlocked the door and stood menacingly in case there should be any attempt to break out. 'Get in,' he snarled at Alice and Lucy.

The inmates of the cell gave way. The sisters moved in under gazes filled with curiosity. They felt hands touch their dresses, feeling material which was so different to the shabby and dirty clothes worn by the other inmates, though there were some who had made attempts to retain a semblance of neatness, futile though they were.

Alice and Lucy looked about them in despair. They recoiled from the sanitation – two buckets in one corner of the cell.

'We tak' it in turns to empty 'em once a day when Lugs lets one of us out,' said one woman on seeing the newcomers' reaction. 'Thee can do it tomorrow.' She indicated Lucy.

Lucy recoiled at the thought of the task. 'But . . .' she started to protest.

'No buts.' The woman, whose dark, greasy hair hung to her shoulders, peered close to Lucy's face, her hooked nose and sharp features reminding Lucy of a drawing of a witch she had once seen in a book. The beady eyes bored into Lucy. 'You'll like that won't you?'

Lucy was too scared to answer.

'Won't you?' The words rapped sharp, demanding an instant answer. 'Say, yes Madge.'

Lucy swallowed hard. 'Yes, Madge,' she whispered.

'I'll do it.' Alice tried to intervene.

'I said she'll do it. You'll do it the next day.' The fierce glare she gave Alice brooked no nonsense and Alice knew it was better not to respond. When she saw that Alice had retreated Madge went on. 'I'm boss in this cell.' She glanced round the faces which crowded in on them. 'Ain't I, lasses?'

'Aye,' came the chorus.

'Is that settled?' She looked at the sisters.

'Yes, Madge,' they both replied subserviently. Though it went against their instincts they had both understood it would be the easiest way for as comfortable a life as possible in these grim circumstances.

'Good.' Madge gave a toothy smile of satisfaction. Her tone eased towards friendliness. 'What's the likes of you doing in here? You ain't been walking the streets like Beck and Lil, or pickin' pockets like Cora and Blanche, though where she found a name like that I'll never know.'

'Better than thine,' snapped a small slip of a girl.

Madge gave her a push in the face. She would have fallen but for the others close around to hear from Alice and Lucy. 'Well?' she demanded. 'Ain't waiting all day for an answer.'

'Breaking and entering,' replied Alice.

'Thieving, thee means?'

'No. We took nothing,' said Lucy, beginning to regain some of her composure.

The rest of the cell laughed.

'Thee means thee got caught.' Madge held her sides as her laughter got louder. 'First time I guess?'

Alice gave a slight nod.

'No need to tell me. I can see it was. First rule about thieving is don't get caught.' She shook her head in mock dismay. 'Ah, well thee's here now and this ain't the Angel Inn. Thee'll have to make the best of it until they drags thee

282

before the magistrate and goodness knows when that will be. There's us lot to deal with and they don't seem in a hurry to move some of us.' She grinned. 'Don't look so glum. Mak' thissens at home.' She bowed in mock politeness.

The group broke up. Three including Madge sat on the only bench, the others slid to the floor with their backs to the walls. Alice and Lucy looked around. There seemed nowhere for them until little Blanche turned to the waif next to her.

'Shove up, Cora,' she said with authority.

Cora sniffed and shuffled sideways on her bottom. Blanche moved closer to her.

'Sit down 'ere.'

'Thank you,' said Alice as she and Lucy lowered themselves to the floor.

'Cold, ain't it?' said Blanche when she saw Alice twitch. 'Thee'll get used to it.' She leaned closer to Alice and whispered. 'Tak' no notice of Madge, she's all wind. Let her think she's boss. I'll see thee all right.'

Over the next two days Alice and Lucy had reasons to be thankful to Blanche. She always made sure they got their rightful rations, meagre and unappetising though they were, and she always kept a place beside her so that they could lean, with a little measure of comfort, against the wall. She encouraged them to take no notice of the uncomplimentary calls that came their way from those who saw them as different to the others. Blanche had told them at the outset to 'muck in' and they realised how right she was, but their loss of freedom weighed heavily on them.

The days were long, the nights longer. Sleep did not

come easily, until weariness took over. Lucy wept, blaming herself for their predicament. Alice had to mask her own fears in order to try and persuade her that things would come right for them.

The only release from the degradation was a few minutes' exercise each day in the open high-walled yard. The sweetness of the air after the stink in the cell only served to make Lucy more miserable once they were locked in again.

On the morning of their fourth day Lucy's misery had deepened. She bewailed the fact that this could go on for years. 'No one will know we are here,' she cried. 'De Northby will see to it that no one finds out.'

'The Smurthwaites know what happened. They'll have told Paul. He'll take word to Robert . . .'

'And if he comes, de Northby will have him arrested as an accomplice,' moaned Lucy.

'He'll be careful and see we are freed.' Alice endeavoured to boost Lucy's morale, hiding her doubt that Robert would be successful against de Northby's strong influence. In spite of Lucy's recklessness, which had landed them in this foul-smelling cell, Alice still loved her sister and was determined to support her.

Lucy scratched at the itching around her body. She felt she was being eaten alive. Her despair intensified. What had they come to? Oh for those peaceful family days in Newcastle, when she could soak in a tin bath in front of the fire. What would she give for that now to rid herself of the fleas? Thoughts of her mother and of life as she had known it only made her feel worse. Tears started to trickle silently down her cheeks. She turned her head away so that Alice would not see her misery.

284

'The Mitchells!' Lugs's coarse voice resounded through the block. It raised curiosity in everyone. Why were the most recent inmates wanted? 'On your feet!' He rattled the bars with his blackjack. 'Yes, you two,' he barked.

Alice scrambled to her feet and helped Lucy. The cell door swung open.

'Move! Move! Can't keep the magistrate waiting!' Lugs growled.

Magistrate! They were going on trial!

His words made an impact on the rest of the inmates and immediately the block was filled with their yells.

'What about me?'

'I've been here three months.'

'Why those bloody bitches? They've just come.'

'Get me in front of that bastard magistrate, I'll give him a piece of my mind.'

Madge tried to stand in the way. 'They don't get out if I don't!' She drew herself up menacingly but Lugs lashed out with his blackjack. The searing pain through her shoulder caused her to retreat. 'You bastard,' she hissed, her eyes on fire with hate.

'Out,' he snarled at the two girls.

Alice paused and looked back at Blanche who still sat in the same place. Their eyes met. Blanche winked and raised her thumb.

'Get a move on.' Lugs gave her a rough push. She staggered and would have fallen if she had not had hold of Lucy's hand. He escorted them out of the cell block and handed them over to two men who were neatly dressed in black coats. They did not speak and obviously wanted no truck with Lugs, viewing their visit to the gaol with disdain.

They walked briskly, one in front of the two girls, the other behind them. They left the gaol and crossed to another building where they climbed the stairs at the top of which they came to a closed door.

'Wait,' commanded the taller of the two men, who entered the room. The murmur of voices drifted to the two girls whose thoughts were filled with apprehension about what awaited them. They gained no relief as voices beyond the door were raised in anger, followed by shouting. The only words they could make out were 'Order! Order!' followed by a loud rapping. The situation settled. Voices continued at a normal level and then were followed by a lot of shuffling. That died away and then the door opened and the man who had escorted them reappeared. He signalled with his hand for them to step past him.

The two girls found themselves in the prisoner's dock, from which steps led to ground level. The steps were closed off by a small wooden door. In the round room seats at three levels occupied a third of the circle. They were filled by the public, some genuinely concerned about the fate of certain prisoners, others merely displaying ghoulish interest in the punishment meted out, and others only there for the fun of deriding the unfortunate ones. Opposite the prisoner's dock, at the same level, was a large carved seat behind a sloping desk. It was occupied by a sombre, heavy-jowled man whose eyes dwelt critically on the two girls. The tiers below him were used by various officials who now sat patiently awaiting his opening of the case.

Alice and Lucy felt embarrassed by all the attention they were attracting. Whisperings went on among the public as heads came close together while eyes dwelt with curiosity on the two prisoners.

'There's de Northby,' said Alice, her voice low as she leaned nearer her sister. She had seen him sitting in the well of the court, a satisfied smirk on his face. Alice concluded that he had arranged for them to be brought before the magistrate without delay. He wanted them out of the way as soon as possible. No doubt the verdict was a foregone conclusion.

'Where's Robert?' whispered Lucy anxiously.

'He won't have had time to get here,' answered Alice.

'But we need someone to . . .'

She never finished the sentence for a sharp rap on his desk by the magistrate quietened the babble of voices. A man on the tier below the official looked up. The magistrate indicated that he wished him to proceed. The man stood up, a paper in his hand. He cleared his throat and read in a high-pitched voice, 'Alice Mitchell, Lucy Mitchell, you are charged with breaking and entering the property of Mr Richard de Northby, an office at his alum works, with the intention of stealing items belonging to the aforesaid gentleman. In the course of that you caused damage to the fabric of the building and to furniture and materials within that building. How say you, guilty or not guilty?'

The girls, dazed, did not answer.

'How say you?' the man asked again, irritated that he had to repeat himself. 'Guilty or not guilty?'

'We took nothing.' Lucy suddenly came alive and spat the words out.

Even more irritated that this slip of a girl had not rightly followed the procedure, he snapped, 'Guilty or not guilty?'

Cries resounded from the public. 'Guilty!' 'Not guilty!' 'Shouldn't have got caught, lasses!' 'Didn't know how to do it. Should have got help.'

The magistrate rapped harshly on his desk. 'Quiet! Quiet!' He glanced with annoyance at a man standing in the well holding a long, polished stick.

The man suddenly pounded the floor with the shaft of his stick. 'Order! Order!' he yelled. The shouting subsided then one wag shouted, 'Woken up, Smiler?' This raised laughter and more catcalls.

'Order! Order!'

The noise fell away.

'Well, how do you plead?' asked the magistrate, glowering at them.

'Guilty,' said Alice at the same moment as Lucy said, 'Not guilty.'

Shrieks of laughter pealed around the room.

Smiler rapped his stick harder. He was not going to be caught out again. 'Order! Order!'

Silence descended as the people in the court waited for the next development.

'It seems you don't know, so I'll ask Mr de Northby to plead for you. How say you, Mr de Northby?'

Richard de Northby stood up. 'Guilty!' his voice rang across the hushed room.

Lucy was incensed. 'You shouldn't be asking him!' Alice pulled futilely at her sleeve as a warning not to antagonise the magistrate.

'You were asked but you couldn't agree,' smirked the official. He turned back to de Northby. 'Sir, will you give us your interpretation of what happened?'

288

De Northby did so in clear terms which left no doubt in anyone's minds.

'You say two of your estate workers caught them?'

'Yes, red-handed.'

'Are those estate workers here?'

'Yes.' De Northby signalled them to stand up.

The magistrate took their names and listened to their recollection of the events which led to the prisoners being caught.

When they had finished the magistrate looked directly at Alice and Lucy. 'Is that what happened?'

Alice sensed that Lucy was going to blurt out the whole story and, fearing that would only bring worse repercussions, hissed at her sister, 'Say nothing!' Lucy stiffened with defiance but held her tongue.

'Can you deny it in the face of three witnesses?' asked the magistrate when the girls did not answer his first question. When they still did not speak he added, 'I will take it that silence means you agree and therefore are guilty. I can do nothing more but sentence you.' He paused, looking grave. 'Thieving is a serious crime. You may have taken nothing but the intention was there and that is just as grave. I therefore have no alternative but to sentence you to be held here awaiting transportation to London and then Australia!'

A gasp ran round the court. No one had expected such harsh punishment though it was within the jurisdiction of the magistrate to punish stealing this way.

The courtroom buzzed with exchanges of comment.

'Ain't right,' someone shouted.

'Don't deserve that,' came from another.

Boos and catcalls bombarded the magistrate but these were counteracted by some who approved the sentence.

'Got what they deserve.'

'Can't let 'em off 'cos they're ladies.'

Arguments started, fists were raised. The magistrate hammered hard on his desk. His officials moved quickly to quell what threatened to become an affray.

The girls heard the noise but it meant nothing to them. They were severely shocked. Australia! It couldn't be. They hadn't heard correctly. But the satisfied look on de Northby's face told them they were condemned. Alice felt weak at the knees. She held on to the front of the dock, her grip so tight, trying to control her shattered nerves, that the knuckles showed white. Lucy uttered a low moan. Her world had caved in. What would Mark think? If only he was here maybe he would be able to do something. Oh, where was he? Where was Robert? What would her mother think? She closed her eyes at the pain she knew her mother would suffer. And it was all her fault. If only she had quelled the curiosity raised by her father's last words. The enormity of what she had brought about overwhelmed her. Why hadn't she heeded her mother? Her head spun. The noise in the court pounded at her mind, louder and louder until it seemed her brain would burst. Everything spun faster and faster in a whirl of mist until her legs began to give way and she slumped against the front of the dock.

Alice saw her sister crumpling. Automatically she grabbed her and appealed for help from the two men who, having escorted them to the court, had stood behind them throughout the so-called trial. They hastened to Lucy's aid.

The officials in the court were restoring order when the commotion in the prisoner's dock caught the magistrate's attention. He realised that the thought of the impending punishment had been too much for one of the condemned. He also knew that the sight of a prisoner so overcome could lead to more trouble with sympathisers.

'Get the prisoners out of here,' he shouted.

Once outside the building they stopped. Lucy had recovered a little and the fresh air helped to revive her further. Her face was ashen. She looked wildly at her sister but words would not come.

Alice realised that she was trying to apologise, to take the blame for the predicament they were in and that she needed her sister's support and forgiveness. 'It's all right, Lucy,' she said in a reassuring voice, disguising all the hurt and confusion she was really feeling. 'We're together. We have each other. Don't give way. Robert will come. I know he will.'

Lucy gave a wan smile. It did her good to hear her sister speak in this way. But could they ever escape from this hopeless position?

'Feeling better, miss?' asked one of the men, a touch of sympathy in his voice. He had escorted many prisoners to the court but every one of them had been a hardened criminal or a first offender whose poverty and hardship had inevitably brought a clash with the law. None of them had had an air of respectability such as these two. It was hard on them. He wished he could ease their burden but there was nothing he could do except return them to Lugs to await shipment in the degradation of their cell.

* * *

Immediately they reappeared in the corridor of the cell block the inmates clamoured to know what the sentence had been.

'Australia.' Alice brought herself to utter the dreaded word. Like a raging moorland fire, the news swept from prisoner to prisoner.

There were sympathetic calls and both Alice and Lucy felt the antagonism, which they had experienced on their first arrival from some of the inmates, disappear. Now they were like them, condemned in the eyes of the law.

When the door clanged shut they felt life as they had known it had ended. The unknown awaited them.

They sank wearily on to the floor beside Blanche.

'That was harsh,' commented Madge.

Alice did not look up but acknowledged the sympathetic tone with a nod of her head.

Others muttered agreement but Madge signalled them to say no more. She had seen cases where too much sympathy had cracked the resolution to cope and had sent the victim into the realms of madness.

After ten minutes Alice and Lucy had not moved . . . Blanche leaned nearer Alice. 'Thee'll be all right, Cora and I will look after thee.'

For a moment Alice did not respond. Then the bleakly amusing side of the situation struck her. Here were two waifs, barely out of childhood, offering to look after her and Lucy. Yet Blanche's advice when they first met had been sound. Maybe they had been fortunate in finding them. She turned her head slowly and looked at Blanche, whose eager eyes told her that she hoped Alice would accept her offer. 'You're going to Australia?'

Blanche smiled and nodded. 'Yes. Sentenced over a week ago.'

Alice was taken by her outlook. Blanche had accepted the verdict as if it was part of life. Here was a change of direction, life had to go on and she would go on living it whatever the circumstances. Was this a lesson she and Lucy had to learn? But then she doubted if Blanche and Cora had as much to lose as they had. Had they friends who would be distraught by what happened to them?

'And from what Lugs has said we'll be shipped out of Whitby in three days' time.'

The news dismayed Alice. 'So soon?'

'Aye,' Blanche nodded. 'Might be better than this hole.'

Alice sighed; their world was crumbling even more quickly. Where was Robert? Hadn't Paul got word to him? He must come or they were doomed. But would he be here soon enough? And if he was what could he do in the face of de Northby's influence?

Robert watched with impatience as Whitby came closer. Anxious to be ashore to help his sisters, time seemed interminable as the ship ran in between the piers and made its way slowly upstream to its quay on the east bank of the river.

All around life was going on as normal but it was unreal to him. His sisters were in danger.

'Calm yourself, Robert.' Mr Palmer offered a word of advice. 'I understand how you must feel, you too, Paul, and you, Mrs Mitchell, but you must keep yourselves under control. We must be careful that our actions do not prevent us achieving our objective. First we must establish a base, so we will go straight to the Angel Inn and get ourselves some rooms. Then, Paul, I want you to go to the attorneys to whom you delivered those letters. Ask them if they have found anything. If not acquaint them of my presence in Whitby and tell them if they unearth something it should be brought to me at the Angel without delay. Robert, you and I will try to find out what has happened to your sisters, then we can plan our course of action.'

'What can I do?' asked Rebecca, anxious to help.

'You remain at the inn and be the base with whom we can leave messages for each other.'

Once ashore they hurried to the inn. The landlord remembered Mr Palmer and Robert from their previous visit and they were soon ensconced in their own rooms, Mr Palmer having persuaded Paul that he would be more use in Whitby for the time being than living at home.

Within a quarter of an hour he was setting out on the mission assigned to him, while Mr Palmer and Robert engaged the landlord in conversation which they gradually directed to enquire if there had been any recent court proceedings.

'Yes, sir,' he replied. 'Quite a stir in the court when two young women were condemned to be transported to Australia. Most of the crowd thought it harsh treatment.'

Mr Palmer sensed the tension mounting in Robert and he shot him a warning glance. 'What were they accused of?' he asked the landlord.

'They broke into Mr de Northby's property. Took nothing, but the magistrate said that the intention was there.' The landlord pulled a face. 'I reckon the magistrate was hard on them, but, you know, with a man like de Northby bringing the charge . . .' He left them to draw their own conclusion from his implication.

294

'They were caught breaking in?' asked Robert.

'Aye. And that's another curious thing. The break-in was at night at the alum works but it was two estate workers who caught them. Now what were two estate workers doing around the alum works at that time? And of course their evidence was strong.'

'Who was the magistrate?' asked Mr Palmer.

'Joshua Hope.' The landlord chuckled. 'Right name for a magistrate.'

'I have some business to attend to and I might need his help, where would I find him?'

'He has an office in Grape Lane. First right after you've gone back over the bridge.'

Following the landlord's directions Mr Palmer and Robert were soon being shown into Mr Hope's office.

He sat behind an oak desk which was strewn with papers seemingly without any orderliness about them. They were in keeping with the man whose clothes were ill-fitting and his cravat askew. His heavy jowls added to his miserable look but Mr Palmer read an astuteness behind those apparently lazy eyes.

'Good day, gentlemen, what can I do for you?' His voice boomed in greeting but he made no effort to rise from his chair nor to shake hands.

Mr Palmer introduced himself and Robert. They both noticed the fierce questioning look which was shot at Robert when Mr Palmer said, 'Robert Mitchell, my assistant.'

'Mitchell?' Mr Hope snapped. 'Any relation to the two girls who were recently brought before me?'

'Brother,' returned Robert firmly.

'And I suppose you've come to plead for them?'

'I will leave that to my attorney friend, Mr Palmer.'

'Attorney, eh?' Mr Hope grunted. 'You should know better than to try to persuade a magistrate to change his verdict.'

'It has been done when certain relevant facts which were missing at a trial have been pointed out,' returned Mr Palmer calmly.

'Not with my initial judgement. To review a case is a waste of time and money, especially this one.' He looked at Robert. 'Your sisters were caught in the act.'

'But I understand they took nothing,' Robert protested.

'The intent was obviously there, and you should know that that is just as serious,' the magistrate said to Mr Palmer.

Mr Palmer ignored the remark and said, 'We'll see what the Misses Mitchell have to say about it.'

'I'm afraid that won't be possible. You need my approval to see any prisoner. It's something we find works well for the good of the community. If we allowed easy access it could lead to trouble. I'm afraid in this case I cannot give permission.'

'That's ridiculous!' Robert's eyes darkened with anger. 'It's not right.'

'It's what I say,' interrupted Mr Hope harshly. 'Be careful what you say or do, Mr Mitchell, or you could be in grave trouble. Your sisters were guilty, they've had sentence passed and they will be taken from Whitby for their journey to Australia. There is no more to be said. Good day, gentlemen.'

Robert would have launched himself at the magistrate but Mr Palmer restrained him. 'Come, Robert. We're wasting our time here.' He eyed Mr Hope. 'This matter isn't finished yet.' He turned Robert towards the door.

Mr Palmer's grip tightened when he tried to resist but Robert's anger was so deep that he could not resist one final remark which he flung with venom from the doorway.

'How much did de Northby pay you?'

Before Mr Palmer ushered him from the room he caught a glimpse of fear flick across the face of the man who thought his position could not be challenged.

Once they were outside, Robert turned his concern to his employer. 'Mr Palmer, what are we to do? I must see my sisters. I must let them know I'm here.'

'We'll get word to them somehow. But we've got to keep calm throughout this sorry business. Do nothing that will jeopardise our position.'

'I'm sure de Northby's behind this. According to the landlord of the Angel his estate workers caught Alice and Lucy. He must have had them watching. And I believe he bribed the magistrate to bring in that verdict. He wants the girls out of the way. To me, it proves he has some family secret to hide and he was frightened they might find out what it is.'

'Be careful he doesn't try to get you out of the way too,' warned his employer.

'But I've got to do something.' There was a desperate tone to his voice. 'I'll go to see Miss Zilpha, maybe she can help.'

'I don't advise that, Robert. Don't go into the enemy camp and remember traits can be hereditary: she might turn as vicious as her father.'

'I know but . . .' He pondered, then, throwing off all doubt, added firmly, 'I'm going to see her.'

Chapter Fifteen

Paul made the rounds of the Whitby attorneys quickly but at each call he met with negative results.

When he left the last office he made his way to the Angel Inn to find Mr Palmer informing Mrs Mitchell of the hopeless outcome of his interview with the magistrate and that Robert had gone to see Zilpha de Northby in the hope that she might be able to get her father to take a more lenient view of the incident.

He left the inn and walked down to the harbour. From what Mr Palmer had said the chances of getting official permission to see the girls was very remote, but maybe there was another way. His courage bolstered by activity, he walked briskly to the prison.

Gaining admittance he asked with some trepidation to see the head gaoler. A few minutes later Lugs walked in and Paul was shocked by the disreputable appearance of this ugly man.

'Well?' Lugs growled.

'I'd like a private word with you, sir,' said Paul, concealing his nervousness.

'What about?' asked Lugs suspiciously.

'I'd like to see two of your prisoners.'

Lugs looked thunderstruck. How dare this young whipper-snapper come here with such an outrageous request? 'Get to hell out of here,' he snarled. He drew himself up to his full height, pulled his blackjack from his pocket and slapped it threateningly in the palm of his left hand.

Paul read the menace but he did not flinch although he felt his nerves quake. 'Hold on, sir.' He used the word again, for the first time he had done so he had noticed Lugs's chest swell just a little and his head go back with a touch of pride. No one ever called him sir, and he liked it. 'I can make it worth your while if I can just see them for a few minutes.' As he was speaking he fished in his pocket and made sure Lugs saw him reveal a half-sovereign. He saw the gaoler's eyes brighten.

'Well,' he said pensively, 'it might just be possible.' He glanced around furtively. They were unseen. He moved closer to Paul. 'And who might thee want to see?' He felt the coin slipped into his hand.

'Alice and Lucy Mitchell.'

Lugs grunted. 'Wait here,' he ordered sharply, and left the room.

Paul glanced round and shuddered. The place was grim, cold and bleak with little light from the dirty windows high up on the stone wall. Time seemed to stretch. Paul began to get apprehensive. Had the gaoler gone to higher authority to report being offered a bribe?

The door swung open and Alice and Lucy, wondering why Lugs had ordered them out of the cell, walked in. Observing they were unharmed, relief swept over Paul, but it was mingled with shock at seeing their dirty, dishevelled appearance so unlike the neat, smart sisters he was used to.

Disbelief crossed their faces but turned to delight at seeing him. Hope soared that within a few minutes they would be out of this hell-hole.

'Paul!' Alice rushed into his open arms. She sobbed with joy, feeling protection in his strength. Their troubles were over.

Lucy, with tears of relief flowing down her cheeks, was beside them. Paul held out his right arm and hugged her. 'Get us out of here, please,' she cried.

'I'm sorry, I can't.' His voice was low, full of pain and regret.

The shock stiffened them. They were condemned after all to stay in these demeaning and degrading conditions.

'You can't?'

'Oh, Paul, help us!'

'We are doing our best.' His sorrow and regret almost overwhelmed him. He was desperate to help them, yet utterly helpless. He had to fight to stop himself breaking down.

'We?' queried Alice between her sobs.

'Your mother and Robert are here and we have the help of Mr Palmer. We are doing what we can. Mr Palmer and Robert went to the magistrate, who refused permission for us to see you, but I thought a bribe might gain me admission. I wanted you to know we were in Whitby. The others don't know that I'm here.'

'Is there any hope for us?' asked Alice.

'The magistrate told Mr Palmer and Robert that there would be no reconsideration of the verdict.'

'Then it's Australia in two days.' Dismay rang in Alice's statement.

'In two days?' Paul was taken aback.

Alice nodded.

'Please don't let it happen,' cried Lucy.

'We aren't giving up. Mr Palmer hopes to find some way of saving you.' To reassure them he explained about their search for the document. 'And Robert has gone to see Miss de Northby to see if there's any chance of her persuading her father to drop the charges.'

'There's precious little chance of her helping,' commented Lucy bitterly.

'Time's up!' Lugs's voice boomed off the walls.

The girls glanced round, desperately wanting Paul to stay longer.

'I'll have to go,' he whispered as he hugged them tight. 'We'll have to work fast. Keep your spirits up. We'll save you.'

Hasty kisses were exchanged and with tears in their eyes they left Paul. At the door they looked round and raised their hands, a dejected action which tore Paul's heart. The door clanged shut behind them, the heavy noise echoing through the room, a sound separating two worlds with a finality that weighed heavily on him.

Back at the Angel Inn he found Mr Palmer trying to reassure a worried Mrs Mitchell over a cup of tea at a table in one corner of the dining room.

'I've seen Alice and Lucy,' he announced, his voice charged with the excitement behind the news.

Surprised, Rebecca looked at him anxiously. 'How are they?' she asked in a tremulous voice.

'Well, but distressed by what has happened. They are relieved to know that we are here to help them.' He spared her the full truth of their condition.

'I must see them.'

'I'm afraid that won't be possible,' said Paul gently. He did not want to encourage any false hope.

'But you did,' Rebecca protested.

'How did you manage it?' Mr Palmer intervened to ease Paul's dilemma.

'Bribed the gaoler.'

Mr Palmer's eyes widened with a mixture of disbelief and horror. Though many gaolers took advantage of their position to bestow favours on prisoners and visitors it was always fraught with danger. 'You took a risk. You could have ended up in gaol.'

'It was worth it to let the girls know we were here,' replied Paul.

'Can't we bribe him again?' Rebecca asked, her eyes pleading with them to agree. 'I want to see my girls.'

'Too risky, Mrs Mitchell,' the attorney advised. 'We don't all want to end up in gaol. We'll be no use to the girls there. Let's wait and see if Robert's been able to achieve anything.'

She nodded reluctantly and looked down at her hands.

'I'll go and have a wash,' said Paul. Taking advantage of Rebecca's diverted gaze, he flashed a signal at Mr Palmer.

He had been in his room only a few minutes when the attorney followed him.

'I take it you wanted to see me?' he said.

'Yes,' replied Paul. 'Alice and Lucy said they are to start the first part of their transportation in two days.'

'So soon?' Mr Palmer felt a cold clutch at his heart.

'I thought it best not to say anything in front of Mrs Mitchell, seeing she does not know the full extent of the sentence.'

'Quite right, my boy.'

'What are we to do, Mr Palmer? The situation is desperate.'

Mr Palmer nodded. 'Everything has happened so quickly, almost too quickly, that it makes me even more suspicious of Mr de Northby.'

'Yes, but how are we going to spike his plans?'

'As I said downstairs, let's see if Robert has any good news. With luck he will be back before too long.'

Robert was filled with turmoil as he hurried to Northby Hall. The thought of his sisters in prison distressed him, the idea of them being transported to Australia was agony to him. He felt sure that de Northby was behind the swiftness of the trial and the severity of the sentence. His one hope was Zilpha. Could she influence her father?

Even as he entertained this possibility he was daunted by the thought that her father might have enrolled her to keep a watch on him. Had she reported what he had told her?

As he approached the portico he saw Zilpha sitting in a comfortable wicker chair sipping a glass of lemonade. It riled him to see her relaxed, enjoying the peace and tranquillity while his sisters were locked up in a stinking gaol among the riff-raff of Whitby.

'Hello, Zilpha,' he said with an edge to his voice as he neared the steps.

Startled, for the grass had muffled his footsteps, she shot upright in her chair and turned to see who spoke.

'Mr Mitchell!' Her expression sharpened when she saw his hostile expression. 'What's wrong?'

'As if you didn't know.' He sneered at what he thought was an attempt to play the innocent.

'Of course, your sisters. I'm sorry about what happened,' she said, her tone placatory.

'Are you? I wonder. What part did you play in it?'

She was hurt by the charge but there was fire in her reply. 'Don't you accuse me. I did nothing. They were caught in the building.'

'Who alerted your father that we are descended from the Wades?' He looked at her with disgust.

'I did no such thing. I'm no informer.'

'You got information from me while pretending to like me, then passed it on to your father who, because of that knowledge, was alerted to what might happen. After that Alice and Lucy were watched, otherwise how was it that two estate workers were in the vicinity of the office at the alum works?'

'You're saying my father set those men to spy on your sisters?'

'Yes.'

'What would he do that for? What was he suspicious of?'

'You know as well as I. He was frightened that we might discover the truth of what happened between our great-grandfathers. Something he wants kept hidden.'

'Nonsense.' The word came automatically out of loyalty to her father but some doubt had been implanted in her mind. Her conversations with her father, the times when the past was related to the present, her talks with Robert, all began to pose misgivings. 'Your sisters shouldn't have broken into the office,' she said defensively. 'That was a punishable offence.'

'It didn't deserve transportation to Australia.'

'That's how the magistrate saw it. It's his decision.'

'No doubt it pleases you. Lucy out of the way so the path to Mark is clear for you.'

She flinched inwardly at his remark but drew herself up and answered, 'He always was mine.'

Robert gave a snort of mockery but at the same time he was annoyed that this interview was not turning out as he wanted. 'I came here hoping you might intercede with your father on behalf of my sisters but I see I was mistaken. You're as bad as he is.'

Zilpha was hurt but she would not show it.

'Confront him,' she challenged haughtily.

'He'd deny everything and have me detained on the spot to suffer the same fate as my sisters. I suppose you'll go and fetch him now and have me arrested.'

'I can't,' she returned. 'He's in Scarborough.'

'But you would have done if he had been here.' He rejected with disdain the protestation he saw she was about to make. 'You're a de Northby. You'd do nothing to help a Wade. I'm sorry I ever bothered to come here.'

She saw hate in his parting look and she regretted that she had experienced any sort of interest in him.

When he reached Whitby Robert was met was solemn faces and despondency from his mother, Mr Palmer and Paul.

'What's the matter?' he queried with concern as he looked from one to the other. He saw his mother's eyes dampen.

'Your sisters will start their transportation in two days' time,' explained Mr Palmer.

'What?' Robert stared disbelievingly at them. 'So soon?'

'I am afraid so. Did you have any luck with Miss de Northby?'

Robert shook his head. 'No, and her father's away in Scarborough. He won't be back for two days. How do you know they are being moved in two days?'

'I saw Alice and Lucy,' said Paul.

'How? Are they all right?' asked Robert eagerly.

Paul quickly acquainted him with what had happened.

'Mr Palmer, what can we do?' There was desperation in his question. He needed assurance from the older man that the situation would not be allowed to stagnate.

'We'll do everything we can,' replied Mr Palmer thoughtfully. 'But I want you two young men to promise me that you will not do anything rash or stupid. We don't want to fall foul of the law. I will certainly go and see the magistrate again tomorrow. He may be in a more congenial frame of mind.'

'I doubt it,' replied Robert. 'De Northby will have told him what to do.'

'We don't know that, Robert,' Mr Palmer pointed out, though privately he was inclined to agree. 'We've got to explore every possibility. We'll start with the magistrate. I'll try to persuade him that we are hoping for evidence to justify the girls' action.'

'If Paul was able to bribe the gaoler couldn't we persuade him to accidentally lose his keys?' suggested Robert.

306

Robert caught the look in Mr Palmer's eyes and knew he had gone too far. 'Don't even think of it again, young man. We've enough to do to try to gain your sisters' release legally. Nothing must jeopardise that.'

'I'm sorry, sir,' Robert apologised. 'A foolish notion. Maybe if you fail with the magistrate I could persuade Miss Zilpha to go with me to see her father in Scarborough.'

'That's a possibility,' agreed Mr Palmer, 'but you would run a risk so let's see what we can achieve in Whitby first.'

Mrs Mitchell looked fixedly at her son. 'You pay heed to Mr Palmer, Robert.' She turned to Paul. 'You too, Paul. I'm grateful for all you've done and are doing but please don't risk anything again.'

For the next hour, under Mr Palmer's guidance, they discussed and marshalled all the facts they knew from the time of the dispute, searching for something they might have missed which would help to find a solution. But they failed.

Finally Mr Palmer leaned back in his chair. 'I wonder if it would prove useful if I went to see Mr Mark Cossart's great-grandmother? There's a chance she might have thought of something since Alice and Lucy visited her.'

They were considering this line of approach when the landlord came to them. 'I'm sorry to interrupt you gentlemen, ma'am.' He inclined his head to Mrs Mitchell. 'There's a gentleman here from Ormston and Peckett, solicitors, asking to see Mr Palmer.'

A ripple of excitement ran through the friends. 'Show him in,' said Mr Palmer.

As the landlord hurried away, Paul said, 'One of the

firms who had not completed their search for a document. Maybe they've found something?'

'They must have, otherwise why be here?' said Robert.

'Calm, boys, calm,' said Mr Palmer, but he felt his nerves flutter with hope.

Mrs Mitchell said nothing. She felt weak. Was there going to be news which would help the release of her daughters? That was all she wanted. She watched the entrance to the room. The landlord returned escorting a man of medium build, slightly stooped at the shoulders. His eyes, which were bright and full of good humour, revealed a man of interest. He was neatly dressed in black trousers and a tail coat. His shoes were highly polished, betokening a man who was careful of his appearance as behove one engaged in a respected profession.

Such was his aura of discreet confidentiality that Mrs Mitchell felt sure he was bringing good news in the envelope he was carrying.

'Mr Palmer, Mr Peckett.' The landlord introduced them and left the group to become acquainted.

Their greetings exchanged, Mr Palmer introduced Mrs Mitchell and Robert. Mr Peckett bowed politely to her and shook hands with Robert. 'You may already have met Paul Smurthwaite,' added Mr Palmer.

'Indeed I have. He was most insistent that this enquiry was of some urgency when I told him that we had not had time to look into it.' He hesitated and sent a querying glance at Mr Palmer.

'It is perfectly all right, Mr Peckett, you may speak openly here for we are all involved in this matter. And please do sit down.'

'Let me apologise for not dealing with this on receipt of your letter but we have been busy, and on first reading your request nothing occurred to me.' He gave a little smile. 'Of course you were dealing with matters before my time. But after this young man,' he indicated Paul, 'called a second time, I recalled my father telling me that there was a box of old documents, mostly from my grandfather's days, in the office attic. They were to be held until further instructions were received. Apparently such instructions were expected fairly soon after the deposit, but, as time went on and none were forthcoming, the documents were stored. I had them brought down from the attic and I found an envelope with the name Mr Jacob Wade written on it.'

Everyone gasped and exchanged charged glances.

'And?' prompted Mr Palmer.

Mr Peckett hesitated. 'Sir, as you will appreciate the document contained in here,' he tapped the envelope, 'is private. Not only that, there is a letter attached which I think must have been sent to our office at a later date with a request that it be placed with the document. Now that letter makes some serious accusations of a very personal nature. I do not think I should hand it over without being completely reassured that it is absolutely necessary. May I ask you, sir, for what purpose do you wish to see the contents of this envelope?'

This sounded serious. The tension round the table deepened. A letter! Was this what they had been hoping for? Something which would explain everything?

Before Mr Palmer could speak, Rebecca burst out, 'Mr Peckett, my two daughters are in prison here and will be transported to Australia unless we can do something and

309

I think whatever is in that envelope will help us. Please let us see the items.'

Mr Peckett was moved by the pleading in her voice. He gazed at the envelope as if considering his position. He looked up at Rebecca with sympathy and understanding but said gently, 'I'm sorry, Mrs Mitchell, but I don't see what your daughters' imprisonment has to do with the contents of this envelope. From what I have read there can be no connection.' He looked at Mr Palmer for an explanation.

'Let me tell you the whole story,' the attorney from Newcastle offered. 'Then maybe you will revise your judgement.'

Mr Peckett listened carefully without interruption as Mr Palmer told him everything that had any relevance from the moment Isaac Mitchell uttered his last words.

Silence descended on the group around the table when Mr Palmer finished his story. Everyone watched Mr Peckett, willing him to make the decision which would end their suspense.

The Whitby attorney pondered Mr Palmer's story and then nodded. 'What you have told me explains quite a lot. Whether what I have here will obtain the release of your daughters, Mrs Mitchell, is doubtful.' He saw disappointment cloud her face and quickly added, 'It might but it's not certain. Your daughters were obviously hoping to find a document like this and did commit a crime in so doing. So that charge may have to stand in spite of what these papers reveal. But there is a chance that with these as evidence the magistrate might look a little more favourably on your daughters. Who was the magistrate?'

'Mr Hope,' replied Mr Palmer.

Mr Peckett raised his eyebrows. 'A hard man. Very rarely does he move from his original verdict.'

'Could he be in the pay of Mr de Northby? We think he is afraid of what we might discover and wants it kept suppressed,' Robert blurted out.

Mr Peckett adopted a severe expression. 'Young man, you need to be careful of your accusations.' Robert looked sheepish, wishing he had kept quiet but then he felt easier when Mr Peckett went on in a more amenable tone. 'I can understand why you think that, for Mr de Northby does carry some power around Whitby.' He lapsed into silence, pondering as he looked at the envelope.

Mr Palmer signalled to the others to say nothing. A wrong word could sway Mr Peckett's judgement against them. The atmosphere was taut.

Mr Peckett looked up and silently cast his gaze around the table. 'Very well, I will let you see these items.' He felt relief replace the tension. 'But I must insist that if they or the information contained therein are to be used for any purpose I must be informed and indeed insist that I should be present if they are produced in any confrontation.'

'Certainly,' agreed Mr Palmer without hesitation.

'Very well, sir. You should read this document of agreement first.' He drew out a parchment which was folded to make four foolscap pages. He slid them across the table to Mr Palmer.

He picked them up and read them silently, aware that all eyes were on him. When he had finished he laid them down thoughtfully, then said, 'They are legal and correct, don't you agree, Mr Peckett?'

'Indeed, sir. Both parties have signed, the signatures being witnessed by my grandfather who drew up the document, and by two men who worked in the office.'

'This,' Mr Palmer explained, 'is an agreement between Jacob Wade and Peter de Northby that all Jacob's interest in the alum works be passed to Peter.'

'And that's it?' asked Robert.

'Jacob was paid a sum of money, which incidentally I consider was totally inadequate for what Peter de Northby was getting.' He glanced at Mr Peckett for confirmation.

Mr Peckett nodded. 'I agree. But Jacob Wade must have consented to the sum – he signed the agreement.'

'You said there was a letter,' prompted Mr Palmer.

Mr Peckett was already withdrawing the paper from the envelope. He passed it to Mr Palmer without comment. Mr Palmer gave it a cursory glance and decided he would read it aloud.

'There is no address on this letter so it looks as if the writer did not want anyone to know where he was living.' He flicked to the signature on the last page. 'It is signed Jacob Wade.' He turned back to the first page. 'It is dated seventeen seventy-one, that is one year after that agreement was made and therefore presumably a year after he and his family left the area. I will read it to you.'

' "This note is attached to the agreement between myself, Jacob Wade, and Peter de Northby, who were partners in an enterprise concerned with the manufacture of alum at Ravenscar, in order that the truth behind the concluding of this agreement may be known to whichever of my descendants comes into its possession.

' "I have no doubt that this agreement would be upheld

312

in a court of law for it is signed and sealed by both parties in the presence of witnesses, but there may be sympathetic readers of the truth who would uphold a rightful justice to my family.

' "Be that as it may, the truth must be told.

' "I, Jacob Wade, had no real interest in nor talent for the progress of the alum industry. My heart lay with the sea, but to please my father who wished for the family name and presence in the industry to continue, I forewent my own desires and took the part of the obedient son. Let me say that this did not inhibit me when it came to putting all my effort and attention into the work. In fact I made some deals which were excellent for the business, outshining Peter de Northby who was scolded by his father for missing equally important deals. This led to a sense of jealousy and, looking back, may have been the start of all the trouble.

' "When our fathers died Peter and I continued the partnership. The sense of power he now felt led him to countermand some of my decisions in spite of my protests. I was tempted to sell my share of the business to him, in fact he pressed me to do so on more than one occasion, but remembering my father's wishes I did not.

' "If I had known what was to happen it would have been better if I had done so. I could easily have turned my back on a position in which I was not truly happy and which was becoming less and less satisfying due to the growing hostility towards me from Peter de Northby.

' "It was shortly after my thirtieth birthday that the events which I am about to describe took place.

' "For once I thwarted a deal he was about to make. It

would not have enhanced the reputation of the firm. He was furious and the confrontation led to a terrible row. Harsh words were exchanged and when we parted I felt that his attitude towards me now contained a degree of enmity. At the time I dismissed it as fanciful thinking.

' "I learned later that his fury at my countermanding the deal was heightened because he had involved some of his friends, may I say gambling friends, and it had made him look foolish in their eyes.

' "I sensed in him a greater desire to have the alum works to himself, but I was not prepared for the lengths to which he went.

' "One day he confronted me with book entries which showed that I had been taking money from the business, supposedly for my own use. I emphatically denied this but there was my signature on a number of withdrawals. I had no answer to this except that of forgery but I could not prove it. To any outsider the evidence was irrefutable especially when our manager, Frederick Wilkins, came forward with evidence of how he discovered a discrepancy in the accounts which could only be due to the money I had supposedly withdrawn.

' "At the time I was not suspicious of Wilkins' part in the affair but it came to me afterwards that he was in the ideal position to carry out instructions supposedly from de Northby. Wilkins was responsible for keeping the books. Though they were always available to the partners, we tended to leave that side of the business to him, regarding him as a trustworthy fellow.

' "My first instinct was to fight, but the more I realised the evidence against me was strong, the more I understood the scandal there would be and the slur it would leave on my family.

' "Therefore when Peter de Northby offered me a way out which would appear to others as a legitimate sale of my share of the business I took it. He used the lever of the possible scandal to the full and gave me very little for my share.

' "If this letter helps to achieve some retribution for my descendants then it will have been worth the time spent in writing it." '

Mr Palmer paused, looked up, and added, ' "Signed, Jacob Wade." '

For a moment there was silence as the meaning of what the letter revealed was digested by the listeners.

'So there was something behind Father's words,' said Robert, preoccupied with his thoughts. He started and a note of excitement came to his voice. 'We can confront de Northby with this.'

'Will it get my daughters back?' queried Rebecca hopefully.

Mr Palmer drew a deep breath. 'In a word, no. This has no bearing on what your daughters did, except that they were hoping to find a copy of the agreement. The document in itself does nothing to lighten their case. But I might just be able to use it to get a stay of implementation.'

'You can't show that letter to the magistrate,' protested Mr Peckett.

'No, but I can wave it at him saying that it is evidence which has come to light and coupled with more we are hoping to get he should suspend his sentence for the time being.'

Mr Peckett looked doubtful. 'Mr Hope is a hard man.'

'Can't we use it to persuade Mr de Northby to drop his charges?' put in Paul.

'This is only a letter written by an accused man. Wouldn't he try to vindicate himself in this way when he wouldn't challenge openly at the time?'

'But surely . . .' Robert started, only to be interrupted by his employer.

'De Northby would deny its truth. It would be passed off as the writing of an embittered man. We need confirmation of its veracity.'

Robert looked downcast.

'This person Frederick Wilkins mentioned in the letter?' suggested Mr Peckett.

'We know he left for France shortly after the affair,' explained Mr Palmer.

'Does that add credence to the statements in that letter? Does it show that he was involved in something to discredit Jacob Wade?' observed Mr Peckett.

'Even if it does we don't know if he is still in France or even if he is still alive.'

Chapter Sixteen

Mark and David, knowing that they should not waste time, quickened their steps through the Paris streets but at a pace which would not attract attention.

They found the house without too much trouble. It lay on the right-hand side of a small courtyard, an archway giving access from the street. Its unprepossessing façade was repeated in the other fifteen dwellings around the cobbled square.

The dull grey door was opened only to a slit in answer to Mark's knock. An eye peered at him. He saw suspicion.

'Madame Wilkins?' he asked, keeping his voice friendly.

There was hesitation and then the question, 'Who wants her?'

'Monsieur Mark. An Englishman on urgent private business.' He withheld his surname in case the fact it was French brought refusal.

'Wait here.' The door closed.

The two men were uneasy. They knew this interview needed to be concluded quickly and Madame Wilkins alerted to the danger in which they had inadvertently placed her. They glanced around the buildings. All was quiet; only a cat slunk across the cobbles to disappear into an alley which led to the rear of the houses on the opposite side of the courtyard.

Mark's eyes flicked expertly across the windows but he saw no one. The silence was almost disturbing. Moments seemed like hours. He began to thrum the side of his thigh with his fingers.

'Someone just peered out of an upstairs window,' whispered David. 'Corner house opposite. Just a slight curtain movement.'

'Could it be someone placed there by the authorities to keep an eye on Madame Wilkins?'

'Unlikely,' replied David. 'With husband and sons executed she can hardly be a threat to them now.'

'True as far as we know,' agreed Mark, 'but we don't know what connections she still has, nor if . . .'

All further speculation was halted by the opening of the door, wider this time. It was held back by an attractive young woman simply dressed in white blouse and black skirt. She gave them a shy glance and said, 'Mother will see you. Follow me.'

She led the way along the narrow corridor from which stairs rose to the next level. She opened the second door on the right and went inside.

'Mother, the gentlemen to see you.'

They found themselves in a room with the minimum of furniture, a table with four chairs, and two armchairs in one of which a woman, whom they judged to be about sixty, was sitting. Her hair, prematurely greying, was neat and well kept and enhanced features which they saw had once been noble and beautiful. Her face was lined by the hardships which had blighted her recent life, but she had not allowed them to overwhelm her; Mark saw determination not to allow life to overcome her as long as she had someone to live for. He guessed that person was her daughter. He could sense the strong relationship between them as the younger woman stood beside her mother with her hand resting on her shoulder.

'One of you is Monsieur Mark?' Madame Wilkins looked from one to the other.

'I am,' he replied, 'and this is David Hughes.'

Madame Wilkins inclined her head in acknowledgement. 'Have you no surname, young man?' she asked.

'Yes, ma'am. I thought if I gave it you might not see me. It is Cossart.'

'Ah, French. I thought my Louise,' she glanced up at her daughter, 'said you were English.'

'So I am, ma'am. My mother is English, my father French. I lived the first eight years of my life in France. My father foresaw the Revolution and took us to England to my mother's parents. We have lived there ever since.' He thought he had convinced her with these credentials but added to make sure, 'David and I are officers in our army.'

'Then what are you doing here in civilian clothes?' Fear touched Claudette Wilkins' voice and she sought her daughter's hand.

'We were on a special mission,' said Mark.

'I thought you told Louise it was a private matter?'

'It is, ma'am.' He went on quickly so as to dismiss the uncertainty in her mind. 'Did your husband ever talk about his life in England?'

319

'Yes.'

'Was it connected with the alum trade?'

'Yes.'

He was hoping she would be more expansive but he pressed on.

'A place called Ravenscar in particular?'

'Yes.'

Mark sensed he was on the verge of an important discovery. 'I have a friend who is anxious to clear up something which happened about fifty years ago. It is of great importance to her family.'

'What is her name?'

'Lucy Mitchell.' He saw the name meant nothing to her but her expression changed when he added, 'but she is interested in her mother's side of the family and the name is Wade.'

Claudette looked up at her daughter. 'Get the book, please.'

Louise left the room.

'My husband was well off when he came to France. He settled in Senlis a few miles out of Paris. I remember the day he arrived. I was a girl of ten and fascinated by this man because I had never seen an Englishman before.' She gave a little laugh. 'As if he would be something different. He was thirty and I never imagined then that we would fall in love and marry when I was twenty.' She smiled at the recollection. 'I can tell you, monsieur, heads shook. A girl of twenty marrying a man of forty and an Englishman at that. We were immensely happy until the Revolution took him and our sons away, falsely accused as spies because of the English connection.' Her last words were filled with bitterness and hate for those who had taken her family.

Louise returned with a notebook which she handed to her mother.

'About the time Louise was born, Frederick became moody and eventually he told me that his conscience was troubling him about an unsavoury matter in which he had been involved before he left England. I suggested that the only way to clear his mind was to return there but he refused, pointing out that it would mean arrest and prison if he confessed to his part in the affair. I did not want that to happen. We stayed living our lives happily though I knew there were times when his conscience troubled him. The Revolution came and when his arrest was imminent with no possible hope of escape he told me that he had written about the affair and made me promise to do all I could to get to England and see justice was given to the family he had wronged. I never got the chance, for Louise and I were closely watched. The situation is easier now but I would need a permit to leave the country and I would not get one. To try to leave illegally would be fraught with danger and the consequences if caught . . .' She left those to the imagination. 'This is the book. I hope it might help your friend.'

Mark took it gratefully. He skimmed through a couple of pages and realised that what he held was exactly what Lucy wanted. 'This is better than I expected.'

'Then take it, monsieur. I will feel that I have fulfilled Frederick's wish.'

'You are very generous, ma'am.' She dismissed the idea with a wave of her hand. 'Ma'am,' went on Mark quietly,

'I am afraid in looking for you we have inadvertently alerted the authorities.' He saw alarm in the glances exchanged between mother and daughter. He noticed their grips tighten as if each was giving support to the other and trying to give reassurance that all was not lost. He went on to explain quickly what had happened. 'I think you should come to England with us.'

The suddenness of this proposal seemed to bewilder Claudette.

'Your husband asked you to take this book to England. Now you have your chance. And your presence will lend authenticity to its contents.'

'But our lives?' She looked at her daughter for help.

'Mother, what have we to lose? Nothing. We face prison or death when the authorities arrive and accuse us of conniving with English spies.'

'You'll be cared for in England. My family have estates and I know my friend will do all she can to help you after what you will be doing for her. May I say action is urgent? As I explained, those men we left unconscious knew where we were coming.'

'Very well. Louise, a few belongings, one bag each. Monsieur Cossart, you keep the book.'

'Very well, ma'am.'

She nodded and hurried from the room. She and Louise were back in a few moments, each carrying a cloth bag.

'That's all you want?' queried Mark.

'You must travel light on an expedition such as this. I take it we are not travelling at leisure. You will have your escape route planned.' She gave him a serious look which demanded the truth in reply to her question, 'Will we be a hindrance?'

'No, ma'am, you won't.' The conviction in his voice persuaded her.

'Very well.'

'First call, Monsieur Lacroix.'

'Ah, a good friend,' commented Claudette. She started for the door without giving the room a second glance. Her sadness at departing had been left upstairs when she had packed a few belongings. But that sadness was not as marked as it would have been if this had been the house she had shared with her husband.

'We'll be less conspicuous in twos,' Claudette suggested. 'You accompany Monsieur Hughes, Louise.' She glanced at David. 'She knows the way in case you lose sight of us.'

'Let us take your bags,' David offered as he reached out for Louise's.

Mark and Claudette left first and when they had passed under the archway David and Louise followed. As they stepped into the courtyard he cast an anxious glance at the house in the corner. There was no movement of curtains, but he would not have felt the same relief had he known that their departure had been observed from a neighbouring house and that at this moment Charles Gravelet, a ferret of a man, was hurrying through the streets rubbing his hands together at the thought of the praise he would receive from his superior.

Reaching a grey stone building which had once been a club, a meeting place for the Paris aristocracy, he demanded instant access to Citizen Tourney. He was irritated when the guard on the door refused, saying Citizen Tourney was busy.

'I have vital information for him. To hold it back will mean prison for you.'

'Wait,' said the guard and turned to the door. He knocked and opened it.

The man behind the desk broke off in mid-sentence and looked up sharply in annoyance. The two men sitting opposite him looked ill at ease.

'Sorry to interrupt, Citizen, but Gravelet is outside insisting on seeing you.'

Tourney nodded. 'Show him in.' He shot a look at the two men. 'Let's hope this counteracts your stupidity in being outwitted by the two Englishmen.'

Gravelet hurried into the room. His face registered surprise at seeing the two men, whom he knew were among Tourney's best stalkers, looking decidedly uncomfortable.

'Well?' snapped Tourney. 'Speak. It may well concern these two oafs,' he added when Gravelet hesitated.

'Madame Wilkins and her daughter have left with two men. They carried bags, and were clothed as if for a journey.'

'Ah,' Tourney leaned back in his chair. The satisfaction he felt was evident, but it did not dampen his contempt towards the two men. 'You knew the Englishmen were . . .'

'Englishmen?' Gravelet gasped. This was more serious than he had thought.

'Yes. They outwitted these two bunglers. Laid them out. Then when they recovered they came whining to me instead of continuing to Madame Wilkins's. Thankfully you were there, Gravelet, and no doubt will be getting a report from Juin before long.' He saw embarrassment cloud Gravelet's face as he looked down at his worn shoes. 'Gravelet!' he shouted. 'Tell me!'

Gravelet opened his mouth to speak but he floundered.

'Gravelet, where's Juin?' Tourney feared the worst and his anger was already rising.

'I left him in the house in case Madame Wilkins returned.'

Tourney's clenched fist thumped on the desk, making his subordinates jump. 'Fool! Nincompoop! I thought you said they carried bags and were dressed for a journey.'

'That only came to me as I walked here,' he replied sheepishly.

Tourney was not listening. 'Now we'll have to cover every known associate of Madame Wilkins and do it fast.' He went to the door and started yelling orders.

Men scurried, grabbing coats and hats and, immediately they received their instructions, raced from the building. In his present mood no one wanted to cross Citizen Tourney again. Men hastened through the streets of Paris to keep watch on people suspected of anti-government views.

It was this haste that saved the escapees. They were nearing the street where André Lacroix lived when Claudette murmured urgently, 'This way!' She turned into a side street and fell into a quicker pace.

'What is it?' asked Mark. His army training had told him that Claudette had been alarmed by something.

'Agent provocateur. Recognised him.' She glanced back and was relieved to see Louise and David. 'The two men you dealt with must have reported to Monsieur Tourney, head of agents. He's learned we've left and put a watch on all possible contacts.'

'So we can't use our designated route.'

'What was it?' Claudette asked. She had slowed the pace

so that they did not attract undue attention, but she was alert, her eyes everywhere.

'Coach to Caen. There we would be met by Marcel Davout.'

'I do not know him.' There was doubt in her voice.

'He is trustworthy,' Mark reassured her.

'My faith is in you.'

'He would drive us to his house. There we would stay until dark, then make our way to the Baie de la Seine to be picked up.'

Even as she was hearing this information she had been formulating their next move.

'You have money, monsieur?'

'Yes.'

Little more was said as they slipped through the Paris streets until they came to a quieter quarter. They were still a hundred yards from a road junction when Claudette stopped.

'Take the left-hand fork. A short distance on the left-hand side there is a livery stable. Hire a carriage for us. Mention my name. We will be walking along the right-hand fork. Pick us up.'

Mark had already admired the calm composure of this Frenchwoman and knew better than to question her instructions. After all, the lives of her and her daughter were just as much in jeopardy as his.

He walked briskly away and turned the corner without looking back.

Claudette strolled towards the fork, allowing Louise and David to close the gap. She crossed the road at the corner to take the right-hand fork. A casual glance to her left told her that Mark had reached the livery stable.

Behind her Louise and David were puzzled by the fact that Claudette and Mark had split up.

'What do we do now?' queried David. 'Who do we follow?'

'Mother,' came Louise's firm reply.

When they reached the corner David was perturbed by the fact that there was no sign of Mark, but his concern was soon dissipated by Louise.

'Mother has sent him to hire a carriage!' David looked questioningly at her. 'Mother's distant cousin runs a livery stable. I think we'd better get closer to her. There'll be no time to waste when Monsieur Mark arrives.'

She was right. A few minutes later when the rattle of wheels and the creak of leather closed behind them Claudette turned and gave them an urgent wave. They were with her by the time Mark pulled the horse to a halt beside them. They climbed on board as if it was an everyday occurrence so as not to attract too much attention.

'Keep straight on,' ordered Claudette.

'The man who let me have the carriage asked no questions on hearing your name and would take no fee. He sent his love and good wishes.'

Claudette gave a little smile. 'A good man. A distant cousin, so distant the authorities do not know of the relationship, and that has proved useful at certain times, though we had to be discreet about meeting when I was closely watched.'

'We are in your hands, madame. You will have to direct us out of Paris.'

'Citizen Tourney is a shrewd man. He will be all out to stop us for he will see this as an opportunity to enhance his reputation as an arrester of spies and a tracker of enemies of the state. We saw how quickly he had put his men to watch possible contacts. I think he will already have instigated watch at the main exits from Paris and probably some of the minor ones.'

'If he knows he is tracking Englishmen won't he have concentrated on the northern and eastern roads?' put in Louise.

'Quite right,' agreed Claudette. 'I'd already decided that to leave by the west might be less of a hazard.'

'But that will take us much longer,' pointed out David.

'We'll arrive at Monsieur Davout's later than intended but still in time to make your rendezvous.'

Claudette guided them to the west side of the city. She had taken a minor road which she knew swung sharply northwest about five miles from Paris. They had cleared the last of the cottages straggling out from the city and Mark had increased the pace of travel. It was late afternoon, cirrus clouds hazed the bright blue sky. Mark was feeling confident that they had made their escape when they rounded a corner to see their way blocked by four carts and a carriage.

Alarmed, he automatically reined the horse.

'Keep moving,' urged Claudette. 'Don't attract attention by stopping. There's nowhere else to go.'

A sergeant was talking to the driver of the first cart and two soldiers with fixed bayonets were examining its contents.

'Monsieur Tourney has been more thorough than I expected,' said Claudette. She had been sizing up the situation ahead of them. 'We've had a good day out in

Paris. Plenty to drink.' Over her shoulder she said to Louise and David, 'You two are in love, cuddle up, and make it convincing.' She glanced at Mark. 'You're sleepy with drink, the horse knows its way home. Leave the talking to me.'

Louise flung her arms round David's neck and lay back on the seat, dragging him with her. 'I don't mind, monsieur,' she whispered as she drew him into a passionate kiss. David surrendered.

Mark let his head drop forward, but all the time kept an alert lookout from beneath the brim of his hat.

Claudette started to hum a tune and sway gently to its rhythm. She let her eyes glaze over while continuing to take in everything in front of her.

One more cart was allowed to pass and then the carriage came under close scrutiny. Protestations from the occupants caused further delay while the sergeant, annoyed at being challenged, exerted his full authority. There were several snappy exchanges before he allowed the carriage to continue. The next two carts were quickly examined and authorised to move on.

Mark halted his horse at the appointed spot without looking up.

'Good day out, citizen?' queried the sergeant with a knowing grin at the state of the occupants of the vehicle.

'The best, citizen sergeant,' replied Claudette, slurring her words. She bent towards him with narrowed eyes. 'Don't expect the night'll be up to much.' She swayed upright and gave Mark a dig on the shoulder. 'Just look at him,' she said with disgust in her voice, 'falling asleep. Can't hold his liquor.' She swayed towards the sergeant again. 'Like to take his place, citizen sergeant?' She gave a little seductive chuckle.

Mark swayed under Claudette's second derisive push. He grunted, looked at the sergeant with mock bleary eyes and let his head fall forward again.

'Like nothing better,' grinned the sergeant looking meaningfully at Claudette. He was already visualising what a night with her would be like.

'Want us to turf them out, sergeant?' asked one of the soldiers indicating the couple on the back seat.

Louise and David gave the impression that they were oblivious to what was going on.

The sergeant grinned at them. 'Ah, no. I'm a romantic. Pity to part them.' He looked back at Claudette. 'Is that what you had in mind for us?'

'And more,' Claudette promised huskily.

'You go, sergeant, we'll look after things here. It's a quiet road, we might not get any more folk.'

The sergeant hesitated, rubbing his chin thoughtfully.

Claudette eyed him encouragingly.

'Go on,' the second soldier egged him on. 'Maybe if you aren't too long, we could get a turn.' He looked up at Claudette leeringly.

She realised she must continue her charade otherwise the situation might get ugly. 'Why not?' she slurred. 'We live only a couple of miles down the road.'

'Right,' said the sergeant. He stepped up beside Claudette, then stopped and eyed his two men. 'Keep alert, citizens.'

'We will,' they grinned back, anticipating the pleasures of the night ahead.

'On your way,' the sergeant ordered and Mark flicked the reins. The soldiers settled himself beside Claudette and immediately put his arm round her. She almost recoiled from his touch but checked herself in time. His tatty, dirty uniform smelt, his unkempt hair straggled beneath a greasy hat, and she felt like shrinking from the thin pointed nose and wet lips which were already nuzzling her cheek.

Her performance had gained them permission to move on but the result had developed further than she had ever expected. Now they must find a way out of this dilemma. There might be only one way, but she shrank from cold killing.

'Faster.' She gave Mark a dig in the ribs.

Mark obeyed while still feigning doziness.

'Can't wait?' grinned the sergeant.

'The sooner the better,' replied Claudette.

The carriage gained speed. The horse's hooves thrummed on the earth. The wheels crashed over the uneven road, jerking them in their seats.

'Steady,' yelled the sergeant, his eyes widening when he saw the man holding the reins was no longer almost asleep but was completely alert. 'What the . . .' He sensed someone close to his back and a glance over his shoulder revealed the lovers sitting upright with the man's hands threateningly close. Two men, two women! Exactly what they had been told to look out for. He swallowed hard. He could feel the guillotine. 'You!'

'Yes,' replied Claudette. 'I'm sorry, there'll be no fun for you tonight.'

'You bastard!' The sergeant grabbed at the knife in his belt but his hand had hardly closed on it before David dealt him a sharp blow to the head. He reeled sideways. The strike had not been as severe as David had intended and he fought the drop into unconsciousness for he realised it had given him a chance, though it was a dangerous one. He slumped sideways, pushed hard with his legs and plunged from the cart. He hit the ground hard and tumbled down a small embankment to lie face downward in a stream.

Mark started to haul on the reins.

'Keep going,' yelled David. 'He won't get up out of that.'

'Hadn't we better make sure?'

'He was unconscious. If the fall didn't kill him he'll have drowned in that water.'

Mark kept the horse running.

The sergeant's befuddled mind thought the whole world had crashed on him when he hit the ground. The momentum rolled him over and over, then he felt the movement taking him downwards. Wetness closed over him. The sharp contrast of the cold cleared his mind somewhat. He must be face down in the stream by the side of the road. Hold your breath. Lie still. Would they stop? Come back? He heard the carriage still rumbling on. They must think he was dead, killed by the fall or drowned. The sound was diminishing. Were they stopping now? No.

He raised his head slowly and drew air into his lungs with a great sense of relief. Then the enormity of what had happened hit him. The two men and two women they should have detained had fooled him. Citizen Tourney would have his head if he didn't do something about it. Wincing, he stood up and was thankful that no serious damage had been

332

done. His head still spun from the blow, and his body ached from the fall, but there were no bones broken.

After he had scrambled up the embarkment he set off along the road.

The two soldiers with nothing to do at the road block were shocked when they heard shouts of, 'Get the horses! Get the horses!' and saw their sergeant coming towards them at a staggering run.

They knew better than to dally, and ran to the three horses which they had tied to a hedge a few yards from the road. Leading the third animal, they rode towards the sergeant.

The two men stared in amazement at his dishevelled appearance. 'What . . . ?' started one of them as he steadied his horse.

'They were the ones we were supposed to arrest,' snapped the sergeant. 'Tourney will have our heads if we don't do something about it. It's no good stopping here. They'll be using this road to swing round Paris to the coast.' He kicked his horse into a gallop and his two men matched his pace.

The road was deserted. Mark decided to keep the ride fast for a while. The two soldiers would at some time question the prolonged absence of their sergeant when their expected place in Claudette's bed was overdue.

After half an hour, Mark eased the pace. He must not overtire the horse; besides, there were more people dotted about in the fields doing evening work and he did not want to arouse their curiosity.

They made good progress at a more comfortable pace

but Claudette realised that they would not reach their destination until the early hours of the morning if the horse could keep going that long.

'It will be better if we stop for the night,' Claudette commented, 'this horse needs a rest.'

Mark agreed but he was wary of stopping. 'But where? We've got to exercise the utmost caution.'

'We'll turn off this road and find a small village with an inn.'

'Won't four of us arriving in such a place attract attention?' put in David.

'It's risky,' agreed Mark.

'We must divide up,' said Louise. 'Drop David and me outside the village, and we'll walk in. You drive to the next one, then return this way in the morning.'

Mark was finally convinced and two miles further on turned on to a minor road which ran west. The tranquil evening scene with dusk settling over the countryside stood in marked contrast to the inner feelings of the four travellers. Cattle grazed peacefully in lush meadows, orchards showed signs that the apple crop would be good.

The unruffled atmosphere around them relaxed the occupants of the carriage. Their escape from Paris had not brought the hazards they had expected. The men at the road block had been outwitted, the sergeant dealt with and by the time the two soldiers realised something was wrong they would experience difficulty in picking up their trail.

The road dipped. Across the other side of a shallow depression a village was caught by the last rays of the sun momentarily released by the clouds of night.

Mark stopped and studied the landscape.

'It looks a likely place,' commented David. 'And there's another village a couple of miles to the north.' He and Louise descended.

'Be on this road at eight o'clock in the morning,' Mark instructed. 'Good luck.'

'And to you.'

Claudette and Louise did not speak but they exchanged a look of love for each other and a hope that all would be well.

The carriage rumbled forward, leaving David and Louise to walk into the village.

'We must look weary as if we had walked far,' said David, pausing to scuff the toes of his shoes, loosen his cravat, slap his hat in the side of the road and rub his clothes with dust. Louise saw the wisdom of his actions and did likewise.

By the time they reached the first cottage they could see the carriage had cleared the village and was moving along the ridge to the north.

Some buildings were in need of repair while others, in marked contrast, looked well maintained. At one an elderly man made the last sweep with his rake before retiring indoors. He looked up on hearing footsteps and passed the time of day. David and Louise smiled but did not stop.

The road they were on led into a small square with houses on three sides and a shop, now closed, and an inn on the other. The grey stonework did nothing to lift the gloom which was rapidly settling as the sun sank out of sight. A sign, creaking on a rusty bar, procaimed the inn with the grand name of The Musketeer.

They found themselves in a large oblong room with a

low ceiling, its beams dark, its windows already shuttered for the night. Four lanterns hung from the beams in the main body of the room and at the long wooden table which served as a bar counter a heavily built man was concentrating on lighting a fifth lamp.

He looked up from his task and stared at the newcomers with his one eye, his right being covered by a black patch below which an ugly gash marked his cheek.

David wondered how he had received it. From the revolutionaries or in the act of promoting their cause? He knew they would have to be extremely cautious.

'Good evening, monsieur. We are weary travellers. Would you have a room we could take for the night?' asked David pleasantly.

The man eyed them suspiciously. It was not often they got strangers in these parts. 'It's possible,' he replied half grudgingly as if he did not want his routine upset. He shouted over his shoulder, 'Marie, Marie.'

A thin woman dressed in black came into the room. A hessian apron was tied around her waist. Her straight hair was drawn to a tight bun at the back. Her face was gaunt with a pointed nose and her eyes lacked life.

'Visitors for the night. Give them the back room,' the man ordered gruffly.

'Yes, Pierre.' She nodded at Louise and David. 'Come with me.' She picked up a lantern and led the way up some narrow stairs. At the top she opened a door to a room, neat, though sparsely furnished with a washstand on which there was a bowl and a ewer, a chest of drawers and a bed covered with a patchwork quilt.

'Will this be suitable?' she asked.

'Yes, thank you,' replied Louise, making a play of being tired. 'That bed looks so inviting.'

'You have come far?'

'Rouen. We go to visit my uncle in Chartres and then on to Orléans,' replied Louise.

'You would like something to eat?'

'Oh yes please.'

As soon as Marie had gone David turned down the lamp and moved to the only window. There was still sufficient light outside for him to see a cobbled yard on the opposite side of which was a building which he judged from the half doors to be the stables. He closed the curtains, turned up the lamp again and surveyed the room.

'You take the bed and I'll sleep on the floor,' he said.

'You'll do no such thing,' she said in a voice which brooked no nonsense. 'You'll need a good night's sleep to be fresh in the morning. We do not know what tomorrow holds for us.'

'But,' David started.

'You object to sharing a bed with me?' She looked coy before putting on a hurt expression.

'Er . . . not at all, Louise, but . . .'

'Buts again. You do not want to finish what we started in the carriage thanks to those soldiers?' There was a teasing twinkle in her eyes which set David's nerves tingling so that he could not refuse.

'I'd like nothing better,' he said with a concentrated gaze of admiration.

'Then that is settled,' said Louise and turned her attention to her bag.

* * *

The danger which hung over them had heightened their desire to seize life and wring from it all the ecstasy they could. Every joy was to be taken while it was possible. Now they lay contentedly in each other's arms and the world of intrigue and violence seemed far removed from the peaceful inn in this tiny French village.

'What will happen to us when we reach England?' asked Louise, quietly running her fingertips up and down his arm.

'That will be for Mark to decide after he has seen how things turn out in Yorkshire,' replied David.

She gave him a playful tap. 'You and me, I mean, silly.'

'Oh, well, I suppose we'll say goodbye,' he answered gravely.

Louise shot up in bed and looked down at him. Her eyes were wide. 'You do not like what we have had? I did not please you? You do not want more?' The questions raced off her lips.

He stared at her for a moment, making his serious expression cast more doubts in her mind. But before she could voice them he started laughing. 'You look so tempting when you are annoyed.' He grabbed her by the shoulders and pulled her down to him. 'Of course we'll be together.'

Her face broke into a broad smile and she kissed him passionately.

Ten minutes later, David was alerted by a noise different to the hum of conversation which had come from the bar as customers came and went. This one was the clop of horses' hooves in the stable yard.

'A moment, Louise,' he whispered and slid from her arms. He crossed to the window where he viewed the scene below from the edge of the curtain.

Figures moved across the cobbles. The first one carried two lanterns. He recognised Pierre's bulk. He was followed from the end of the inn by three men leading horses. The soldiers? He couldn't see them clearly. They couldn't be. He must be mistaken. But he waited. They moved into the stables. Out of earshot, David eased the window slightly open. Maybe he could hear a snatch of conversation when they returned.

'What is it?' the whisper came from behind him.

He turned. 'Quiet.' His voice was low but Louise could tell from the tone that she had to exercise the utmost caution. She lay still, anxious to know what had aroused David's attention.

The minutes passed. The men must be seeing to their horses. Then a light appeared, carried by Pierre. He paused in the yard. A man came into view. The light fell across his face. The sergeant! David stifled his reaction. How had he survived? How had he managed to follow them? The other two men came from the stable. David fought to control his feelings. This was no time for panic. Words drifted up to him, catching and concentrating his attention.

'Seen any strangers this evening?' the sergeant asked.

'Two. They're here now. Young man and young woman.' He gave a little chuckle. 'I'd say they were newly married, eager to have a bed for the night.'

'Only two?'

'Yes.'

'See any more?'

'No.'

'These two, did they say where they were from?'

'Told my wife they were from Rouen on their way to Chartres and Orléans. You looking for more?'

339

'Four, out of Paris.'

'You expect them to come through this village?' Pierre showed surprise.

'Yes. We know they came this way. I've been after them ever since they broke through my checkpoint. They were in a carriage, which made them more conspicuous, people notice things. They were last seen turning on to the road to here. You saw no carriage?'

'No.'

The sergeant grunted.

Just before they passed out of David's hearing and into the inn he heard the sergeant say, 'We'll sleep here the night, chairs downstairs will do. We'll question the two strangers in the morning. If they've come from Rouen they might have seen a carriage with four people.'

The words drifted away.

David stayed, still listening to the footsteps below, followed by increased sound as more voices joined in.

He went and sat down beside Louise.

'What is it?' she asked.

'The sergeant and his soldiers.'

'Oh, my God.' Fear tinged her voice. 'What can we do? How have they found us?'

'They haven't. They don't know we're here. Pierre said he thought we were newly married.'

Louise gave a little giggle. 'Near enough.'

'We must leave here,' said David.

'How? They'll see us.'

'Wait a minute.' He went to the window and peered out. His quick examination over, he returned to her. 'We can drop out of that window. It's not too high. I'll go first,

340

you throw the bag down and then I'll catch you. We'll take their horses so they can't pursue us.' His eyes clouded with concern. 'You do ride?' he asked hopefully.

'Mother's relation where Mark got the carriage taught me.'

'Good. We'll get ready and then wait until things are quiet downstairs.'

They dressed quickly, packed their belongings and sat down to wait, listening to the noises below.

The night drew on. David and Louise became restive. Was there to be no respite in the drinking? Louise was growing more and more anxious, for she knew their fate should they be caught. If Mother hadn't got involved with these Englishmen they could still have been living quietly and safely, though under a certain surveillance from the authorities in Paris. She then chided herself for such thoughts. Her mother had seen this as the right thing to do and had never considered the risk. She needed all the support she could give her. Besides, she wouldn't have met David; but at this moment the priority was to escape the attention of the soldiers and warn her Mother and Monsieur Mark.

A door banged. Footsteps scrunched across the yard. They faded round the end of the building. The door crashed again. More footsteps, this time accompanied by some indistinguishable words. The intensity of the noise below had diminished considerably. Now there was only a slight hum of conversation.

Another uneasy half-hour passed and then they heard footsteps on the stairs. There was a low exchange of words, the noise of a sneck and the closing of a door.

'Landlord and his wife coming to bed,' whispered David.

The voices below gradually faded and a few minutes later snores signalled the time for David and Louise to take their chance.

He left some money as payment for their lodging and crossed to the window to look out. Half the yard was saturated with the deep shadow cast by the inn. The moon bathed the stable block in a pale light. He eased the window open as far as it would go. He swung his leg over the windowsill and turned until he was hanging by his arms.

'Come out the same way,' he whispered.

Louise nodded.

David dropped to the ground. He glanced round quickly then held up his arms. First Louise dropped the bag out to him, then David braced himself as she released her hold. He staggered as he took the force of her fall but he held her. A tense moment while they listened passed and then they crossed to the stable.

They were thankful that the landlord had left a lantern. It was low but rather than risk turning it higher they managed with its dim light to saddle the three horses. With everything ready, David made a quick survey outside. Satisfied that no one stirred, he took the reins of two horses and led the way, keeping to a slow pace to minimise the sound until they were clear of the yard.

They mounted their horses and, leading the third, rode out of the village at a walking pace, curbing their desire to put as much distance between themselves and the soldiers as quickly as possible. Careful checking assured them that nothing had disturbed the sleeping villagers.

David gradually quickened their speed, formulating a

feasible plan of action to contact Mark and Claudette on reaching the next village.

They passed some dilapidated cottages with roofs falling in, timbers stark in the moonlight. A mile further on they came to a small hamlet of a few cottages straggling along the roadside.

'No inn! Where can they be?' The concern in Louise's voice begged David to come up with an answer.

David tried to put himself in Mark's place as he checked the restless movements of his horse. Mark's instructions had been that they would be picked up in the morning along the road where they had been dropped. That meant that Mark and Claudette would have to return this way. Was it likely that they would have gone to the next village, not knowing how far it was? Could they have found accommodation elsewhere in this hamlet?

'We must find them, David. When those soldiers see their horses have gone they'll realise it's us at once.'

'I know, my love.' He started to turn his horse. 'Come on, I have an idea.' He led the way quietly back through the hamlet.

Louise was concerned that they were riding back towards potential danger but she stifled her desire to protest. She knew she must trust David's judgement.

When they reached the dilapidated cottages David left Louise to hold his horse's reins and walked towards the ruined buildings.

He moved cautiously along the side of the first cottage to the back. He paused at the corner, listening intently. The only sound came from the rustle of leaves as a gentle breeze soughed through nearby trees. He stepped round the corner and stopped. Excitement gripped him. His supposition had paid off. In the deep shadows he could make out the shape of a carriage. No doubt about it, this was the one in which he had ridden from Paris. Mark and Claudette must be in one of the cottages.

He eased past a door hanging precariously from its hinges. He looked into a room on his right and saw a horse, no doubt brought in through the hole in the wall at the front of the building. He slipped outside to find the door of the next cottage. It gave a little and grated on the ground as he opened it. He moved inside and entered a room on his left.

The deep shadows at the back were accentuated by the moonlight which filtered into the room past the odd pieces of tattered sacking draped across the two front glassless windows.

Two figures, one on each side of the room, lay huddled on the earth floor.

'Mark!' David's whisper was sharp.

Mark was already awake. He had slept lightly and the first movement into the cottage had alerted him that there was an intruder.

'David! What brings you here?' He was bewildered and alarmed by his friend's presence.

Before he could answer Claudette's sleepy voice came from across the room. 'What is it? What's the matter?'

'It's David,' replied Mark.

'Where's Louise?' she asked anxiously.

'She's outside with the horses,' David quickly reassured her.

'Horses?' asked Mark in surprise.

David quickly explained what had happened and before he had finished Mark and Claudette had gathered their things together.

'We must go away from here now, as far as we can before daylight.'

'But the carriage horse has no saddle,' she pointed out.

'I'll ride that,' said Mark. 'Help me, David. Madame, you go to Louise, she'll be getting anxious.'

She hurried away, leaving the two men to make the final preparations.

Mark let Claudette be their guide and she led the way unerringly, travelling in a northwesterly direction to join the Paris-Caen road, where, though it was still the early hours of the morning, they assumed the role of a group of amiable travellers, whenever they met anyone on the road.

The eastern horizon was beginning to lighten when Caen came in sight and, in territory more familiar to him, Mark took over as leader. He guided them east of the town where, with the sky brightening quickly as the sun rose, Marcel Davout's house came in sight.

Halting the party where there was suitable cover he scouted the area around the house. Satisfied that all was well he signalled his friends to join him. By the time they reached him he was being welcomed by Marcel.

'I expected you before this,' he said. 'I was worried but thank God you are safe.' He looked beyond him in surprise when he saw two females and the unexpected mode of travel.

'We ran into trouble in Paris,' Mark said. 'Let me introduce you to Madame Claudette Wilkins and her daughter Louise. It is imperative that I get them to England.'

Marcel ushered them inside his house where Mark quickly explained what had happened.

'You are picked up tonight?' Marcel asked.

'Yes.'

'Then you can rest for the day. No doubt you'll be ready for it after your night's ride. But first you need food.'

'What about the horses?' asked Mark.

'I suggest that you take them with you. It will be dark. Release them in different places and let them run. The saddles, leave with me. I will bury them.'

Mark nodded. 'You're a good man, Marcel. You will not be forgotten.'

The sergeant yawned and stretched his aching limbs. His head felt thick and he was beginning to wish that he hadn't consumed so much wine the night before, but who could refuse such a pleasant landlord?

He scratched his stubbled chin and pushed himself upright in the chair which had served as a bed. He groaned, stretched once more, and blinked. His gaze settled on his two subordinates still stretched out in sleep. He stood up and, remembering that there were two people upstairs whom they had to investigate, gave them both a hefty kick on their feet.

Reluctantly, cursing, they clambered to their feet, scratching at their chests and arms while bemoaning the fact that their heads were not as clear as they should be.

A few moments later, with the night's drinking still heavy on them, they followed their sergeant up the stairs.

The noise had attracted the attention of the landlord who, seeing the condition of the soldiers and knowing what they were about, deemed it wiser to keep out of the way.

The sergeant knocked at the door of the room which had been occupied by Louise and David. On receiving no reply he hammered with his clenched fist. When there was still no response he went in to find the room empty. He saw the money David had left, and that and the open window left him in no doubt about the former occupants of the room. His loud curse resounded off the walls.

'The stables, quick,' he yelled to his two men, and pushed roughly past them, cursing them for being in the way.

They clattered down the stairs and out into the cobbled yard followed by the landlord, who had now come to see what all the commotion was about. They stormed into the stables to pull up short. The horses had gone.

The sergeant turned on the landlord. 'Did you hear anything during the night?'

'Nothing, nothing,' came the quick denial.

'Who were those two?'

'I don't know,' replied the landlord. 'They arrived wanting a room. I ask no questions. I want no trouble.'

'There were only two of them? You saw no one else?'

'No one.'

He strode out of the yard to the front of the inn and looked around almost as if he was hoping to see them, yet knowing they would be far away by now.

'Something the matter?' A voice broke into his thoughts. He looked round to see an elderly man nodding a greeting to the landlord.

'Did you see any strangers yesterday evening?' snapped the sergeant.

'Yes.'

'Who?'

'I was doing a last bit of gardening before it was too dark when a man and woman driving a carriage came by. Then a couple walking.'

The sergeant let out a savage cry heavenwards. If only he had carried out his investigation last night he would have had his prisoners and been a hero in the sight of Citizen Tourney. Now there would be only one outcome. He shuddered at the thought.

'Did you see which way the carriage went?' He put the question automatically, even though he knew the answer would be useless to him.

'Through the village and then they turned north.'

The sergeant grunted his thanks. 'Come on,' he barked to his two men.

Beyond the houses he stopped and eyed them both. Having served with them since the Revolution, he thought he knew them well enough to make what would appear to be an outrageous suggestion. 'We've no chance of catching them, they could be anywhere. We'll be interrogated, why did we leave our post, how we lost our horses, there'll be too many questions. Do you feel like going back to Paris to face Citizen Tourney?' As he put the question he drew his right hand sharply across his throat.

The two men shuddered, knowing they could finish on the guillotine, even though the sergeant was ultimately responsible for their inefficiency. They shook their heads.

'Then I suggest we disappear in the countryside, each sworn to keep the secret of what happened.'

* * *

The sea lapped gently on the beach. Four people stared into the darkness, thankful that clouds still covered the moon, just as they had on their walk to the appointed place.

Little had been said. Though they all felt that safety was within their grasp these were tense and taut moments, when trust in each other was essential.

'There!' Louise's gasp was low.

Mark had seen the light – a pinprick, visible and immediately gone. He stooped to the lantern sheltered in a hollow in the sand, lit it and raised it so that its light could be seen only from the sea. He lowered it. Blackness. Then an answer for the briefest of moments. He extinguished the lantern and buried it.

They waited. Watching.

The faint dip of oars into water. A shape darker than the surrounding night. A boat running into the shore. Mark started forward, followed by the others. The vessel grounded. Not a word was spoken as David and one of the sailors helped Claudette and Louise into the boat. Mark and David pushed it away from the beach and, as it floated free, clambered on board. Oars dipped into the water and were pulled strongly to send it skimming across the water to the ship. Preparations to sail immediately the passengers were on board were already under way.

Mark climbed the rope ladder first and was greeted warmly by the captain.

'Sir, I have two more passengers for you.'

Mark helped Claudette and then Louise on board, then said, 'Sir, may I present Madame Wilkins and her daughter.'

The captain bowed. 'It is a pleasure to have you on

board, madame, mademoiselle.' He called over his shoulder, 'Casey!'

A sailor stepped smartly forward. 'Aye, aye, sir.'

'Take these ladies to my cabin.'

'Aye, aye, sir.' Casey took the bags and led the way aft.

'The ladies, sir . . .'

The captain held up his hand to stop Mark continuing. 'I may wonder who they are but I need no explanation for their presence. You have your reasons for bringing them. My orders are to pick you up and take you back to England. Let us make a good voyage.'

Chapter Seventeen

Mr Palmer, with Robert beside him, faced Mr Hope across the magistrate's desk. He had frowned when they were announced by his clerk and he was still frowning as they sat down. He saw the attorney from Newcastle as a threat to his comfortable position in Whitby. He was able to do favours for the right people in order to make his life a little more luxurious. He wanted no outsider upsetting his 'arrangements'.

'Mr Palmer, if you are here again about these two girls, I will not and cannot change my mind nor alter my punishment. Their crime merited transportation and . . .'

'Mr Hope,' he interrupted, 'I have a right to be heard.' He held up the agreement between Jacob Wade and Peter de Northby, folded so that Hope could not see what it was, and motioned with it to emphasise his words. 'I have here evidence to exonerate the Misses Mitchell.'

Hope had his doubts about this statement. The girls had been caught in the office where they had no right to be.

How could there be evidence to prove otherwise? He was suspicious of Mr Palmer's allegation.

The attorney noted it and added, 'I agree with what you are thinking, that they were caught on the premises having been seen to enter illegally, but what I have here will show that they had a perfectly good reason for what they did and that their objective could not have been achieved any other way.'

'Then let me see it so I can judge.' He still looked sceptical as he held out his hand.

'I'm sorry, I cannot do that at this moment,' replied Mr Palmer, who went on calmly in spite of Mr Hope's look of triumph. 'I am expecting another piece of evidence which, linked with this, will prove beyond any doubt that the girls had a perfectly legitimate reason for being in that office. This paper would not give you the whole picture but it is sufficient for me to insist that you hold the punishment in abeyance.'

The magistrate still thought Mr Palmer's assertions were dubious but misgivings had been sown in his mind. Dare he oppose this man? He was an attorney who could exert some authority which could jeopardise his whole career. If he went along with his request he would incur the wrath of de Northby, an influential man who would not trust him with future lucrative favours.

'Well, I don't know. Sentence has been passed.' He drew the words out slowly, playing for time, considering his options.

Mr Palmer looked at Robert. 'When do you think we'll get confirmation of this evidence, Robert?'

'Well, sir, it seems certain within the week,' he replied, having been primed for such a question.

Mr Palmer plunged in. 'There you are, Mr Hope. Surely a stay of execution, as you might put it, would not be amiss for a week?'

The magistrate saw his chance. Agree and he would appease this interfering attorney. He would be seen to be doing what he could to help. After all, a week was not long, surely Mr de Northby could not take umbrage at that. The girls would still be transported.

'Very well, I'll issue orders for the girls to be held in Whitby for a further week.'

'Thank you,' replied Mr Palmer gratefully, then added a little more forcefully, 'I also suggest that you have the Misses Mitchell released into my custody.'

'Now see here . . .' blustered Mr Hope indignantly.

'No, you see here,' Mr Palmer interrupted him. 'This paper implicates certain people in what the Misses Mitchell were trying to achieve and I feel that those people would be grateful if their names were kept out of the matter in case it became public knowledge. I can only do that if you authorise their release into my custody.'

Mr Hope eyed Mr Palmer with suspicion. Was this man trying to hoodwink him? He would dearly love to see that piece of paper the attorney was flaunting in his face.

Mr Palmer saw him looking at it and gave a cold understanding smile. 'There's no chance of you seeing this until I am prepared to release it, but dare you risk your reputation by ignoring what I have told you and not acceding to my request? Do you think he dare, Robert?'

Robert was still joyously contemplating the news that his sisters would not be moved for another week and he almost missed the unexpected question.

'Er . . . I think Mr Hope would make a tragic mistake.'

The magistrate looked sharply from one to the other then, with marked reluctance, said, 'All right, but you will be responsible for them and you must see that they don't leave Whitby.'

'Very well. You'll give me a note for their immediate release?'

As Mr Hope began to write, Mr Palmer exchanged a glance of triumph with Robert.

Mr Hope finished writing the authority for the releases, then took another sheet of paper and started to write again. When he had completed this one he shoved it across the desk to Mr Palmer.

'I require a signature making you responsible for these two young women for a week.' He held the pen out.

Mr Palmer took it but before signing he perused the wording. Satisfied, he put pen to paper with a flourish.

Mr Hope took the paper, glanced at the signature and then eyed the attorney. 'I expect these two prisoners in front of me a week today, at this time.' He pulled a watch from his pocket, looked at it and announced, 'Eleven in the morning.'

Mr Palmer agreed. 'The authority for release, please.'

Reluctantly Mr Hope slid the paper across the desk. Mr Palmer read it to make sure that the gaoler could not mis-interpret its purpose.

He stood up. 'We'll bid you good day.' They left the magistrate seething as he stared after them.

'Mr Palmer, that was marvellous,' exlaimed Robert with admiration as they walked away from the magistrate's office. 'At one time I thought he would not give way, but you seized that moment for our advantage.'

Mr Palmer beamed. 'If you're going to bluff be positive, Robert, and don't show any signs of wavering.'

'But what are we to do? Where can we get evidence to back Jacob's note?'

'I don't know,' admitted Mr Palmer, 'but we've gained a week in which to do more investigating. Maybe you should see Miss de Northby again. But first things first. Let's get your sisters out of prison and give them and your mother and Paul a happy surprise.'

Their demand to see the head gaoler brought a slow response and their patience had been tested almost to the limit by the time he appeared, yawning loudly.

'What d' y' want?' he grunted, scratching his stomach.

'That order carried out immediately,' snapped Mr Palmer, making no attempt to diguise his distaste and contempt for the man.

Lugs took the piece of paper and squinted at it. He stared at Mr Palmer and, seeing authority standing before him, shuffled reluctantly to a door on the opposite side of the room, unlocking it and slamming it behind him.

Ten minutes passed in which their agitation heightened but that was all forgotten when Alice and Lucy, mystified at what was happening, appeared.

Bewilderment turned to surprise and that in turn to joy on seeing Robert and Mr Palmer. They rushed forward and hugged the two men, then remembering themselves they turned to Mr Palmer with apologies. 'We are sorry . . .' they stammered with embarrassment.

He laughed. 'Nonsense. I'm delighted that you thought

me worthy of a hug.' He put his arms round their shoulders. 'Now, let's take you out of here.'

'Out?' They both gasped and turned to Robert for confirmation.

'That's right,' he said, delighted at having to break such momentous news.

'How? Why? What's been happening?' Questions, filled with elation, poured from them.

'Come on. We'll tell you everything on the way to surprise Mother and Paul,' Robert urged.

They hastened from the prison. The girls, while breathing deeply in the salty air and revelling in the vast space of freedom around them, tried to tidy themselves up, though it was a somewhat forlorn attempt after the unsavoury prison conditions.

While their attention was on their deliverance from harsh prison life, Robert gave Mr Palmer a querying look. The attorney knew instantly that Robert was wondering if they should break the news that they might have to return to their cell after a week. He mouthed the words, 'Not yet.'

The reunion at the Angel Inn was a joyous and exciting one. Even though shocked by their dirty and dishevelled appearance, Rebecca wept with happiness at having her daughters with her again. She held them, hardly daring to let go in case they were whisked away once more. Paul's throat was tight, his emotions ran high as he hugged Alice. There was much he wanted to say but this was not the time.

'I'm longing to know how you got them out of prison, Mr Palmer, but I'm sure the girls would like a good wash.' Rebecca turned to her daughters. 'You can do that in my room and get your fresh clothes when you go to Mrs

Smurthwaite's. Robert, order us some hot chocolate and Mr Palmer can tell us all that has happened while we have it.' Linking arms with Alice and Lucy she started towards the door.

'One moment, Mrs Mitchell,' Mr Palmer stopped them.

Mother and daughters looked askance at him when they saw his serious expression.

'Anticipating the outcome of our interview with the magistrate, I took the liberty before we went out of booking a room here for Miss Alice and Miss Lucy. If what I expected came about I knew they would not be able to go to Mr and Mrs Smurthwaite because they would be in my custody. You see, I have gained their release for a week only.'

'Oh no!' The cry of despair came from Lucy.

Alice was speechless. Her world was collapsing around her again. She looked at Paul for strength to help her bear this awful news but saw that he was as astounded as herself.

Rebecca let out a low moan. She felt as if a weight had been thrust on her shoulders and it was pressing her down into depths from which she would never escape.

As soon as Mr Palmer started to reveal the truth Robert was ready to step in with reassuring support. 'That is not as bad as it sounds.' He made his words crisp, penetrating. 'You are free of that horrible place and it gives us a week to seek a permanent release. We have some ideas and you might have more suggestions when you hear all that has happened.'

Rebecca had watched her son closely. She had seen confidence in him and realised that she too must be strong. Her children needed all the support she could give them. She must not show any weakness. 'Robert is right, girls.

All is not lost, far from it. We have a lot to do, but first let us tidy ourselves.'

Alice and Lucy copied their mother's example and threw off their despair though the thought of what might happen at the end of a week still hung over them like an oppressive cloud.

Half an hour later they were in possession of the encounter with the magistrate and its results. Mr Palmer then acquainted Alice and Lucy with the document and the note from Jacob Wade.

'It bears out what Mark's great-grandmother told us,' said Lucy. 'Maybe we could get her to give evidence.'

'It's a possibility,' agreed Mr Palmer, 'but her memory might be challenged if she was the only witness we had.'

'But who else can we get?' asked Rebecca.

'That's the problem,' said the attorney, 'but we have to try everything. Now this is what I propose as a course of action. I will accompany Miss Alice and Miss Lucy to Mrs Swinburn's and talk to her again. Paul, you will see your parents, explain what has happened, tell them we don't want to implicate them because of your father's work but ask them if they can think of anybody who might be able to help, who might be old enough to remember anything connected with the Wades leaving.'

'There's Amos, the man I saw in Robin Hood's Bay,' put in Robert.

'Good,' said Mr Palmer. 'You might have to contact him again. We may need him. I would also like you to see Miss de Northby once more, to see if you can persuade her to plead with her father.'

'Zilpha?' Lucy was astounded. 'She'll do nothing. She'd like to see me on the ship to Australia.'

'I don't think it will do any good,' said Robert, 'not after my last stormy meeting with her.'

'We must try anything and everything,' pleaded their mother.

Paul left immediately for his parents' home where he collected Alice and Lucy's clothes and returned to Whitby. He had reassured his mother and father that all would be done to prevent de Northby's wrath being turned on them for harbouring the two girls who had broken into his property. But he was disappointed that they could think of nothing which might help Alice and Lucy.

The following morning in a hired carriage Mr Palmer, accompanied by Alice, Lucy and Paul, drove to see Mrs Swinburn. They arrived to find Mrs Cossart taking a cup of chocolate with her grandmother in the morning sunshine.

She showed surprise at seeing Alice and Lucy while welcoming them warmly. 'I'm so pleased to see you are no longer in that terrible prison. I heard you were to be transported. I couldn't believe you were guilty.'

'I'm afraid we were,' replied Alice, her voice contrite.

'But . . .' Mrs Cossart looked bemused.

'It's a long story,' said Alice. 'We'd like to tell you it in a moment for it's possible that Mrs Swinburn may be able to help us.'

'Grandmother?'

Alice nodded. 'We hope so. But first can I introduce Mr Palmer? He is an attorney from Newcastle.'

'Ma'am.' Mr Palmer had already removed his hat and now bowed politely.

'Mr Palmer, you are welcome. I hope you are here to help these girls. I could not believe that the trouble they were in was true. Come, please sit down. I'll tell the maid to bring some more chocolate.'

With the rest of the introductions over, Mrs Cossart was informed of the facts and of the happenings. Mrs Swinburn seemed to be listening carefully but occasionally interrupted with something completely irrelevant to the conversation.

Alice and Lucy feared that this old lady would not be able to add any more to what they already knew. She kept looking at the two girls as if trying to place them. She had given them a pleasant greeting but it was only now that she had fully comprehended where she had seen them before. She pointed a finger at them. 'You came with Mark. Where is he?' She looked around.

'He was called away. I told you,' said Elphrida gently. 'You are right, the Misses Mitchell visited you with him.'

Mrs Swinburn nodded and said wistfully, 'Jacob Wade was a nice man. He would never do anyone any harm.'

Everyone's gaze turned on the old lady at this unexpected remark.

'Sad he had to go away.' Her eyes were fixed, appearing to be seeing the past.

'Do you know why?' asked Mr Palmer quietly.

Mrs Swinburn's face took on a savage look. 'Peter de Northby forced him, I'd swear on it.'

'Why are you so sure?'

The old lady looked a little vacant, as if she was confused with the task of trying to remember.

'Would it help you if I mentioned the name Frederick Wilkins?' said Mr Palmer, leaning forward in his chair and watching Mrs Swinburn closely.

'Wilkins? Wilkins?' She whispered the name, trying to jog her memory. 'That man was no good. Hired by de Northby for his own ends, no doubt. Jacob didn't like him, he told me so. I am sure he had something to do with the scandal.'

'Did you talk to Jacob during the trouble?' asked Mr Palmer.

'No. But I did talk to his wife.'

'Did she tell you anything?'

Mrs Swinburn looked thoughtful.

'Think carefully. It might be important,' said Elphrida, taking her grandmother's hand in hers.

Tension mounted among the listeners as they waited hopefully.

'Yes.' The word was drawn out as if she had not fully recalled the conversation. 'She said Jacob was being forced out because de Northby wanted everything for himself.'

'This Frederick Wilkins . . .'

She cut Mr Palmer's words short. 'Went to France, and good riddance I say.'

'You never heard of him again?'

'No. Didn't want to.' She looked at her granddaughter. 'Are these people staying to lunch?'

At that moment they all knew that the past had gone from her mind and that it was no good trying to return to the subject.

Mr Palmer spoke quietly to Mrs Cossart. 'If your grandmother does think of anything else please let us know. We are all at the Angel.'

361

'Was that of any use?' asked Paul as they drove back to Whitby.

'Helpful in verifying, up to a point, certain aspects of what Jacob wrote in that letter but,' Mr Palmer pulled a face and shook his head, 'it is no proof of what happened. Challenge de Northby with it in court and it would be laughed at. If only that man Wilkins was still here. I'm sure he's the key to the story. I'm afraid we must rely on Robert's interview with Miss de Northby and hers with her father.'

'Who is due back today,' said Lucy.

'Welcome home, Mother.' Zilpha gave her mother a kiss on the cheek and linked arms with her as they walked up the steps at the front of the house. 'I hope you had an enjoyable time.'

'I did indeed. I took the waters and relished the company while your father had his meetings.'

'Profitable, I hope?' Zilpha called over her shoulder.

He laughed as he said, 'They always are when a de Northby's dealing.'

Zilpha stopped and turned to him. 'Then you deserve a special hug and a special kiss.'

He loved being fussed by his daughter and felt the closeness of the family when she linked arms with them both to walk into the house.

'Has everything been quiet while we've been away?' he asked.

'Yes,' she replied, 'but there is something I want to tell you when you get settled in.'

'Very well. I'll be down in a few moments.' He and his

wife followed the servants who were carrying their luggage up the stairs.

'I'll be in the drawing room,' Zilpha called after them. When they joined her she had hot chocolate awaiting them.

'Before you say anything, we brought you a present from Scarborough.' He handed his daughter a small package neatly wrapped in pink and tied with a pink ribbon.

Zilpha, her eyes wide with excitement, took the paper off quickly to reveal a square red leather box. Her fingers shook as she moved the lid on its hinges. She gasped when she saw the beautiful string of pearls neatly curled on the velvet covering.

'Oh, they're so beautiful.' She stood staring at them.

'Here, let me put them on.' Her father, delighted by her reaction, stepped forward.

Her mother, smiling, watched him carefully place the pearls around her daughter's neck and deftly fasten them.

There were tears of pleasure in Zilpha's eyes as she kissed her parents in turn and thanked them. She went to the mirror over the fireplace and admired the gift gleaming around her neck.

'Now, what is it you have to tell us?' de Northby said as he sat down comfortably in his favourite wing chair.

'Robert Mitchell came while you were away.'

Richard's lips tightened; his eyes smouldered with annoyance at the mention of this name.

'What for?'

'He hoped I would ask you to reconsider the charge you brought against his sisters.'

'What? The audacity of the man. His sisters commit a

363

crime and he wants them letting off! Has he no respect for the law? I hope you told him to go.'

'Yes, I did. I told him it was not my affair. He would have to see you.'

Richard gave a little chuckle. 'Let him try and I'll pack him off with his sisters. No doubt he was behind it all. He's as guilty as they are.'

In the depths of the house a bell rang and a few moments later a maid came into the drawing room.

'There is a Mr Robert Mitchell asking to see Miss Zilpha.'

Zilpha was startled. After his last visit she had not expected him to come here again. She had told him then she could not help. Now he was spoiling this pleasant homecoming with her parents.

'What?' Richard was on his feet in an instant. 'What insolence, to come here again. Tell him he's not welcome.'

'Very good, sir.' The maid left but a few moments later the door crashed open.

Startled, the de Northbys stared at a furious Robert striding into the room, his body vibrant with anger.

Richard's jaw muscles knotted. His eyes were hard. 'How dare you burst in here. Get out!'

Robert drew himself up defiantly. 'You'll listen to me. You'll drop those unfounded charges against my sisters.'

Richard gave a snort of derision. 'You don't tell me my business. Your sisters were found guilty and will be shipped out of Whitby today.'

'They won't!' Robert felt pleased at the shock registered on de Northby's face.

'Won't? What are you talking about?' he snapped.

'We've gained a stay pending further evidence,' Robert replied. He saw suspicion mount in de Northby's eyes.

'Evidence? Of what?'

Robert realised he must carry out the bluff. 'Evidence of what you are afraid might come out.'

'Me afraid of . . .' He threw his head back with deep-throated laughter. 'Nonsense. There's nothing to come out.'

'We'll see what my sisters have to say when they return from seeing Mrs Swinburn.' Annoyed by de Northby's mocking laughter Robert had let the words slip before he realised it.

'Your sisters? From Mrs Swinburn's?' He eyed Robert suspiciously.

'Yes. We've got them out of that stinking gaol for the time being.'

'What?' de Northby exploded. 'What's that fool of a magistrate done? You bribed him?' De Northby started to tremble with rage. 'Well, let me tell you, you'll be taking the ship with your sisters. You've admitted trying to divert the course of the law. You won't get away with it. You'll end up in Australia, a convict like your sisters.'

'Try it and you'll rue it forever!' Robert glared threateningly at the man then strode quickly from the room. There was nothing more to be gained here.

Chapter Eighteen

Richard de Northby did not like what he had heard. What information had the Mitchells about the past? Dare he call their bluff? They had got the two girls out of gaol. He'd soon make that fool of a magistrate countermand his release note. But what about Robert? He needed to be dealt with. He no doubt was the driving force behind everything. Remove him, and the probing of the past would collapse.

'Zilpha, tell the groom to saddle my horse. I'm going into Whitby.' His clipped tone brooked no questioning. As his daughter hurried to do his bidding he glanced at his wife. 'I'll settle the Mitchells once and for all.'

'Be careful, Richard, that young man could . . .'

'I know what I'm doing.' He cut her short. This was no time for caution. He strode from the room to change.

Richard grabbed the reins from his groom and mounted without a word. Once out of the stable yard he rode to the coppice where he knew Albert Johnson, Edward Norton and Jarvis White were cutting back the young trees.

They straightened from their task when they heard the sound of a galloping horse. They recognised de Northby immediately and wondered what brought him to them in such haste.

'Forget that job,' he called as he reined in the horse. It twisted and turned, his powerful wrists fighting to keep it under control. It quietened but was still irritable at having its run stopped. 'Young fellow needs dealing with. He's on his way to Whitby on foot.' He gave them a quick description of Robert and what he was wearing. 'See to it. Better if he's quietened forever. Extra money in it for you all.'

There was no need to wait for questions. He whirled the animal and stabbed it into a fast ride towards Whitby.

Satisfied that his workers knew what to do, he kept away from the track he knew Robert would take. He did not want to be seen anywhere near it.

The three men dropped their tools and hurried away from the coppice.

'We'll take him where the path is near the cliff edge. Make it look like a fall, then there'll be no evidence to point at anyone,' said Albert.

The other two agreed and Jarvis added, 'Better if we get ahead of him, come back to meet him.'

They quickened their pace to cut across country to the cliffs.

As they neared them they saw a figure in the distance.

Albert searched the rest of the landscape. 'No one else about,' he observed.

'He's striding out,' commented Edward. 'I'd say he's in a temper.'

'Good,' said Albert, 'his mind must be on what has happened. He won't anticipate any more trouble.'

Robert's thoughts were on what possible course of action they could take against de Northby. He had called his bluff but he would soon see through that when no more evidence against his ancestors was forthcoming. If only Frederick Wilkins was here.

He was barely aware of the three men walking towards him until they were close. They were spread across the path, and he soon realised they were not prepared to give way. What was this? Robbers? He had little money, but they would not know that. His step faltered. They kept to their threatening pace.

Then he saw it all. Their attitude, the way they barred his path, the very fact that they were here, on this trackway to Whitby – de Northby had arranged it! His thoughts raced. It had been done so quickly, they could only be de Northby's workers. He glanced round. There was nowhere for him to go. To his right the cliff fell sharply for a few yards and then less steeply towards the sea. There was rough open ground to his left and behind him the path along which he had just come. From their look these men would be relentless until they caught him.

He braced himself. The men stopped three paces from him. He weighed up the situation. There was little he could do but stand and fight.

Albert launched himself forward. Robert sidestepped and brought his fist round to hit him on the nose. Blood spurted. Albert staggered under the impetus of his own movement and the blow. Robert half turned but he felt himself gripped round the waist, a shoulder came into his stomach and he fell backwards. Edward kept his grip but yelled with pain as Robert brought his knee into his groin. Robert felt the weight ease and tried to twist away but the breath was driven from him by a blow from Jarvis into his side. Albert was back, gripping his shoulders, throwing his weight to pin him to the ground. Robert struck out. He felt something soft surrounded by bone. Someone's eye. He hit out again. Suddenly he was free of hands and bodies. He rolled to one side and sized up this situation as he scrambled breathlessly to his feet. He felt the ground crumble. A quick glance revealed that he was on the edge of the cliff. The men, one with an eye half closed, another with blood streaming from his nose, came at him in a half crouch. He was trapped, but didn't want to die yet. Attack was all he could do. He flung himself forward. As he moved the men stepped back, causing him to lose his balance. He was helpless. Hands gripped his arms and legs. Strive as he would he could not loosen their vice-like hold. They lifted him bodily and moved towards the cliff edge. He fought desperately, his legs and arms pumping hard for release. One leg came free. He kicked hard at the man at his feet and caught him in the groin. The man doubled up, gasping at the pain. Both legs were free. As they touched the ground he exerted pressure to hold back the two men holding his arms. They pushed harder, forcing him forward, closer and closer to the cliff edge. The sea was far below. A final thrust.

Robert was free, falling, falling. The horror struck him. This was the end. It seemed as if he was suspended in air for eternity but it was only a matter of seconds. He struck something hard but he felt it give under the impact. He was suddenly aware of clay spurting around him from the blow. He bounced. Then he felt the cliff give again and he was sliding. He skidded over a hump and dropped into a slight depression, softer this time. His hands tried to find a hold. In spite of the lacerations he felt nothing, only the earth through his clawing hands. He felt a jerk and a pain as if his shoulder had been torn out of its socket. Another jerk and his fall had stopped.

He lay still, gasping for breath, not daring to believe his luck. In a moment his sense of the immediate had returned and he was able to review his situation. Earth and small rocks in a whirl of dust still tumbled to the sea.

He glanced up expecting any minute that his attackers would hurl rocks at him to break his hold and send him on his final plunge to death. But he could not see the top of the cliff. When he had tumbled into this hollow it had been over an overhang which now hid him from view. He was holding on to some strong tufts of grass and if he was careful he could pull himself into a safer position from which he could reassess his situation and consider a means of extricating himself from it.

He eased himself upwards and in doing so set some rocks and clay crashing to the sea. If those men were watching and wanted more proof that he had gone to his death they should have it. He slipped out of his coat, kicked some more earth and boulders away and let his coat tumble in the falling mass.

After it had hit the sea an eerie silence settled, broken only by the sound of the lapping waves and the plaintive cry of circling gulls.

He listened intently for any sound from above. Nothing,

then he picked up intermittent words among the groans and grunts.

'Bastard, hurt me.'

'You'll have . . . eye.'

'Hope . . . isn't broken.'

'Well, he's gone for good.'

'Wouldn't survive . . . fall.'

'Sea has him . . .'

'De Northby should pay us well for . . .'

Robert tensed. So de Northby was behind the attempt on his life.

'Come on let's . . .'

The voices faded and Robert relaxed, taking a few moments to regain his strength and subdue the shock which racked his body and mind.

Reviewing the situation he realised how lucky he had been to hit this hollow the way he did. Five yards either way and he would not have had a chance. Examining the cliff face he saw that there were a series of small ledges, really small protrusions of the layers of rock, leading to his right and offering a possible chance of reaching the cliff top.

Making sure that his body had suffered no more than the shock of the fall he twisted himself over, reached up and felt the first ledge. He put some weight on it with his hand and flakes of soft rock came away in his hand. His heart sank. Were they all like this? If so, there was no chance of reaching the top this way.

He inched his way to the right and tested another. This was firmer. He pulled himself to his feet. For a moment his head swam. He fought the giddiness. He must keep his senses sharp.

He felt for another ledge with his left hand. That too was strong. He pulled. His feet left the ground and he scrambled to find the lower footholds which he had thought might support his feet. He found them, tested them and, satisfied, pushed so that he could reach higher.

Slowly and painfully he moved upwards as if he was using two ladders, one for each foot. Rock broke loose under the pressure and tumbled ominously downwards. A foot slipped, causing palpitations and panic. He found a foothold again. Slowly, ever so slowly, testing each hold before putting full weight on it, he moved upwards.

One more heave and his eyes would be level with the cliff top. Eagerness to finish the horrendous climb came so strongly that he had to fight hard not to overdo the last few steps which could still prove fatal. The last few movements to take him to safety seemed to be a lifetime. Then he was there. The final heave brought him sprawling on to the path on the cliff top. He lay panting for breath, easing his aching limbs and staring at the sky in the joy of survival.

When he reached Whitby Richard de Northby went straight to the magistrate's office and burst in without any formality.

'Hope, what the hell do you think you're up to?' he stormed at the magistrate, who was so startled by his sudden appearance that he almost tumbled backwards off his chair.

Blustering, he straightened himself, trying to assume some dignity. 'What do you mean?' he spluttered.

'You know damned well what I mean.' De Northby

loomed over the desk staring darkly at him. 'Those two girls should be on board a ship out at sea heading for London.'

'I could do nothing about it but they'll be in the next shipment of criminals.' He hoped he was pouring oil on troubled waters.

'You could do nothing about it? You're the magistrate.'

'My position was threatened,' Hope whimpered.

'By whom?' snarled Richard in disbelief.

'An attorney from Newcastle and a Mr Mitchell.'

De Northby smacked the desk so hard the magistrate recoiled. 'I knew he'd be behind it.' He gave a little chuckle. 'He won't bother me any more. He's bluffed you, man. He'll never do it again. So get those girls back in that gaol or you'll get your just dues.'

De Northby strode from the office leaving the man quaking at the threat. But he'd have that damned attorney, Palmer, to contend with. He moaned and held his head in his hands. Whatever he did he could not win.

Robert's limbs hurt, the lacerations were sore and his body bruised from the fall. He limped his way back to Whitby with vengeance in his heart.

The sound of an unexpected carriage on the drive brought Elphrida out of her chair in the drawing room and on to the portico. She scrutinised the occupants but they were too far away to make a positive identification. She waited, watching. Two ladies and two men as well as the man driving the carriage.

The carriage drew nearer. She did not know the ladies

and as yet could not see the men's faces. The carriage swung round the drive.

Mark! Elphrida's mind raced with joy at seeing her son. Mark, home again! And that was David with him. But who were the ladies? She studied them closely as the two horses were guided towards the steps. An older woman and a younger one. Mother and daughter? Their outdoor clothes were plain but of a good cut, their bonnets small and neat. Why was Mark bringing them here?

Her son was out of the carriage almost before it had stopped. 'Mother!' His cry was full of sparkle and love. He swept her into his arms and hugged her tight. 'It's good to see you.'

'And you.'

Still holding her hand he turned to see David helping Claudette and Louise from the coach.

'Mrs Cossart.' David inclined his head respectfully.

'David,' she returned, 'it's good to see you again.' Her eyes strayed to the ladies who were standing looking a little embarrassed, awaiting introductions.

'Mother, I'd like you to meet Madame Wilkins and her daughter Louise.'

'Wilkins!' Elphrida gasped and looked at her son as if seeking confirmation that she had heard correctly.

'Yes, Mother.'

'Any relation to Frederick Wilkins who used to . . .'

'His wife and daughter.'

'But . . .' Elphrida pulled herself up. There were so many questions she now wanted to ask, so much to tell Mark, but first . . . 'I forget my manners,' she said as she held out a hand to Claudette. 'Madame Wilkins, welcome to my

374

home.' Her smile was warm as she shook hands with Claudette and Louise.

'They will be able to stay here, won't they?' Mark asked.

'Of course. How did . . . ?'

'It's a long story, Mother. Suffice to say for the moment that David and I have been in France on military matters. We came across Madame Wilkins and she was willing to come to England to tell her husband's story. We have been in London a day. David and I made our reports and then we came by sea to Whitby and by coach from there.'

'Come along in. I've so much to tell you.'

Mark, surprised by this statement, looked curiously at his mother but realised she would say no more until they were inside.

She started to usher them into the house then stopped and called to the coachman who was following with the luggage. 'Take the carriage into the stable yard. I'll tell a maid to inform the cook to give you a meal before you return to Whitby.'

'Thank you, ma'am.'

Inside, Elphrida fussed while a maid took Claudette's and Louise's outdoor clothes. She ordered some tea to be brought to the drawing room.

'Now, Mother, what's this you have to tell me?' asked Mark once they were settled.

'Alice and Lucy Mitchell were arrested for . . .'

'Arrested?' Mark was incredulous.

'Yes. For breaking into Mr de Northby's office at the alum works.'

'Breaking in? What on earth for?'

'They were looking for some document relating to the

agreement when their great-grandfather sold his share in the alum works. They didn't find it.'

'And what happened to them?'

'They were arrested, tried and condemned to be transported to Australia.'

'My God! They can't be. Where are they now? I must see them, tell them I found Madame Wilkins and that she is willing to talk.'

Claudette nodded. 'The truth must be told. And I hope it will help these young ladies.'

'I'm sure it will,' said Mark. 'Mother, where are they? Not in that awful prison?'

'Thankfully no.' The relief on Mark's face confirmed her suspicions about his relationship with Lucy. 'They were, but an attorney from Newcastle, a Mr Palmer, gained their temporary release. They are in his custody at the Angel Inn in Whitby. I have seen them. They are well but the sentence still hangs over them.'

Mark jumped to his feet. 'Mother, please look after Madame Wilkins and Louise.' He started across the room. 'David, be a good chap and ask a groom to get me a horse ready immediately. I'll fetch a change of clothes.'

As the door closed behind the two friends, Claudette gave a knowing smile, 'Madame Cossart, I can see you love your son dearly as I do my Louise, so I must tell you what a gallant gentleman he is, as indeed is Monsieur Hughes. Without them we would never have got out of France and I would not be able to fulfil my husband's wishes. It is a long story and I have no doubt he will tell you all in time. He has also been exceptionally generous in fitting us out with new clothes when we were in London. We had to leave our home in Paris in a hurry.'

'It sounds as though you won't return,' observed Elphrida shrewdly.

Claudette gave a wan smile. 'It would not be safe, madame.'

'Then allow my husband to take care of things for you here.'

'That is most kind of you.'

Mark's ride to Whitby was fast and as he dismounted at the Angel Inn he flung the reins to a stableman. 'Look after him.'

'Aye, sir,' the man replied, knowing that there would be a good reward if his attention to the horse was first class.

Mark hurried into the inn. 'Good day, landlord. The Misses Mitchell?'

'They're in there, sir.' He indicated a door on the right.

Mark knocked and opened the door. Five people looked in his direction. Lucy and Alice he knew. He recognised Paul Smurthwaite but the older man and woman he did not know, though he guessed the man must be Mr Palmer.

'Mark!' Lucy's cry at seeing him was filled with an upsurge of uncontrolled emotion. She was out of her chair and, unembarrassed, in front of the others, flung her arms round him. 'Oh, Mark, Mark!' She sobbed with the joy of seeing him. Suddenly she felt that here was a knight in shining armour to rescue her from an enforced journey to the other side of the world, never to return.

'Lucy,' he said, his voice soft. He held her a moment and then eased her away but slid his hand into hers, imparting comfort and reassurance. 'Mother told me briefly what has happened. We've got to do something about it.'

'We're trying so hard, but seem to be making little progress.' Rebecca's statement carried a hope that he could help.

'You must be Mrs Mitchell. I'm pleased to meet you.' He inclined his head gracefully.

In these few moments Rebecca knew why Lucy had fallen in love with this handsome young man, for he had already revealed sincerity, concern and charm.

'And you must be Mr Palmer. My mother mentioned your name.' He extended his hand and in the grip Mr Palmer read a trustworthy young man.

'Sir, I'm pleased to know you. This is a sad case and indeed one of gross injustice by a man who desires to see these two young ladies transported. We have great reason to think it has something to do with some past action by one of his ancestors. We just need the final verification. With that we might be able to bring pressure to bear on de Northby.'

'I might be able to provide what you need,' said Mark.

They all stared at him in disbelief. What could he possibly know? He'd been away from Whitby.

Mr Palmer looked seriously at him. 'Please, don't raise our hopes unnecessarily.'

'Trust me. I have important news which I think we can turn to our advantage. It's to do with Jacob Wade and Peter de Northby.'

'What?' There were gasps all round and everyone's attention was riveted on Mark.

'Robert is missing.' A questioning look came to his face. 'I would have liked him to hear what I have to say.'

'He went to Northby Hall, to make one last effort on behalf of his sisters,' Mr Palmer explained. 'De Northby was due home from Scarborough and Robert hoped he might see Miss de Northby before her father returned and persuade her to plead with her father.' He shook his head slowly. 'But I have little hope. He has tried before and she refused.'

'She did what?' Mark was startled by this unexpected revelation.

'Mark, don't you see, she saw that my transportation would leave the way clear for her with you.'

Before he could comment the door opened and Robert staggered in.

'Oh, my God!' Shocked at the state of her son Rebecca was on her feet, reaching out to help him. His clothes were dirty and tattered, his face swelling with ugly bruises and his hands marked by streaks of coagulated blood.

'What happened?' everyone questioned at once.

He sank wearily on to a chair, acknowledging Mark's presence, and then went on to explain. 'Three men tried to kill me.'

'De Northby?' Mr Palmer voiced his immediate suspicions.

Robert nodded and went on to tell them of the events since his arrival at Northby Hall. While he did so, his mother carefully bathed his wounds with the water Paul had brought into the room.

'Would you recognise the men?' asked Mr Palmer.

'Certainly. They made no attempt to disguise themselves. No need when they expected me to be dead.' He went on to describe his assailants.

As he did so Alice and Lucy exchanged glances. 'Two

of them sound like the men who followed us. They were Mr de Northby's estate workers.'

'Good.' Mr Palmer nodded with satisfaction. 'Then we can press charges of attempted murder against them and implicate de Northby.' He paused slightly. 'But that won't mitigate the charges against Alice and Lucy.'

'Maybe not,' put in Mark, 'but with what I was about to tell you when Robert arrived, we might be able to bring pressure to bear on Mr de Northby.'

He had everyone's concentrated attention as he went on. 'I've been in France on army business and while I was there I traced Frederick Wilkins.'

'Mark!' cried Lucy, eagerly anticipating what she hoped would follow.

'I'm afraid he went to the guillotine, branded as a spy, and his sons suffered the same fate. But his widow and daughter are still alive and I have brought them to England. They are at Howland Manor with my mother.'

'But can they help?' asked Mr Palmer cautiously.

'Apparently Mr Wilkins wanted to return to England to ease a troubled conscience by confessing the part he had played in instigating the accusations levelled at Jacob Wade, but he could not escape the attention of the French authorities. However he confessed to his wife, signed a paper relating the facts and asked her to come to England to put things right. She was closely watched and was never able to do so.'

'But you've brought her,' said Lucy with admiration.

'That's another story for another time.' Mark drew some paper from his pocket. He handed it to Mr Palmer. 'Sir, I'd like your opinion.'

When he had finished reading Frederick Wilkins's confession he announced, 'This throws a different light on the situation. While it cannot negate the agreement between the two men, it backs up and gives authority to Jacob Wade's letter.' He explained quickly to Mark what they had found.

'So we have proof that Jacob was subjected to a type of blackmail,' said Mark.

'Yes,' agreed Mr Palmer. He was looking thoughtful as he added, 'If we handle this correctly I think we might solve several things at once.'

He put forward his ideas and over the next hour they were discussed thoroughly. When Mark left the Angel everyone was in a happier frame of mind.

He reached home to find David and Louise sitting on the portico delighting in each other's company and enjoying a peaceful evening after their recent traumas. When he went inside he was immediately struck by the friendly atmosphere between the three people taking a glass of wine. He knew that there was empathy between his parents and Mrs Wilkins. They had made her feel at home and he sensed her gratitude to them and to him for his help in getting her out of France, enabling her to fulfil her husband's wishes.

He called David and Louise inside and quickly explained to everyone what had happened to Robert and what had been planned in Whitby. 'I have arranged a meeting to take place here tomorrow morning. The company can only be completed by inviting all the de Northbys, so, Father, I would like you to send someone over with an invitation to visit us for an important occasion at ten o'clock in the morning.'

Mr Cossart complied. 'I'll say it concerns Mark and Zilpha. I'm sure that will bring them.'

Zilpha was in a buoyant mood as she drove with her parents to Howland Manor. Mark was home and this invitation could mean only one thing as far as she was concerned. Her father's news that Mr Hope was to rescind his release of the Mitchell girls immediately had pleased her, though she had kept that delight to herself. She felt satisfaction with the way her father had dismissed Robert's attempts to sully her family's name. If he escaped transportation with his sisters he would never show his face in Whitby again.

Now she looked forward to seeing Mark and to a future as his wife. They had always been close. They made a handsome couple. Didn't everyone say so? Their lives were compatible. Wouldn't both families be pleased? And wouldn't all her friends be envious? She sighed contentedly.

The horses trotted briskly, guided by the skilful hands of the coachman. The wheels crunched on the drive which curved towards the front of the house. Their noise drew the attention of the butler, who had been waiting in the hall for this expected arrival. He went out and stood, waiting to help the occupants out of the carriage. A few moments later he was joined by Mark and his father.

'A fine morning, John,' commented Emile.

'It is that, sir. It will have been a pleasant ride for Mr and Mrs de Northby and their daughter.'

The carriage rolled to a halt. All its occupants descended and exchanged greetings with their host.

Elphrida had come on to the portico to greet their

friends, and as she engaged Adeline in conversation Emile held out his hand to Richard.

De Northby shook hands and as the two men walked up the steps he asked, 'What is this all about? You want something settling between Mark and Zilpha?'

'All in good time, Richard. It may be something we will have to leave to them.'

Richard shot him a look of curiosity but could take the matter no further for they had entered the house.

'Let us go in here,' said Emile, indicating the drawing room. He opened the door and stood aside to allow his guests to enter.

Adeline was taken aback when she saw the room occupied by others. She had not expected anyone else to be there.

Zilpha received a jolt. Lucy and Alice, Paul Smurthwaite, three ladies and a gentleman she did not know. Why were they all here? What had they to do with this meeting? If they were here, why not Robert?

Richard walked into the room and pulled up short. 'What are you doing here?' His glare at Lucy and Alice was full of dark anger. 'You should be back in gaol by now.'

'Not yet, Mr de Northby,' said Mr Palmer, 'they're still in my custody.'

'What's that fool of a magistrate done now?'

'You expected him to take action before my time as custodian was up?'

De Northby read the implication behind the question but he ignored it and turned on Emile. 'What's the meaning of this?' he thundered. 'Why are you harbouring thieves in your house?'

'They are not thieves, Mr de Northby,' said Mark quietly but firmly, as he stepped forward.

'You keep out of this, young man,' snapped Richard. 'You know nothing about it.'

'Indeed, sir, I know a great deal about it.'

'Only what these mountebanks have told you,' scowled de Northby.

'And more, sir.'

'There is no more,' he insisted, irritated by Mark's assured attitude.

'Please let us look at this reasonably,' Emile intervened.

'I've no wish to stay,' snapped Richard, starting to turn towards the door.

'I think you should,' said Emile. 'The situation for you might worsen if you leave, at least that is my opinion; I am an independent witness to what these people are saying and I would certainly like to hear your side of the story.'

De Northby grunted and nodded at Emile.

'You know Mr Palmer and you'll remember David Hughes, Mark's army friend, so now let me introduce you to the people you don't know. Mrs Mitchell, mother to Robert, Alice and Lucy.' He went on to introduce Mr Palmer to Adeline and Zilpha and then turned to Claudette and Louise as he said, 'Richard, Adeline, Zilpha, now I want you to meet probably the most important person at this gathering, Mrs Claudette Wilkins, widow of Mr Frederick Wilkins, and her daughter Louise.'

De Northby was thunderstruck. He stared at Claudette disbelievingly. He couldn't be hearing right.

'It is perfectly true, sir.' Mark gave a little smile at Richard's confusion. 'I found Madame Wilkins and her daughter

384

in Paris while I was there on army duty with David. He was a witness to that and to what Madame Wilkins told me.'

De Northby shot a glance at David and received a nod of confirmation in return. 'I was there throughout the whole meeting, sir.'

'Now, I would like you to hear what Madame Wilkins has to say,' said Mark.

Claudette told her story and when she had finished she gave a contented sigh of relief. Louise, who had held her mother's hand all the time she was speaking, gave her a smile of approval at having come through the ordeal with quiet dignity. 'I have been pleased for you all to hear this,' Claudette went on. 'It is a great relief that I have been able to carry out my husband's wishes and I hope that as a result of his confession, by which he has incriminated himself, Mr de Northby will have the goodness to see that Mrs Mitchell and her family, as descendants of Jacob Wade, receive just compensation.'

A momentary silence enveloped the room as Claudette's story and final plea sank in.

Richard's face was a mask of thoughtfulness. He still scowled. His mind toyed with ways to extract himself from the unsavoury situation that faced him. 'You say that your husband left a written statement, a confession. May I see it?'

'Mark handed it to me for safe keeping,' Mr Palmer put in. 'Certainly you may see it.' He handed the book to Richard.

He read it quickly, his nimble brain taking in the details. 'This is all very well, and in your eyes may constitute hard evidence, but may I point out that it could be the writing of a man who delighted in making things up.'

385

Sharp protestations sprang to Claudette's lips but she caught Mr Palmer's look warning her to say nothing.

De Northby gave a little smile. 'I think it would need more to confirm its contents.' He thought that he had put himself into an unassailable position, for he could not see where any of these people could have corroborating evidence.

'We have that, Mr de Northby.'

Richard glowered as he watched Mr Palmer extract some more paper from his pocket.

'This is the document of the agreement between Peter de Northby and Jacob Wade assigning the alum works to Peter de Northby.'

'Where did you get that?' asked Richard with suspicion.

'This was Jacob's copy. We traced it to Ormston and Peckett, solicitors here in Whitby.'

'Yes, yes, I know of them,' said Richard testily with an impatient wave of his hand. 'That will prove nothing.'

'True,' granted Mr Palmer, 'but the letter attached to it will help.'

Richard looked askance and took the paper handed to him. He read it quickly.

When he judged that de Northby had almost finished reading Jacob's letter, Mr Palmer continued. 'You will see from the dating of that letter and that of the statement made by Mr Wilkins that there could have been no collaboration between the two. They are both completely independent statements of what happened, written at completely different times, one here in England, the other in France. Neither man could have known of the existence of the other statement, in fact Jacob was dead when Mr Wilkins wrote his.'

'That is perfectly true, monsieur.' Louise added strength to Mr Palmer's observations. 'My father never returned to England so he could not know what happened to Monsieur Wade, never mind what he wrote.'

Richard's feelings were a mixture of anger that the past had been uncovered, annoyance that his own attempts to keep it secret had been unmasked, and that his bribing of a magistrate had also been discovered.

'As an attorney,' Mr Palmer went on, 'I grant you that the agreement between the two parties is legally binding. The other two statements have no power to reverse that, but I think you will agree that they prove that the agreement was made under undue duress. I also think you knew this to be the truth and, fearing you would lose a great deal, were prepared to go to great lengths to keep the Mitchells quiet when you learned they were descended from the Wades and were making enquiries.'

'Nonsense,' snapped Richard. 'These two girls,' he glanced contemptuously at Alice and Lucy, 'broke into my property and got what they deserved.'

'You went to greater lengths than having them followed. Even though they had transportation hanging over them there was still their brother to deal with and you attempted to murder him.'

Attempted? De Northby was confused. According to his estate workers Mitchell was dead at the bottom of the cliffs. He kept a tight rein on his reaction.

Zilpha was flabbergasted by this final accusation. She had been bewildered by Mark's part in all this. Her hopes for a future with him were shattered. It was obvious that he had thought more of Lucy than her or he wouldn't have

387

bothered to support her claims by searching for Madame Wilkins while on an army mission.

Adeline had paled at all that was being thrown at her husband but this latest accusation brought indignation pouring from her. 'Richard, I've heard enough falsehoods obviously condoned by people who were supposedly our friends. I'm not going to stay here a moment longer.' She started towards the door.

'Murder? What a ridiculous idea.' De Northby's laugh rang round the room and he turned to sweep after his wife.

'I think you had both better stay.' The commanding voice was cold, pulling them up sharp. 'What Mr Palmer said was true.'

The room had gone quiet. Recognising the voice de Northby's bravado began to evaporate but he marshalled himself. He must keep control.

Robert walked in from a neighbouring room.

Zilpha gasped at the sight of his battered appearance. Her thoughts tumbled in confusion. Was the claim of attempted murder true? Surely not. Her father wouldn't – not the man she knew and loved.

'Have you suffered a fall?' asked de Northby with an air of feigned surprise.

'You expected me to be at the bottom of a cliff, thrown there by three of your estate workers,' replied Robert coolly, his eyes never leaving de Northby.

De Northby met his gaze. He drew himself up indignantly. 'Young man, I'll have you for slander.'

'I think not, sir. We have proof of what we say and also of your attempts to influence the course of law.' Robert called over his shoulder, 'Come in.'

388

The three estate workers and the magistrate shuffled into the room.

Everyone was aware of de Northby's thunderstruck expression. Robert noticed Zilpha's mystified, questioning glance of horror at her father. He could tell the truth was striking home, she was hurting and he was glad she was being punished for the attitudes she had adopted when he wanted help.

'Mr de Northby, I persuaded your estate workers to come here. Robert's description matched those of Alice and Lucy.' Mark explained the presence of the three men.

'And I couldn't refuse, Mr de Northby,' bleated Mr Hope. 'Mr Palmer had the power to ruin me.' He shuffled uncomfortably.

De Northby did not speak. He needed to come out of this as best he could. He could be sent to gaol, lose everything, his wife and daughter left in poverty. The thought was too horrifying.

'Father,' Zilpha's quiet voice broke the silence. 'Please do the right thing.'

He saw disgust and condemnation in her eyes. He did not want that and if only he could do something to alleviate it he would be satisfied even if he had to make sacrifices.

He nodded and looked around the room. His eyes finally rested on the four men who were last to enter. 'You can go,' he said calmly but with the authority which would never leave him, though from now it might be used differently.

Having been forewarned by Mark that they should only leave when he personally dismissed them they did not move.

'I will tell them to go only after I have reassurances that

389

you will never, whatever the outcome, seek revenge on these men,' said Mark.

'You have it,' replied Richard humbly.

Mark nodded to the four men who left.

De Northby hesitated while he gathered his thoughts together. He looked round the faces who watched him expectantly. His gaze finally rested on Zilpha. This was the one person he did not want to hurt; he wanted her faith in him restored.

'I knew my grandfather to be a ruthless man, always on the lookout to gain as much for the de Northbys as he could. I knew he had gained the whole of the alum works and land belonging the company from Jacob Wade and I thought there might be some truth in the rumours that he had acquired it by foul means, but that was no concern of mine. The agreement was legally binding and I thought it would never be challenged. And then these two young ladies came on the scene followed by their brother.' He paused. 'Well, you know the rest.' He paused again. No one spoke, for all sensed that he was about to add something.

'It seems to me that Jacob Wade should not have left the business, and therefore his ancestors should still be sharing the profits.' He glanced at Rebecca. 'That is you, Mrs Mitchell, and following you, your son Robert, no doubt. Mr Palmer, if this family can ever forgive me for what I've done, I would like you to draw up the necessary documents so that Mrs Mitchell and I have equal shares in the alum business.'

Rebecca glanced quickly at her son and daughters and received a nod from them. She knew they were satisfied by fulfilling their father's dying wishes and were against revenge. 'Very well,' she said.

'Thank you, ma'am.' Richard bowed his humble thanks. 'Also, Mr Palmer, I would like you to arrange the transfer of some land, as a compensation for the injustice of the past. We hope that the Mitchell family will build a property there and live among us, and that we can work together in a partnership that will be profitable to us all.'

'Very well,' agreed Mr Palmer. 'I will be sorry to lose Robert but I can see where his future, and indeed the future of the Mitchell family, lies.'

'Come to see me tomorrow at Northby Hall and we'll discuss the details.'

'Will you see to everything for us, Mr Palmer?' Rebecca asked. 'I would like to return to Newcastle and settle everything there quickly, for I know my daughters will want to be back here as soon as possible.'

'I will take care of everything,' Mr Palmer reassured her.

'Very well. Eleven o'clock, Mr Palmer.'

Satisfied with the look of approval given by Zilpha, knowing that his final move in the drama would eventually outweigh her memories of what he had tried to do, he turned for the door.

'Mr de Northby.' Alice stopped him. 'There is something Lucy and I discussed last night. It depended on the outcome of today. Things have turned out as we hoped and that leads us to make one more request of you, if you will agree to use your influence.'

'You think I still have some?' he queried with a doubtful smile.

'I'm sure you have,' she returned. 'When we were in prison there were two young girls, Blanche and Cora, who were kind to us and helped us to get through our ordeal.

They are condemned to be transported to Australia, their crime thieving to stay alive. They are hardly out of childhood. They are orphans. I would like you to use your influence with Mr Hope to obtain their release. They can come to us and can work for Mother when we come to Yorkshire to live.'

'You can trust them not to return to their old ways?' asked de Northby cautiously.

'Yes, for they will be shown a love they have never had.'

'I will see to it.'

As they drove away from Howland Manor Zilpha kissed him on the cheek, then sat back and wondered about her own future now that it was obvious that Mark had chosen Lucy.

Three days later Zilpha turned up the collar of her coat against the freshening breeze as she walked along the edge of the cliffs. She was in no hurry and let Rupert and Bracken enjoy their run.

After the upheavals life had settled down and now she was beginning to feel the rejection she had suffered. Oh, why did the Mitchells have to intrude in her life?

The dogs chased each other in wild pursuit. They raced ahead and were lost to sight as the path dipped. She could still hear their bark when suddenly it stopped. Had they chased some poor rabbit down a hole and were now trying to scrabble the hole wider? She quickened her pace, only to stop suddenly on the edge of the dip.

Robert Mitchell crouched on his haunches with the dogs, tails wagging wildly, fussing around him. His hands ruffled their heads and they were enjoying it.

She started to turn away. The dogs would follow in their own good time. They knew their way home.

Aware of a presence, half knowing that it would be Zilpha, he stood up slowly. She was moving away. She was not going to speak.

'Miss de Northby,' he called softly.

She stopped and turned round. 'Mr Mitchell,' she returned without feeling.

He came to her, the dogs walking alongside.

'I thought you would be in Newcastle,' she said casually.

'Mother and my sisters sailed yesterday but I decided to stay.'

She raised a surprised eyebrow.

He gave no reason but said, 'I want to thank you for asking your father, when we all met at Howland Manor, to do the right thing.'

She shrugged her shoulders.

'I know how much he thinks of you and I'm sure you had a great influence on his decision.'

'I hope you're satisfied with what you got out of it,' she said testily.

'The money, the land, mean nothing if we are to hold a bitterness towards each other. After all, we are to be neighbours and one day partners in the alum works.'

The dogs fussed at him as if they wanted to be off with him.

'You've certainly made a conquest,' she commented.

'You know what they say, if you like my dog you like me.'

She met his intense look, and saw the desire for friendship. Maybe there was more.

'They were instrumental in us first meeting,' he went

393

on. 'Could you and I start at that moment again and forget what has happened in between?'

She looked down at the dogs still rubbing against him. 'I don't think I am going to control them easily unless you come home with me.' She looked up and saw that he had read a deeper meaning in her suggestion and she did nothing to contradict it.